D0871797

No Forwarding Address

NO FORWARDING ADDRESS

Elisabeth Bowers

Douglas & McIntyre
Vancouver/Toronto

Douglas & McIntyre Ltd.
1615 Venables Street
Vancouver, British Columbia V5L 2H1

Published in the United States of America by The Seal Press, 3131 Western Avenue, Suite 410, Seattle, Washington 98121

Canadian Cataloguing in Publication Data

Bowers, Elisabeth.
    No forwarding address

    ISBN 0-55054-007-6

    I. Title.
PS8553.092N6   1991   C813'.54   C91-091625-X
PR9199.3.B69N6 1991

All the characters and events in *No Forwarding Address* are entirely fictional. Any resemblance they may bear to real persons and experiences is illusory.

Design by Clare Conrad

Printed and bound by D.W. Friesen & Sons Ltd.
Printed on acid-free paper

Acknowledgements

Many people helped me write this book. They answered my questions, shared their expertise, did research on my behalf, edited and criticized the manuscript, suggested plot changes and gave the book a title. I am indebted to all of them.

No Forwarding Address

1

EVEN NOW, MORE THAN a year later, when I'm driving across town or at home washing dishes, I'll suddenly become aware that I'm reiterating the details, explaining the circumstances, justifying my actions to some invisible judge. It makes me sick to hear myself. Won't I ever get over it?

When you grow up as I did, in a middle-class Canadian home, you are taught that evil exists elsewhere, in other neighborhoods, other countries. You see it on television; it stays on the other side of the glass. Now, of course, I know that behind those closed suburban doors of my childhood the usual atrocities were being committed: wife battering, child abuse, murder, rape. Even so, those early years have had an indelible effect. Like jello, I've set—I'm too trusting, too complacent. Intellectually I know what people are, what they do, but on an emotional level I can't quite assimilate that knowledge. No matter how paranoid and cautious I am, I'm never quite paranoid and cautious enough.

My name is Meg Lacey. I'm a white, middle-aged divorcée; I have two (almost) grown up children. I live and work in Vancouver, which is a city of about one million on the Pacific West Coast. For the last ten years I've been scrounging a living as a private investigator. I do better now than I used to—sometimes I almost believe I'm getting good at it. Despite my mistakes.

But we all make mistakes, right? The problem is that when I look back, I can't point to any one moment and say: There's where I went wrong. I can't feel sure that it won't happen again. And that's the part that scares me.

I could blame someone else, of course—like Vicky Fischer, who hired me to do what I did. She swept into my office one March afternoon—a solid, handsome woman in her mid-thirties—filling the room with her presence: her gaudy, expensive clothes, her musky perfume. She had a broad face, fair skin and thick, tawny hair. She gave an impression of competence and self-reliance, as if she'd learned long ago how to fend for herself. When she smiled a deep, fat dimple popped into her left cheek, but her eyes looked wistful and bitter lines were etching into the skin around her mouth.

In my business you meet a lot of busybodies, people that love to manage other people's lives. At first, Vicky seemed typical. She wanted me to find her sister, Sherry, who had left her home and husband, taking their son with her. Sherry was eight years younger than Vicky, and it was clear that Vicky had been looking after her all her life, tying her shoelaces, holding her hand across the road. But now Sherry had escaped her surveillance.

"I don't look for adults," I explained, "unless they've skipped out on their debts. They don't get lost. And if they're dead, the police are much better at finding them than I am."

But when Vicky elaborated on the situation I began to understand that Sherry's case was different, that Vicky's interference might be justified. Sherry was mentally ill, and getting progressively worse. According to Vicky, her sister had always been rather moody and high-strung, but in the last few years her difficulties had become so severe that she was unable, at times, to care for her child by herself. Sherry refused to consult psychiatrists and had never been institutionalized, but she'd only escaped that fate because Vicky stepped in whenever Sherry couldn't function.

"But now she's decided that all her problems are our fault," Vicky said, sounding a little exasperated. "She came to see me— oh, about a month and a half ago. She told me that she'd decided to leave Glen—that's her husband—and she didn't intend to tell anyone where she was going. She said that the people she knew

4

were like mirrors, keeping her stuck in the same pattern. If she could get away from us all, she'd be able to be different."

"Maybe she's right," I said.

"But she's always coming up with new theories, trying out new cures, and none of them do any good. Several times a month I get a phone call from Glen asking me if he can drop their kid off at my house because Sherry's gone off the deep end again and he doesn't want to leave him alone with her. She locks herself in the bedroom and won't come out, won't eat. . . . And she can go on like that for days."

"When she told you she was planning to disappear, did she say that she was planning to take her little boy with her?"

"Yes. And when I asked her what Glen would think about that, she said that Glen was so busy with his restaurant he wouldn't even notice. You see she doesn't have a very good sense of reality. I said to her: 'Mark is Glen's son. You can't just walk off with him and disappear. That's called kidnapping.' "

She paused, waited for me to agree.

"Mm." I was noncommittal.

"But she never listens when she's got some new idea in her head. She gets mad at anybody who criticizes her. I didn't know whether to take her seriously or not, but I told her that if she did move out, she'd have to phone me every week. I promised that I wouldn't tell anyone that I was still in touch with her as long as I knew that she and Mark were O.K. But I said that if she didn't phone, I'd have to come looking for her. She can't take care of Mark on her own. I've been looking after him—looking after both of them—ever since he was born."

I watched her, thinking: Would I want to be looked after by a big sister like this? "Why you? Isn't that Glen's job?"

"Oh he does what he can. When he's home," Vicky added disparagingly. "But he opened up his own restaurant about a year ago and he's managing it single-handed. He's sunk thousands of dollars into it and borrowed every penny he could get to capitalize it. If it fails, he'll be bankrupt. So he can't look after Mark every time Sherry has a bad day."

"And you can?"

"Well, I've got three kids. I'm at home anyway."

5

"What did Glen do when Sherry disappeared?"

"He phoned me, he phoned my parents, he phoned all their friends. . . . Finally he phoned the cops."

I picked up my pen. "When was this?"

She frowned, and I pushed my desk calendar towards her. She consulted it, counting backwards under her breath. "February 2nd, I think. That's right—it was a Friday."

"And when did she tell you she was planning to disappear?"

"A few days before that. She phoned me about a week later."

"After she'd disappeared?"

Vicky nodded. "And she phoned me the next week too. She told me she'd found an apartment and a job in a restaurant, and a babysitter to look after Mark while she worked. She said everything was fine and I shouldn't worry. But she wouldn't tell me where she was living, and she said she had no phone."

"Did you tell Glen about these phone calls?"

"No," Vicky answered with an edge of defiance. "And I didn't tell the cops about them either."

I put down my pen and sat back.

"I told you—I'm on her side," Vicky defended herself. "I'm looking out for my sister, not Glen. I don't know why she left him—that's her business. But she can't expect me, after our history together, to let her drop off the edge of the world. She wants to be independent; I can understand that. But even if I were willing to let her take that risk—what about Mark? It's not fair to him. She doesn't realize what he goes through because when she's going nuts, someone else is looking after him. I keep thinking of him alone with her when she starts shouting and—"

She broke off with a gusty sigh, tried to discipline the shape of her mouth. "When she gets frightened, he gets frightened too," she continued in a small voice, "and now there's no one there to reassure him anymore."

Some of my clients sob and scream and I don't turn a hair—but at the sight of Vicky's troubled blue irises, I was touched, in spite of myself.

"When did Sherry last phone you?" I asked.

"Not since I went to see her."

6

"You went to see her where?"

"I got those phone calls, right? And then nothing. She didn't phone. I didn't panic—not right away—but after two weeks of not hearing from her, I thought: Well, this is it. What am I going to do? I found this book in the library about how to find people, like a private detective does?"

"Really?"

"You know, a do-it-yourself book."

I wondered if I should read it.

"And since she'd told me she was working in a restaurant, I tried phoning all the restaurants in the yellow pages."

"You found her?"

"She was clearing tables in a place called Copper's, on Clark Street." Beginner's luck, I thought jealously. "Just one of those breakfast and lunch places—where working people go. I drove over there and talked to her."

"How did she seem?"

Vicky hesitated. "She seemed O.K. She was angry at me for coming to find her, and she wouldn't tell me where she was living or anything. I warned her that if she didn't phone me, I'd come looking for her again. Finally she promised to call me twice a week."

She looked down at her hands and began twisting one of the opulent rings that weighted her fingers.

"But she never phoned," Vicky went on, sounding increasingly discouraged. "Two days ago I phoned Copper's restaurant again and they said she'd quit. I went down there and talked to her boss. I explained the situation and he gave me the address that she'd given him. I went to the address but no one was living there anymore, and the neighbors told me she'd moved."

"How old is Mark?" I asked.

Vicky's eyelids lifted. "Four."

"Is Sherry a competent mother—when she's functional?"

"Oh, sure—she takes good care of Mark. But it's a constant struggle for her to stay in control. She knows herself pretty well by now, she has all these tricks and strategies . . . but if something catches her off guard, she's over the edge before she can

7

stop herself. It's hell for her," Vicky protested with sudden vehemence. "I hate watching her go through it."

"Does she get violent?"

"She yells sometimes—she gets pretty upset—and sometimes I'm afraid she'll do damage to herself. But she'd never hurt Mark."

"Why won't she get treatment?"

Vicky sat silent for a moment, and I found myself watching her as if she were a piece of sculpture, studying the planes of her face, taking satisfaction from the solidity of her form. "She's scared, I think. We have an aunt.... When we were kids she'd show up at the house every once in a while, and she'd sit in the kitchen, like a zombie. She didn't move, didn't say anything—I think she was probably on a heavy diet of tranquilizers. Sherry used to hide whenever she came; she was scared of her. When Sherry was about twelve, the social workers finally put Aunt Karin into a mental institution, and Dad made us go visit her. It was awful. She looked like an old soccer ball, all beat out of shape—and she didn't even know who we were anymore. Sherry had nightmares for years afterwards. I think Sherry's afraid that if she goes to see a shrink, that's how she'll end up too."

"Have you talked to her about getting help?"

"Oh, of course. I read all these articles; there's this new kind of therapy where the patient directs each stage of the treatment, where you don't have to take drugs.... But Sherry doesn't want to hear about it. She's going to leave us no choice but to sign her into some medieval institution with bars over the windows."

"You've discussed this possibility?"

Vicky sighed. "We don't have to discuss it. We all know it's there."

"Does Glen feel the same way you do?"

"Approximately."

"You're on good terms with him?"

"Good enough."

When I continued to regard her expectantly, Vicky added: "I don't really like him or dislike him. He's just someone I have to work with. For Sherry's sake."

This was pretty faint praise. "Look." There was something I'd been mulling over right from the beginning of our conversation, and it was time I brought it up. "When a wife disappears she usually does so for one of two reasons. Either she's having an affair with someone else, or her husband beats her up. Or both."

"She's not sleeping with anybody else." Vicky made this sound like a fact.

"How do you know? In disappearing from her husband, she's only doing what thousands of other women do every year. Since her behavior isn't unique, maybe her reasons aren't either."

"You have to understand that she's already walking a tightrope," Vicky answered impatiently. "When you're afraid that you're going to end up in a loony bin, you're not looking for extra stress."

"Then why did she leave her husband?"

She watched me, lifting a finger to her mouth as if to wipe away a smudge of lipstick.

"He beats her," I said.

"No." Her finger dropped, she shook her head. "At least—I don't think so." Then she frowned. "Don't you think she'd tell me if something like that was going on?"

I thought this was a question she should answer for herself.

"She knows I'd be on her side. I'm not crazy about Glen—and that's no secret. When she told me she was going to marry him, we got into a big fight about it. Ever since then, she's been pretty defensive about their relationship. But now that she's become so dependent upon me, I'm really careful not to say anything; I don't want to sound like I'm telling her how to run her life. But if she were really in trouble. . . ." Again Vicky was waiting for my opinion. Obviously this was a question that had been bothering her for some time.

"You've never seen any signs that she was afraid of Glen? She's never said anything about him having a bad temper? She's never seemed afraid to go home or. . . ."

Vicky was shaking her head.

"Sometimes," I said, "a woman won't tell anyone that she's

9

being beaten because she's afraid that if she does, her husband will kill her. And sometimes she won't tell because she can't stop loving him, can't stop hoping he's going to change."

Vicky looked perplexed. "She certainly did love him once. But I don't know how she feels about him anymore."

"What don't you like about him?"

Her forehead wrinkled. "I don't really dislike him. And we get along well, at least on the surface. But he's—he does all the right things, but he's. . . . He's just not my type, I guess. I know that being with my sister hasn't been easy for him. It would be nice if he spent more time with her—but with the kind of business he's in. . . . Well, it's hard. I mean, he's home more than my husband is, so. . . ." She shrugged, made a gesture of acquiescence, defeat.

"Did you tell Glen that you were coming to see me?"

"I thought I'd talk to you first and see what you said."

"How do you think he's going to react? After all, he'd be the first person I'd want to talk to."

"I think he'll do everything he can to help you. I mean, he's as worried as I am—that's why he went to the police. He wants to find them as much as I do."

I watched her, debating—and seeing me do so, Vicky pressed on: "Look, if you find her, you don't have to tell me where she is. If she wants to keep her whereabouts a secret, that's fine by me—as long as they're O.K. I just need some way to check up on her. If she won't phone me, maybe you could visit her once a week, or I could arrange something with a social worker."

I considered the situation while sketching a fat tulip in the margin of my notebook. "Well. . . ." I added another leaf, shaded in a petal. "As I told you, I don't usually take on this kind of case. But since there's a child involved, I'd be willing to look for her to see how she's doing. But if she doesn't want anyone to know where she is—that's her decision."

"If she's falling apart," Vicky pointed out, "you'll have to tell someone. For Mark's sake."

I was silent, imagining the scene: Sherry hiding in her bedroom, defending herself against a legion of invisible enemies, the small boy crying, afraid of her and for her. . . . "If I think someone's got to be called in to help, I'll either get you, or a social worker—whatever I think best."

Vicky relaxed visibly and subsided into her chair like a deflating balloon.

I went over the dates in more detail, questioned her about their family, got a description of Sherry's history and character, her habits, interests. I outlined my usual procedure; Vicky wrote me a check. We agreed that she would talk to Glen and try to arrange a time for me to see him the next day.

I asked Vicky if she could find me a good recent photograph—preferably a snapshot of both Sherry and Mark. She produced one on the spot; she'd brought it with her just in case. It was a portrait from the waist up: a slim, smiling young woman holding a solemn little boy in her arms, his cheek resting against her shoulder, her cheek resting against the top of his head. The photograph had been taken the previous summer; Sherry was wearing a sleeveless blouse, the child, only a pair of shorts. Sherry's name suited her. Her honey-colored hair hung loose and straight to her shoulders; her eyes were amber, her bare arms golden. The child was several shades darker than she was—with dark brown hair and eyes.

I accompanied Vicky to my office door, then sat down at my desk and typed up her contract. In it, I said I'd try to persuade Sherry to agree to some means of regular communication with Vicky, either through me or through phone calls or whatever. But I made it quite clear that if Mark was being adequately cared for and if Sherry seemed able to cope on her own, I wouldn't betray their hiding place.

It's a document that doesn't bear rereading.

2

THE BLUE HERON RESTAURANT was crammed in among all the other trendy businesses on Robson Street: cappuccino bars, boutiques, bistros, specialty shops. Robson caters to the West End, Vancouver's Manhattan; its denizens are fashionable and flush, its store windows heaped with hand-crafted luxuries— bought for peanuts in the Third World, sold for big bucks in North America. Here materialism gets gussied up, disguised by so-called good taste, and the consumers like to think that their ability to purchase "quality" absolves them from the charge of greed.

I entered the restaurant through a handsome carved wooden door and found myself in a tiny lobby, a nook to my left, furnished with low-backed armchairs and a coffee table. An empty cashier's stall confronted me; above it was a framed photograph of the restaurant's namesake, its huge wings outspread, its long neck curved, its ungainly body lifting into the air. The great blue heron is one of the most exotic-looking birds on the West Coast, but I guess there's never been any profit in killing them since they're still a common sight on the city's beaches. They stand in the shallows, their toothpick legs encircled by coils of kelp and tattered plastic bags, their beaks thrusting after contaminated fish.

I peered around the corner into the restaurant and saw that about two-thirds of the tables were occupied. Not bad for two o'clock on a Friday afternoon. The decor was aquatic, a subtle intermingling of soft blues and purples, with highlights of pink and mother of pearl. I glanced through one of the menus on the cashier's desk. Fish, being the staple of the heron's diet, was the specialty.

A hostess appeared. By her accent I identified her as a recent immigrant from Hong Kong, and she was so beautifully groomed that I felt like a member of a completely different species. Where do women find the time and energy to make themselves look like that? I justified my presence in her elegant foyer by explaining that I had an appointment to see Glen Hovey.

"Please have a seat," she said, indicating the armchairs. "He's on the phone at the moment, but I'll tell him you're waiting. Would you like coffee?"

"Thank you." I never turn down a free cup of coffee, especially if I have reason to believe it might be a good one.

It was. And when I was about halfway through it, Glen Hovey came out to find me.

He had a pleasant face, thin, rather lined—a dark complexion for someone with an English surname. He looked about thirty-eight, which would make him a good ten years older than his wife. His clothes were casual but expensive, and he moved like a man who keeps himself fit. He stood about five-foot-eleven, but when he greeted me I noticed that his hands were disproportionately large—like the hands of someone much taller, bigger-boned.

He led me to a coffee pot, where he refilled my cup and helped himself. Then he escorted me, opening doors and hovering at my elbow, through the restaurant to the back, where his office was located. On leaving the dining room, the aquatic blues were replaced by stark white walls and gleaming linoleum floors; I got a glimpse into the kitchen, where everything looked very clean and orderly. I've been behind staff doors in many expensive restaurants and I've grown accustomed to the sight of walls flecked with food, bags of garbage and laundry piled in the corridors, lakes of dirty water seeping from defective dishwashers. But Glen's restaurant wasn't like that.

Vicky had told me over the phone that Glen was looking forward to meeting me, but his behavior gave no indication of this. Keeping his face slightly averted and his eyelids lowered, he took my jacket, pulled up a chair nearer to his desk for my convenience, waited till I was seated before sitting down himself. He let me ask all the questions, answered them in detail, spelling out names, looking up dates and addresses. But I noticed that whenever I looked down at my notes, he watched me furtively, as if hoping for something from me in return. His wife?

After I had all the facts straight, times, dates, names of police officers and so on, I said, "Tell me about Sherry. The whole story—right from the beginning."

He hesitated. But I think he'd realized that it would be politic to enlist my sympathy, and once he got going he seemed relieved to be able to talk about Sherry, and made a thorough job of it.

Glen said that he'd met Sherry seven years ago when he was working for Shamrock's, a local chain of family-style restaurants. He'd been promoted to the position of manager at their location on Oak Street, where Sherry was a waitress. "She was one of the best waitresses we had," he said. "She'd been working there for several years so she was pretty experienced, and we'd get her to train the new girls. She was a bit disorganized sometimes, but quick to see what needed to be done, always cheerful and friendly—and very popular with the customers.

"But as I got to know her better, I discovered that her cheerfulness was sort of an act—underneath, she was pretty moody. Sometimes, when I took her out, she'd start running herself down, telling me that she was no good, saying that I should stop seeing her. When I met her parents, I thought I understood what the problem was. Her Dad's an alcoholic and he orders her mother around from morning till night. My parents' marriage wasn't much better, so I knew what she was going through. I persuaded her to move out of home and try living with me. And it seemed to work out fine; she was definitely much happier. When we decided to get married, I know we both believed that our marriage would be different."

And it *was* different, according to Glen, right up until Mark was born. "You've heard of postpartum depression?" he asked, looking uncomfortable. "Well, I'm not a psychiatrist, but I guess it was something like that. Sherry became very listless, withdrawn—she didn't even bother getting dressed anymore. And she was a complete slave to the kid. Mark had colic—"

"That wouldn't help."

"It didn't," he agreed fervently. "We were told that colic is normal, nothing to worry about—but for the first eight months Mark cried almost constantly, and despite what the pediatrician said, Sherry felt that his crying was her fault. She became obsessed by Mark—even when he slept, she wouldn't leave his room. I tried to help out, I hired babysitters, but she wouldn't go out. I heard about a group for mothers who were having similar problems—but she wouldn't go to that either. She wouldn't leave Mark with anyone—not even me.

"By the end of the first year, Mark was over the worst of it, but Sherry never really recovered from that experience. She hasn't been what you'd call 'stable' ever since. She's totally paranoid, she flips out over little things. . . I never know what I'm coming home to. I've begged her to get help, but she refuses to see anyone. She talks about shrinks as if they were torturers."

"Vicky told me about her aunt, the one who ended up in an institution."

"Yes." He was quiet for a moment, as if letting me know that he was not dismissing his wife's fears, and sympathized with what she suffered. "But ignoring the problem is no solution. She's never normal anymore; she's getting worse and worse. And there doesn't seem to be anything I can do about it. Sometimes—" He broke off, propped both elbows on his desk and burrowed his fingers into the roots of his hair. "I don't even know if I want you to find her," he confessed.

"I can understand that."

He gave me a grateful look.

"It's amazing what kids can get used to," he continued, after a pause. "Some days I come home and it's way past Mark's bedtime but he's still up and dressed. 'Mummy's sick today,' he says. 'I'm making a rocket.' And sure enough, he's got his Leggo blocks spread out all over the landing outside the bedroom door and she's locked in the bedroom, arguing with herself, or hiding under the blankets. Sometimes she's been

15

there for hours, and he's had no supper—nothing. He climbs up onto the kitchen counter and helps himself to the crackers. Not the cookies." Glen smiled faintly, to himself, and shook his head. "Mark knows the rules. Crackers are O.K. I'd phone home from work, I used to check up on them several times a day. And if she wouldn't come to the phone, I'd ask Mark: 'How's Mummy? Is she talking to you? Have you had lunch?' If things didn't sound too good, I'd try to leave work, or I'd phone Vicky and ask her to look in on them. I don't know how I would have got by without Vicky. She's pretty much the only person who can cope with Sherry anymore."

He paused and gave me a cautious glance. "Have you ever known someone who was mentally ill?"

"I have some experience with it."

"The worst part of it is that—it's not exactly that I don't love her anymore—I still love her, I know that. But after a while, you lose hope, and you start dreaming...imagining what it must be like to live with somebody sane. Someone whose moods you can predict, someone who'll answer when you talk to them, someone who doesn't sit there, staring at you as if you'd sprouted fangs. It gets pretty exhausting."

"Do you think that Sherry's capable of looking after Mark on her own?"

He leaned back in his chair. "No." One of his long brown fingers tapped irritably on his desk. "But I don't know what to do about it. A lot of people have been telling me that I should get custody and in a way I agree. But if I take Mark away from his mother, he'll hate me. They're thick, those two. It's like they hold onto each other for survival. So even if I find them—what am I going to do? He won't want to leave her. I'm not close to him, not like she is. I want to find him, I want to visit him regularly—you know, give them as much support as I can. I wish he was older—old enough to phone me if he needed help. But I don't think I should separate them.

"Now that I've got this place going—" He gestured towards the dining room beyond his office walls. "I'll be able to delegate more and take some time off. But first I've got to get my bank loan paid off—by July at the latest. Once that's over with. . . . " He saw the look on my face, and decided he'd better be more frank.

"I haven't been much of a father—I know that. I don't know what it is—I guess I'm not very patient. Mark whines so much, and his mother always defends him. Maybe if she were different, then. . . . But I don't want to be blaming everything on her. I hope that as Mark gets older we'll get along better. After all, I haven't really been around much. . . . " He grimaced, gave up. "A typical masculine confession, right?"

You said it, I thought. And he'd gauged me well—I prefer people who dispense with the excuses and acknowledge their faults.

"There's one thing I should make clear to you," I said. "Vicky's hiring me to make sure that Sherry's O.K. We've agreed that if Sherry's managing to cope on her own, and if she doesn't want anybody to know where she is, I'm not revealing her whereabouts."

He dropped his eyes. "I see." He said nothing for a moment. "I guess I can live with that. Tell her—if you find her—that I want to see Mark. I have a right to see him," he added, as if challenging me to disagree.

Sure, I thought, but that's not my department. Leave me out of it.

"And what about money?" he asked. "She's got nothing but her savings—"

"Where? Which bank?" My pen was poised; Vicky hadn't been able to tell me anything about Sherry's financial situation.

He named the bank, the branch, dug through his wallet and produced the account number. "She's been putting her Family Allowance checks into it for years. I put some more money into it—a couple of thousand—"

"Into her savings account?"

"Yeah. But I don't know if she's using it."

I stared—thinking that I'd underestimated him. Deserted spouses aren't usually so generous. "Does she get a bank statement on that account?"

"It usually arrives about the middle of the month." He checked the date on his watch. "I've got last month's statement at home. I'll bring it in to show you."

We went over the list of people Sherry knew. It wasn't very long—Sherry's illness had isolated her. The friends Glen could name were his friends rather than hers, mostly business acquaintances. We talked about places she'd lived, visited, wanted to go. But according to Glen, all Sherry's connections were here in the Lower Mainland; she was born and raised in Vancouver, and had never been far from home. "I find it hard to imagine her leaving this city. She's not very adventurous; she doesn't like going anywhere that she hasn't been before."

He gave me the names of her dentist, doctor, hairdresser. I made him root through his memory for other leads: the name of the community center where Sherry and Mark went swimming, the address of their local health unit, the names of her favorite stores. It's one thing, after all, to run away from your husband—but quite another to abandon your favorite fabric store or butcher. Finally, when I figured I had enough, I rose to leave.

"You know," he said, also getting up, "I think I know why she ran away."

"You do?" I wondered why it had taken him this long to bring it up.

He came around from behind his desk. "I've been thinking about it." A muscle in his cheek twitched. "She was desperate—she must have been. It took a lot of courage for her to walk out like that. And she's very perceptive—she knows what's going on. I think Sherry realized that Vicky and I can't handle her anymore, that we've reached the point where we're going to have to force her to get treatment."

"Maybe you told her as much?" I reached for my jacket.

"No. That's my point." He took the jacket from me, helped me into it—and I tensed, expecting his touch. But he didn't touch me. "She didn't need to be told. And the other day I realized that if we put her into a psychiatric hospital or whatever, they'll separate her from Mark."

I glanced up. He was gazing into my eyes with an intensity

that was almost hypnotic. "And you think that Sherry has realized the same thing."

"Like I say—she's not stupid."

He showed me out through a staff door. As I walked back to my car I reviewed our conversation and discovered that my reactions to him were mixed. Sherry should have little to fear from a man who put money into her bank account, admitted he was relieved to be rid of her, and said that he didn't want custody of their son. But I wondered if, despite Glen's denial, he'd warned Sherry that if she didn't seek treatment voluntarily, he'd consign her to an institution where she'd be separated from her child. If so, his plan had backfired. And he struck me as the kind of man who wouldn't like to admit it.

On Monday I started making my usual, official inquiries—which the cops would have made too—but maybe they'd missed something. Sherry didn't have a driver's license, so the Department of Motor Vehicles couldn't help me; she hadn't filed a change of address form with the post office, or turned up in any of the hospitals. She hadn't visited her doctor, her dentist, or Mark's pediatrician; she hadn't applied for hydro, cablevision, or a telephone; she hadn't even used her library card. I took her photograph around to all the food banks and soup kitchens—but no one recognized her.

I went to talk to Sergeant Oliffe at Missing Persons. He was gruff and taciturn, the type of man who will only help you if you let him lecture you first. After reminding me that he was under no obligation to talk to me and pointing out that any Tom, Dick or Harry (not to mention Jane) could obtain a private investigator's license, he pulled out Sherry's file. But already I knew more about Sherry than the cops did.

When I got back to my office there was a message from Glen on my answering machine; he'd received the March bank statement for Sherry's savings account and had brought both the March and February statements with him to work. I went down to The Blue Heron to take a look at them. According to the February statement, Sherry had withdrawn seventeen hundred and fifty dollars on February 2nd, the day she disappeared, leaving only the ten dollars necessary to keep the account open. Glen's deposit of twenty-five hundred dollars, dated February 23rd, was recorded on the March statement. There were no other transactions.

So. Sherry hadn't touched Glen's money, probably didn't even know that it was there. She had worked for about three weeks at Copper's restaurant; in total she couldn't have much more than twenty-four hundred dollars, which would last her about two months. And she'd already been gone for six and a half weeks. She'd have to go back to work again, soon.

I debated my next move. Her parents? Friends? Finally I decided that my best bet would be to visit Copper's restaurant, since that was where she was last seen.

3

COPPER'S WAS A TYPICAL Canadian-style restaurant, run by a Greek immigrant, heavy on the hamburgers, fries and hot turkey sandwiches. But they cooked these staples well, and the restaurant was in a good location, surrounded by light industry, on one of the busiest truck routes out of town. When I arrived there at one-thirty, the lunch rush was just ending.

Alexis, the owner, was propped on a stool behind the cash register, ringing in the money, keeping an eye on his staff and chatting up the customers. His joviality was forced, his jokes were sexist, but his employees treated him with good-natured familiarity, so perhaps a heart of gold beat somewhere beneath his curly grey chest hairs.

"Ah—Sherry," he said, when I asked about her. "Everybody wants to find Sherry. But she left!" He raised his eyebrows and gave a nearby waitress a glance of mock despair. "She didn't like me, I guess." The waitress, who had skin the color of milk chocolate and the kind of good looks that usually condemn women to parade floats, smiled obligingly. She continued writing up her bill.

"Have other people been in here asking about her?"

"There was her sister—" he began, but was interrupted by a customer who demanded a pack of cigarettes. The customer paid for them, grumbling at the cost.

I repeated my question. But now a group of overalled workers was assembling in front of the till, arguing and joking with each other, emptying change, gum wrappers and miscellaneous bits of metal from their pockets. The tallest of the workers, a young black man, laid a bet with Alexis that the Edmonton Oilers would win the hockey game tomorrow night. I waited, wondering if I'd ever get Alexis to myself.

Finally most of the lunch crowd left, and Alexis surrendered the till to one of his "girls," sat down and had a cup of coffee with me. I asked him how he'd come to employ Sherry. He told me that he'd had a "Help Wanted" sign propped in the window and Sherry had walked in, holding a little boy by the hand. She'd said she was an experienced waitress. "Maybe she was," Alexis conceded, "but she had some kind of problem. I don't know what was wrong with her. I stuck her in the back with Luisa, washing dishes. And I got her to set up, clear tables, stuff like that. But there were still problems—I knew she wasn't going to work out." He ran his tongue around the inside of his bottom gum, making his lower lip bulge.

"She quit?"

His eyes kept flickering past me, watching the door, the till; even now, I had only half his attention. "One morning she just didn't show up. She gave no notice. Nothing. I didn't even have a phone number for her." He nodded to a customer who was walking by our table, gave an inscrutable signal to a pair of cops as they were leaving. "I've still got her last paycheck sitting in my office. I don't know what to do with it. I sent it to the address she gave me, but it came back."

"What were the problems?" I asked. "Can you describe them?"

He considered, narrowing his eyes against the smoke spiraling from his cigarette. "She was touchy," he said finally. "She put people off—not just customers—the other staff too. She tried too hard; she went too fast, forgot things. 'Relax,' I said to her. 'Take it easy.' But she couldn't." He tapped the side of his head, significantly. "She made the customers uncomfortable."

Again I confirmed dates: when had Sherry started working there, when had she quit; how many days after that had Vicky showed up asking about her. I asked him if he'd mind if I talked to his employees. "It's up to them," he said. "That's the staff table—over there." He jerked his chin in the direction of the corner table near the kitchen, where several of the staff were just sitting down to lunch.

I went over and introduced myself. I asked if any of them knew where Sherry had moved to, or why she'd quit—and drew blank looks. "Tell me what she was like to work with," I invited, pulling up a chair at their table.

Sherry's co-workers described her as "nervous" and "disorganized"; when one of them said the word "crazy," the rest of them nodded. "She acted like she was afraid of me," said Tabib, one of the kitchen staff. "She made me feel like I was a bad guy or something." He shook his head sorrowfully and decorated his chips with generous squiggles of ketchup.

"She was always trying to do too much," complained Angela, the waitress who could have graced a parade float. "She tried to do other people's jobs as well as her own. Then she'd get mad at herself when she messed up. I was always saying to her: 'Leave it—that's my job!' It bugged me."

They described Sherry as unfriendly, evasive, and quick to take offense. "She didn't like questions—that's for sure," said Patty, a middle-aged white woman. She had slipped off her shoes and was surreptitiously massaging her swollen ankles under the table.

"What kind of questions?"

" 'Where do you live? Are you married?' She as much as told me to mind my own business."

"Did she ever mention her little boy?"

"She never told *me* anything about a little boy." Patty looked around the table, as if daring anyone else to have heard of him.

"I saw the little boy the first day she came in here—when she was asking about the job," Chi Ming offered, smoothing a strand of hair under his cook's cap. "But I never heard her talk about him."

"Who took care of him when she went to work?" I asked. They shrugged, shook their heads.

"She didn't talk about that stuff," Angela explained, flipping her hair over her shoulder. "She acted like she didn't want to have anything to do with us."

There was a short silence, broken by Tabib. "She talked to Luisa."

"About what?" Patty demanded.

"I don't know. But I used to hear them in the back. Yak, yak, yak." He gave Angela a flirtatious grin and stuck another forkful of chips in his mouth.

"Luisa is the dishwasher?" I asked.

"She's on holiday right now," said Angela. "Visiting relatives in Thunder Bay."

"Italians," Patty explained; it was as if she'd said, "Scum."

I gave her my best ingenuous gaze. "You don't like Italians?"

She answered with a glare. You don't like anyone, I thought, and you say so whenever you think you can get away with it.

Again I addressed the group: "None of you have heard from Sherry since she stopped working here?"

None of them had.

"Talk to Luisa," Tabib suggested.

"I will," I said. "When does she get back?"

They all looked at Angela. She preened a little under the attention, twirling her fingers in her luxuriant black hair. "She took two weeks off and this is the second week—so, she should be in on Saturday."

When I was back outside on the sidewalk, I stopped, and debated. What next? Sherry's parents? (Parents are always worth a visit.) But I should call them first. I noticed a phone booth nearby—one of the enclosed, old-fashioned kind.

But the booth was occupied. I waited, deafened by the roar of passing trucks, surrounded by swirling grit and litter, while the man inside it finished his call. Semi-trailers belched, dump trucks changed gears, cars dodged around them, changing lanes and squealing their tires as they turned the corner onto Hastings.

The man had one ear jammed against the receiver, the other plugged with a thick forefinger, a cigarette sticking out from the side of his mouth. He glanced around, saw me waiting and abruptly hung up. He pushed out the door of the booth and walked away, his right knee held rigid, the leg swinging out to the side with each step.

I went into the phone booth and closed the door behind me—immediately opened it again. The booth, smogged with cigarette smoke, reeked with the overpowering smell of... Camels, that was it. I know the smell of Camel cigarettes well; my former mentor, George, used to smoke them, and I'd know which rooms he'd been in by the residual stench he left behind.

As I waited for the booth to air out a bit, I thought about George. I do this occasionally, in the same spirit that war veterans remember their fallen comrades. It was George's idea, really, that I should become a private investigator. When I met him, I was fresh out of the divorce courts and wondering what to do with the rest of my life. George took me on as an apprentice, taught me everything he knew, and when he died he made me the heir to his business. I still miss George—when I remember him—but I no longer feel like I'm trying to fill his shoes. I've discarded some of his methods, improved upon others. He was a very nice man, but I've come to realize that he wasn't a very good detective. It's my business now, and it's worth a lot more than it was when I inherited it.

When the air in the phone booth was fit for human consumption, I closed the door and made my call.

Vicky had told me that her father was a driver for an automotive parts company, and that her mother worked part-time in a discount department store. When I phoned, only Mrs. Svendsen was at home. She agreed to talk to me, and said that if I came by around four, I'd catch her husband too. He was usually home from work by four-thirty.

The air in the Svendsen's house was sickening—saturated with cigarette smoke, perfumed with air fresheners. As soon as Sherry's mother opened the front door, it hit me like a bank of fog, and I held my breath as I entered it. Obviously no one had opened a window in years.

Betty Svendsen received me nervously. "Oh—a woman," were her first words. "I didn't expect that."

I get so sick of hearing this. "Did I sound like a man on the phone?"

"Well no, but—"

But you thought you'd mention it anyway, I thought.

Her face was putty-colored (except for a livid smear of lipstick), her eyes a watery blue, her permed hair faded to an indeterminate grey-blonde. Once, I suppose, she'd looked a lot like Sherry, but the years had blurred her features and sucked the luster from her skin.

As I talked to her, seated on her plastic-covered couch, trying to see around the huge, plastic-wrapped lamp shade beside me, I remembered Glen saying that Sherry's Dad "orders her mother around from morning till night." The description fit. Betty Svendsen's speech and gestures were habitually placatory. As she talked she chain-smoked, stubbing out the lipstick-smeared cigarettes before she'd even finished them, her hands constantly moving from the cigarette pack to the lighter to the ashtray and back to her lips.

On the mantelpiece were high school graduation portraits of both her daughters: Vicky, determinedly smiling, her cheekbones tinted an unlikely shade of pink; Sherry, also smiling, but looking stiff, her eyes evasive, as if wishing she were somewhere else. No wonder, I thought, returning my gaze to her mother. This was not a happy home.

But Betty Svendsen wasn't about to admit it. Yes, they were both lovely girls, they had made good marriages and she now had four darling grandchildren. Yes, Vicky had always been "a little mother" to Sherry; and yes, Sherry was a bit moody sometimes, but when she was feeling a bit blue, she knew she could always ask Grandma to come and sit with her little boy. I let her go on like this for some time—wanting to find out how long she could keep it up. I finally realized that if I left it up to her, we'd never get around to talking about Sherry's disappearance.

I asked her, point blank, why Sherry had left her husband. "Oh yes," she said, vaguely, "well, she's just taking a little break. She's always been like that. When she was a little girl, she used to go for long walks, just take off—" She tried to chortle, but it turned into a cough. Her eyes started to water; she flapped a hand in front of her face, dispersing the smoke. "She'd go so far she'd get lost and we'd have to go looking for her. We used to call her our little explorer!" She gasped, and started coughing again.

"I guess she got lost again," I said, when she'd recovered.

"Oh she'll be back—I know she will. She just needs some time to herself."

"Vicky thinks Sherry needs psychiatric help."

Betty looked affronted. "If I were you," she advised me, "I'd take what Vicky says with a grain of salt. She's always interfering in things that are none of her business. When Sherry decided to get married without asking Vicky's permission—well! You should have seen the way Vicky carried on. And now she brings in complete strangers. . . ." Then she remembered who she was talking to. "I know you're just doing your job, but I really don't think that any of this is necessary." She crushed another cigarette.

"You think Sherry is perfectly capable of looking after herself?"

"Of course she is!"

"Her husband doesn't seem to think so."

This gave her pause—she'd already told me how wonderful Glen was. "Oh—men!" She shook her head patronizingly and reached for another cigarette. "They always think that we can't do anything without them."

At this moment her husband walked in the door. Betty dropped the lighter and cigarette, jumped up, walked heavily across the living room to greet him. "Oh, Karl—you're home. This is Mrs.—" She looked at me.

"Lacey," I reminded her.

"The detective Vicky's hired, you remember? A woman." (She wasn't going to let me forget it.) "She's come to—"

"You found her yet?" her husband interrupted her, looking at me. He pulled off his jacket and handed it to his wife to hang up.

"No. I haven't."

"Stupid kid," he commented. He lumbered into the living room, sat heavily into the big lazy-boy chair opposite me, the only chair in the room that wasn't coated in plastic. *His* chair, I thought.

Vicky had inherited her good looks and dimples from him, but like many drivers he'd run to fat: his rear end had spread, he'd developed a big beer belly and heavy jowls. He was now bent over, untying his shoelaces, grunting with the effort to reach them. "You won't find her here," he commented helpfully, sitting upright again. He kicked off his shoes, his face was a dangerous shade of red. "Get me a beer," he said to his wife. She disappeared into the kitchen.

"But perhaps Sherry talked to you before she left, gave you some hint of her plans?"

He leaned back into the lazy-boy chair, his feet rising in front of him. "Nobody tells me a bloody thing," he said with satisfaction.

I believed him. I watched, resignedly, as he reached into his shirt pocket and pulled out a package of cigarettes. "Why do you think she disappeared?" I asked.

He lit a cigarette, put the lighter on the coffee table beside him. His wife reappeared with an open beer bottle and handed it to him. He lifted the bottle to his lips, took a long draft, and as the alcohol went down, his eyes closed—just as a baby's eyelids droop when it latches onto a nipple. Finally he pulled the bottle from his lips and remembered his manners. "You want one?" He indicated the bottle.

"No. Thanks."

He heaved himself up, adjusted the cushion behind him. "Playing games, I figure," he said in response to my question. "Everybody should ignore her—leave her alone. She'll be back."

"That's what I was telling her," Betty Svendsen chipped in. "About how Sherry used to run away all the time when she was little. Remember how we'd have to send Vicky out looking for her?"

He didn't respond. He was exuding smoke from his orifices

like a somnolent dragon, examining his feet in their brown-striped socks.

"Do you think that Sherry is happy with Glen?" I asked him.

Betty Svendsen jumped in. "Of course she's—"

"She's asking *me*!" Karl snarled at her, stabbing his chest with his thumb. Betty's mouth drooped.

Her husband gave me a long, sardonic stare. "I wouldn't know," he said, as if he made it his business not to. He held up his bottle, squinted at its contents. "They've got a pretty fancy house."

"That's not what I'm asking."

He heard—but chose to ignore me. "In Shaughnessy," he added, giving me an appreciative leer. "You know what that costs."

I did. Shaughnessy is a neighborhood of established money: solid upper-middle-class homes, big lots, tree-shaded streets—and in Vancouver's booming real estate market, houses like that cost a fortune. No wonder Glen was in debt.

"He's going up in the world," Karl mused, complacently, as if watching his son-in-law's progress from a comfortable seat on the sidelines. He took another sip of beer, savored it. "So they don't come round here much. Do they, Mother?" He gave his wife a belligerent look.

She decided not to answer.

"Do you think Sherry's capable of living on her own and looking after Mark?" I asked.

His lower lip curled. "She babies that kid."

"Now Karl, he's only four," Betty remonstrated.

"There's four-year-old kids who live on the streets," he pointed out, roughly. "They feed themselves, everything."

I thought it an odd remark. Was this what he was recommending?

Since he wasn't answering my questions, I decided to try a little provocation instead. "I understand that there's a history of mental illness in the family."

Betty gaped. Her husband's cigarette stopped in midair.

"Vicky told you that?" Betty protested.

29

"Whose sister is it," I asked, "who ended up in a mental institution?"

Karl narrowed his eyes at me. His wife, standing just behind him, was looking at the bald spot on top of his head as if expecting it to erupt.

"Yours?" I suggested.

Betty chose this moment to slip out of the room and return to the kitchen, where something was sizzling. When she was gone I tried, one more time, to get her husband to talk. "I'm told that Sherry's very moody, and easily upset. You know anything about that, Mr. Svendsen?"

He lifted a calloused hand, waving me away. "I don't know," he said disgustedly. "How do I know what in the hell's wrong with her?"

"Then there is something wrong with her."

He glowered at me—upended the beer bottle into his mouth.

"When did you last see Sherry?"

He extracted the bottle from his mouth, ground out his cigarette in the ashtray beside him. He muttered something I couldn't hear. "Pardon?" I leaned forward.

He was staring down at his bottle, enfolding it tenderly with his stubby, thick hands. "Get out," he said softly.

"With pleasure," I assured him. The plastic squeaked as I stood up.

4

I DIDN'T LIKE Glen's friends. They were business people, for the most part: a woman who owned a chain of fashion boutiques, a real estate agent, a junior stockbroker. They were all ambitious and upwardly mobile; Glen seemed much nicer than any of them. Yet they were his friends, not Sherry's. They agreed that it was "just terrible the way that Sherry had treated him." They all knew that Sherry had "mental problems," although they told me that Glen didn't talk about it much, the subject was painful for him.

The real estate agent seemed to be already grooming herself for the position of Glen's second wife. She was eloquent on the subject of Glen's sufferings with Sherry and told me that she'd occasionally looked after Mark when Sherry was ill. "But he never wants to be with anyone but his Mum. He's a very insecure little boy. He still wets his bed, apparently. I've told Glen that he must step in, must do something or that boy will grow up twisted. And she can't have custody. She's not fit!"

The stockbroker told me about the time she'd gone clothes shopping with Sherry. The trip went fine, right up until Sherry locked herself into a fitting room booth and wouldn't come out. "I was so embarrassed," the stockbroker said. "Standing there in that stupid dressing room, talking to her through the door, everybody looking at me, wondering what was going on. After that day, I really understood what Glen must be going through, living with her."

The woman who owned the chain of fashion boutiques

coolly informed me that she didn't invite Sherry to her dinner parties anymore. "I explained to Glen that I just can't run that risk. The last time they came she behaved so oddly that she made everybody else very uncomfortable. She spoiled the evening for all of us."

"Now you invite Glen on his own?"

"I have. But it's an awkward situation."

When I'd finished with them, I phoned Glen and asked him if he could give me the names of some of Sherry's old friends, the people she'd known when he met her. "She hasn't seen any of them for years," he objected. But when I insisted, he finally came up with one name: Mei Ling. He didn't remember her last name, and no longer had her phone number, but thought that if I called the Shamrock on Oak Street, someone there would be able to tell me how to reach her.

At the Shamrock they told me that Mei Ling was now a manager at another Shamrock in West Vancouver. When I showed up there, she abandoned her invoices for a few minutes, sat down and had coffee with me. But as Glen had predicted, she hadn't seen Sherry in years. "You know how it is," she said, "I was still involved with work, and she was in a another world, with her baby. We just drifted apart."

"How well did you know Glen?"

"Actually, I've known him for years—before he met Sherry even. When I was in high school I used to work weekends at the Shamrock on East Broadway and he worked there too, although our paths rarely crossed. The first time I ever really talked to him was at a staff Christmas party; at that time he was involved with some other girl. . . she was at the party too, I remember. But I didn't really get to know him until he became a manager at Oak Street."

"Did you like him? What was he like to work with?"

"Oh sure—he's an excellent manager. If he applied to work here, I'd hire him on the spot. Although, personally, I don't think I'd want to get *married* to him. . . . ." She wrinkled her nose.

"Why not?"

"Well—" she cocked her head. "When he and Sherry started

dating, I saw another side of him. Even at work, he wanted Sherry all to himself; he didn't like to let her out of his sight. We used to tease him, butt in on their tête-à-têtes, stuff like that. Sherry never minded, but he did. He'd get all poker-faced."

"Do you think they were happy together?"

"They seemed so, back then."

"This other girlfriend—the one who came to the Christmas party—what was her name?"

"Oh, Jeez—I never knew. I only met her that one time. But I remember someone told me that they were living together."

"How long ago was this?"

"I was in high school—grade twelve, I think. So that was. . . . " Her eyes went past me, considering. "Thirteen years ago?"

Still, I thought it might be interesting to have a chat with this ex-girlfriend.

On my way home that evening I stopped off at Tom's place. Like me, Tom is divorced, and we've been lovers for many years. We've never lived together, but we see each other at least once a week, usually more often, and we know most of each other's friends. For a long time Tom kept expecting our relationship to become something else—a marriage, for example. In the early years of our relationship we fought about this at regular intervals, Tom insisting that a relationship couldn't work without commitment and security, while I tried to make him understand that living with me would never provide him with either. "You'll expect me to be home every night at five-thirty, like you are," I pointed out. "You'll expect me to be there for supper—to cook supper! You'll get upset when I leave the house and go to work at what you consider to be bedtime. But I don't work regular hours; I don't live like you do. And I don't see why I should."

Tom has tried, we've both tried—and failed—to replace each other with someone more compatible. But like most people, we're the victims of our inconsistencies. I don't really trust men who don't come home for dinner every night, and Tom resents women who try to make him change his habits. So as the years have gone by, we've accommodated to each other; I've learned to appreciate the emotional and sexual security that our relationship provides, and Tom has acquired a new self-image. He's the kind of person who likes being in a rut, but he knows that others mock him for this trait. Therefore it pleases him to have to explain to all his staid, married acquaintances that I'm his lover—not his wife. It makes him feel unpredictable.

I found Tom standing outside the entrance to his apartment building trying to get his cat, Mozart, down from a tree. He explained that he'd brought Mozart outside to have a little romp on the grass (usually Mozart is confined to Tom's balcony), and a brutish white dog had attacked the cat and driven him up this tree. I don't like Mozart. He's a big, thuggish tabby; he steals onto the kitchen counter at every opportunity; he demands to get in and out at least thirty times a day; and he jumps into my lap every time I sit down. He'll do just about anything to get Tom's attention—this tree climbing stunt being no exception. Tom had been standing there for the last half hour, calling: "Come on, kitty, I'll catch you. Come on—you can do it," oblivious to the people who'd come out on their balconies to watch him.

"Just leave him," I said, "and he'll come down by himself."

"But he's in shock, Meg. He's too scared to come down."

"Don't be ridiculous. Remember when you took him to the park and he climbed up that fir tree? He was twice as high up. And as soon as he was good and ready he came headfirst down the trunk. But as long as he's getting so much sympathy for staying up there, he has no reason to come down."

Unconvinced, Tom continued to gaze upwards, besottedly, while Mozart, yowling, prowled back and forth along the branch. "I'll have to phone the fire department," Tom decided, in distress.

"No," I said firmly. "As a tax payer I object to having a whole truckload of firefighters diverted from their duties to rescue a stupid cat who's perfectly capable of rescuing himself."

"You should have seen that dog, Meg," Tom said worriedly. "I'm sure it was rabid—"

"Then you should have phoned the pound."

"It was growling and foaming; it would have killed Mozart if it had caught him."

Too bad Mozart escaped, I thought. But if Mozart had fallen prey to the dog, I'd have been called upon to support Tom through his time of grief—which would have been beyond my capacities.

Finally, when Tom said that he was going to drive halfway across town to his friend's place to borrow a ladder, I took matters into my own hands. "Give me a boost," I commanded, taking off my jacket.

He stared at me.

I threw my jacket onto the ground. "Come on—like this." I made a stirrup, interlocking my fingers.

"What are you proposing to do?"

"I'm going to rescue your damn cat!"

"But—" He looked up; his cat looked down. They were like lovers divided by an insuperable abyss. "How will you get up there?" he asked me.

"You're going to help me," I explained, trying not to lose my temper. "Now give me a leg-up."

"You'll be able to hang onto that bottom branch, but where will you go from there?"

"I'll pull myself up."

"Then I should do it," Tom decided. "Mozart won't come to you."

"But you haven't climbed a tree since you were in primary school," I reminded him.

"Have you?" he inquired, looking at me with new interest.

Having reminded him that as a student of martial arts, I was much better qualified to fall out of a tree than he was, I convinced him to boost me up. I got hold of the bottom branch, kicked my feet up the tree trunk and hoisted myself over it. From there, standing up, I could just reach the cat.

Mozart's ears pricked attentively. He greeted me with a poignant mew. But since I only had one hand, the other being needed to embrace the tree trunk, I had to grasp the cat awkwardly around the stomach to get him off the branch, and Mozart rewarded me with a good scratch.

I dropped Mozart hastily into Tom's outstretched arms and he scrambled onto Tom's shoulder, digging his claws into the thick material of Tom's suit.

"Poor kitty," Tom consoled him, stroking him from head to tail. Mozart started to purr. "There you are now—safe and sound."

I sat back down on the bottom branch, rolled over onto my stomach, swung myself down and dropped to the ground. I brushed myself off and picked up my jacket.

"Good work, Meg," Tom congratulated me, while Mozart butted against his hand to remind him to keep patting. "Very resourceful indeed. An intrepid and selfless act."

"Thanks," I said, sucking the scratch on my hand. Tom turned back to the cat and nuzzled him affectionately.

"He scratched me," I said.

"He was scared," Tom commiserated, scratching Mozart behind the ear. "Look at him—he's trembling."

"I'm trembling too," I accused. It was true. My knees felt weak.

Tom came over and put an arm around my shoulder. "You have my undying admiration," he murmured into my ear as he escorted me towards the door.

Which was why I'd climbed the tree.

The next morning I visited the neighborhood where Sherry used to live when she'd worked at Copper's restaurant. It was about two kilometers from the restaurant, near Trout Lake Park. The street was uninspiring: a grab bag of sagging, wood houses, built before World War II, and mass-produced stucco boxes, circa 1975.

I went up and down the block, knocking on every door. A third of the residents weren't home, another third didn't know enough English to understand what I wanted, and of the remainder, only two people recognized Sherry's photograph. They remembered seeing her on the street with Mark. But nobody had ever talked to her, nobody knew where she'd moved to, nobody knew who'd looked after Mark when Sherry went to work.

I went to the house where Sherry had lived, which was sub-divided into suites. Three barefoot children, probably refugees recently arrived from Southeast Asia, were playing on the sidewalk out front. Their grandfather opened the basement suite door. He stared at my photograph of Sherry and Mark, nodded, came out onto the sidewalk in his slippers and pointed to the rickety upstairs suite where Sherry used to live. "Gone now," he said. That was as far as we could get. I knocked on the door of the main floor suite, but no one was home. Finally I climbed the stairs to the top floor, where the door was opened by a white youth who smelled of beer. He said he'd moved in a week ago and suggested I talk to the landlord who lived on the next street. But the landlord wasn't home, and his wife said the tenants were his department, not hers. I got his phone number and left.

Again I phoned Glen. This time I wanted to know if he employed a cleaning woman at his house. He said that there was a woman who came in once a week, on Tuesdays, to do the laundry and heavy cleaning. I told him I'd like to talk to her. He received this news in silence.

"It makes me uncomfortable," he admitted at last, "the thought of you going around talking to everyone about us."

"Washing your dirty linen in public."

"Something like that. And you're not going to learn any-thing from Teresa. She hasn't worked for us for long and she speaks almost no English at all."

"I'd still like to talk to her. I admit that it's a long shot—but long shots are about all I've got left."

"All right," he said. "But I'm warning you—she hasn't said more than two sentences to me the whole time I've known her." He finally gave me Teresa's phone number and address.

I phoned her, but the person on the other end of the line said that Teresa wouldn't be home until after six. I said that I'd stop by that evening to see her. If her English was poor, it would be easier to talk to her face to face.

Meanwhile I visited the community center where Sherry and Mark used to go swimming, the local health unit where Mark received his vaccinations, and Sherry's favorite fabric store on 41st Avenue. At all of these places they recognized Sherry's photograph, but said they hadn't seen her in some time. It was the same story at her hairdresser's. Finally I gave up, stopped in at the Old Budapest for a bowl of goulash, then headed over to Teresa Minero's house.

It was another of those ugly stucco boxes, an up-and-down duplex designed to provide the maximum amount of space for the minimum amount of money. As I walked up the front sidewalk I could see the blue light of a television illuminating the ceiling through an upstairs window, and downstairs, to my right, a curtain lifted, then dropped. Someone had heard me coming.

I knocked on the downstairs door and it opened, but the chain was left on the latch. A shadow, silhouetted in the crack, asked me what I wanted. I told the shadow that I'd like to speak to Teresa Minero and passed my card through the gap. Slim, brown fingers accepted it; the door closed again. I waited.

The door reopened—but still the chain remained in place. This shadow was shorter. She had a husky voice and a heavy Spanish accent. "What you want?"

"I understand that you work for Glen and Sherry Hovey. I was hoping that you might be able to tell me something about Sherry. She's disappeared, and no one knows where she's gone."

"Mr. Hovey said?" She seemed puzzled.

"Yes, he gave me your address. But I'm working for Sherry's sister. Did you know that Sherry Hovey had disappeared?"

"Yes. No," she said abruptly. "I don't know. Sorry." The door shut; she locked it. I'd reached another dead end.

Theoretically, it should have been easy to find Sherry. But I'd now been looking for her for a week and I'd made no progress at all. Maybe Glen was wrong—maybe Sherry had left town. But I didn't want to face that possibility until I'd exhausted every other alternative.

This time I phoned Vicky. "About this babysitter," I began.

"What babysitter?"

"The one who looked after Mark when Sherry was working at Copper's. Everyone I've talked to has told me that Mark is extremely insecure and never wants to be with anyone but his mother. So how did Sherry get Mark to spend five days a week with some woman he'd never even seen before?"

"You know, I wondered about that too. But of course it depends on the person—children find some people much less threatening than others. And Mark is getting better. He's always been much better with women than men."

"Really? Why?"

"Oh some kids are afraid of men. My eldest was the same. Men are bigger, louder; they tend to tease kids more and—Oh, I've just remembered something. Sherry told me that the woman who was looking after Mark had a boy the same age. That would help."

"He likes other kids, does he?"

"Yes. I know when I'm looking after him, it's much easier if my own kids are at home."

But how am I going to find this babysitter? I wondered, as I hung up the phone. All I know is that she has a preschool-aged son and lives somewhere within a two mile radius of Trout Lake Park. "How about a house-to-house search?" I suggested sarcastically, getting up from my desk. I treated myself to a good stretch, and tried to remove the pain lodged between my shoulder blades.

Later that afternoon, Sherry's ex-landlord finally returned my call. "I know nothing about Mrs. Hovey," he complained. "She moved in and moved out, just like it was a hotel or something."

"Had she already paid rent for the month of March?"

"Yep."

"Did she collect her damage deposit from you before she left?"

"I didn't see her. She didn't even tell me she was leaving!" He spoke so loudly that I had to hold the phone two feet away from my ear.

"Then how did you find out that she'd gone?"

"I went over to the house to fix the sink for the couple on

39

the main floor. While I was there I remembered Mrs. Hovey had told me that the tap was dripping in the bathtub upstairs. I went up to her place to take a look at it. All her stuff was gone, and she'd left her apartment key in the middle of the kitchen table."

"She'd cleaned up?"

"Sure! But how about giving me notice?"

"But the rent was paid in advance—and you still had the damage deposit," I reminded him. It seemed to me he'd done pretty well out of the deal.

Before going home that day I returned to Sherry's old neighborhood, hoping to talk to the couple who'd lived below her on the main floor. This time they were home. They were a soft-spoken pair; the man was native, the woman looked white. They recognized the photograph of Sherry and Mark, and told me that they'd said hello to her on several occasions, but not much else. "They were very quiet," the woman said. "When they moved in we thought, Oh no, a little kid above our heads—you know what that's like. But they weren't noisy at all. I wish they'd stayed." She lifted her eyes to the ceiling, through which we could hear the dull thumping bass of a stereo.

"You've no idea why she moved?"

"We never talked to her at all."

"We actually saw her moving out," the man added. "But we didn't realize that she was leaving for good. We just thought she was going on a trip. She didn't have much—two big suitcases, and some bags. I offered to give her a hand with them down the stairs."

"The upstairs suite is furnished," the woman explained.

"How did she move her stuff? Did she have a car?"

"She'd called a taxi," the man said. "We saw her and the little boy get into it."

"Ah." Finally. I tried not to look too greedy. "What company was it—do you remember?"

The man frowned, glanced at the woman. "I'm not sure."

"What color was the cab?"

Again they looked at each other. "Green?" the woman suggested. "But I'm really not sure."

"About what time was this?" I'd pulled out my notebook—for the first time in days.

"We were on the way to work so it was early—about eight-twenty in the morning."

"It would really help," I said, "if you could figure out exactly what day that was."

The woman produced a date book, and together they studied it, heads almost touching, consulting each other in murmurs, like a couple in a television ad debating the color of their next capital expenditure.

Finally they decided on Thursday, March 8th, which was the same day that Sherry had failed to show up for work, and three days after Vicky had visited Sherry at Copper's restaurant.

As I headed home, it occurred to me that Sherry might have quit working at Copper's in order to elude her sister and might have moved for the same reason—knowing that, through Alexis, Vicky would be able to get hold of her address. If so, Sherry was going to a lot of trouble to keep her whereabouts a secret.

It was a thought that made me uncomfortable. She wasn't going to like it when I found her.

5

THAT EVENING AROUND nine o'clock, I started spring cleaning my kitchen cupboards. I've noticed that whenever I get stuck on a case, I undertake some project, usually something that I've been putting off for months. I need to feel that in at least one area of my life, I'm getting something done. In this case, however, this sudden urge to clean my house indicated something more: an end to months of irresolution, and a decision not to move.

When Brian and I divorced, I moved into an absolute dump just off Kingsway, where the kids and I huddled among our unpacked boxes, eating cereal out of the carton and listening to the drunks beating each other up in the apartment next door. It was a traumatic introduction to my life as a single parent. Fortunately, two months later, a friend found me this townhouse where I've lived ever since. It's nothing special: it was poorly constructed and is starting to fall apart; the north walls are prone to mildew and the landlady neglects everything except the collection of rent. But it's relatively cheap and peaceful, and I'm on speaking terms with most of my neighbors. It's home. I've painted it twice; I've put up shelves and made lots of nail holes in the drywall. But practically speaking, now that my kids have gone and I no longer need three bedrooms and a patio on which to store their bicycles—I should move. The problem being that I'm not, when it comes right down to it, a very practical person.

It makes sense to move. I could find something smaller, but better designed, with higher ceilings and bigger windows. I could live within walking distance of my office, and save myself many liters of gas a month. My daughter, Katie, left home over three years ago and will certainly never live with me again. Ben, who's two years younger, has only been gone for a year and might decide to move back for financial reasons—but his current living arrangement seems to be working out fine. In Vancouver, housing of any kind is in short supply—especially rental housing that's suitable for kids—so it's wrong, really, for me to continue to inhabit this three-bedroom townhouse. Whenever I turn on the news and get confronted by yet another story about the urban homeless, I feel like hiding my face in a pillow.

But I hate transience, this shucking off of possessions and homes, this lack of connection to a place. When I was a child, we went twice a year to visit my grandparents' house in Victoria, where I'd find children's books inscribed with my mother's wobbly handwriting. I played with the doll's house that used to belong to my great-aunt Edith, I laid myself out on the bed in which my uncle William had died. On the walls were photographs of great-grandparents and second cousins; on the Christmas tree were ornaments that had been made by my aunts. My grandparents' house was a familial museum, a place where every year I rediscovered a sense of history. When they died, the house was sold—and all that history went with it.

And somehow, that's my problem—the feeling that I'm losing my identity, becoming yet another anonymous, self-sufficient city-dweller—the kind of person who could get scooped up by a flying saucer and no one would ever notice. Sometimes I find myself standing in the doorway of Katie's bedroom, looking at the china horses lined up on her shelves, at the grubby dolls propped at the end of her bed. Her room is an impenetrable clutter of memorabilia: peacock feathers, seashells, old Halloween costumes, posters of endangered animals and rock stars, garments she designed and never finished making, abandoned macramé projects and paint-by-number pictures, lists of New Year's resolutions. . . . She never threw out any of it. If I moved—what would I do with it all? Katie would lose that tangible connection to her past, which is my past too—just as, when Brian and I sold that house in suburbia, we never found her charm bracelet, or Ben's cowboy belt or my favorite Miriam Makeba record. Somehow, somewhere they got lost.

Meg, I admonished myself, squirting more soap into my bucket of water, in order to advance spiritually you're supposed to purge yourself of your attachment to the material world.

But I'm not dead yet, I retorted, climbing up onto the counter so that I could reach the top shelf. I was taking comfort from the fact that this was my grease, my dirt, and that I'd be the one to benefit from all this scrubbing. I was reclaiming my territory, reasserting my right to a permanent home. I'd stay here another year and see how I felt then; I'd buy some tubs for the patio and plant basil and dahlias. Maybe I'd even replace those rotting tiles in the bathroom. Then I thought of Sherry, who'd done just the opposite—who'd walked out of her home in the hope that she'd be able to leave a part of herself behind. Is that it? I wondered. Do I feel that if I moved somewhere else—to a place where my kids had never lived—I'd begin to wonder if I'd ever been a mother at all? Just as now, sometimes, I can no longer remember what it was like to be Brian's wife.

I finished another set of shelves, looked up at the clock. It was one-thirty in the morning.

But I woke up bright and early the next day, thinking about my shining clean shelves and the blood-red dahlias that were going to bloom on my patio. Or how about a wisteria? Would it grow in a tub? Then my thoughts moved on to taxi cab companies, which are wonderful sources of information; their drivers keep trip sheets and write everything down: times, dates, addresses. I felt that the case was about to break.

I made myself a generous pot of coffee and sat down beside the telephone. While the rain drove in gusts against my living room windows, I phoned every taxi company in town. A couple of them gave me what I wanted over the phone, and assured me that no driver of theirs had picked up a party on East 14th Avenue at about eight-twenty on the morning of Thursday, March 8th. A few others declared that such information was confidential, and was only given out to "authorized personnel" (meaning, the police). And most of them told me that I'd better come down and speak to the manager.

I armed myself against the deluge outside and drove through the flowing streets, my windshield wipers thrashing. I spent the rest of that day talking to the managers of taxi cab companies, waiting in their offices while they went to look through their trip sheets. Sometimes, when they'd let me, I'd do the work myself, attempting to decipher the illegible scrawls of taxi drivers. By four o'clock in the afternoon, I was way out in southeast Burnaby and ready to give up. I parked in front of a donut shop, hefted my phone book under my arm, went into the donut shop and ate a long john that made me feel sick as soon as I'd finished it. I washed it down with tea, consulted my phone book and my map. There was one more taxi company in this area: "Star Taxi"—I'd never heard of it. But like the good trooper my father always told me to be, I put on my soggy jacket, went back out into the rain, climbed into my car and headed south into New Westminster.

An hour later, in a dingy back room with blackened, wire-meshed windows, I found the entry I was looking for. A driver by the name of K. Sidhu had picked up a party on East 14th Avenue at eight-twenty-five on the morning of March 8th, and had deposited them a few minutes later in the 800 block on East 6th.

I copied down the information, then took the trip sheet out to the front office and waited for the manager to find a moment to talk to me. She finally glanced up. "Found something?" she inquired. I showed her the entry. She glanced at the driver's name on the top of the sheet. "He should be coming off shift in about half an hour. You want me to tell him to call you?"

"Maybe I'll just wait."

"Be my guest." She gestured to a chair in the corner and went back to work.

While I waited, I pulled out my notebook and flipped through the pages. I found myself staring at a shopping list. Oh. Right. I'd invited my kids to eat brunch with me tomorrow morning, which obligated me to purchase some food for them to eat. I then reread all my notes on Sherry's case to see what I'd missed. "Talk to Luisa, the dishwasher," my notes said. "Back

45

on the 24th." That was today. But Copper's Restaurant closed at five—so Luisa would have to wait until Monday.

K. Sidhu was a plump, spectacled man with a nest of worried wrinkles permanently embedded in the center of his forehead. I showed him the entry on his trip sheet, then the photograph of Sherry and Mark. He had no difficulty remembering them. "As soon as she got into the car she said, 'Make sure we're not being followed'—like we were in a movie or something. Then all the way there she kept turning around and looking out the rear window. I figured she was nuts, but she made me kind of nervous so I kept a lookout just in case. Was she kidnapping the kid or something?"

He hadn't written down the address Sherry had given him, but he described the block and the house where he'd stopped. "It was on the south side of the street—about halfway up. It shouldn't be hard to find—most of that street has been turned into apartment buildings."

Returning through Burnaby the traffic was heavy, long line-ups accumulating at every crosswalk and red light. By the time I got back into East Vancouver, an early dark was closing in and the rain had diminished to a drizzle. I went a few intersections past Clark and turned right onto St. Catherines Street.

I happen to hate this neighborhood. Most of its heritage homes have been demolished and replaced by utilitarian three-story apartment buildings; the few houses that remain have been subdivided into suites, providing a temporary refuge for the transient and poor: refugees, unemployed youths, single mothers who can't afford the rents anywhere else. There is never anywhere to park, the streets are clogged with cars attempting to circumvent the traffic jams on Broadway; the neighborhood feels like what it is: an overflow site for people who've been displaced. There are much worse areas of town, but I always find this one particularly depressing.

St. Catherines Street skirted the edge of a park, then came to an abrupt end at the edge of a bluff. Below me, Great Northern Way hissed and thundered with traffic; beyond it were the rail yards, spot-lit and ghostly in the drizzling mist. I turned left onto East 6th.

46

I drove the length of the block. As the cab driver had said, there were few houses left on this street, and only two on the south side. I rejected the one on the corner at the end, made a U-turn and double-parked in the middle of the block opposite a stolid, unprepossessing grey house. Then a car pulled out of a parking space behind me so I backed up—ignoring the vehement beeps of a van that was trying to get around me—into the spot it had just vacated. I turned off the engine.

It was Saturday night. There were lots of people about, coming in and out of the apartment buildings. Four youths were smoking cigarettes and socializing over the hood of a vintage Dodge that was parked across the street. Over the crest of the hill behind me, the sky had broken into blinding yellow strips which were reflected in the rear-view mirrors of my car. But the valley in front of me was still packed in with mountains of charcoal-colored cloud.

The top floor of the grey house was in darkness, but windows were lit on the main floor and in the basement. The house was typical of its age and genre; older Vancouver homes are almost as predictable as new ones. There were two front doors opening off the main porch, one of which led to the main floor suite, the other to a staircase going up to the second floor. The third suite was in the basement, with its own door below ground level—probably around the side or at the back of the house. Assuming, therefore, that this was the right house, I still had three suites to choose from.

I glanced at my watch. It was now six-forty-five. I hadn't done my grocery shopping, and I'd agreed to meet Tom for dinner at eight. Why not come back tomorrow?

You're just afraid she's going to get mad at you, I said to myself. Go get it over with.

I unpacked my voice-activated tape recorder, checked that it was working, clipped it into the breast pocket of my jacket. I got out of the car, walked up the front sidewalk to the house, mounted the porch steps. Judging by the darkened windows on the top floor there was no one home upstairs, so I ignored the right-hand door and approached the door on the left. Through the living room windows of the main floor suite I could hear music playing, and the sound of children—plural?—running and shouting. In houses like these, the main floor suite is usually the largest and most expensive, so I didn't expect to find Sherry behind this door. Gaining confidence from these deductions, I knocked.

A boy opened the door—but his hair was curly and he was at least seven years old. "I'm looking for Sherry Hovey," I said, as a woman appeared behind him in the doorway. "Does she live here?"

The woman was tall, had an angular face and black hair raked back into an untidy ponytail. "She lives in the basement," she answered. "You have to go around the side."

"Thanks," I said.

As I started down the porch steps, a man turned in on the front path from the street and came towards me with long strides as I descended the porch steps. We reached the bottom step at the same time. He gave me a startled look—and I stared, almost stopped. He was a black man, and therefore easy to remember in a city where blacks comprise a very small percentage of the population. But perhaps he recognized me too because he frowned and glanced at me again before continuing up the porch steps.

Now that's interesting, I thought, as I started around the path that skirted the front porch. When I reached the corner of the house, I lingered and watched him, surreptitiously. He pulled a key out of his pants pocket, unlocked the door to the top floor suite and let himself in.

I'd last seen him at Copper's restaurant. He was the worker who'd made a bet with Alexis that the Edmonton Oilers would win the hockey game Tuesday night. Since Sherry had quit working at Copper's the day before moving to this house, he and Sherry probably knew each other.

I followed the narrow side path around the house. A chain-link fence and some meager, sun-starved shrubbery separated this lot from the lot beside it, through which I could see into the kitchens of the ground floor apartments in the massive, liver-colored building next door. Drips fell on my head from a rotted gutter overhead; I passed one small, lit but curtained window that was at the height of my knees. I stopped outside it and listened. A chair leg scraped. A woman's voice said, "Just wait a minute, it's almost ready." Ahead I could see the recessed steps that led down to the basement door.

The cement steps were cracked and crumbling, the door was dark green and stood in need of new paint. From the darkened hulk of the apartment building behind me I could hear the cumulative sounds of people at suppertime: the clatter of dishes and cutlery, voices, doors slamming, taps gushing, televisions. By contrast, down here in the crevice between the two buildings, the silence was intense—only the dripping from the gutter, the occasional distinct and isolated sounds from the room where Sherry and Mark went about their lives, not two feet away from me through the green door.

Well, Meg?

I stood in the cement stairwell, staring at the places where the paint had chipped off. Now that I was about to confront my prey, I felt as squeamish as a meat-eater who's been invited to tour a slaughterhouse.

Finally, I knocked.

6

THE DOOR OPENED; her face appeared around its edge. "Yes?" she asked warily.

"My name is Meg Lacey," I said, showing her my card. "I'm a private investigator and I've been hired by your—"

"No!" She tried to push the door shut but I'd wedged my foot into the gap and it slammed into my shoulder. Shocked, she dropped the doorknob as if it had scorched her, stumbled backwards and started yelling: "You've got no right! Get out of here! I'm calling the cops—get out!"

"Just listen to me for a moment—"

"You're trespassing! Get out! You've got no right barging in here!"

"Will you just listen—" I said, as I stepped across the sill. I was worrying that we'd be overheard in the apartments next door. I closed the door behind me and stood with my back against it.

Her little boy, Mark, began to cry. His bottom lip wavered, his eyes brimmed, he gazed at me with reproach. He was sitting at the kitchen table, a clean, empty bowl in front of him, waiting for his soup, which was heating up on the stove.

Sherry gave him a panic-stricken glance. "I'll scream," she threatened. "I'll scream so they can hear me all the way around the block. Plug your ears, Mark. . . . "

Mark's wails ascended; he cowered, his eyes widening.

"Wait," I commanded, with all the authority I could

muster. I turned to Mark, lowering my voice. "Hey. It's O.K. I'm not going to hurt you—or your Mum. I just gave her a bit of a shock. I want to talk to her for a few minutes and then I'll go away again. Your aunt Vicky sent me because she hasn't seen you for a long time and she was worried about you. She wanted to make sure that you and your Mum were all right."

It worked. Mark gulped, Sherry released her breath—but she stood braced against the kitchen counter, her eyes darting around the room as if seeking an escape route. "Your sister hired me to look for you," I explained to her quietly. "She doesn't want to know where you are, but she asked me to find out how you were doing."

She turned her back on me, lifted the pot of soup from the stove—but was trembling so violently that the soup slopped over the sides and sizzled onto the burner. She dropped the pot with a clatter.

"Is that for Mark?" I asked. She didn't move, kept her head lowered, face averted. "I'll do it," I said. "You sit down."

She hesitated—but then went and sat down at the table beside Mark. I picked up Mark's bowl and carried it to the stove, ladled some soup into it. I showed it to him. "Is that enough?" He watched me, the tears still clinging to his eyelashes. "There's more if you want it." I put the bowl in front of him.

I sat down at the table opposite her. She had the same amber brown eyes, the same features as the young woman in the photograph that I'd been carrying around with me. But there the resemblance ended. The woman in the photograph would have been described as pretty—this woman was haggard. Sherry had lost weight, she looked unhealthy and tired. She wore a stained grey sweatshirt, blue jeans with frayed hems, a pair of cheap plastic shoes.

I repeated the essential pieces of information: that I'd been hired by Vicky to check up on her, that I wouldn't tell anyone where she was living. Again this recital seemed to have a calming effect; Mark set about the business of eating his soup, and Sherry, ignoring me, watched him as if every spoonful were critical to his health.

51

I pulled out the tape recorder from my jacket pocket and showed it to her. "Our conversation is being recorded for your sister. That way she'll be able to hear for herself what you have to say."

Sherry gave the tape recorder a furtive glance and watched me clip it back into my jacket pocket. Then some soup missed Mark's mouth, dribbled down his shirt front and Sherry sprang up: "Now look what you've done!" She fetched a dishcloth and wiped the soup from his shirt. "I told you—you should have had it in a cup. Now eat over the bowl—like this." She moved the bowl closer to Mark's chest. "See?" Mark's dark gaze lifted and met hers, impassively. He sucked up another spoonful of soup.

"He does much better with a cup," Sherry explained, still careful not to look at me. "He wants to do everything the hard way." She sat down again.

I looked around the room. The kitchen table was in the center of it, dividing the kitchen area from the living room; against the wall to my left stood the fridge, sink and stove. On the other side of the room was a hide-a-bed couch, a lamp and coffee table under the window. Two doorways opened off the room, into the bathroom and the bedroom. That was the whole apartment. There were three small, high windows, with curtains that didn't match; the ceilings were low; the furniture looked like it had been salvaged from a back alley. The apartment smelled like the inside of damp boots.

"Sherry," I said, turning to her. "Vicky wants to know if there isn't some way that she can communicate with you. She's asked you to phone her, but you don't seem to want to do that. She suggested that maybe you wouldn't mind if I came and looked in on you once a week or so, just to make sure that you and Mark are getting along all right." I waited, but Sherry's gaze was still fixed on Mark's soup bowl. "She understands that you don't want her to know where you are, and she accepts that. But she's worried that you might need—"

"You think I don't know what's going on?" Now, finally, Sherry looked me full in the face and abruptly pushed herself up from her chair, barricading herself behind it. "You think I can't see the way that people look at each other when I say something?" She was breathing hard, jerkily, as if she'd just crossed a finish line. "Then I know, don't I? That's why I have to get away from everyone—everyone! Because when they give each other those looks—then I know—" Her voice rose, "*I* know what they're thinking."

"What are they thinking?"

"They think I should be locked up—that's what they think!" She pushed aside the chair, advancing towards me menacingly. "How did you find me?" she demanded. "Who told you?" I glanced at Mark. But he didn't seem worried; he had his spoon twisted in his mouth and was watching his mother with interest. "Did *he* tell you?" Sherry hissed.

"Who? Your husband—Glen?"

Doubt entered her eyes. She frowned, her gaze slid away from mine.

"Nobody told me," I answered. "And it's taken me more than a week to find you. But someone at the last place you lived told me you'd left in a taxi cab, and I managed to track down the driver who moved you here."

As I watched her, I realized that she was no longer listening. Her expression was attentive, but remote—as if she'd been distracted by a different line of thought. "That's all right," she said absently. She moved away from me across the room. "I can deal with that. Just got to keep moving, that's all. Keep them guessing."

"Sherry," I said, pointedly. She turned, looked at me. "Sherry, I'm the only person who knows where you are. And I'm not telling. I'm not telling Vicky, I'm not telling Glen—"

"Don't worry," she said magnanimously, waving me away. "I'm not mad at you. Don't worry about it."

"But I want to make sure you understand. Vicky and I signed a contract. I am not going to tell her where you are."

She watched me with a smile of disbelief.

"But she would like to find some way that she can keep in touch with you. Why don't you phone her?"

"I don't have a phone." Then her eyes grew serious. "But if I needed her, I'd phone. You tell her that. She'd be the first person I'd call." She made it sound like a matter of life and death.

"But couldn't you call her from a phone booth or something? Just once a week—that's all she's asking."

Sherry sniffed, tossed her head. "That's all," she repeated, sarcastically. "That's all she wants. Phone her, visit her, tell her all my problems—" She broke off. "I don't tell anyone my problems." Again she was getting angry. "My problems are my business. Mine! I don't have to tell anyone!"

She marched back to the table, picked up her chair and moved it beside mine, sat down so that our shoulders were almost touching. "There's a pattern." She spread her fingers wide, pressed her hands together with the fingers crossing each other. "I've just got to break the pattern. But I'm woven in there, see?" She lifted her hands, watched me through the crosshatch of her fingers. "I have to break the threads and make a new pattern—my own pattern. One that will be better for me." Her eyes, not six inches from mine, searched my face questioningly.

She smelled nervous, the sour reek of her body overlaid by the shampoo scent of her hair. "Do you find it easier," I asked, "now that you're living on your own?"

Her expression became closed, calculating. She laid a hand on my forearm, put her lips up against my ear and whispered, "Who told you where to find me?"

I exhaled, slowly. "Nobody," I said. "Nobody knows where you are. Only me. And I'm not telling."

"Mummy." Mark was holding up his empty bowl. We both looked at him.

"No more soup, eh?" Sherry said, reverting to her more normal, mother mode. She got up, took the bowl from him. "You want more?"

"No," he said, getting down from his chair.

"Then go to the bathroom and wipe your face and hands." He trotted out of the room. Sherry put his bowl and spoon in the sink, turned on the tap.

"They've still got a paycheck waiting for you at Copper's," I said to her back. "And Glen has been putting money into your savings account. He's worried that you're going to run out. I'm sure he'll give you more when you need it."

Sherry wrung out the dishcloth, turned off the tap, came over and wiped Mark's place at the table. She must have heard me, but she gave no indication of it.

"Taking the money doesn't mean that you have to go back to him. It's not Glen's money—he owes it to you. For child support. If you divorced him, you'd split the money, half and half."

Mark reappeared in the doorway, ran over to the couch and jumped up onto the cushions.

Sherry tossed the dishcloth back into the sink. "I may be crazy, but I'm not stupid," she said, with resentment. "I'm not going near that bank."

She stood there for a moment, looking at me intently. Then, for the second time, she spread her fingers and laid them across each other, held them up before her face, as if warding off evil. "Can't you see?" she implored. She took a step towards me and extended her hands closer to my face, as if I were shortsighted, as if this gesture should explain it all. "It's like a web. There's the money and the house and the furniture and our families. . . . We're tangled up in there. Like flies," she whispered. "But I'm the fly who got out." Her hands dropped, her expression was almost vindictive.

"Glen is trapped in there too?"

She gave me a strange smile, shook her head, said nothing.

"You want to cut off every connection to him."

"I have to cut *all* the connections!" Abruptly she returned to the kitchen table and sat down.

I looked over at Mark, the connection that couldn't be cut. He was upending a bucketful of Leggo blocks into his lap. As if following my thoughts, Sherry said, "His father never had anything to do with him."

Mark held up an unidentifiable structure—something he'd made out of the blocks, and cast me a secretive glance. He wanted me to notice it without wanting to acknowledge that he was showing it to me.

"*I'm* the one who looks after him!" Sherry argued, as if I were disputing this fact.

55

Now that I'd seen his whatever-it-was, Mark began dis-assembling it. I said, "Glen told me that he wants visiting rights."

There was a silence, and I glanced at her.

Sherry was staring at my face with a fixed, frightened ex-pression; her eyes were like vortices. "What's wrong?" I put a hand out towards her.

"No!" She jumped up from her chair and started backing away across the room, just as she'd done when I arrived. "I think you'd better go now," she pleaded, nervously. "You've been here long enough."

"Sherry—what happened? What are you afraid of?"

Her eyes closed, her lips set. She shook her head so vehe-mently that her hair flew out around her head.

"Look," I said. "If you're in trouble, there are safe places you can go, there are people who can help you. Here—I'll write down some phone numbers. . . . "

"Go away!" she screamed, then covered both ears with her hands as if trying, belatedly, to shut out the sound of her own voice.

I got up. Sherry continued standing in the middle of the room, eyes tight shut, elbows pressing into her breasts, hands flattened against her ears. I waited—she didn't move. Afraid that I'd precipitated something, that she'd plummeted into some psychological abyss and wouldn't be able to extricate herself again, I walked over and touched her, tentatively, on the shoulder. As if I'd pressed a button, she inhaled; her eyelids flickered.

"I'll go," I said. "I'll tell Vicky that both you and Mark are . . . doing well," I finished, uncertainly.

"Oh we're fine," Sherry agreed, as if there had never been any doubt.

"Do you mind if I come and look in on you from time to time?"

She shrugged. "That's your problem."

"Does that mean you don't mind?"

"I won't even be here."

"Sherry," I protested. "There's no reason to move again. I

56

am not going to tell Vicky where you are—I explained that. And if you don't like the idea of me coming, just say so. I promise I won't come back."

"But someone else will."

"I'm not going to tell anybody else where you are."

"Actually—" she waved her hand, "Mark and I don't really like this neighborhood. The last place was better. It was near the lake."

I gave up. I'd done my best; if she wanted to move again, that was her business. "I won't bother you again," I said, moving towards the door. "Maybe I shouldn't have come at all. But Vicky was very worried about you."

"It was nice to see you," Sherry assured me, warmly.

I stared at her, giving her one of those "looks" she didn't like. "Wait. Here's my card." I dug into my pocket, produced a business card and handed it to her. "If you need anything, just phone me."

She took it, read it carefully, as if memorizing every punctuation mark. Then she handed it back to me.

"No, you keep it," I said.

But she continued holding it out to me, her face grave, as if it were an object of symbolic importance, like an engagement ring. I finally took it back.

"Bye Mark," I said.

He looked up from his blocks. "Bye," he called cheerfully, and for the first time he smiled—a cute, crooked grin. He was glad to see me go.

By the time I came out of Sherry's apartment, it was dark. As I walked back to the car, I took several deep breaths, tried to make the muscles in my shoulders relax. Thank God that's over with, I thought. But I had no feeling of relief. My visit had obviously disturbed and upset Sherry—and what had been achieved by it? Now she'd move again. What was she afraid of? And was she fit to have sole care of that child? (How should I know?) But these were the questions that I'd have to answer tomorrow when I wrote up my report.

I glanced at my watch—it was seven-thirty. No time for a shower; I'd have to go straight to the Ashiana restaurant, where I was supposed to be meeting Tom for supper. And buy the groceries afterwards? Oh, what the hell, I thought, I've made good money this week, I'll take my kids out to a restaurant tomorrow morning. They'll like that better anyway. I unlocked my car door, then stopped. I heard children's voices nearby. It sounded like they were coming from right behind my car.

I'd parked my car just east of the entrance to an underground parking lot. At the edge of this entrance, where the curb dipped, two children were squatting in the gutter, not two feet from my rear bumper. If I hadn't heard them talking, I would have climbed into my car and backed right over them.

"What are you doing?" I asked sharply—though the answer was self-evident. In the gutter behind my car was a heap of white stuff—about eight inches high. It looked like some kind of powder, and the children were spooning it into a plastic bag. "What is that?"

The little girl looked up at me, her dark eyes gleaming in the streetlight. "It's flour," she said, and continued spooning it into the plastic bag that her younger brother was holding open for her. The boy looked no older than Mark, the girl was about six.

I squatted down beside them, gingerly fingered the white powder, pressed it between my fingers. It felt like flour all right, smooth and silky to the touch, pasty where it had gotten wet, flecked with grit and drops of muddy water. There were no tire marks in it, so it must have been dumped here after I parked. "How did it get here?"

"A man dropped his grocery bag," the girl answered. Strands of greasy hair fell over her eyes. She was working quickly, determinedly, as if wanting to get as much flour as possible before the supply was cut off.

Her brother looked up. "All the cans rolled away. Some went under the car. We helped pick them up."

"And he said we could have the flour," the girl added, as if I'd questioned her right to it.

That was real nice of him, I thought.

"Hold it straight!" the girl ordered her brother. "How can I put the flour in it if you don't hold it up?" The boy shifted position, tried to hold the bag more upright.

"What are you going to do with it?" I asked.

"We're going to make muffins!" The boy looked up with a delighted, triumphant smile; as he did so, his grip on the bag slipped, and they almost lost their flour.

"Watch what you're doing!" his sister scolded. She gave an exasperated sigh and pushed her hair out of her eyes with a grubby, floury hand.

"But you can't eat that flour," I remonstrated. "It's dirty."

The boy looked at me, uneasily—then, like his sister, pretended he hadn't heard. They bent their heads over their work.

I glanced around, and discovered that we were being watched. A man was sitting behind the driver's wheel of the car behind us, ostensibly reading his newspaper—but observing us over the top of it. His eyes were shaded by his hat, but as he took a drag on his cigarette, the lower half of his face was illuminated. Just as I was thinking that there was something familiar about him, he turned the page, lifted the newspaper higher and disappeared behind it.

I remembered that the police had put out an alert—something about a man in a car—I'd heard it on the radio that morning. Two children had gone missing in the last month and parents were being advised not to let their kids go out alone. I looked at his car—but since I'd paid no attention to the police description of the vehicle, I was no further ahead. It was after dark. What were these children doing out here anyway?

I turned back to the kids. "It's pretty late. Don't you think that it's time you went home?"

"We're almost finished," the girl answered, then decided that they were. "There. That's enough." She lifted the sagging, dirt-smeared plastic bag, tried to gather the top of it together, twirling it awkwardly. The bag bulged with the air trapped inside it.

"Where do you live?" I asked her.

"Not far," she answered, cagily.

"My brother will be home soon," the boy reassured me. "He's got the key."

"You mean your parents aren't home?"

The girl was now anxious to escape. "Come on," she ordered her brother, and set off down the sidewalk, clutching the top of the bag with both hands, its rotund weight bumping against her thigh. Her brother followed. "Bye bye," he called to me, reminding me of Mark.

For a little while longer I continued to stand beside my car, watching the kids proceed slowly up the street. It occurred to me that Vicky had just spent hundreds of dollars to ensure that her nephew was being adequately cared for—while out here, on the streets, children no older than Mark wandered around, unsupervised and unprotected. I remembered Sherry's father saying: "There's four-year-old kids who live on the streets. They feed themselves, everything."

But I'd thought he was talking about Calcutta.

7

AT THE ASHIANA RESTAURANT, I drank Indian beer, ate pakoras, chicken moghlai and warm buttered naan. Bliss. I couldn't tell Tom about Sherry, of course, but I told him about the two kids scooping flour out of the gutter and Tom, who's a biologist, told me about the pulp mill industry's latest ploy, whereby they'd get to keep pumping lethal levels of dioxins and chlorine into our coastal waters for another five years. This, despite the fact that the government has already banned shell fishing in most of the local inlets. Cheerful topics.

On our way out of the restaurant, Tom started discussing spices with the man at the cash register, so I asked to use the phone and gave Vicky a call. She wasn't home. I left a message with her babysitter, and said that I'd phone her again tomorrow. Then Tom and I drove to my place, made love, got up and watched a late movie, which was so bad that we started playing cribbage halfway through it. When it became obvious that I was winning the game of cribbage, Tom decided that it was time to go back to bed. Remembering that I'd told the kids to come at ten the next morning, I set my alarm clock for nine-fifteen.

When I woke up my daughter and son and some girl I'd never seen before were standing in my bedroom doorway. "Mum!" Katie hissed at me, indignantly.

"Hi," I said blearily. "Aren't you early? What time is it?" I elbowed Tom; he rolled over, flung an arm across me, buried his head against my shoulder.

Ben, with belated tact, escorted the strange girl away. "It's ten-fifteen," Katie informed me, in the icy tones of a professional disciplinarian. At that moment my alarm clock started beeping.

I reached for the button on top of the clock, peered at the numbers. "It says nine-fifteen."

"The time changed, Mother." (Katie only calls me "Mother" when I'm in trouble.) "You know—Daylight Savings Time? The clocks moved forward last night."

"Did they?" I said innocently, looking at my clock.

"Ours didn't," Tom rumbled from under the bedclothes.

Katie was not amused. "Very funny. Now get up—both of you. Ben's brought his new girlfriend."

"Is that who that was?" I was intrigued. I knew that Ben went on the occasional date, but I'd never met any of his girlfriends before.

"I'll go make the coffee." Katie disappeared from the doorway.

"There's no milk," I called after her. "I didn't go shopping. I thought we'd go out for brunch."

"Where?"

"I don't know. You decide. We'll be down in a minute." I heard her descending the stairs.

Ben's girlfriend was not what I would have expected. She was a very pretty, upper drawer WASP, who said all the right things in the right places. This I could forgive—after all, she was only nineteen and couldn't help her upbringing—but she treated Ben with a mixture of condescension and disdain, a characteristic that I found less endearing. She corrected his grammar, blushed at his table manners (which do, sometimes, leave something to be desired), and re-worded practically everything he said in order that we should understand him better. In return, Ben worshipped her. He referred all decisions to her greater wisdom, included her in every topic, and couldn't tell the rest of us enough about her. I learned that she was a hotshot tennis player, got the best marks in her computer programming course, and had a brother who had been on the second-string skiing team for the 1988 Olympics. In short, Ben told us that she was the most wonderful girl in the world while she, keeping her eyelids modestly lowered, picked at her fruit salad. (She didn't like the melon bits.)

Later, after we'd dropped the kids off at their respective destinations, Tom and I went for a walk along the Stanley Park sea wall—as did half the population of Vancouver on that sunny Sunday afternoon. There was stiff breeze blowing, the inlet frothed with white-caps, the freighters tugged at their anchor lines. "She's like Katie," I lamented, zipping up my jacket, "like Katie at her absolute worst. Why is he going around with someone like that? She treats him like dirt!"

"I think they're lovers," Tom said.

"She'd stoop so low?"

"She's probably the first girl he's ever slept with."

"What a splendid introduction to the female sex!"

We rounded one of the high, mossy bluffs, and I looked up at the mountain tops, still sparkling with snow, where, if I had a telescope, I'd see thousands of spring skiers swarming over the slopes like brightly colored microbes.

"Well. . . ." Tom sighed.

I'm familiar with these sighs. They're an indication that Tom is approaching a topic that makes him uncomfortable, and he's going to require prodding to get through it. "Well—what?"

"The first girl I ever slept with," he began—then paused. "A young woman, I guess. We were both twenty-one." Another pause.

"Yes?"

"I think—well, I suppose that we were rather like that."

"Like Tiara and Ben?" (What a name—Tiara!) "You mean, you adored her and she treated you like a door mat."

"Something like that," he admitted reluctantly. "And it was because . . . I was quite overwhelmed, you see. By sex, really, but I thought it was her. I felt blessed—so grateful to her. What I didn't realize, of course, was that I probably would have felt similarly about any other young woman who'd slept with me. Young men, you know, are pretty much all penis."

"So I've heard," I said, dryly. "They've been excused all kinds of atrocities because of it. Gang rapes and so on."

"No, no." He took my arm, steered me around two families who had recognized each other and stopped to talk in the middle of the walk. "I'm not excusing anything. I'm just saying that a young man's first experience of sex can warp his judgement."

"What happened to this relationship?"

He cleared his throat. "She—er—dumped me. Naturally."

"And you were devastated."

"For a while. But I got over it." He smiled at me. "I met another young woman."

"And worshipped her instead."

"Yes, but this time the infatuation wasn't all on my side."

"You're saying that Ben is in love with sex, not Tiara."

"I'm saying that, at this point, I think he's got the two things confused."

"All the same." It was my turn to sigh. "I feel sorry for the boy's mother."

Tom kissed my cheek.

At about five I went down to my office to type up my report on Sherry. As I parked the car, I remembered that Vicky still didn't know that I'd found her sister. This time when I phoned her, she was home. When I told Vicky that I'd found Sherry, there was a sudden, odd silence. "Vicky?" I inquired. "Are you still there?"

"Sorry," she said finally. "Yes, I'm here. Just a little overcome. I guess I've been more worried than I realized. How is she? Is she O.K?"

I said yes, and told her that I'd come visit her tomorrow afternoon to give her a more detailed account. Then I sat down to write up the report. In the end I avoided making any judgement about Sherry (after all, Vicky would hear the tape for herself); I only said that Mark seemed adequately cared for, that Sherry did not want her address known, and did not wish to communicate with any of her family.

I got home at eight-thirty. I made myself a salad, dumped plenty of dressing on it, and was halfway through it when the doorbell rang.

Two plainclothes detectives stood on my front porch.

"Meg Lacey?"

"Yes?"

They introduced themselves, showed me their badges and asked me to accompany them down to the police station.

"Why?"

They glanced at each other—but knew they had to tell me. "May we come in for a moment?"

Unwillingly, I let them in. One of them didn't look much older than Ben, the other was in his fifties. As they entered my living room, they glanced around the walls as if I were offering the place for rent. None of us sat down. "What's this all about?" I asked.

The older man, who'd introduced himself as Detective Baker, pulled out his notebook. "I understand that you were hired by Mrs. Vicky Fischer to find her sister, Sherry Hovey. Is that correct?"

"Yes."

"And that you did indeed find Mrs. Hovey—last night." His small grey eyes lifted from his notebook; his partner was chewing gum and watching me, impassively. "At what time was that?"

I hesitated. "I think you'd better tell me why you're asking me these questions."

"Was that the last time you saw Mrs. Hovey?"

I looked at him in silence. He cleared his throat, shifted his weight to the other foot. "Mrs. Hovey is dead. She was killed this morning."

I hate shocks. I was kicked into a void and left hanging in white noise, minus my stomach. The older detective was still talking; I could see his lips moving—but the volume had been turned off. Then, suddenly, Sherry was right there beside me, her breath on my cheek, her eyes searching my face; she was trying to warn me, pleading with me not to give her away. I watched the younger officer walk towards me in slow motion; he was at my elbow, guiding me to an armchair. He tried to make me sit down, but Sherry was tugging urgently at my arm. I turned my head to look at her, but she slipped sideways, evading me, holding her fingers up before her face to ward off the evil I'd brought upon her.

"Where's Mark?" someone said, as I was pushed down into the armchair. But I wasn't sure who'd spoken—Sherry or I? "Where's Mark?" I repeated.

"The boy is fine, Mrs. Lacey. He wasn't there at the time."

I looked at the man standing on my living room carpet, and wondered why I could hear him again. His eyes reminded me of the eyes of an elephant: small, curious, shallow-set in a web of wrinkles. He was about thirty pounds overweight and was losing his hair. "Killed how?" I asked.

He swallowed, shifted his weight again; he didn't enjoy being the bearer of bad news. "Murdered," he said, and watched me apologetically. It was his job, after all, to see how I took it.

I stared at him blankly. I couldn't believe it. Sherry stood charged in my mind like a tree on fire, crackling and exuding sparks.

"How?" I said aloud, but Detective Baker was talking again, saying that since I was one of the last people to see her alive, and since I was the only person, apart from her neighbors, who knew where she lived—

"You've told Vicky?" I interrupted him.

He looked down at his notes. "Mrs. Fischer? Yes, she's at the station now. She was the one who told us that you'd been—er, working for her."

"And...?" Suddenly I couldn't remember his name. The detective looked at me inquiringly. "Mr. . . . her husband."

"Glen Hovey is also down at the station. We're questioning everyone involved. So—are you ready to come with us now?"

I found my jacket, made sure that I had my keys, locked my front door behind me. They escorted me down the sidewalk and into the back seat of their car.

There was little traffic and few pedestrians were out on the fluorescent-lit sidewalks. The storefronts of Main Street passed by my window like a movie set. I saw the red sign over my butcher's shop, the second-hand store where I buy most of my clothes. But I felt like I'd sidestepped into a different universe. I remembered where the paint had chipped on Sherry's basement door; I saw the patched piece of linoleum in front of her sink, the dent in the metal over the handle of the fridge—a dozen little details that I hadn't consciously noticed when I was there in her apartment. Who'd killed her? Someone she knew?

I was escorted through the large lobby on the main floor of the police station, past the receptionist's area, into the elevator, up to the third floor, down a wide, khaki-colored hall, through a door marked "Major Crimes Division," past another cluster of partitions and desks to another door labeled "Homicide," to a row of chairs where I was told to sit and wait. Detective Baker disappeared down the corridor, the other cop walked over to the window and gazed down into the street.

A couple of minutes later, a door opened down the hallway and I heard Vicky's voice. I stood up and as I saw Vicky step into the corridor, I called to her (to the consternation of the cop at the window). Her head jerked around. She hurried down the corridor to meet me while a uniformed cop, appearing through the doorway behind her, rushed to catch up to her.

Vicky crushed one of my hands between her ring-studded fingers. "You saw her," she accused, as if implying that because I'd seen Sherry alive last night, I should be able to disprove this report of her death. Her eyes looked wild—like the eyes of a spooked horse—and a network of fine lines scored the skin around her lips.

"I'm sorry," I said. "When I saw Sherry she was fine." Our escorts were now joining us, the cop coming up behind Vicky was clearing his throat, loudly.

"What did you—"

My cop interrupted, taking hold of my elbow. "You're not allowed to—"

"I'll phone you tomorrow," I called as I was firmly escorted down the hall, towards the door from which Vicky had come.

As I entered the bare, windowless interrogation room, I looked at the two detectives sitting behind the table and felt like I'd stepped off a five meter diving board. To my right sat Detective Baker, who'd preceded me into the room and was already slumped in his chair like an old sea lion. Beside him, sitting back from the table with his legs crossed, was Detective Dikeakos. And I could tell by the way his eyes stopped at my face that the recognition was mutual.

I had plenty of respect for Detective Dikeakos. He had presided over what was, undoubtedly, the worst experience of my life. I felt that I knew him, intimately: the eyes that tilted slightly down at the outside corners; the rough, sallow, acne-scarred skin; the outline of his beard shadow, like a continent drawn on the map of his face. For hours I'd sat, pinned under his unflickering stare, telling lies left, right and center, trying to save my own skin without betraying my friends. I'd succeeded in doing so, but not without considerable cost to my mental health. And I was sure that Nikolai Dikeakos hadn't forgiven nor forgotten what a lousy liar I was.

I took a deep breath, sat down in the chair that was obviously intended for me. Meg, I reminded myself, you have nothing to hide. You can tell the truth, the whole truth, and nothing but. Relax.

Detective Baker wanted to see my security business license, then asked for a summary of my movements for the past twenty-four hours. I described these, meanwhile wondering if I'd have time to phone Tom before the cops went to see him to verify my statement. If the cops got to him before I did, Tom, with misguided chivalry, would probably refuse to tell them anything about me.

When Baker had written down Tom's name, address and phone number, as well as the names of my kids and Tiara (whose last name I didn't know), he took me back over the past nine days. On what date had Vicky hired me, who had I seen, where had I gone, how had I found Sherry and what had I learned about her in the process. When I said that I'd talked to Sherry on Saturday night, I saw that I'd fulfilled their hopes. Baker wriggled his body in anticipation, like an overgrown boy who knows he's got the right answer to the teacher's question; and Dikeakos' gaze dropped for a second before resuming its fixed, imperturbable surveillance of my face. Baker said, "We'd like you to describe that conversation in detail—as much as you can remember of it."

I gave them the bare bones of my conversation with Sherry: that she wasn't pleased to be found, didn't want me to tell anyone where she was, didn't want to communicate with any of her family or former friends. "She said that she'd been trapped in a pattern that wasn't good for her, that she had to get out of it. She said that she wanted to break off all connections with her husband, didn't even want to take money from him."

"Did she say why she'd left him?"

"She wouldn't answer that question, only talked in generalities—about patterns and so on."

"Did she seem afraid of him?"

"I'm not sure. At one point, when I said that Glen wanted visiting rights to his kid, she looked very frightened. But I would describe her as being generally fearful, which made it difficult to separate out any specific fear from all the rest. Her answers didn't always make much sense."

"You agree then that she's—ah—mentally unbalanced?"

I hesitated. "Yes—although I didn't see her at her best. My visit upset her and she seemed to think that now that I'd found her, she'd have to move again. But I got the impression that something—something apart from my visit—had scared her."

"Mrs. Lacey—" Baker lifted his shoulders and eased his big belly up over his belt. "Who knew that you had found Sherry Hovey?"

"Vicky Fischer," I said promptly. "I phoned and told her so shortly after five o'clock this afternoon."

"Who else?"

"No one."

"Are you sure about that?"

"Quite sure. I can show you my contract with Vicky. It specifies, clearly, that I won't tell her where Sherry is if Sherry doesn't want her to know. And I certainly didn't tell anyone else."

"Did you write down the address?"

I shook my head. "Nope."

There was a short silence; they were both watching me.

"You're sure," said Baker.

"Look," I said. "As far as I was concerned, Sherry had a right to her privacy. I wouldn't have looked for her at all if there hadn't been a child involved. But Vicky Fischer convinced me that Mark's welfare might be in jeopardy. I thought I'd better check it out."

I paused, remembering Mark as I'd left him, sitting on the hide-a-bed couch, his lap full of Leggo blocks.

"How is Mark?" I asked. "Who found her?"

I was looking at Baker, but he looked at Dikeakos, and it was Dikeakos who finally answered, speaking for the first time. "The neighbor who lives on the main floor found her. She was taking of care of Mark this morning. Sherry was planning to go out, and had told the neighbor that she'd be back by noon. At two-thirty this afternoon the neighbor went down to the basement suite and found the body."

"So Sherry was killed this morning?" Again I directed my question to Baker—but it seemed to be Baker's job to ask questions, Dikeakos' job to answer them.

"Sometime between eight-thirty, when the neighbor picked up the kid, and eleven, when she got back. We may get a more exact picture after the autopsy."

"And how—?" I stopped. I couldn't believe that I was getting answers to these questions—although I was determined to ask them. "How was she killed?"

Dikeakos lowered his smooth, olive eyelids; his long, curly eyelashes contrasted oddly with the papery, bruise-like shadows beneath his eyes. "She was beaten up."

I took a sharp breath, exhaled, carefully. His eyelids lifted. "She received several blows before she went down, to the body as well as the head; then she cracked her head on the edge of the counter as she fell. We won't know the exact cause of death until after the autopsy."

"Brain hemorrhage," I suggested, with distaste.

"Probably."

"No weapon?"

"No weapon. It may have been manslaughter."

He saw the expression on my face.

"Accidental," he elucidated, thinking I hadn't understood.

"That's not my idea of an accident," I retorted. "Did she fight back?"

"She tried, but—" He shrugged. "Looks like he killed her pretty much right away."

"No prints?"

"Everything was wiped. There's hardly a fingerprint in the whole place. Must have taken him half an hour to clean up."

"Him?"

"Women don't usually hit each other like that. But anything's possible. Of course," he added, "none of what I'm telling you goes outside this room."

"Of course." I was amazed that he'd told me as much as he had. Perhaps he was practicing disarmament maneuvers, letting me in on a little inside information in order to lure me into being candid myself.

Dikeakos glanced at Baker, then tipped back in his chair, as if abdicating from any further part in this interrogation.

Detective Baker warned me not to leave town without telling them, and phoned down to the lab to check that they'd got my fingerprints on file. He told me that they wanted to see my contract with Vicky, and any reports that I'd written up on the case. Then they sent me downstairs to wait while a clerk typed up my statement. By the time I got out of the station, it was after midnight.

On the way home in the cruise car, we drove past the same deserted sidewalks and storefronts, and as I stared through the car window, I thought of Sherry's clammy, emaciated body stiffening on the autopsy table, of the bruises staining her greyish-white flesh. But even as I was contemplating this image, I felt the pressure of a gaze against the side of my face, a whisper tickling my ear. "Who told you where to find me? Did *he* tell you?"

Who?

I'd given the cops the facts—which were all they'd wanted to hear. But I hadn't told them the whole truth, the one I'd absorbed by osmosis, through my hair follicles and nerve-endings.

Sherry had seen this coming.

8

ALTHOUGH I DIDN'T get to bed until after two, I woke up before six and lay there, going over and over my conversation with Sherry, reviewing everything I'd heard about her, everything I'd learned about her death. Then I remembered that I'd made a tape of my visit with her—a tape that the cops would certainly want to hear. But before I offered it to them, I wanted to listen to it myself. At six-thirty I finally got up, threw last night's soggy salad into the compost bucket (the contents of which I donate to my neighbor's garden), and drove down to my office. I stopped to buy gas and a cup of dishwater coffee on the way. Then I sat at my desk with my jacket on, sipped my coffee and warmed my hands around the cup, waiting for the electric baseboard to heat up my office. At seven-thirty I phoned Tom, and to my relief he hadn't yet heard from the cops. That could only mean one thing: even without my alibi, they knew I hadn't done it. I told Tom what had happened and warned him to expect a visit from the cops. I phoned my kids too, just in case. When I told Ben that the cops might want to talk to Tiara as well, Ben got huffy and said that he wouldn't give them her phone number. "Don't be ridiculous," I snapped.

"But this has nothing to do with her! And she'd be just—"

"Mortified?" I suggested. "Shocked? Well, of course, if you'd rather see your mother charged with murder. . . ."

Then I listened to the tape that I'd made of my interview with Sherry.

The tape was lousy. My questions were clear enough, but

Sherry had moved around so much that her voice faded in and out, and it was often difficult to hear what she said. Nevertheless, it brought her back to me vividly: her tense, abrupt movements, her disjointed remarks, the panic in her eyes. Now that she was dead, everything she said seemed to foreshadow her murder: "Just got to keep moving . . . keep them guessing . . . if I needed her, I'd phone . . . she'd be the first person I'd call." Christ, I thought, I should have got her out of there. Dragged her into my car? Phoned her sister to come and get her? Let's face it, I concluded, you should never have looked for her in the first place.

Meaning what? That if I hadn't found her, she wouldn't be dead? "Come on, Meg," I scolded myself, "stop being so egocentric."

When Julio opened up his delicatessen next door, I went over to buy a cappuccino and a Portuguese bun and saw that the morning newspapers had arrived. Sherry's death took up half the third page. I strolled back to the office, reading the reporter's version of events, which were predictably inaccurate. He said that Sherry had recently separated from her husband, but didn't mention the fact that she was in hiding; and he made a lot of the fact that she was mentally ill, as if women who were mentally ill were more likely to be murdered than others. According to the paper, none of the neighbors had heard anything, and the police had no suspects. As I opened my office door, the phone started ringing.

It was Vicky, and her voice had a tight, smothered quality, as if she were trying not to breathe. She wanted me to stay on the case and find out who had killed her sister. I told her that Sherry's death was now a police matter and they wouldn't appreciate my interference.

"Who cares about their stupid protocol!" she demanded, recklessly. "Did you see the paper? There was a bank robbery in Kerrisdale, some drug pusher knifed in a hotel downtown, and they still haven't found the guy who's kidnapping those kids. With all that going on, how much time are they going to spend on Sherry? No, I want you to do it; I'm paying you, personally, so that you won't do anything else until you've found out who killed her. I mean, that's what money's for, isn't it? What else am I supposed to do with it?"

"Vicky," I said. "You haven't slept yet, have you?"

"How can I *sleep!*" she yelled at me.

And, I thought, you've had too much to drink.

"Look. Have a bath and go to bed. Phone me when you wake up. Meanwhile, I'll get those copies made. After you've had some sleep, I'll bring you the tape and we can talk about what to do next. O.K? Where are your kids?"

"My neighbor drove them to school. I haven't told them. What should I tell them—the truth?" Her tone was resentful.

"Where's Mark?" I asked.

"He's with Glen."

"Then take advantage of the opportunity and go to bed. I'll come see you this afternoon."

I got her to give me directions to her place. After I'd hung up, I walked down to the local library and made photocopies of my report and my contract with Vicky. Back in my office, I copied Sherry's tape onto a regular cassette. Then I went down to the police station again.

I took the elevator up to Homicide, gave the clerk at the front desk a bulky manila envelope, asked her to pass it on to Detective Baker. Just as I was turning away, Dikeakos walked through the door behind me, moving so fast that he almost missed me. He did a double take, wheeled to a stop and back-tracked. He didn't waste time on greetings. "Have you got your report?"

I indicated the clerk, who held the manila envelope out to him. He took it. As he started to turn away, I said, "I forgot to tell you that when I talked to Sherry on Saturday, I taped our conversation." He stopped, stared at me, then glanced down at the envelope and fingered the bump that the tape made inside it. "It's in there," I said.

He opened the manila envelope and peered into it, frowning, gave an abrupt nod. "Come on," he ordered, and strode off down the corridor. I followed, wondering if I'd been given a choice.

He led me to his office, which had one window (with a view

of the police parking lot) and was about eight by eight feet square. His desk took up most of it. The walls were lined with shelves which were crammed with books, papers and overflowing files. He moved a stack of books from the visitor's chair to the floor so that I could sit down, produced a pocket-sized tape recorder from one of his drawers and cleared a space for it on top of his desk, which was about three inches deep in paper. He scanned the contract and leafed through the report, chewing the inside of his cheek. Then he extracted the tape from the envelope.

He stuck the tape into his machine, turned it on, sat back and pulled a pack of cigarettes out of his jacket pocket. As the tape kicked into life with a crash ("You've got no right! Get out of here!...."), he sat back and lit his cigarette. He heard the whole thing once through, then rewound the tape and started it again. This time he kept stopping it, asking me questions: "What did she say?" "What was that noise?" "What did she look like when she said that?" I answered as best I could. When he'd been through the whole thing again, he shut the machine off and looked at me. "Sounds to me like she was hiding from someone."

"Yes," I said. "But then hindsight helps."

He leaned back in his chair and reached for the file that was on the top of his filing cabinet. He opened it, shifted a few pieces of paper aside, then turned the file around and placed it before me on his desk. The piece of paper confronting me was a mug shot of a young black man. I recognized him immediately, although the photographs must have been taken several years ago.

"In the course of your investigation," Dikeakos said, "did you run into this guy?"

I glanced at the vital statistics at the bottom of the page: his name was Ed Jeffreys—which meant nothing to me. "I saw him going into the top floor suite of Sherry's house. He had his own key." This much, I thought, they'll have found out for themselves.

There was a silence; I glanced up. Dikeakos seemed to be waiting for more. "Who is he?" I asked.

Dikeakos tipped back in his chair. "He's a welder. Twenty-four years old. He has a record for assault."

Uck, I thought. In the mug shot he looked belligerent, but I was remembering him as I'd seen him at Copper's restaurant: a big man with an engaging, insolent style, and a chipped front tooth.

"He was charged five years ago," Dikeakos said. "He got off with a suspended sentence."

"Who did he assault? A woman?"

"No." Dikeakos let his front chair legs hit the floor, butted out his cigarette. "A white guy who insulted him."

Oh, I thought. Well that's a bit different.

Dikeakos read the expression on my face. "It's not a good idea to get into the habit of using your fists."

I conceded the point. "You've talked to him?"

"Uh-huh. When we questioned him, he told us that he knew nothing about Sherry Hovey, didn't even know what she looked like. But the landlady had a different story. She said that when Sherry phoned her to inquire about the suite, Sherry told her that she'd heard about it from this guy, Ed—" he nodded at the file in front of me, "who lives in the same house."

I winced. Not good. And when I'd recognized him at Sherry's house, I'd thought the same thing—that he and Sherry must know each other. Then why was I protecting him?

"Actually," I admitted, "I saw him twice—once at Sherry's house, but also in Copper's restaurant. It was lunchtime and he was leaving with a bunch of his co-workers. He seemed to know the staff; he probably goes there every day."

"Copper's is that restaurant where Sherry worked?"

I nodded.

"On Clark, near Hastings."

I nodded again.

Dikeakos looked out the window at the sky; a seaplane was flying overhead, descending into the harbor. "Ed Jeffreys works about a block away from there—a place called 'Coast Welding.'"

"There you are then."

He gave me a sharp, appraising glance, and for a moment we were both silent—a silence that grew to almost oppressive

76

proportions—so that the next question seemed to get forced out of me against my will. "How's his alibi?"

"Rotten. He was asleep."

"People do sleep," I reminded him. Now I definitely wanted to change the subject. "What about Glen Hovey?"

Dikeakos' lips quirked as if I'd just said something amusing and the tension between us dropped so abruptly that I realized, retroactively, how uncomfortable I'd just been.

"What about him?" But he knew what I wanted, and enjoyed holding the answer, like a carrot, out of reach. The room was warm; there was a faint flush across his cheekbones.

"What's *his* alibi?" I persisted.

He raised an eyebrow. "He didn't know where the hell she was—remember? Unless you told him."

Of course. I felt irritated. "What was Glen doing yesterday morning?"

Dikeakos dug his fists into his eyes and yawned, giving me a firsthand view of his fillings. "Sorry," he said, belatedly. "No sleep." His mouth snapped shut. "He was at his Dad's house, washing the kitchen floor."

"His Dad says so?"

"Says he arrived at eight-forty and left at ten-thirty. Apparently this is a regular thing; his father is nearly eighty and Hovey drops in on him several times a week to help him with his chores. Then Hovey went to work, showed up at the restaurant at quarter to eleven. His employees say so," he added, anticipating my next question.

"Where does his Dad live?"

"Below 49th and Fraser."

At least two miles away from Sherry's apartment. "And Sherry died between eight-thirty and . . . "

"Eleven a.m., when the neighbor got back with the kids."

"No later?"

"No. They finished the autopsy this morning, and all the indications are that Sherry Hovey died Sunday morning, when the rest of them were down at the park. And she was alive at eight-thirty when the neighbor picked up the kid."

Then Glen couldn't have done it. He couldn't have killed

Sherry, wiped up his fingerprints and made it to his father's place in ten minutes. "Did the autopsy say how she was killed?"

"As you guessed—a brain hemorrhage. She really hit that counter when she went down. Died instantly. But if you were trying to kill someone, that's not how you'd go about it. I figure they started arguing about something, he lost his temper and things got out of control."

"I notice he didn't call an ambulance."

"No," he agreed. We watched each other, speculatively; his eyes were so dark that the pupils were almost indistinguishable from the irises. Abruptly he turned to the tape recorder, ejected the tape and reached for the manila envelope as he stood up.

I stood up too, but tried to squeeze in another question. "Nothing under her fingernails?"

"She didn't get near him." He was re-packing everything into the manila envelope. "Thanks," he said, giving it a flick with the back of his fingers. He opened the door for me.

As I walked away down the corridor I noticed I was feeling flustered. It felt odd to be working with the police, instead of against them. I entered the elevator, gazed up at the flashing red numbers, and a nasty thought suddenly exposed itself—like a slug inside a lettuce leaf.

Dikeakos' confidences were manipulative, deliberate—and flattering to my ego. He knew that, like all outsiders, I was susceptible to the condescensions of those on the inside. By pretending to consult me, by treating me like a colleague, he was turning me into an informer. But he hadn't succeeded—had he?

I remembered Ed's grin as he'd stood in front of Alexis' cash register, extracting grit, wads of kleenex, and bits of metal from his pockets, and finally—like magician pulling a rabbit out of a hat—one scrumpled up five dollar bill.

I felt like someone had thrown a pie in my face.

I tried to persuade Vicky that I was no longer useful to her. I sat on one of her deluxe sofas in her barn-size living room, drinking tea and arguing with her. I pointed out to her that I was not trained in homicide, that I didn't have access to criminal records or laboratories, that the cops were much better qualified to find Sherry's killer than I was. "Nowadays it's all science," I said. "Blood and hair analyses, fingerprints, international data banks. And people will talk to the cops who won't talk to me. Using me is like counting on your fingers when you've already got a calculator. You're wasting your money."

Vicky's eyes were like stones. Grief had intensified her natural presence; she seemed to have acquired solidity, a force, like gravity, which I was finding difficult to resist.

"As far as the cops are concerned," she said, "Sherry was a statistic. Another nutcase. I could tell by the way they talked. You care. They don't."

"They do care," I objected. "Cops hate murderers, and there's nothing they like better than catching them. What's more, they're quite good at it. Whereas I'll just be—"

"You're afraid that if the cops find out that you're working on this case, they won't like you anymore. Is that it?"

I opened my mouth, closed it again without speaking. I resented her tone—but understood the anger that fueled it. But what I'd said was also true—no amount of empathy was going to qualify me for this job.

"Are you telling me you won't do it?" she asked, with hostility.

Was I? I gazed out the giant picture window that looked over her sloping front lawn across to the lawn on the other side of the street, beyond which I could see another giant picture window in a house that was not quite identical to this one. Vicky lived in one of those new subdivisions in Richmond where the houses are all over two thousand feet square, and where individualism is confined to superficial details: brick facades, cedar siding, a balcony on the left instead of the right, a rockery instead of a swimming pool.

"No," I said finally, emptying my teacup, "I'm not saying I won't do it. You're right—I care, and I want to get the guy who killed her. But you shouldn't be paying me to satisfy my blood lust. The cops are doing the job for free, and they've got resources that I just don't have. I mean it—you'd be wasting your money."

"Then let me waste it," she said, with cynical satisfaction. "My husband can always make more."

"Hey." I reached out, but didn't actually touch her. She looked too much like a bomb that might explode upon contact. "I think you could use some support. Where is your husband, anyway?"

"In Bangkok." She gazed at me as if to say: Where else would he be?

"Did you phone him?"

"Of course I phoned him!" Her lips fluttered in a self-deprecating smile.

"When's he going to be back?"

"Oh, who knows?" She glanced down at her hands, which looked shrunken, too frail for the rings that imprisoned them. "I'll be all right. I've got a friend . . . and a good neighbor across the street." She lifted her chin in the direction of the picture window opposite. "That's where the kids are right now. She's cooking them supper." She sat silent for a moment. "I just want to know that someone's out there, *doing* something. Sherry was the only one in my family who I—" Suddenly her eyes flooded. Her mouth gripped, her eyelids closed; she fought for control.

I emptied my teacup and set it down on the coffee table. "All right," I said, carefully. "But when you're tired of paying me, feel free to stop. Because if Sherry was killed by an escaped homicidal maniac who just happened to be roaming through her neighborhood last weekend, I haven't got a chance. The police have files on such people—I don't."

Slowly her eyelids lifted; then, in a gesture that was eerily reminiscent of her dead sister, she leaned forward, placed a hand on my forearm, gazed at me intently. "Is that what you think? That it was just some psycho, that it could have been anybody?"

I looked into her burning, pink-rimmed eyes and shook my head. "I think someone was out to get her. Which means you have a job to do. Think," I commanded. "Chances are that Sherry knew him, that she talked about him." Vicky stared at me voraciously, as if trying to suck the thoughts out of my head. "You may know him too."

Her pupils seemed to magnify behind the film of tears, her fingers tightened around my arm like claws—and for a split second I felt that I'd walked into a trap. Then she let go of me and went to get her check book.

9

BEFORE I LEFT HOME on Tuesday morning I stood in front my mirror and appraised the image confronting me: a sturdy middle-aged woman, five foot five inches tall, one hundred and twenty pounds, round-limbed, square-shouldered. I have a rosebud mouth (which conceals thousands of dollars of dental work), an arched nose (which imparts, I like to think, a certain dignity to my profile), and a mess of frizzy brown hair which refuses to be styled. I feel silly dressed up; I prefer clothes that I can move in: wide-cut cotton pants, sweaters, suit jackets when I want to look businesslike. Despite my size, I'm strong—but that morning I was wishing that I was five inches taller, thirty pounds heavier, and looked a lot more intimidating.

Finally I went into the hall and started searching through the backlog of mail and other significant pieces of paper that I keep stashed in the top drawer of the dresser beside my front door. Eventually I found what I was looking for: the green registration form for an upcoming Aikido workshop. I read the fine print, and was relieved to discover that there was still time to sign up. I'd been slacking off lately, missing more Aikido practices than I attended, but if I registered for this workshop I'd feel obliged to get back on the mats to prepare for it. The senseii giving the workshop was a sixth dan black belt, and rumor had it that his assailants slipped off him like melted butter, an attribute that I hoped was contagious. I'd been startled out of sleep that morning by the realization that I'd just agreed to go after someone who was pretty handy with his fists. And I'd lain in bed feeling queasy, until I remembered this workshop and resolved to sign up for it.

On my way down to 6th Avenue, I delivered my registration form to the community center where the workshop was scheduled to take place. As I walked through the parking lot a soft breeze lifted my hair, warm sunlight bathed my face; I squinted up at the infinity of sky. In this part of the world spring goes on and on and on—and some years it stops raining long enough for people to really appreciate it. Even in my neighborhood, far from the big landscaped lots on the west side of town, daffodils bobbed in the flowerbeds and plum blossoms showered the sidewalks like confetti.

But the grey house on East 6th had been passed over by spring; it was set back from the street and shaded by the apartment buildings on either side. Apart from the trampled grass on the front lawn, there was no sign of the drama that had recently taken place there. I assumed that Ed Jeffreys would be at work, but I was hoping that the woman on the main floor would be home.

She was. Even before I knocked I could hear the sound of the television: the extra-loud, enthusiastic voice-over of a commercial. Not surprisingly, she inspected me through the window that gave onto the porch before she opened the door.

It was the woman with the ponytail, the one I'd talked to before. She had a French-Canadian accent, an olive complexion—that slightly misshapen, bruised look, characteristic of people who grow up undernourished. I showed her my license, gave her my card, explained my business and told her who I was working for. "I was wondering if I could ask you some questions," I said. "I know you've already given a statement to the police—but I would really appreciate it if you'd talk to me too."

The commercials finished, the show resumed; it sounded like I'd interrupted her in the middle of a soap opera. "All right, I guess," she said reluctantly. As she opened the door, I heard the patter of bare feet running down the hall and a little girl materialized and planted herself in front of me, staring up at me expectantly. "Hi," I said.

The child smiled, stuck a finger in her mouth, backed up

bashfully into her mother's thighs. Her round brown belly protruded through her pajama top, which was missing two bottom buttons.

The woman looked down at the little girl. "Vas t'habiller," she scolded her and moving the child aside, she led the way down the hall to the back of the house. Entering the kitchen, we stepped into dazzling light; the sun streamed through the south windows, highlighting the dirty dishes stacked beside the sink, the children's drawings tacked on the walls, the pile of laundry in the middle of the floor waiting to be washed.

"Since I can't seem to think about anything else," the woman said, kicking the pile of laundry out of the way into the corner, "I might as well talk about it. It's scary to have someone killed right underneath you like that. I don't feel safe here anymore. I want to move."

"You won't be any safer anywhere else."

"I know." She nodded at me. "That's what I keep telling myself. Sit down," she added, and cleared a heap of colored felt pens off the kitchen table.

In the living room I could hear the protagonists of the soap opera pleading with each other, but my hostess didn't seem to mind having abandoned them. "I was just going to make some instant coffee. You want some?" She plugged in the electric kettle. I didn't, but accepted anyway, because I thought she'd feel more comfortable talking to me if I had some with her.

Her name was Corinne. She told me that she'd lived in the neighborhood for nearly two years; she was a single parent and had two children, a boy of seven, a girl of three. "My daughter, Sylvie, would be out in the back yard here, and Mark started hanging around, looking over the gate, so I told him to come in and play if he wanted to. I don't think his mother liked it, but after a couple of days she saw him getting along and having a good time, so she just kind of ignored it. It was great for Sylvie— because he wasn't much older. They got along real well."

"Why didn't Sherry like it?"

"I don't know why." Two vertical wrinkles creased Corinne's narrow forehead. "She always acted like she didn't want to know me."

"Did she ever have visitors?"

"Not that I ever saw."

"Do you know if she had job?"

Sylvie, now more or less dressed, came running into the kitchen and climbed into her mother's lap. Corinne adjusted her position to accommodate the child's weight. "I don't think so. She hardly ever went out. To the laundromat, to go shopping—nothing else." She glanced down at her daughter, did up the buttons at the neck of her shirt, then noticed that one of her feet was bare. "Où est ton bas?" she asked, wrapping her hand around Sylvie's bare, plump foot. "Je n'sais pas," answered the child, reaching up to touch one of her mother's long, beaded earrings. Corinne captured her hand and pushed her down onto the floor again. "Vas chercher ton bas." The child ran away into the living room.

"Did it ever occur to you that Sherry might be afraid of something? Or somebody?"

"Of course I think of that now," Corinne agreed. "But before, no. I just thought she was unfriendly. Too bad, I thought, because with kids the same age, we could have helped each other out."

"So you never talked to her at all?"

"Not until that last night—like I told the cops."

"What last night? When was this?"

Corinne told me that on the Saturday night before Sherry was killed, about an hour after I'd talked to her myself, Sherry had knocked on Corinne's front door and asked if she could use her phone.

"Had she ever used your phone before?"

"Never." Corinne was emphatic. "I showed her where it was—right over there." She swiveled and pointed to the telephone mounted on the wall just outside the kitchen doorway. "Then I went back to the dishes. I wasn't listening," she defended herself, "but I couldn't help hearing a little bit. And it sounded to me like she was looking for another apartment—like she wanted to move, eh? I heard her say, 'Does that include the hydro?' 'Can I come see it tomorrow morning?' And I thought, Jeez, she only moved in here a couple of weeks ago. She made more than one phone call—three or four, I think—and when she finally got off the phone, she came into the kitchen and I saw she had a newspaper folded in her hand. But I didn't say anything—I didn't want her to think I was being nosey."

Corinne glanced at me; when I nodded, she went on: "Then she sort of stood there, like she felt awkward, you know? And suddenly she says, 'I just found out my grandmother had a stroke.' She seemed pretty upset. She said she wanted to go to the hospital to see her grandmother, but the nurse told her over the phone that no kids were allowed in the ward. She asked me if I'd mind looking after Mark the next morning so that she could go visit her grandmother."

"But you'd just heard her on the phone making an appointment to view an apartment."

Corinne smiled a little, shook her head. "Yeah, well—I wasn't about to argue with her."

"But why would she lie?"

"Maybe she was going to visit her grandmother and then see the apartment on her way back. Anyways, it didn't matter to me where she was going. I was just glad she was being friendly for a change."

"But you must have been surprised."

"Yeah—I was. But you know how it is—" Corinne gave a philosophical shrug. "Suddenly she needed me. But also she was upset—because of her grandmother. And sometimes when people get upset about something, they change their behavior."

"You believed this story about her grandmother?"

Corinne didn't answer immediately; she rubbed her thumb across a picture of a kitten that was embossed on the side of her mug. "I did, you know. Because she seemed pretty shaky—like she'd had a shock."

But that might have been the effect of my visit, I thought.

Corinne took a sip of coffee. "So I told her that Mark could come to the park with us. My son plays T-ball down there every Sunday morning, and I knew that Sylvie would be glad to have someone to play with. I said we'd have to pick Mark up from her place at eight-thirty, and since we're usually back by eleven, she could just come up for him whenever she got home."

"You're quite sure of the time?" I asked. "Eight-thirty?"

"Oh definitely. Because we lost an hour that night, remember? So it was actually seven-thirty and I had a hell of a job getting the kids ready on time. The game is supposed to start at eight-thirty, but everybody else is always late, so now I am too. It's too early, anyway—especially on a Sunday—but the older kids take over the field at ten and we get squeezed in before them."

"And what time did you get back?"

"Just after eleven."

"Did you check to see if Sherry was home?"

"No. I wasn't expecting her back until noon. And the kids had gone up to the top floor to see Ed."

"To see Ed? The guy who lives upstairs?"

"Yeah. They go visit him all the time. He doesn't mind—he likes kids. Sometimes he looks after them for me if I have to go out."

"Did Sherry know Ed?"

"Sherry? No—at least, I don't think so."

"You never saw them together?"

Corinne shook her head.

At twelve-thirty, Corinne said, she called the kids down to eat lunch. "It wasn't till around one o'clock, I guess, that I started to wonder why Sherry wasn't back yet. I went down to her suite and knocked on the door. Then I noticed that the door wasn't locked. That's funny, I thought. Nobody leaves their doors unlocked around here. I looked in, I called . . . the breakfast things were still out on the table, the dishes weren't washed, and I saw what looked like that same piece of newspaper—it was the classified section, with the ads, you know?—on the floor under a chair. I went back upstairs; now I was getting worried. I thought: Has she had an accident or something? I don't know her last name, I don't know anything about her. An hour later, I couldn't stand it anymore. I went back to her apartment and looked all around, trying to understand what was happening—where she was. And then I saw that someone was sleeping in the bed. I went—"

"In bed?" I interrupted. "You found her in bed?"

"Yes. All tucked up just like she was asleep. On her side, you know? I shook her a little bit and then . . . well, I used to work in an old folk's home. So right away I guessed—I knew that she was dead." Remembering, she took an unsteady breath. "Well—you can imagine. I started to shake—at first I thought she must have taken sleeping pills or something. But then I turned on the light to look—and I saw the swelling along here," she lifted a hand, brushed her palm along her cheekbone, "and there was blood on the pillowcase, behind her head. I lifted the eyelid to look, to make sure—"

"Her eyes were closed?"

"Yeah—like I say—she looked asleep! Eyes shut and everything."

"But she—" I stopped myself, remembering that what the cops had told me was in confidence.

"And for sure she was dead. I ran back upstairs to phone the police. Then I sat in the living room, staring at the kids—they were watching a T.V. show. And all I could think was: What am I going to tell Mark when he sees the cops going into his place?"

Again I became aware of the television in the next room, the music and muted voices indicating that the plot had taken a sentimental turn. The front door opened, closed; I glanced at Corinne and found her watching me.

"It's my friend," she explained, getting up abruptly and carrying our cups to the sink. I heard Sylvie's feet padding through the living room, a woman's voice in the hallway, and then a stocky woman with close-cropped blonde hair appeared in the kitchen doorway, carrying Sylvie in her arms.

Corinne introduced us. The woman nodded at me, then walked over to Corinne and gave her a gentle kiss on the lips. A serious, inquiring look passed between them—which was interrupted by Sylvie, who was clambering, monkey-style, from one woman to the other. Sylvie, I noticed, was still missing a sock.

I thanked Corinne for her help; she and Sylvie accompanied me to the door.

I climbed back into my car, drove around the park to Great Northern Way, joined the barrage of cars charging up the hill to Clark Street. I turned north and sat at the traffic light on 1st, looking up through my windshield at the mountains where big brown patches were slowly spreading, like mold, over the lower ski slopes.

Sherry had decided to move—again. That was my doing. She'd fabricated a story about her grandmother for Corinne's benefit, because she didn't want to take Mark apartment-hunting with her. But before Sherry got out the door that Sunday morning, the guy she was hiding from caught up with her. He smashed her against the kitchen counter, then scooped her up in his arms and carried her to bed, committing her to eternal slumber, like a princess in a fairy tale.

The traffic light changed; I dodged through the narrow side streets and parked in front of my office. But he must have realized that she was dead, I thought, as I unlocked the door and collected my mail off the carpet. Because after he'd tucked Sherry under the blankets, he'd gone around the apartment, wiping everything he might have touched.

I sat on my desk, perusing my bills, while I listened to the messages on my answering machine. Various people wanted to talk to me—but I ignored their requests and phoned Vicky instead.

"Have you got a grandmother?"

"None living."

"Did one of them die of a stroke?"

"Yes. About ten years ago. How did you know that?"

"Just a guess. Have you told Glen that you're keeping me on this case?"

"I told him this morning when he came to drop off Mark."

"*You're* looking after Mark?"

"Well—Glen has to get back to work. And this doesn't seem like a good time to introduce Mark to someone new. But it's a temporary arrangement."

"How did Glen react to the news that I was still working for you?"

"Well—I don't think he approved."

No, I thought. And he's not going to like it any better when I start questioning his employees. "How is Mark, by the way?"

"Um . . . well, he's O.K. as long as he's sitting in my lap.

89

That's where he is right now," she said, letting me know that this wasn't a good time to talk about his welfare.

My next project was Ed, who'd probably had a number of unpleasant interviews with the police by now, and wouldn't welcome any further conversation with me. I decided to proceed formally, starting with a phone call.

I found the number for Coast Welding in the phone book and called him at work. It went better than I expected. I explained who Vicky was, and why she had hired me; he swore he knew nothing about the circumstances of Sherry's death. "I've been through enough about all this," he objected. "The cops have been hassling me every day since. I tell you I didn't even know this woman!"

"I know that," I assured him, though of course I didn't—and his telling me so didn't make me believe it. "But I'm trying to get a full picture of everyone's movements in the house that day, what happened before, what happened after. I talked to Corinne this morning, and she told me that the kids went up to your place around eleven. . . . "

Finally, unwillingly, he agreed to see me, and we arranged that I'd stop by to talk to him that evening.

After that I went grocery shopping, and when I got home I treated myself to a home-cooked meal. I made up a stir-fry with gai-lan, tofu, bean sprouts and soft Shanghai noodles, ate it while watching the six o'clock news. Interest rates were going up, another plane had fallen out of the sky, they were still murdering each other in the Middle East. As the news was ending, Ben walked in my front door and slumped onto the couch beside me. "Hi," I said. "What's up?"

"Nothing." He stared at the screen, which was providing us with a synopsis of the weather all over the province. Sleet on the Hope-Princeton highway, snow flurries in Penticton . . . the rest of the country had disappeared under an Arctic front.

"Did the cops come talk to you?"

He nodded.

"Did they want to talk to Tiara?"

He shook his head.

The weatherman said that here on the Coast we were experiencing unseasonably warm temperatures. "Have you eaten?" I asked him.

"Not hungry."

This was unusual. But he didn't look sick—a bit glum, maybe. His legs seemed to stretch halfway across my living room. We were now getting recaps of the day's hockey games.

"How's it going at school?" Ben was enrolled in a computer science program at Vancouver Community College.

He shrugged.

I got up, went into the kitchen, put my dishes in the sink, the food back into the fridge. I went to the bathroom, got my jacket and car keys, stopped in the living room doorway. "Bye," I said.

Ben looked up. "Where are you going?" he asked, with a momentary relapse into childish imperiousness.

"Work."

For a moment he stared at me, remembering (with difficulty) that I lived a life of my own. "Bye," he said, his eyes returning to the screen.

I hesitated. "How's Tiara?"

"Huh?"

"How's Tiara?"

"She's O.K.," he said indifferently.

I gave up playing guessing games. "Lock the door when you leave."

He grunted assent.

10

As I DROVE over the Knight Street hill I caught the last of the sunset: blood-colored clouds over a silvery sea. By the time I parked outside the grey house on East 6th, it was dark. From Corinne's apartment came the plaintive strains of a country and western ballad; a shaft of light from a gap in her living room curtains cast a long, yellow stripe across the floorboards of the porch. Pushed up against the wall under Corinne's living room windows was an old-fashioned armchair, which I didn't remember having seen there that morning. This time I knocked on the door to my right.

I heard Ed's feet come thundering down the stairs, gathering momentum like an avalanche; the porch light came on over my head, the door opened explosively. He stood there staring at me, blinking in the light.

"You!" he greeted me, and stepped back a pace. "You were here before."

"Yes," I admitted. "I was here on Saturday—the evening before Sherry Hovey was killed. As I told you over the phone, her sister has hired me to find out who killed her."

"I thought the cops were supposed to be doing that."

"She wants me to conduct an investigation of my own. I'm just asking the same questions the cops asked—trying to find out what happened, who was where, who saw what."

I was struck by his size. He was large, as well as tall, more than two hundred pounds and built like a football player: big shoulders, big thighs. He was not somebody you'd want to get into a fight with.

"You're wasting your time with me," Ed said curtly. "I was asleep. I didn't see anything or hear anything."

"I understand that," I said. "But I'm trying to figure out what was happening to Sherry, and why she was hiding. Because if I knew why she was hiding, I might be able to find out who killed her." I lifted my eyes to his, tried a straightforward appeal. "Please. Can I talk to you?"

He slowly backed up, opening the door for me to enter. He turned; I followed him up the stairs.

Light shone through the kitchen doorway, illuminating the small landing at the top of the stairs. But Ed directed me left, into the living room at the front of the house, which was in darkness. With the aid of the streetlight that shone straight into his front window, I could make out a couch, a low chest, a wall of shelves stacked with audio-visual equipment, an electric guitar leaning against a cushion in the corner. I walked over to the couch, sat down resolutely, and waited for him to turn on the light. But he stopped in the living room doorway and stood there, watching me—as if still debating whether to throw me out.

"Tell me," I said, "how Sherry came to be living here. I understand that she gave the landlady your name when she phoned about the suite."

Ed leaned against the doorjamb with his hands shoved in his pants pockets. There were no lamps in the room, only the main overhead ceiling light, and I could see the switch on the wall not two feet from where he stood. But he made no move to turn it on.

"How'd I get into this?" he protested. "The police ask the same questions. 'You must have known her—she gave your name as a reference.' "

"I'm not accusing you of anything," I said. "I want to know about Sherry—not you. Why did she move? Why did she choose this place? Why did she quit work on the day that she moved here?"

"I don't know—that's what I'm saying to you!"

"Then tell me what you do know."

I received a swift, sideways glance—which I wasn't sure how to interpret.

"Where did Sherry get your name?" I repeated, reasonably, as if I were prepared to go on asking this question all night, if necessary.

Ed winced. He was fingering something in his pocket; I could see the material stretching and shifting over the knuckles of his right hand. "At first I couldn't figure it out either," he admitted, finally. "The cops were harassing me, and it just seemed like a bad joke. Because as far as I knew, I'd never even seen this woman."

"Really? But she lived right here—in the same house."

"Yes—really!" he retorted, widening his eyes, mocking me. "The cops don't believe me either—but hell, she only moved in here a couple of weeks ago and her door's around the side so she probably used to go out the back way, through the alley. Besides, I'm a single guy—I'm not home very much."

"Then—"

"But now I know what happened." Ed stopped, as if I'd interrupted him, and glared at me as if to say: You want to hear this or not?

I tried to look patient.

"Today the cops finally saw fit to tell me that this same woman—Sherry—used to work at Copper's restaurant, which is where me and my buddies go three times a day for coffee breaks. They showed me her picture, and now—yes—" He nodded, exaggeratedly, "I do remember her. But." He lifted a cautionary forefinger. "I have never talked to this woman in my life." He gave each word emphasis, then paused dramatically.

"But now I remember," he went on in a more conversational tone, "that one day when I was on my break, I was at the same table with Ahmed, who works in the body shop across the street. He was telling us that he was getting kicked out of his apartment and needed somewhere to move to, fast. So I told him that the people who lived in the basement of my house had moved out and that the place was probably for rent—cheap.

Well, Ahmed wasn't crazy about living in a basement, but I wrote down the landlady's phone number, because I said it's better than nothing, and you can always move again if you find something better. Right?"

As the headlights of the cars moved up and down the street, long rectangles of light converged and circled the ceiling, making Ed's face flicker in and out of the shadows. "Well, she overheard us, eh?"

"Sherry?"

"Yeah—Sherry. I paid no attention at the time—but she'd been round to give us refills right when I was talking about the suite. So she heard what I said. And she was right there when I was writing down Mrs. Cheung's phone number."

"You think she saw the phone number, memorized it?"

"I figure Ahmed left the phone number right there on the table!" Ed answered indignantly. "We left—and a minute or two later Sherry came by to clear the table and picked it up. Simple."

"Have you talked to Ahmed about this?"

"I saw him today, on my coffee break. And sure enough, he doesn't remember what happened to that piece of paper. That night he went home and his wife had found someplace else to live, so he never thought of it again."

"Then how did Sherry know your name?"

He shrugged dismissively. "They all know my name at Copper's. I've been going there for years. Even though she never talked to me, she would have heard it."

The tension between us had eased; I no longer had the feeling that Ed was waiting to throw me out. But why hadn't he turned on the light? He didn't want to expose himself more than he had to?

"She quit working at Copper's the day she moved in here."

"So you said. To tell the truth I hardly noticed her. Now that you point it out—yeah, I realize that she doesn't work there anymore. But I couldn't have told you when she quit."

"And you never even knew that someone had moved into the basement?"

"Oh sure, I knew—because Corinne told me that some lady

and her kid were living there. And I met Mark myself. But I never saw her. I figure if she was hiding or something, she didn't want to be recognized and was keeping out of my way." He glanced at me diffidently, offering me this theory on a take it or leave it basis.

"Tell me what happened on Sunday morning," I said.

Ed's eyes moved to the window, following the headlights of a car down the street. "Not much to tell. The kids came up from downstairs a little after eleven and woke me up."

"You were still asleep at eleven o'clock in the morning?"

I was only surprised, but he thought I was being moralistic. "It was Sunday, remember? I was out partying Saturday night, didn't get home till four a.m. I was dead to the world until those kids came banging on my door. Too bad, eh?" He stuck out his lower jaw—this was the pose he'd presented for his mug shot.

"Too bad for my investigation, yes," I answered equably. "Was that the only time you met Mark?"

"Once he came up with Sylvie—but I didn't have time for visiting that day, chased them away again. He was a shy kid—wouldn't have come up by himself."

"I'm amazed he came up at all. I was told he was afraid of men."

"That so?" For a second, Ed looked interested. "He kept his distance—I noticed that. But I thought it was—" He stopped.

"You thought it was?"

He shrugged.

"Finish the day for me," I said. "They came up here at eleven and . . . ?"

"We watched the hockey game for a while. I made coffee, ate breakfast—then Corinne called them down for lunch. About one o'clock I went out, did some shopping. When I came back it was around four, and the place was crawling with cops."

"So you have no idea why Sherry moved here or who she was hiding from. . . ."

He pushed his weight off the doorjamb, finally dropped the pose of indifference. "Look," he pointed out, "if I knew any-thing about it, I'd tell the cops. I didn't know this woman—but that doesn't mean I'm not sorry for her. And the kid too. I got no reason to be protecting her murderer. But I don't know anything! That's what I keep saying—to you, and to the cops. But for some goddamn reason," he added, with sudden vehemence, "nobody seems to believe me. So I'm fed up with the whole business. You hear?"

He crossed his arms and turning away from me, settled his shoulder against the doorjamb again.

"I understand that you have a record for assault."

His lips tightened. He was staring out the window at the ski lights on Grouse Mountain, which were just visible over the tops of the apartment buildings across the street. Finally he said, "Word gets around—doesn't it?"

"Tell me how it happened."

He debated, surveying me with half-closed eyelids. "I was in a bar one night—" he began, speaking so softly that I stilled, as if we were in the presence of danger. "Pissed, I admit it. And when I went to sit at the bar, this well-heeled white dude beside me starts complaining to his friend that there's a funny smell around here. He says it to the bartender: 'Hey, George—something smells bad around here.' And George looks at me, eh?—like he's nervous. So I lost it. The guy I punched turned out to be a lawyer. *My* mistake—eh?" His eyelashes meshed.

"They gave you a suspended sentence?"

"That's right. I acquired a criminal record and a debt that took me six months to pay off. So you can understand—since then I stay clear of trouble."

"You seem to be in it now."

"Don't I?" he agreed, bitterly. He lifted his chin, and I found myself staring at a thin line of shadow that lay across his neck like the weal of a rope.

I decided I'd had enough. "Thank you very much for talking to me," I said, getting up. "I really appreciate it."

Ed's expression became resentful. "Three times," he said, holding up his three middle fingers. "Three times they've dragged me down to that station. And what is this—Tuesday? Three times in two days. They stick me in a chair in front of those lights and start going after me like a swarm of deer flies— question after question after question—the same things over and over again. Why this? Why that? It's enough to drive you crazy."

"I know," I said, quickly. "I've been through it myself."

I'd stopped a few feet away from him; he was blocking the doorway. "Yeah. But you didn't have a little voice whispering in your ear, saying: 'Maybe they're after you because you're black, eh? Maybe they don't like black men.' Now don't get me wrong—I don't usually think like that. But after three times in two days—you start to wonder. I got the police on the one side of me, and I got this voice in my ear . . . and by the time they're both through with me—Hey—I'm getting pretty scared. Maybe a little paranoid, huh? Or maybe it's not paranoid. What do you think?"

Another car came down the block, the shadows swung, the illuminated rectangles veered around the walls. His face leapt into light and hung there, as if severed from the rest of him—then was obliterated by the darkness. Suddenly I was scared; I think it was his fear communicating itself to me.

"I don't know—" I hesitated. "I can see why you'd start to wonder. . . . "

"Thank you," he said sarcastically. But he finally stepped aside so that I could get by him. As I passed through the doorway, I made myself meet his eyes. "I do know what it's like. By the time they get through with you, you don't even know what your name is anymore."

His gaze flickered over my face—an insolent, intimate appraisal. There was a glaze of sweat on his upper lip.

I thanked him again, then fled down his stairs, back to the security of my car.

Although Ed had just captured a significant chunk of my attention, I believe in being methodical, and I didn't let him distract me from my original plan. The next morning, therefore, I turned my attention to Glen Hovey. I'd decided to question his employees, but was going to try to be discreet about it by starting with someone who was no longer in touch with him, preferably an employee who had recently quit. I tried a ruse—

and it worked. I phoned The Blue Heron and, posing as a customer, I told Kaye, the hostess, that I'd been in there "some while ago" and had talked to one of the women working there, who was pregnant. "She wrote down her name and phone number for me—but now I've lost the piece of paper and for the life of me I can't remember her name. But I promised to get in touch with her because I know her baby must be born by now and I have this playpen that I said I would pass on to her—"

"She was pregnant? But I don't think any of our—Oh you must mean—but that would have been a long time ago. Shigeko—one of the waitresses? Was she Japanese?"

"Yes," I breathed. "Shigeko—that was it."

"But her baby's nearly seven months old now."

"Seven months! No! Is she working again? She'll think I've forgotten all about it. . . ."

But fortunately, Shigeko hadn't come back to work, and her baby already had a playpen. It was brand new, plastic padded, bedecked with mobiles and other enticing educational toys, and had been placed, like a showpiece, right in the center of her living room. Her baby, a black-eyed boy with fat red cheeks, was already trying to stand up.

Shigeko told me that she'd never met Sherry, but she'd heard of her death through another waitress, Doreen, who still worked at The Blue Heron. "Are you planning to go back there to work?" I asked her.

"Oh no," she said, decidedly. "We are starting our family now. Yukio will soon be a big brother. Won't you?" she asked, wrinkling her nose at the baby in the playpen. Yukio chortled and flexed his fat knees, then sat down inadvertently, with a well-wadded thump.

Shigeko had nothing but compliments for Glen. He was a wonderful employer, very thoughtful and considerate; he always paid on time, and treated his employees "like a kind father." Before Glen, she'd worked for a man "who shouted and swore at us when we made mistakes. But Glen always treated us with respect. And everything in the restaurant was very organized. We never ran out of things; he took care of everything himself, personally."

I asked her if she could give me the names of other people who had worked at The Blue Heron. Shigeko said that she didn't know the new people—but through Doreen she knew the names of everyone who had left. She told me that she used to help Glen with the payroll, and as a result she knew many of the employees' last names, sometimes even addresses. She had a phenomenal memory. ("Now Olivia used to live on Wall Street, but then she moved to...I think it was Kitchener.") She provided me with such a wealth of information that I felt that, like the cops, I should have reminded her that she was under no obligation to answer any of my questions.

But she made my task a lot easier. With the help of the directories in the library, I found phone numbers for most of the names that Shigeko had given me and I made appointments to visit several of Glen's employees. I started with those who'd quit sometime in the last year, then moved on to those who were still working for him. And I learned something that surprised me— Glen had many admirers.

I heard the same things over and over again. Glen cared about his employees, treated them like family, inquired after their personal problems, proffered help and advice. "We tell him our problems, he tells us his—we always work out solutions together." "One time Alberto, our dishwasher, got very sick in the middle of his shift. We were already short-staffed; Glen couldn't find anyone to replace him. He sent Alberto home and washed the dishes himself." "He knows the business inside out. He has very high standards in everything, but he doesn't sacrifice his workers in order to maintain those standards." Glen had a medical/dental benefit plan for his workers (rare in the restaurant business), paid good wages (by industry standards), and prided himself on running a clean and safe work place.

"He is a wonderful boss. We felt terrible when we heard about his wife; all the girls cried."

This last was Doreen, Shigeko's friend, who also told me that Glen was "a broken man. He's devastated. He just adored his wife. He used to phone her every day."

"He never went after other women?" I asked.

Her greenish eyes, lavishly decorated with pink and gold

eyeshadow and encircled with black liner, widened expressively. "Never! That's what I'm saying. I don't think he ever even *looked* at anyone else."

Over the course of these interviews, I became aware that most of Glen's employees were female—he hired waitresses rather than waiters, and employed very few men. And I noticed that the men I talked to were less enthusiastic about Glen than their female co-workers. The dishwasher, Alberto, pronounced him "a good boss," but looked uncomfortable when he said it and wouldn't elaborate. The bus boy, Sayed, spontaneously sang Glen's praises, but then admitted that he was "too fussy." Michel, one of the cooks, told me that Glen was the best employer he'd ever had, "except for one thing," he amended. "He is always spying on us. He pretends he's being friendly—but really, he's checking up on us." But I found only one employee who was downright critical: Dan Reisler, the sous-chef who had recently quit.

Dan was a thin, sandy-colored young man who had narrow features and a slightly arrogant air. He didn't like Glen, and made no bones about it. "He knew his job—I'll give him that. But I don't know—maybe it was just a personality conflict or something. We didn't get along."

"What didn't you like about him?"

"He was always trying to get personal. A boss is a boss—not a friend."

"But that's what everyone else tells me they liked about him. They tell me that he treated his workers like people, and cared about their problems."

"Yeah—a little condescension goes a long way with some of them. But I don't want my boss butting in on my personal life. We may like each other or not—that's irrelevant. But Glen wanted everyone who worked for him to be his friend, and he didn't leave you alone until he figured he'd won you over. I felt like he was trying to manipulate me all the time, trying to worm his way into my confidence. I'm gay—I don't advertise the fact, but I don't hide it either. Glen would make remarks sometimes—as if he figured he had something on me."

"What kind of remarks—can you give me an example?"

"Oh—" He made a gesture of contempt. "I don't know—it was pretty subtle. When I came in looking tired he'd say, 'More sleep, Danny-boy, less hanky-panky,' or I'd be getting cleaned up, changing to go home and he'd whistle and say, 'Who's the lucky date tonight?' Stuff like that. It doesn't sound like much when I repeat it—but it added up, and he knew I didn't appreciate it."

When I figured I'd got enough information out of Glen's employees and could now afford to come out into the open, I approached Kaye Wong, Glen's hostess, who'd just been promoted to the position of assistant manager. Up until Sherry's death Glen had done all the managing himself, but now that he had to be at home in the evenings to look after Mark, Kaye managed in his absence. I gave her a long spiel about how Glen had promised to cooperate and how I'd talked to everyone else and wanted to get her views as well. . . . She said she'd think about it and call me back.

Two hours later, I got a phone call from Glen.

"I hear you've been questioning my employees."

And I know who told you, I thought. "Yes. I have."

"I wish you'd asked me first."

"I'm just doing my job."

"But there's no need to go behind my back. I told Vicky that I'd be more than willing to assist you in your investigation. So now—come down to the restaurant and ask me your questions in person. Why don't you have lunch with me?"

"Sure," I said—and made a face at the receiver as I hung up.

11

LUNCH WAS EXCELLENT: pan-fried sole, new potatoes, a green salad sprinkled with tarragon vinegar, a glass of white wine. Just eating it made me feel svelte and chic. Or was it the company? Glen seemed a little subdued, but was otherwise the perfect host. He was one of those men who, when they are with you, seem to give you their entire attention; he ate little himself, but personally supervised every mouthful I took. And he possessed all those lost, gentlemanly arts (which I can do without): he held out my chair, helped me out of my jacket, ordered my food (after, of course, checking out my preferences). Despite the reprimand on the telephone, he seemed to bear me no grudge and answered my questions without hesitation, treated my opinions with respect. Doreen served us. And he treated her exactly as he treated me—as if, by being there, she were doing him a favor. It was a technique that worked with both of us.

Taking him at his word, I asked him what he'd been doing on the Sunday morning that Sherry was killed. He said he'd risen early, around seven-thirty, showered, ate breakfast, then drove over to his father's place, arriving there at about eight-forty. "At least that's what my Dad says. I didn't notice—but it sounds about right. He's always watching the clock." He talked about his father at length. "He's an obstinate old codger. He's lived in that house for . . . well, my brother and I were both born there—and he refuses to move. But he can hardly get around any more, can't get down the back steps at all—so I go in there three or four times a week, take out the garbage, mow the lawn, wash the floors. As if I didn't have enough to do at my own house," he added, almost fretfully. "But he won't let me hire a cleaning woman. No strangers, he says."

"Where does your brother live?"

"He's dead. Died in a car crash when he was seventeen. So there's only me."

"He was older than you?"

"A year older."

"And your mother?"

"She died about twelve years ago. Cancer."

That leaves Mark, I thought. "How's Mark doing?" I asked.

He interlaced his fingers on the table, inspected them. "Not so good." I waited, and he went on. "He's a mess. Very insecure, cries all the time, wets his bed—you name it. The doctor told me to expect this—but I'm finding it hard. I'm only just hanging in there myself—and I can't stand it when he cries. Makes me want to start bawling myself."

"Maybe that's what you need to do."

"Yeah sure, but—" His voice broke. "Life has to go on," he protested, huskily, gesturing around him.

"You mean the restaurant."

"The restaurant—everything."

He was silent for a moment, then, as if making a decision, burst out, "You know what? I'm mad at her. Furious. It's unreasonable, I know—but I can't seem to get over it."

"Mad at her because . . . ?"

"Because she died, dammit! Unnecessarily. She had a good, safe home, a nice little boy—and she threw it all away, everything she had. Just to get herself killed by—by—well, who knows who he was?"

Again he lowered his eyes, leaving me staring at the crisp, dark waves on the top of his head. Finally he continued: "That bothers me too. Who was he? It sounds insane—but I think I'm jealous of him."

"No idea who it could have been?"

He hung his head and shook it for a long time, as if the action were affording him some relief. "I've no idea. And that hurts. She had a life of her own, I guess." He tried to smile, but only succeeded in looking miserable.

Doreen arrived and cleared away our plates; Glen asked her to bring us coffee. After she'd left again, neither of us spoke for some time. We sat in an island of silence while the sounds of the restaurant—the voices of nearby diners, the muted clink of glass and crockery—lapped around us. The waitresses glided like priestesses bearing offerings through the crowded tables; the atmosphere of the restaurant was calm and unhurried, the service smooth and efficient.

Our coffee arrived. Glen gave Doreen a grateful smile, offered me cream and sugar.

"You've got a nice place here," I said.

"Yes." He sat back, glanced around, stirred sugar into his cup. "My staff have been wonderful. They've kept this place going while I try to reorganize my life." He took a sip of coffee. "You're really the first person I've talked to about what I'm going through. But that's what they say, isn't it?"

I looked at him inquiringly.

"That it's easier to talk to strangers at times like this. And you're a good listener." He fingered his teaspoon, adjusting it so that it was exactly parallel to the handle of his cup. "But I guess that comes with the territory, doesn't it?"

"Meaning?"

"It's part of your job. The more you find out about me, the better. Right?"

"Yes," I admitted.

"Which is why you've been running around questioning everyone about me."

"It's nothing personal," I said. "The spouse is always a suspect."

"But I would have appreciated it if you'd warned me first. When Kaye told me that you'd approached her, I was kind of upset."

I was silent. He'd succeeded in making me feel guilty.

"Now tell me," he challenged. "What have you found out about me that you couldn't have learned by talking to me personally?"

"Lots," I said. "You're an excellent manager, thorough, fastidious, extremely responsible, fair, kind, sympathetic, loved and admired by almost all your employees. I don't think you—"

I stopped at the sight of his face. He looked almost horrified—then acutely uncomfortable. A dark red flush was mounting up his cheeks and into his forehead; a tic started hammering just below his left eye. Abruptly he covered his face with his hands. Wow, I thought. This man is really on the edge. When he dropped his hands, his face was still pink—but he managed to offer me a embarrassed smile. "Well!" He shook his head. "You caught me out that time." The smile remained fixed to his lips—but faded from his eyes like a sunset. "You said 'almost.' "

I stared at him, puzzled.

"You said 'almost all my employees.' "

"Yes," I said, not understanding.

"Who were the exceptions?"

"I'm not telling!" I said, amazed that he should think I would.

"But if I knew—perhaps I could do something about it."

I shook my head. "No one gets to be loved by everyone."

"No," he agreed, automatically. He touched his unused knife, straightened it. "But I'm an idealist, I guess. I always think that dislike is just a matter of misunderstanding. That something can be done about it." Now that the knife was correctly placed, his hands moved to his napkin, defining its folds, smoothing its creases. "Sometimes I'm right, too."

And sometimes you're wrong, I thought, remembering Dan Reisler, who didn't want to be his friend.

"Have you ever been married before?" I asked.

He lifted the napkin to his mouth and wiped his lips. "Before Sherry?"

"Yeah."

"No—" He sounded uncertain.

"Ever lived with anyone else?"

He took another swallow of coffee.

I said, "I heard that you were involved with someone a long

time ago, when you were working at the Shamrock on East Broadway."

"East Broad—" He broke off, gave me a dubious look. "Hey—you're going way back."

"Yes." Then when he didn't answer, I tried again. "There was someone—wasn't there?"

"Yeah," he admitted. "Kassie. I'd almost forgotten about her. It seems so long ago now—like someone else's life, not mine. We were both so young. She was barely out of high school."

"Her name was Cassie . . . ?" I was writing it down.

"K," he said, looking over at what I'd written. "Short for Kasia. But I don't remember her last name anymore."

How convenient, I thought.

"I'm telling you—we didn't last very long. And she left town after we broke up. I don't know where she is now."

"Kasia," I wrote. "When were you involved with her?"

He ran a hand through his hair. "Twelve, thirteen years ago? At least. She probably doesn't even remember me anymore."

"Was she from Vancouver? Does she have family here?"

"She went to school in North Van—I remember that. Her family lived down near the water somewhere. She had a younger sister, and a kid brother—but I don't remember the sister's name either. Like I say—this was all a long time ago."

"Sure you don't remember her last name?"

He shook his head and tried to look sorry.

I recapped my pen, closed my notebook.

"That's it?" He seemed disappointed.

"For now. But I'm sure I'll be back with more."

"No problem," he assured me, resting both forearms on the table. "Really. I want to give you all the help I can. I realize that I lose my temper sometimes—this process is kind of hard to take." His gaze rested on my face, soliciting sympathy. "You're not out to get me personally, I realize that. But please—if you can talk to me rather than my employees, I'd appreciate it. I'd like them left out of it as much as possible."

107

"I think I'm pretty much finished with them by now." I put my notebook away. "But there is one thing you can do—probably you're already doing it. There's a good chance that Sherry's murderer is somebody you know. Please go back—think over the past year, two years. . . . Is there anyone Sherry was afraid of? Did she ever say anything. did you ever suspect anything—"

"You think she had a lover?" His voice was rough.

"A lover, an enemy, a persistent admirer. . . . Hey, it's wide open. Who wanted her dead?" We stared at each other and our eyes got stuck; they disentangled with difficulty.

"That's a tough one," he acknowledged.

"But you're better qualified to answer it than I am."

When we parted, we shook hands. His clasp was warm, strong. After he'd left, I went to the cashier and tried to pay for my lunch—but Doreen had been instructed not to give me a bill.

Leaving, I wondered if Glen had got his money's worth.

I went to an Aikido practice that evening, and was given a thorough workout. We were practicing high-entry rolls and breakfalls: how to flip through the air and interface, gracefully, with the earth. I'm usually pretty good at these, but as I said, I'd been slacking off, and by the time the practice was over, my knees and feet were chafed raw by the mats, and my body felt like a beanbag. I drove home, looking forward to a long, hot bath.

But it wasn't to be. My front door was unlocked, there were lights on in the kitchen, and I could hear the washing machine churning at the back of the house. That meant Ben was here—doing his laundry and monopolizing my hot water supply. "Hello?" I called, kicking off my shoes.

This time he'd brought Tiara; they were making tea in my kitchen. Tiara was warming the teapot, Ben was rooting through my cupboards, trying to find something to eat. "What happened to those cookies?" he greeted me as I walked into the kitchen.

"Ben!" Tiara smiled at me, shaking her head.

"You ate them," I said. "When you were here the other evening."

"I didn't eat them all."

"No," I agreed. "You left me one and a half cookies."

He closed the cupboard door. "I guess it's peanut butter sandwiches," he grumbled.

"*I'm* not hungry," Tiara admonished him, carrying the teapot to the kitchen table. "Do you always eat your mother out of house and home?" She gave me a conspiratorial glance over her shoulder. Today her dark hair was scooped back with bright colored combs; she was wearing skin-tight black pants, pink socks, and a sweatshirt the color of egg yolks. She was young, healthy, privileged, and very pretty. Surely I wasn't jealous?

"I've learned to live on vegetables," I explained to her, "which Ben won't eat."

"I told him he should be ashamed to be still dragging his laundry home to his mother."

I glanced at Ben, who was cutting himself a slice of bread. "Did it do any good?" I asked her.

Ben gave me a dirty look. "I told you," he said to Tiara, plastering his bread with peanut butter, "I hate laundromats. And she doesn't do my laundry—*I* do. In fact, sometimes I do *her* laundry as well."

"Sometimes," I demurred.

"Last week," he said.

"Last week?"

"I washed your towels."

"Ah yes. My towels." I smiled at his sullen face.

Ben took a bite of his sandwich, walked around the counter, sat down at the table with Tiara. She reached for the teapot and poured a little liquid into her cup to see if it was steeped. "Would you like some?" she asked me. "It *is* your tea," she pointed out.

She poured out the tea and I talked to them for a while, then, feeling that I'd discharged my social obligations, I went into the living room and put my feet up on the couch, unfolded the evening newspaper. I wanted to ignore them, but snatches of their conversation drifted in through the open doorway and I found myself straining to overhear what they were saying. Despite my attempts to be indifferent, I was intensely curious about their relationship, and had noticed that the balance of power seemed to have shifted since I last saw them together. Today Ben seemed rather morose, withdrawn—and Tiara's behavior, although still condescending, was less secure, almost placatory. I got the feeling that Ben was brewing for a fight and that Tiara was trying to head him off.

I read the comics first, glanced at the personals, read Ann Landers and my favorite columnist, leafed through the business section, finally made it to the front page. The washer was silent now, but the dryer was rumbling, and Tiara's soft, mellifluous voice blended into it. I couldn't hear Ben's voice; Tiara seemed to be doing all the talking. I scanned the front page . . . as usual, the provincial government was blaming the federal government, which was blaming it back; there were riots in the Gaza Strip, more elections in Eastern Europe. Then a photograph on the second page caught my eye, and I glanced at the caption. "Fred Dunbar, killed in his home at 3553 St. Joseph Street." The features were blurred and indistinct; the photograph could have represented almost any heavy-set white male between the ages of fifty and seventy. Yet it seemed to me that I'd seen Fred Dunbar before. I read the article.

According to the police, Fred Dunbar had been murdered last Monday but his body hadn't been discovered until yesterday afternoon. An elderly neighbor had been alerted by the behavior of his dog, a small terrier, that had started hanging around her back porch, obviously wanting food. She knew the dog and its owner by sight—and thinking that her neighbor might have abandoned his dog, had finally gone over to his house to investigate. Anyone who'd seen Fred Dunbar last weekend was asked to contact the police.

"That's not what you said at the time!" Ben's voice, surmounting the dryer's rumble, intruded into my consciousness. I glanced up, listening—but again there was only Tiara's indecipherable murmur. I glanced at my watch. Surely his clothes must be almost dry? I do hope that they're not going to have their fight here, I thought. Then my eyes drifted back to Dunbar's photo.

Why did he look familiar? He had small eyes and a heavy,

rectangular chin. He looked a bit like Detective Baker. I didn't think that I knew him—I'd just seen him somewhere.

The dryer stopped. A chair scraped across the floor, the kitchen tap gushed. "Your shirts will get all wrinkled," I heard Tiara protest. "So what?" Ben snapped. And the tone of his voice carried me back to the fights that I used to have with his father. I remembered the evening that I'd spent scrubbing my kitchen shelves and I tried—just as an exercise—to recall the young wife I'd once been, content to stay at home with my two small children, taking them to the YWCA for swimming lessons, driving to the supermarket once a week. I used to listen to my neighbors complain about their marriages and think: Thank God, Brian and I aren't like that. Then I got raped. And as if God had spun a kaleidoscope, my world-view shattered. When it reassembled again, everything looked different. I took up martial arts, made new friends, acquired new thoughts—and somewhere along that process, Brian discovered that he didn't want to be with me anymore.

Now, when Brian phones—which isn't very often—it's like talking to an ex-colleague, someone I know well, but was never very close to. This bothers me—I feel like I've rewritten history, lobotomized myself. And when my kids, like archaeological artifacts, reveal unexpected glimpses of Brian's bone structure, gestures and argumentative tactics, I notice that I get irritated at them—as if I were being reminded of faults that I've outgrown.

When Ben had finally finished his laundry, he and Tiara made a farewell appearance in the living room doorway. "Thanks, Mum," he said. "Thanks for the tea," added Tiara.

"Bye," I answered, and wanted to add (but didn't): Have a nice fight.

Then I went upstairs and soaked the bruises out of my bones.

12

SINCE I CAN'T STAND waiting for my first cup of coffee in the morning, it's my habit to put on the kettle, spoon the coffee into the filter and then, while waiting for the kettle to boil, pace restlessly around my house, tidying up. I empty the compost, put out the garbage, pile the dirty dishes in the sink, collect yesterday's newspapers and add them to the pile on the back porch. On Saturday morning, six days after Sherry's death, I drew the curtains in the living room, stooped to pick up the paper from the couch and then stopped—found myself staring, once again, at the photo of Fred Dunbar. Goddammit—I'd seen that man somewhere before. I was sure of it. But where?

I carried the paper back into the kitchen where the kettle was now boiling; I poured the water over the coffee grounds. As the liquid dripped into the pot, I stood leaning against the counter staring at the grid of tiny dots that, from a distance, coalesced into the blur of Dunbar's face. What a crummy photograph. Surely the police had a better one.

My coffee cup now securely in hand, I sat down by the telephone and called the police station. I asked the receptionist to put me through to Major Crimes. I told the next voice on the line that I wanted to speak to someone in Homicide concerning the investigation of Fred Dunbar's death. This time I got a male voice. "Homicide. Dikeakos speaking."

I was startled. "I thought you were working on Sherry's case."

"I was—am," he said. "It's Lacey, is it?"

Trying not to feel flattered that he'd recognized my voice, I told him that I'd seen the photograph of Fred Dunbar in the paper and thought he looked familiar. I said that if the police had any better photographs, I'd be willing to come down and take a look at them, on the off chance that I might be able to tell the police where I'd seen Dunbar before.

Dikeakos said that I could see the original of the photograph they'd published in the paper, "and we have a few more—mostly group shots, though." He said he'd leave the photos with the clerk at the front desk, and that he'd be in and around the station all morning if I wanted to talk to him.

So instead of going straight to the office that morning, I made a detour to the police station. The clerk at the Homicide desk gave me a file. I sat down in one of the chairs near her desk and extracted the photographs.

At first I thought someone had made a mistake, and had given me their kid's collection of hockey team photographs. But after about the fifth photo, I noticed that although the teams kept changing, every team had the same coach. But Fred Dunbar looked less familiar in his hockey team sweatshirt; I only knew it was him because he resembled the man whose photograph was in the newspaper. Then I found the original of the photograph that the newspaper had printed, and again I experienced that slight tugging feeling. But this, the original photograph, wasn't much better than the reprint in the newspaper. It was overexposed and slightly out of focus.

A shadow crossed my lap; I glanced up and found Dikeakos beside me. "There's one on the bottom you might like to look at." He leaned over, enveloping me in the stench of cigarettes, and shuffled through the pile until he got to a photo of Dunbar standing on a podium, grinning and holding a trophy in front of his stomach. He watched my face as I studied it. "I don't know," I said doubtfully. I shifted position, and a much smaller, color photograph slipped sideways out of the pile. I picked it up. It showed a big man wearing an overcoat and a hat, standing in someone's back yard with his arm draped over the shoulders of a dumpy, anxious-looking woman. The upper part of his face was shaded by his hat—but it was the line of his jaw that jumped out at me.

"Yes!" I cried, looking up at Dikeakos. "That's the guy who—"

His palm went up; his eyes stopped me in mid-sentence. "Not here," he said. "Come down to my office."

Again the visitor's chair in his office was piled with papers. Dikeakos scooped them up, then gazed around, wondering where to put them. "Sit down," he said, finally balancing the stack of papers on top of the display terminal. He settled himself behind his desk, pulled out his cigarettes. "O.K.—shoot."

"This guy," I said, holding up the photograph of the couple in the back yard, "was sitting in a parked car outside Sherry's apartment on the Saturday night before she was killed."

Dikeakos lit his cigarette and narrowed his eyes at me through the smoke. "You sure?" he said, snapping the lighter shut.

"No. I'm not sure. It was dark, he was wearing a hat—just like here in the photograph. Could have been the same hat even. But I recognize that chin."

Dikeakos sighed. "This was around . . . ?" He had pulled out a pen, was opening his notepad.

"Seven-thirty."

"What kind of car was it?"

I squirmed a little. I remembered that I'd taken a good look at the car, but I'm not very good at identifying vehicles—although in my job, I should be. Sometimes I practice, and I now know all the older makes—but they keep producing new ones. "American," I said. "A big American sedan. Greyish color."

"That tallies," Dikeakos said cautiously. "Fred Dunbar drove a 1986 grey-green Oldsmobile."

"And he smoked," I remembered.

Dikeakos lifted his eyes from the notepad. "Uh-huh," he agreed.

I sat back, feeling vindicated. "There were two kids playing near his car. Maybe they noticed him too. They probably lived in the neighborhood."

Dikeakos took down a description of the children. "Light brown hair, dark eyes. . . . Race?"

"White," I said. "If you show Dunbar's photograph up and down the block, you might find the kids too while you were at it. Or try the local school. The girl would be in kindergarten or Grade One. And I'll—" I stopped, remembering that the cops didn't know that I was investigating Sherry's death. "Dunbar was a hockey coach?"

"He coached kids." Dikeakos was inspecting the cone of ash at the end of his cigarette. "His walls were covered with hockey pictures—stars, teams, trophies—you name it. But he gave up coaching a long time ago."

"How did he make his living?"

Dikeakos took a last inhalation on his cigarette, searched for his ashtray under the papers on his desk. "He used to work as a security guard in a warehouse on the docks. He injured his knee on the job—retired early with a disability pension."

"Wife? Kids?"

Dikeakos shook his head. "Never married. Next of kin is a sister in Winnipeg—I think that's her in the photograph. And the dog."

"Do you—"

"Would you have noticed if he had a black eye?" he interrupted me.

"A black eye?" I thought for a moment, remembering the bands of dark cloud at the top of the hill, the man behind the newspaper with the shadow across his face. "I couldn't see his eyes—it was too dark. You're saying he had a black eye *before* he was killed?

"The eye had already started to heal. If we could find out when he got it, we'd be able to pin down the time of—" He stopped, realizing that he was being more communicative than was necessary.

"Death," I finished for him.

He said nothing.

115

"But you're sure that he was killed on Monday?" I asked.

"Give or take twenty-four hours. Maybe Sunday night. Unfortunately, he wasn't found until Thursday. That makes it hard to be exact." He stood up. "Thanks for coming down." He held out his hand for the file of photographs.

I rose, slowly, giving him the file. "Since I saw Fred Dunbar outside Sherry Hovey's apartment, I assume that their deaths are connected. Is that why you're working on both cases?"

He had opened the door, was standing beside it, waiting for me to leave. "No. I'm working on both of them because we're short-staffed, as usual. Now, if you'll excuse me—"

"How was he killed?"

Our eyes met—deadlock. A uniformed policewoman passed down the corridor, glanced at us curiously.

"You're investigating Sherry Hovey's death," Dikeakos accused me. "Aren't you?"

I realized then, that my honeymoon with the cops was over. We stared at each other for a few seconds longer; without saying anything more he ushered me out.

As I drove along Hastings Street towards my office, I continued my discussion with Dikeakos. But maybe there is a connection, I argued. Maybe whoever killed Sherry killed Fred Dunbar too, because he knew too much about Sherry's death. Or maybe Dunbar killed Sherry, and someone else, knowing he'd done so, killed him. It's either that, I said, or Dunbar's presence outside Sherry's door on the night before she died was a coincidence. And Dikeakos, who was more cooperative in my imagination than he'd proved in reality, agreed that detectives don't believe in coincidences.

On the way into my office, I bought the morning paper, which was running the same photograph of Fred Dunbar. Reading the accompanying article, I learned that Dunbar's dog, "Rocket," had been kindly adopted by Mrs. Irma Storey, the neighbor who'd found the body. "I feel sorry for the poor little thing," she told the reporter, "he's had a nasty experience." Some minor league hockey official was quoted as saying that

"Dunbar almost single-handedly brought hockey into the lives of the boys of Vancouver. It's not like in the East," this official explained, "where you can just walk out the back door, step into your skates and hit the puck down the river. Here we've got to have rinks, the money to build them and the money to maintain them. It took a lot of hard lobbying—and Fred Dunbar never quit." He said we were all in Dunbar's debt. All except us girls, I reminded him, who were never allowed to play.

I cut out the photograph of Dunbar and taped it to a sturdy card, meanwhile listening to the messages on my answering machine. Now that I was unavailable, it seemed that all sorts of people were longing to hire my services. This is where detective agencies with half a dozen employees have the advantage over individual operators, and they often hire extra investigators on a contract basis, only using them when they need them. Of course I could do the same—but I want to be my own boss, not someone else's.

Then I drove, once again, to the 800 block on East 6th. It was a wan, hazy sort of morning, the sunlight smeared by high, thin clouds; the squat, bleak apartment buildings lined both sides of the street, facing off like antagonists. I was feeling kind of depressed, and the task that confronted me did nothing to raise my spirits.

I started at Ed's door, but even though it was Saturday, he wasn't at home. Then I tried Corinne's door—and got her friend instead. The woman's short hair was tousled, she wore a man's green plaid dressing gown. "Yeah?" she said, squinting at me.

"Is Corinne around?"

"She's out shopping with the kids."

Since this woman obviously spent a good deal of time at this address, I showed her the photograph of Dunbar. I explained where I'd seen him, and why I wanted to know more about him. She listened attentively, but when I'd finished my explanation she just handed the photograph back.

After that there was no alternative but to start at one end of the block, buzz every apartment in every building until I reached the other end of the block, and then head back down the opposite side of the street.

117

Despite the intercoms I managed to talk to a fair number of people. I met plenty of kids—but not the ones I was looking for—and nobody recognized the photograph of Fred Dunbar.

I drove over to Copper's restaurant. As usual, Alexis was lounging behind the till, his cigarette smoldering in the ashtray beside him. "You're back," he said, as if he'd been missing me. I sat down on the stool nearest him and ordered a corned beef on rye sandwich to go. I wondered if Alexis knew that Sherry was dead, and thought I'd better mention it.

"One of the girls saw it in the paper. Some of the customers read about it too—they recognized the picture. She had just left her husband, the newspaper said. She never told us that. Guess he caught up with her, eh?" A knowing look crossed his face.

"Why do you say that?"

"She left him, didn't she?" Apparently Alexis could have predicted the consequences.

"She deserved it?" I spoke gently, but my voice quavered, and I knew that I'd better not continue this conversation or I'd end up screaming at him. I wasn't in good shape that morning; every jerk I talked to was getting under my skin. I handed Alexis Dunbar's photograph.

"What's this?" He frowned at it.

"You ever seen him before?"

"Maybe." He made a dubious face. "But I don't know him. Is this her husband?"

"No," I said. "Mind if I show it to some of the others?"

He waved me away.

I collected my sandwich, then went back into the kitchen to talk to the staff. Today I had to answer a lot of questions before I could ask any of my own. "Are you looking for the guy who killed her?" "Have they arrested anyone yet?" "I never knew anyone who was murdered before." Finally I produced my photo of Dunbar and showed it to them, one by one. Chi Ming wasn't working that day; Tabib and Patty didn't recognize Dunbar, but Angela thought that she might have once served him. Angela and Patty got into an argument about it. "I never forget a face," Patty declared. "Names, sure—but never a face."

"But you don't always work on the same days, do you?" I

118

intervened, diplomatically. "Maybe he came in on your day off."

But as far as Patty was concerned, if she couldn't recognize Dunbar, Angela couldn't either.

I asked them if they knew a customer named Ed.

"What's to know about him?" sniffed Patty.

"Of course we know him," Angela said, "he comes in here every day."

But neither of them had ever seen him talking to Sherry.

"I wouldn't put it past him," Patty warned, darkly—whatever that meant. The global village, when it arrives, will have to commandeer another planet for diehards like Patty.

When Patty had left us, Angela said, "Remember you told us that if we thought of anything else, we should call you?"

"Yes?"

"But it wasn't really important so I didn't know. . . . "

"What was it?" I demanded, looking into her eyes, which were so huge, so luscious that they gave me a feeling of vertigo.

Angela told me that on the last day that Sherry had worked at Copper's she was "worse—much worse than usual. She kept forgetting things; she dropped a whole tray of cups, and she talked to herself nonstop. Alexis told her off several times. He'd warned her before to put a zipper on her mouth."

I thanked her for the information—though I wasn't sure where to file it—then asked if Luisa, the dishwasher, was now back from vacation. Angela said yes, and offered to introduce me to her.

Luisa, a middle-aged, barrel-shaped woman, took advantage of my appearance to sit down for a moment. The area around the dishwashing machine was warm and steamy; tiny droplets of water had condensed onto her hair, which was neatly compressed into a hair-net; a pair of thick-lensed glasses sat halfway down her nose. Angela introduced me, and I produced Dunbar's photograph. Luisa took off her rubber gloves, wiped her hands on her apron, accepted the card and holding it out in front of her, peered down through her lenses at it.

"No," she decided, handing it back to me. "I don't know him."

119

"I was told that you probably knew Sherry better than anyone else who worked here."

"Maybe," she agreed. "We talked a little bit."

"Did Sherry ever say anything to you about her husband, or about why she had decided to leave him?"

"I thought she was married because she had a little boy—but I knew she didn't want to talk about it. I didn't know if the husband died or what."

"Do you know who Ed is? I understand that he's one of your regular customers."

She watched me uneasily.

"A big black guy," I added. "He works just down the street, comes in here every day."

"Oh yes. I know."

"Did Sherry know him? Did you ever seem them talking or—"

"No," she answered, guardedly.

She wasn't liking this process, and I tried to figure out how to draw her into conversation. "Angela was telling me that on the last day that Sherry worked here, she seemed to be disturbed about something. She kept forgetting things and talking to herself."

Luisa nodded. "She was upset." She took off her glasses, wiped them on her apron, set them back on her nose.

"Do you know why?"

"She told me she didn't feel good."

"She felt sick?"

"She was upset," Luisa repeated, firmly. "I don't know why."

I bet your neighbors don't invite you over when they want a good gossip, I thought. "Do you know what she did with her little boy when she went to work?"

"She took him to a neighbor's house. She found a woman to look after him."

"Someone who lived near her?"

"Yes." Suddenly she became communicative. "Quite close, she said. She could walk there from her house. And the woman had a little boy the same age—so it was good." She nodded, her whole body rocking with the movement. "She told me she met the woman in the park and their boys started to play together."

Mentally, I crossed my fingers. "Did she ever mention the babysitter's name?"

Luisa squinted, staring straight ahead of her as if trying to see something through the haze of steam. "Hn," she grunted. "She did say it—yes. But I can't remember." She pushed her glasses up her nose. "It was a funny name—I never heard it before. She said the woman came from...it wasn't India, but it was somewhere near there. But she spoke English very good, Sherry said." She paused, considering. "Something like Annie, or Danny—but it was longer."

"Danny?"

She glanced at me, her eyes magnified behind the thick lenses. "Danniyanni-something. Like that. That's as good as I can remember."

"Did she come from the Punjab?" I suggested. "That's part of India. Or Pakistan?"

Luisa was shaking her head. "She looks East Indian, Sherry said. But she's not from India. Somewhere near there." Finally she agreed that it was possible that she'd remember more when she had time to think about it, and she accepted my card.

"I feel very bad about it," Luisa said as she rose and inserted her hands back into the damp rubber gloves. She tugged the wrinkled rubber over her fingers; I glanced up and found her staring at me fiercely. "She was in trouble—I knew it. I feel very bad now that I did nothing to help her." She turned away abruptly and went back to work.

Luisa's mood followed me out of the restaurant. That makes two of us, I thought glumly, climbing back into my car.

13

As I DROVE OUT to Vicky's place, I ate my sandwich, trying to contain the crumbs to the napkin on my lap. I opened my window; finally the sun had burned off the clouds and the air was getting positively warm. A premature summer? The greenhouse effect? Crossing the bridge over the Fraser River, I glanced down at the sturdy tugs plowing against the muddy current, at the fish boats setting out for the open sea. Smoke blossomed upwards from the factory chimneys; sunlight dazzled off the water; a jumbo jet, defying gravity, mounted inexorably over the airport.

In Vicky's neighborhood the sun had brought the residents out of doors. Children were careening unsteadily down the side streets on their skateboards and bicycles, teenagers were washing their cars in the driveways. There was no visible activity at Vicky's house, but there were three cars in the driveway and I could hear the sound of children playing in the back yard. I mounted the wide, brick steps and rang the gilt doorbell. It chimed musically inside the house. No one answered.

When no one responded to a knock either, I followed a path through the azalea beds around the side of the house, and was almost run over by a herd of galloping girls who were stampeding in the opposite direction. "Is your Mum home?" I asked, as the herd parted around me. "She's on the back deck," called one of the bigger girls, shaking her blonde mane. I continued around to the back of the house.

I heard their voices before I saw them. "You figure my arm

is the driveway, do you?" a male voice was saying. My breath stopped; I stood transfixed—then stepped out from behind the screen of espaliered, flowering quince and stared up at the sun deck about four feet above my head. Through the railing I could see two people reclining in deck chairs, and a small dark-haired boy standing beside one of the chairs, driving a truck along its armrest. Vicky had her back to me—but her guest was staring straight into my eyes.

Ed Jeffreys stiffened, lifted his head—then let it fall back against the white webbing of the chair. "You have a visitor," he said to Vicky.

I was already mounting the steps. "Oh!" Vicky exclaimed breathlessly as my head appeared above the deck. "Hi," she added hastily, getting up. She was wearing a halter top that exposed the sun-flushed skin of her upper chest and arms, and tight pedal pushers that creased at the top of her thighs. "Come join us—we're enjoying the sunshine."

But at the top of the steps, I stopped. "How the hell did *you* get here?" I asked, pointing a finger at Ed.

Our gazes crossed like swords in midair. Ed placed his drink beside his chair and glanced sideways at Mark, who was watching him anxiously, as if suddenly wondering the same thing. He addressed Vicky in tones of venom. "Would you tell this goddamn private eye of yours to get off my back."

"I see you've met," said Vicky. "Sit down, Meg, would you like a drink?" She indicated an empty deck chair. "We're having cider. Would you like some?"

I held out a hand, palm upwards, towards each of them. "Explain the connection—please."

"Yeah, Vicky." Ed's feet hit the deck. "You explain. I'm leaving." He got up.

"Ed!" Vicky protested.

"I'm not going to sit around being insulted by your staff. Thanks for the cider." He started towards the steps.

"Wait!" a child cried. We all turned and stared at Mark. He was sitting on the deck, struggling to get his running shoes on his feet. "Wait for me."

"Hey," Ed said gently. "I'm going home now. I'll come see

you some other day, O.K?"

"I'm coming too!" Mark's voice was shrill with panic. He'd got one shoe on, didn't bother to tie it up, was ramming his foot into the other one.

"No, darling." Vicky moved towards him.

But now Mark had his second shoe on and he scrambled to his feet, dodging past her to Ed. He stood, like a little chick, right up against Ed's leg, under the shadow of his body.

Ed dropped a hand on top of the child's head; Mark looked up at him. "I'm going home now, Mark. You can't come. You don't live in my house anymore. You live with your Daddy now. Remember?"

"No!" Tears were imminent.

"I'll come visit you again real soon. You can phone me if you like. Your aunt Vicky—she's got my phone number. You ask her and you can phone me."

"I want to go home!" Mark's voice rose dangerously.

"But Mark," Vicky remonstrated, "you don't live in Ed's house anymore. You live with your Daddy."

And then it came, of course—the words we were all dreading. "I want to go home! I want my Mummy! Mum-meee...!" Mark pressed his face into the side of Ed's thigh; his shrieks of anguish grated up our spines like fingernails scraping across a blackboard. Vicky stooped over him; Ed squatted. The boy flung his arms around Ed's neck, clung to him as if he were drowning.

Ed stood up, lifting the child into his arms. He gave Vicky a look, then turned and walked through the French doors into the kitchen. The sound of Mark's wails moved through the kitchen and into the hall; we heard Ed's feet mounting the carpeted stairs. A door closed somewhere deep inside the house and the cries were muffled.

Vicky stood staring after them as if Ed were a ship that had disappeared over the horizon. I deposited my bag on the deck and sat down in the chaise longue behind me. I closed my eyes. The warmth of the sun pressed against my eyelids; somewhere upstairs, a child was crying lustily—not shrieking anymore—

but sobbing his heart out. I heard—felt—Vicky sit down beside me.

Without opening my eyes I said, "You told me he was afraid of men."

There was a silence. "You mean Mark," Vicky said. "He is. Was." Her voice was unsteady. "But I guess he thought Ed would take him back to Sherry. From the moment Ed arrived, Mark didn't let him out of his sight."

I opened my eyes—Vicky's eyelashes were damp. "You didn't tell me that you knew Ed Jeffreys."

"I don't," she said quickly.

"Then explain."

The explanation, when it was given to me, was remarkably plausible. A couple of days previously the cops had given Glen the key to Sherry's basement suite and he, in turn, had given the key to Vicky, saying that he couldn't face going there. He wanted to abandon Sherry's possessions and hire a cleaning company to clear the place out. "But Mark still has toys there— toys he's been asking for," Vicky said. "Especially. . . . " She glanced around. "Now where did he put it?"

She got up, walked across the deck. "Glen told Mark he'd buy him new stuff—but that's not the same. Kids get attached to their toys." She stooped behind the patio table and produced a stuffed toy dog, reminiscent of a spaniel, with long, floppy ears. "This." She gave it to me. "Mark has been asking for it all week."

I placed Mark's dog in my lap, looked into its mournful, brown button eyes, fingered its velvety ears. My daughter used to have a favorite blanket, and Ben had a teddy that he dragged around everywhere until the poor thing had no more fur on its legs. This puppy looked similarly well-worn, and loved. Then, out of the blue, I remembered the toy I'd cherished: a long-haired white rabbit. I used to sleep with it every night, tucking its deliciously silky fur up against the bare skin of my neck. I just about burst into tears at the memory of it. Good God, I thought. I must be premenstrual.

Vicky explained that on Thursday evening she'd gone over

to Sherry's place with a couple of boxes and packed up everything she thought should be saved. "It was mostly Mark's stuff, but there were a few things of Sherry's. Then, as I was carrying the stuff out to my car, the woman who lives on the main floor—Corinne—came out and showed me the armchair that the Salvation Army had left on her porch. They'd delivered the chair on Tuesday afternoon, saying that Sherry had bought it the week before. Since Sherry had paid for it, they insisted on leaving it there. It seemed a shame to just abandon it—it's a pretty chair, in perfect condition—but Corinne didn't want it and I had no room for it in my car. Then, as we were talking, Ed came out of his place and said that since he happened to be driving out this way on Saturday, he'd bring it over in his van."

"That was nice of him," I commented.

"I thought so," Vicky agreed, coolly. "And if you want to see the armchair, it's in my garage."

"I've seen it." I remembered the chair that I'd noticed on the porch underneath Corinne's living room windows. I dug my fingers into the nap of the puppy's fur and listened—realized that the sound of Mark's crying had stopped. Was Ed still up there? I remembered, belatedly, that I'd wanted to show him Dunbar's photograph.

Vicky's thoughts were running along the same lines. "If you'll excuse me," she said, "I'd better go see what's happening."

While I waited for her to return, several thoughts occurred to me, none of them reassuring. The information I'd been given didn't quite jibe with the scene that I'd just witnessed. Vicky and Ed had addressed each other without formality—like friends of long standing—and Ed had gone upstairs, without asking directions or anything, as if he knew the house well. Either Ed had an extraordinary ability to ingratiate himself into other people's homes, or he knew Mark, Vicky (and Sherry) much better than he and Vicky were admitting.

Vicky returned, her eyes evading mine as she came through the glass doors. "Where's Ed?" I asked.

"He seems to have left. At least his van's gone. And now,"

she said, as if we were finally getting down to business, "would you like that drink I offered you?"

I debated—but wasn't in a hurry to go anywhere else. Vicky described the contents of her liquor cabinet, but I said cider would be fine. She went back into the kitchen.

If, I speculated, Vicky knew Ed much better than she was admitting—what would that mean? As I was trying to concoct a plausible scenario based on a secret alliance between them, Vicky reappeared carrying two tall glasses of cider.

"What happened to Mark?" I asked, taking a sip from my glass. Unfortunately the cider was sweet.

"He's asleep." Vicky sat down in the chair that Ed had vacated and glanced at her watch. "I should go wake him up. Glen doesn't like it if I let him sleep in the afternoon. He's trying to get him onto a regular schedule." Again she looked at her watch, as if hoping it would say something different this time. "But I feel he deserves a little. . . . "

"Recovery time?" I suggested.

She made a gesture of defeat.

I reached into my bag, pulled out the photo of Fred Dunbar and handed it to her. "Have you ever seen this guy before?" While she studied it, I explained that I thought I'd seen Dunbar sitting in a parked car outside Sherry's place.

Vicky passed the photograph back to me. "Sorry—I don't recognize him."

"Neither does anyone else." Discouraged, I let the photograph drop back into my bag.

A flock of tiny birds scooped over our heads; we both looked up. Displaying a flash of white on the underside of their wings, they veered in unison over Vicky's garage roof and vaulted into the sky. "I notice that Ed made himself right at home here," I said. "Took right over."

Vicky turned back to me and gazed, fervently, straight into my eyes. "He was great, wasn't he? Just swept Mark up into his arms . . . I wish more men were like that. I know Will isn't. The moment one of the kids starts to cry, he hands them over to me."

I tried, and failed, to discomfit that gaze. This wasn't quite the answer I'd been expecting.

Vicky got up, took a generous swallow of cider and deposited her glass on the patio table. "I'd better go wake up Mark."

I let my head rest against the plastic webbing of the chair. I've worked hard today, I thought. Why don't I just stay here for the rest of the afternoon, lounging on this nice peaceful sun deck in suburbia? If I'd remained married, I might now be living in a house like this one. My ex-husband, Brian, and his second wife, Barbara, own something very much like it in Tsawwassen—a little less ostentatious, but with a view across Georgia Strait. We divorcées pay a price.

When Vicky reappeared she was carrying Mark in her arms. His face, crumpled and flushed, rested close against her neck; his hair stood up in damp tufts. As she walked onto the deck, he saw the dog in my lap and pointed at it with a dimpled brown arm. "Mine," he whimpered, like a child half his age.

I handed him the toy, and he clutched it possessively. Vicky retrieved her glass of cider and returned to her chair, settling Mark in her lap. He yawned, widely.

"Mark," I said, "do you remember when your mother went to work in the restaurant?"

He lifted his gaze and studied me.

"That was when you lived near Trout Lake, wasn't it? Do you remember the lake—in the park?"

This time he nodded.

"When your Mum went to work, you used to go to the babysitter's house, didn't you? And the babysitter had a boy your age."

His eyes had brightened, just a little, and the nod was more confident.

"Do you remember the name of the woman who looked after you?"

"Yanni," he whispered, then glanced up at Vicky's face.

"What was it?" Vicky prompted.

"Yanni," he repeated shyly.

"Yanni?"

He nodded again.

"Danni, Anni, Yanni." It sounded like he and Luisa were talking about the same person all right. But one mispronounced first name wasn't going to get me very far. "Did she have any other name? Did you ever call her Mrs . . . ?" I paused hopefully.

"Yanni," he repeated. Again he looked up at Vicky. "She had a candy box," he told her. "On the shelf."

"Ooh," said Vicky. "Did she ever give you any candies?"

"Only after lunch," he answered with a serious expression. I remembered Glen's words: "He helps himself to the crackers. Not the cookies." Mark was a child with a conscience.

The front door slammed; there were children's voices in the front hall, feet pummeling up the stairs. The voices faded, then became much louder again as the children entered one of the back bedrooms, directly above our heads. Their words wafted down to us through an open window. "So where is it? You had it last." "And I put it right there." Mark slid down from Vicky's lap and, taking his dog with him, trotted off to investigate.

I settled back in my chair, gazing out across Vicky's manicured lawn to the fringe of pampas grass that screened the swimming pool, which was hibernating under a tarp at the bottom of her back yard. "It's odd," I began. "Did Ed tell you? That Sherry found that basement suite through him?"

"Mm-hmm." Vicky was being circumspect. "And she seems to have gotten him into a lot of trouble. He says the cops are still questioning him about it."

"Well, his story was a bit suspicious."

She frowned at her glass. "Do you think so? Why?"

"Because they've been around each other almost every day for the past month—seeing each other in the restaurant, then living in the same house—but he swears he's never even talked to her."

"But he explained—"

"Yup," I interrupted, nodding. "He made it all sound quite plausible."

Vicky eyed me in silence. "You think Ed killed my sister?"

"You don't like that idea."

"Hey—" She feigned innocence. "I've got no opinion. What do I know?"

"That's what I'm trying to find out," I retorted, in that fake "nice" voice that little girls perfect, because kicking people isn't ladylike. "You heard his story—what did you think of it?"

Her lips parted—but the question seemed to deprive her of the power of speech. "I don't know!" she insisted, like a child accused of something. "He seems all right—quite a nice guy, actually. But then, don't go by what I say," she warned with sudden acrimony. The sun disappeared; Vicky looked up at the big cloud that had obliterated it. "I'm a bit of a sucker."

I thought of that absent husband who handed her the kids when they cried, and who seemed to reside, permanently, in Bangkok. Vicky too paid a price.

A little breeze came up, the pampas grass swayed. Vicky shivered and massaged her upper arms, went inside to find a sweater. I looked at my glass of cider, decided to relinquish the rest of it and followed Vicky inside to ask if I could look at her telephone directory.

I found Glen's father's name listed in the directory just before Glen's. The address wasn't exactly on the way home, but it wasn't far out of my way. I glanced at my watch. Should I phone first? But Glen's father would probably be home; when I'd talked to Glen, he'd made it sound as if his father was practically housebound.

I was still doggedly following my plan—which included a little talk with the man who'd so conveniently provided his son with an alibi.

14

GLEN'S FATHER LIVED in an older working-class neighborhood which consisted of stucco bungalows, each precisely centered in a square of neat lawn. There were no trees on his street, and few of his neighbors had compensated for the deficiency—although an avid rose gardener obviously lived next door. Glen's father, however, was not a gardener; there were no flowerbeds around the house. The only vegetative ornament was a prim privet hedge that bordered the front sidewalk.

I knocked, and heard him shuffling towards the door— which opened inward. He stood peering at me through the mesh of the screen door like a caged animal. "What do you want?" he greeted me.

I launched into my usual explanations, said that I'd talked to Glen and was hoping that he would talk to me too. "What do you think *I'm* going to be able to tell you?" he inquired testily. But he was already opening the screen door and gesturing me in. I guess when you're housebound you accept any company that's offered.

"I can't even get down my back stairs and you think I've committed a murder," he complained, leading me into the living room. He still had a faint, northern English accent, although by Glen's account he must have lived in this country for at least forty years.

The decor in the living room dated back to the early fifties. There was a seascape, an old-fashioned couch and armchair set (looking a little threadbare), a stereo, a television, a bookcase, two spindly side tables, an antique clock on the mantelpiece. Everything was very neat and spare. A newspaper had been tossed down on the square, padded footstool in front of the armchair. It was the only item out of place.

Mr. Hovey carefully settled himself back into the armchair, where, judging by its placement in relationship to the lamp, the television, and the footstool, he probably spent most of his life. I sat down on the couch. "She was an odd girl," he began. Obviously, he'd need no prompting to talk.

"Sherry?"

"You know in Japan—they look into these things. Beforehand."

I had no idea what he was talking about and felt uneasy, anticipating some racist slur. "They look into what?"

He tapped the side of his head. "Insanity," he said, significantly. "Before they get married, they check the family history. She had an aunt went the same way, you know."

"Glen told you that, did he?"

"If we bred ourselves as we do our livestock, these things wouldn't happen. The race is degenerating, and we've only ourselves to blame for it."

Since I hadn't come to argue about eugenics, I changed the subject. "I understand that Glen was here on the morning she was killed. Does he come every Sunday morning?"

"Whuff!" he exhaled, contemptuously. "When he can spare time from that la-dee-da restaurant of his. Can't think why he went into a business like that. Restaurants!" he sneered. "Can't eat the stuff they serve there, personally. Not even a decent plate of roast beef. It's no job for a man—at least, that's *my* opinion."

And I bet Glen loves to hear you say so, I thought, feeling a new sympathy for Glen.

"I had two boys, you know." The expression on his face was a mixture of calculation and self-pity.

"Yes. Glen told me."

"Brad was killed in a car crash," he went on, as if I hadn't spoken. "Seventeen years old." He paused. "I got left with the runt." He sighed, feeling sorry for himself.

I stared at him, appalled.

"But it's up to him to see I'm not wallowing in filth," he continued, in tones of martyrdom. "Eating pet food and such like. It happens, you know." He glanced at me reprovingly. "After all, I cleaned up after him for twenty years, didn't I?"

I finally found my tongue. "Wasn't that your wife's job?"

"That's right! But who paid, eh? Who saw that they had food on the table and a roof over their heads? Now it's his turn. And he grudges it. He does!" he added, as if I'd denied the charge. "He wants to hire one of them so-called refugees that the government doesn't know what to do with. They keep letting them in, and then expect people like me to give them a job. They can't even speak English! So what good are they to me? I don't know where they think we're going to put them all!"

"It *is* a big country," I couldn't help saying, though I knew I was only letting myself in for more.

But before he could lecture me further there was a knock at the front door. It opened. "Hello? Dad?"

I recognized the voice and cringed. This afternoon I seemed doomed to meet people in places where they weren't supposed to be. Yet again Glen had caught me asking questions behind his back. He now appeared in the front hallway, which was visible from where I sat; he was carrying a big paper bag. "I can't stay. I'm just dropping off your—" He saw me. He stood there with a face as blank as a sheet of paper—then gave me a thin smile. "So you've found my Dad," he commented affably, coming into the living room.

"Did you get my sausages?" the old man demanded.

"Yes—I got your sausages," Glen assured him laconically. He moved through the living room towards the kitchen at the back of the house.

"Pork or beef?"

"Pork," Glen answered, with audible exasperation.

"Last time you got beef."

"I told you—they were out of pork."

"And the bread?"

Glen had disappeared through the kitchen doorway.

133

"Not that gritty stuff, I hope. The bits get stuck in my dentures. I swear they put sand in it," Glen's father added, in an aside to me.

"It's called fiber, Dad," Glen called from the kitchen.

"Who's eating it?" the old man shouted, with surprising vigor for someone who looked so fragile. "You or me?"

There was no answer.

"I said—who's eating it!"

"You." Glen's voice was sulky. A cupboard door slammed, a drawer squeaked—wood against wood.

"What else did you buy?"

Again there was a silence, but now Glen reappeared in the doorway, folding the paper bag. "A bag of frozen peas, half a dozen eggs, butter, a lamp chop, some tins of soup—"

"What kind of soup?" his father asked suspiciously.

Glen ignored the question, disappeared back into the kitchen, returned empty-handed. "Enough to last you till Monday anyway." He stopped in the living room, looking towards the front door.

"Well, what are you hanging around here for?" his father jeered. "I thought you were in a hurry." He gave me a covetous glance. He didn't get many visitors and now that he had one, he didn't want to share me with anyone else.

"Yes—I'm off to go pick up Mark," Glen agreed, but then continued to stand there, gazing around absent-mindedly—and I finally realized what his problem was. He didn't want to leave me alone with his father.

Mr. Hovey, meanwhile, was considering his next line of attack. "I notice you didn't get to the grass last Sunday, though you were here long enough."

"Dad, the grass hasn't even started growing yet—"

"Then why are all my neighbors out mowing their lawns? I suppose you'll tell me that their grass grows faster than mine?"

"Look—I can't do it today, but I'll get to it next weekend."

"That's what you said last weekend. And remember that tap you told me you fixed?"

"What about it?"

"What about it?" the old man mocked him. "It's leaking again—that's what!"

Glen swallowed, his face darkening. "I'm not a plumber," he said resentfully. "If you want a plumber, I'll phone somebody."

"I'm not paying somebody thirty dollars an hour to change the bloody washer!" his father exploded.

"I changed the washer!" Glen's voice was high-pitched, defensive. "But it needs—"

At that point I reached my limit, feeling that I'd been subjected to quite enough. "Before you go," I interrupted them, forcibly, looking at Glen (who showed no signs of going anywhere), "there's something I want to show you." I opened my bag.

Glen's eyes slid sideways under his lowered lids. I held Dunbar's photograph out to him.

Slowly he came over, took the photograph and turned away. He stood with his back to me, studying it.

"What is it?" his father demanded.

Neither of us answered—I wished I could see Glen's face.

"Who is he?" Glen asked.

"Do you recognize him?"

"No." He seemed to make an effort, turning to me and raising an interrogative eyebrow. "Should I?"

"Let me see it." Mr. Hovey extended a trembling hand.

Glen gave his father the photograph. The old man grunted at the sight of Dunbar's face.

"Who is he?" Glen repeated. Again I explained.

When I'd finished, Mr. Hovey was still looking ruminatively at Dunbar's photo. "Do you know him?" I asked.

"Well, I'm not sure," he answered slowly, judiciously, mouthing his dentures. There was a brief silence while we all paid homage to Mr. Hovey's cogitative processes. "There *is* something familiar about him."

Glen was staring at his father, an unreadable expression on his face. "He looks a bit like Doman—remember him, Dad? The mechanic who used to live across the street?"

135

His father rejected the hint. "Not a bit like Doman." He fingered the stubble on his chin. "Rings a bell," he decided, and held out the photograph.

Glen took it, handed it back to me. He shook his head, almost imperceptibly, apparently warning me not to put too much stock in anything his father said.

I stood up to leave. We hadn't gotten around to the subject of Glen's alibi—but with Glen here, we weren't going to. I was sure, however, that Mr. Hovey would be more than happy to talk to me again. Pity the pleasure wasn't mutual.

When I said I was leaving, Mr. Hovey looked offended—but Glen was obviously relieved. "I'd better get going too," he said. I thanked Mr. Hovey; Glen told him that he'd come by again on Monday. We left.

"See what I mean?" Glen said, looking a little shamefaced, as we walked down the front sidewalk. "He's quite a character."

I said nothing. I'd been struck—shocked—by Glen's subservience to his father. If my father had treated me like that, I would have left him to rot.

We reached my car, I pulled out my keys.

"And now it's all the way out to Richmond and back," Glen said. I found the right key, glanced up.

"It's quite a drive," I agreed.

"Takes me a good hour each time. I'm trying to come up with an alternative."

"Like what?"

"I'm looking for someone who'll come to my house. A woman who'll take care of Mark and do some housekeeping as well."

"I thought you'd made an arrangement with Vicky. Isn't it working out?"

"Yeah, but it was only intended to be temporary. There's the drive—which is too much, especially at rush hour. But also—" He stopped.

"Also?" I prompted.

"Her husband is due back soon."

"So?" I don't like innuendoes.

"I—uh—I don't really like the thought of Mark being there

136

when Will is around. And I don't think Sherry would have liked it either."

"Why not?"

"Well. . . . " Glen scuffed a bit of grass off the sidewalk with his toe. "Will is . . . a lush, for one." He smiled disparagingly. "A lecher too. Sherry hated him."

He'd finally got my interest. "She hated him?"

"A couple of years ago he was really making a nuisance of himself—coming on to her all the time, sitting too close to her, accidentally brushing up against her. . . . You know—stuff like that. Finally Vicky clued in to what was going on and put a stop to it."

"How did she do that?"

"Hey—" Glen raised his eyebrows appreciatively. "You don't fool around with Vicky. When she gets mad—watch out. She caught Will in the basement one night—he had Sherry cornered—and Vicky lit into him. I was upstairs at the time—heard it all."

I watched him curiously. "How did you feel about what was going on?"

"Like I said—he's a slime-bag. You should hear him talk when there's no women around. And I knew it wasn't Sherry's fault; she'd always tried to stay out of his way. The whole thing really upset her—I think she was afraid that Vicky would blame her, maybe. But Vicky's got no illusions about Will. He's like a kid in front of a candy counter; he just can't keep his fingers off the merchandise."

Glen watched me with something malicious in his eyes, and I returned his gaze, with interest. When men use imagery like this to describe how other men behave, I'm reminded of children who find it necessary to say "Shit!" in order to accurately describe what some other, "bad" child said to them.

"I told you to tell me if Sherry was afraid of anyone," I reminded him.

"Yeah, well . . . I always thought of Will as more of a nuisance than a danger. And I think Sherry mostly hated him on Vicky's account. She didn't want Vicky's feelings to get hurt."

I dug a pen out of my pocket, pulled my notebook out of

my bag. I didn't think much of this story and didn't want to pursue it—but my conscience had already informed me that I was going to have to. "His name is Will Fischer, right?"

"Hey—" Glen looked startled. "I'm not saying that he had anything to do with Sherry's death. I was just explaining that I didn't want him around Mark."

"No stone unturned, Mr. Hovey," I said, uncapping my pen. "Where does he work?"

"Vicky wouldn't want you to be doing this."

But you wanted me to, I thought.

"All right." Glen looked exasperated, stuck his hands in his pockets. "Pacific Rim Imports—that's the name of his company. There's two of them that own it—the other guy is a Thai. He looks after the Asian side, and I think he's the real brains behind it all. Will is mostly a p.r. man."

"Do you know when Will went to Bangkok?"

"No, I—"

"Before Sherry's death, right?"

"Yeah. About two weeks before."

"And when is he expected back?"

"Next weekend, I think. I'm not sure."

"Was he in town at the time that Sherry moved out of your house?"

Glen scratched his neck. "You know—he was. That's right. Because I remember that when I phoned Vicky to ask her where Sherry was, he answered the telephone."

"And he was in town from then until he went to Bangkok?"

"No—there was another trip. But I don't know where, or when. He's always coming and going—I lose track."

"Thanks." I closed my notebook.

"You're not going to question Vicky about her husband's movements?" he asked, as if objecting to the impropriety of such an act.

I didn't answer. I'd found my car key again.

"Will was in Bangkok when Sherry was murdered."

"And you were in your father's kitchen," I pointed out equably.

"What's that supposed to mean?"

Again we were staring into each other's eyes, like inmates imprisoned in the same cell, forced into a relationship that neither of us wanted. I shrugged. "Everybody's got some excuse."

I tried to take Sunday off. It was the day of Sherry's funeral, a private, family affair to which I hadn't been invited. I lay in bed for a while, and finished the science fiction novel that I'd been reading, then got up and decided to clean the inside of my oven. But as soon as my mind had nothing to occupy it, it went back to work—circling, prowling, revisiting everyone I'd talked to, concocting and rejecting theories. Sherry had been dead for a week now and instead of eliminating suspects, I kept finding new ones. Glen, Ed, Fred Dunbar, and now, Will Fischer, who'd been added on at the last minute, like a sales tax at the cash register.

But I found myself thinking about Vicky more than any of them—still bothered by that scene on her sun deck the day before. My instincts told me that Vicky had been lying—but lying to what purpose? If, as I suspected, she knew Ed, had known Ed for some time, then logically it followed that Ed must know Sherry. Ed might have told Sherry about the job at Copper's, about the suite in the basement. In which case, why had Vicky hired me to find Sherry? This was the real poser. If Vicky was lying—to any purpose, or any degree—if Vicky was in any way implicated—why had she involved me? It just didn't make sense.

It was a relief to go over to Tom's place for supper, where I was forced to think and talk about something else. After fifteen years of living on his own, Tom had decided to learn how to cook—and I was often invited over to try out the results. Dishes that turned out perfectly when I wasn't there, seeped liquid or coagulated into lumps the moment I laid eyes on them. Tom is an adventurous cook, always choosing the most complicated recipes, the most unlikely combinations of ingredients, and then improving upon them as he goes along, saying, "I can't wait to see how this turns out." By the time supper was ready, he'd dirtied every pot and bowl in his apartment.

But dinner that night was relatively successful: a sort of Singapore-style chicken with homemade dumplings and Vietnamese salad rolls. The rolls disintegrated, but were still edible, the dumplings were a pasty mess—and the chicken was delicious. After I'd done about half the dishes, we retreated to bed.

We slid into a lazy, leisurely lovemaking, then lay awake talking, listening to the monsoon-style rains which dumped from the sky, hammered the rooftops, ricocheted off the streets. As I drifted into sleep I had visions of drenched plum blossoms and rain-battered daffodils, and I pictured Sherry's profile, boxed deep under wet earth. Then my mind moved to Mark, also lying in darkness, trying to come to terms with the intolerable void that had consumed his mother.

I think I fell asleep. But suddenly I was awake again, my senses taut—in one of the apartments across the street, a child had woken up, crying. Tom stirred, rolled over. And again I thought of Mark, groping in his dreams for some presence of his mother, waking in fright at the prospect of a world without her. Rain thrummed on the lids of the garbage cans beneath the balcony, a window slammed—the crying stopped. Yet I continued to hear it, as if it hung over the city like an everlasting echo, as persistent as the rain.

15

First thing Monday morning I called Vicky.

"When you found Sherry working at Copper's restaurant, you said you didn't tell Glen. But did you tell your husband?"

"Well . . . in confidence, of course."

"He was in town?"

"Yes he was."

"Maybe he told Glen," I suggested.

"He wouldn't do that."

"Why not?"

"They—ah—they don't get along."

"And then he went to Bangkok?"

"Yes." She was beginning to sound wary.

"When?"

"Um. Around the second week in March. But—"

"Do you know the date?" I interrupted.

"I'll get the calendar," she offered, unenthusiastically. When she came back she asked: "But why this sudden interest in my husband? How did he get on the suspect list?" Her tone was amused—but I don't think she was.

"I'll explain in a minute," I said. "Did you figure out the date?"

"It was a Saturday—the 10th."

I wrote it down—March 10th. "Does Will always use the same airline company on his trips?"

"Sky Pacific—usually."

"When he gets back, I'd like to talk to him. Sherry may have

141

told him something—or he might have gone to see her himself if he knew where she was."

"But he didn't know where she was."

"He knew she was working at Copper's, right?"

"Yes, but then she moved again. And why would he go to see her, anyway?"

"To offer help, or support?"

I could tell by the quality of the silence at the other end that Vicky didn't like this idea. "I don't think. . . ." she began. "He wouldn't do that—at least, not without telling me first." It sounded like a threat.

But you're the one who told me you're too trusting, I thought.

"Anyway, you can talk to him," Vicky concluded firmly, as if trying to suppress the anxieties I'd stirred up. "He'll be back again next Monday."

I wrote that down too.

Then, posing as a bookkeeper for Sky Pacific, I phoned Pacific Rim Imports and asked if I could confirm Will Fischer's flights in and out of town over the past two months. It was an unorthodox request—but as one secretary to another, I explained that our computers were down and I needed the information right away to sort out a mess with my invoices. It worked. I learned that Will was in town on February 2nd, the day that Sherry left Glen's house, and that he flew to Taipei ten days later, returning on February 25th. He was still in town on March 5th, when Vicky went to see Sherry at Copper's, and he didn't leave again until March 10th, two days after Sherry had moved to the basement suite on East 6th. He'd been in Bangkok ever since.

In other words, Sherry might have disappeared in order to escape Will, and she might have moved again when Vicky told Will that she'd found Sherry working at Copper's restaurant. Most women don't go to such lengths to avoid a lecherous brother-in-law, but if Will was really making a nuisance of himself, it was easy to imagine that a woman in Sherry's condition might have convinced herself that she had no alternative.

Will, however, had the best alibi of all—and breaking it

wasn't going to be easy. He may well have returned from Bangkok on the weekend of Sherry's death—but if he had. . . .

I paused in my speculations, interrupted by new thought. Will and Sherry had been lovers? And terrified that Vicky (or Glen) would find out, Sherry had gone into hiding—while continuing to keep up the affair with Will? Or determined to break off the affair with Will? Or. . . .

Regardless, I argued, firmly suppressing these imaginative flights, the problem is that if Will returned to Vancouver on the weekend of Sherry's death, no travel agent is going to tell me so. Airlines maintain tight security over their passenger lists and don't talk about them to anyone—lest some terrorist have a specific traveler in mind.

But there are ways, and means, and it's my job to know them. There's an ex-cop by the name of Randy McConnell who now works as a private investigator. He's not a nice man and I don't like dealing with him—but he has management level connections with various airline companies, and for a price he'd probably do a little research on my behalf. A steep price. Was it worth it? I decided to put off that decision and go for a walk.

I drove up to Trout Lake and parked near the community center. It was a crisp spring day: the breeze wrinkled the reflections on the water, clouds played leap-frog with the sun. Numerous dogs and joggers were out getting their exercise and three small children were climbing and crawling over the equipment in the playground. There were two little girls with their grandmother (the girls talked only English, the grandmother only Cantonese—but they seemed to understand each other), and a little Sikh boy, his hair twisted into a knot on the top of his head. His mother and another woman were standing a short distance away beside the jungle gym, talking.

I approached them and explained that I was looking for an East Indian woman named "Danniyanni or something like that," who lived in this neighborhood and had a four-year-old boy. They regarded me uncertainly and shook their heads.

For the next two hours I walked the neighborhoods around Trout Lake Park. I investigated the community center (and looked in on the preschoolers' Adventure Gym class), visited the library (and seeing a notice for Story Hour, made a note of the day and time), and talked to the clerk in an East Indian grocery store. I also found a drop-in center for parents with young children—but they'd never heard of "Danniyanni" and her son. Finally, when I'd had enough, I retrieved my car and drove back to the office.

Now, I thought, for my next exercise in frustration: Glen's ex-girlfriend, Kasia. Fortunately the name wasn't common—or I wouldn't have tried to trace her. I pulled out the telephone directory and looked up North Vancouver secondary schools. There were seven of them. Then, remembering Glen's comment that Kasia's family lived "down by the water," I spread my city map out over my desk, located the seven high schools, and eliminated three from my search. I phoned the remaining four, and discovered that one of them had only been in existence since 1981. That left three. I explained to those three that I was trying to trace the daughter of an old friend, and obtained permission to look through their year books. Then I set off again.

I drove northeast, past the exhibition grounds, up and over the Second Narrows Bridge. The harbor was bustling, cranes swinging, a big freighter being eased, slowly, alongside the dock where the grain elevators towered. The cloud shadows rushed across the forested slopes in front of me—and for a brief, happy moment I imagined I was setting off on a trip, going to . . . Pemberton, Powell River? Unfortunately, the roads heading north don't go very far. The mountains crowd together, high and sheer-sided; the highways peter out into logging roads, which switchback up the mountainsides and invariably end in the middle of some slash-strewn clear-cut—a fitting end to so-called civilization.

If Kasia was "barely out of high school" twelve or thirteen years ago, she must have graduated in 1977 or '78. At the first school, I found the annuals in the school library and sat down with a 1977 year book, perused the pages of graduates, then the photographs of the grade eleven students. I looked through the 1976 and 1978 annuals as well, just to make sure.

At Capilano Secondary the yearbooks were kept behind the counter in the school office—but a helpful volunteer stacked the books I wanted on the counter for me. By now it was three-fifteen and, as if a dam had burst, the school halls were in flood, the office like a back eddy under increased pressure from the cacophonous current of youth going by. One secretary was typing, obviously trying to get something finished before the end of the day while the other was dealing with a long line-up at the counter.

By three-thirty the halls had emptied, and I was staring with disbelief at a photograph of a girl whose name was Kasia Jekubik. She had lightly freckled skin, a snub nose, wide-set eyes and a diffident smile. According to the paragraph printed beneath her name, she wanted to become a flight attendant. "Fasten your seat belts," the blurb enthused. "We know Kassie will fly high."

My finger marking the page, I joined the line-up at the counter. The secretary was talking to a boy who wanted to drop Biology. "It's a bit late in the year for that!" the secretary informed him. The next girl in line was paying for a textbook she'd mutilated. Finally, it was my turn.

I was told (no surprise) that it was against School Board policy to give out students' addresses and phone numbers—even defunct addresses and phone numbers—to members of the general public. Yes, the secretary said, she could think of three teachers, offhand, who had taught at this school for the past fifteen years—but she wasn't going to give me *their* names or telephone numbers either. Finally she said that she'd write out a message for each of them, asking them to get in touch with me if they remembered teaching a Kassie or Kasia Jekubik back in the mid seventies. And with that I had to be satisfied.

When I got back to my office, there was a cryptic message on my machine. "Hi. It's Georgia. I want to talk to you about something. Give me a call." She'd left a number. As I dialed it, I tried to remember who Georgia was. But after I'd talked to her, I was no further ahead. "Good," she said when I identified myself on the phone. "I came by your office earlier, but you weren't there. Are you going to stick around for a while?"

"For a while," I said, glancing at my watch.

"Twenty minutes?"

"Sure. But is this—"

"I'll be there in fifteen." She hung up.

While I waited, I pulled out my telephone directory again and looked up Jekubik's. Fortunately there were only six of them and, miracle of miracles, someone was home at every number. But none of them would admit to knowing a Jekubik named Kasia.

When I answered the knock at my office door, I found out who Georgia was. She was the woman I'd met at Corinne's place, the one I'd last seen in a green plaid dressing gown when I was going up and down East 6th with my photograph of Fred Dunbar. And it was about that photograph that she'd come.

"I didn't want to go to cops," she said as soon as she was in the door. "Because I know Corinne likes Ed—you know, the guy who lives on the top floor—although I don't really know him. But hell, I don't know what's going on and that woman was murdered, so when you showed me that photograph. . . ."

"This one?" I asked, digging the photograph of Fred Dunbar out from under the phone directory.

"Yeah. Him." She looked around my office; I gestured to the chair opposite my desk. We both sat down.

"I saw him—" she pointed at Fred's picture, "the Saturday night before Sherry was killed. I was coming to see Corinne—this was about. . . nine? And I'd parked at the end of the block, by the park—because I couldn't find anywhere closer, you know? And the guy from upstairs—Ed—he was coming down the sidewalk and that other guy, the one you've got the picture of—it looked like he was hassling him. The old guy was following him, calling him names—nigger, cocksucker—stuff like that, and Ed was—" She nodded, meaningfully. "Getting pretty pissed off, eh? Telling him to get lost. Then Ed gets to his van and he's trying to unlock the door when the old guy grabs him by the jacket and starts yanking at it—like he's a stupid dog or something! And Ed—well—" Abruptly she ran a hand up the side of her head, making her short-cropped hair stand on end. "He just turned around and slugged him. Punched him in the face, gave him a karate kick in the gut—and the white guy—I

146

mean, he's old, eh? He went down like a ton of bricks. Then Ed jumped into his van and tore off, left him lying there on the sidewalk."

I gazed at her, rendered almost breathless by this account. "Did Dunbar get up again?"

"Yeah. Eventually. I guess he saw a few stars, but then he hauled himself back onto his feet, grunting and wheezing, looking around to see if anyone had noticed. As soon as I saw he was still alive, I split. I told Corinne, but she didn't think I should talk about it to anyone since it didn't seem to have anything to do with the woman who was killed, and Ed is already in enough trouble as it is. But when you showed me the picture of the other guy too, then I thought, well—maybe this old guy is a suspect. I don't know. Is he?"

"Maybe," I said. "Can you remember any words—exactly what they said to each other?"

She frowned. "It's hard, because they were both yelling and it was mostly swear words. But the old guy was threatening him—that much was obvious. I remember him saying things like, 'Don't think I've forgotten,' and 'I'll get you back.' Whereas Ed was just telling him to fuck off or he'd smash his face in."

Georgia bestowed upon me a smile that was charming, intimate, and altogether unexpected. "You know," she said, as it were, woman-to-woman. "Boy talk."

I returned the smile. "But they definitely knew each other?"

"Yeah—at least, I got that impression. It seemed like they'd had some history together, and the old guy had a bone to pick."

As soon as Georgia had finished answering my questions, she got up to leave. But on her way out the door, she asked a question of her own. "Are you going to tell the cops?"

"If I don't think it's relevant to Sherry's death—then no."
She waved.

"Bye," I called after her. "And thanks."

The door shut. I continued to stare at it, thinking about Fred Dunbar's black eye, the one that had started to heal before he died.

I glanced at my watch, opened my notebook and found Ed Jeffreys' home phone number.

"Hello?"

"Hi, it's Meg Lacey. I—"

He'd hung up.

That evening, when I got home after my Aikido practice, I once again found Ben propped on my living room couch in front of the television.

"Hi. More laundry?" I kicked off my shoes in the hall, hung up my jacket.

"Hi," he said without enthusiasm, staring at the television.

I walked into the living room and stood looking down at him, expectantly—finally he glanced up.

"Um—" He looked uncomfortable. "Do you mind if I—ah—stay here for a few days?"

"No." I waited for more.

"I put my stuff in—ah—my old room. That O.K?"

"Yes." I wondered if I could be accused of having planned for this moment. Ben had been gone for a whole year—yet his bed was ready and waiting for him, and his room looked as if he'd walked out of it that morning. "There are sheets in the cupboard."

He nodded, his eyes on the television again.

Apparently that was all the explanation I was going to get.

Ben had turned twenty the previous January. He shared an apartment with two high school friends, Aziz and Luan. Like Ben, Aziz was taking classes at Vancouver Community College, and Luan was working as an apprentice electrician. As far as I knew, the three of them got along well together—which made me wonder if Tiara had something to do with Ben's sudden retreat home. Would he sleep with her here? I cringed at the thought. Was that the problem—that there wasn't enough privacy at their apartment for lovers?

I went to bed shortly after eleven. When I got up to go to the bathroom at two-thirty in the morning, I heard the television, and noticed that a light was still on in the living room. Didn't Ben have any classes tomorrow? He'd told me his exams were starting next week. None of your business Meg, I reproved myself, he's a big boy now. I went back to bed.

The next morning at ten, I was in the library on Commercial Street. I was browsing through the new titles and meanwhile conducting a surreptitious surveillance of the young children of the neighborhood, who were waiting for Preschool Story Hour to get under way. But "Danniyanni's" son did not appear to be among them. Most of the children were milling around in the picture book section, selecting and rejecting books, distributing them over the floor, while their parents followed after them, remonstrating and restocking the shelves, trying to impose some order on the process. Finally a young librarian appeared and placed a grown-up's chair in the middle of the area, asking the parents to help her set up the rest of the chairs. Within a few minutes the children were seated, more or less, and gathered around the storyteller, who favored them with an abridged version of *The Ugly Duckling*.

I waited ten minutes or so, then, tearing myself from the pages of a book that promised to teach me how to think positively about menopause, I left the library and walked back out into the sunshine. On my way to the car I passed a laundromat that I hadn't noticed before, and I dropped in and looked around. A very old native woman sat hunched in the corner, staring with sad eyes at a dryer, a black transvestite was leafing through a fashion magazine, and a young white woman with dyed magenta hair was smoking cigarettes and watching television, her young son sitting on the floor between her feet, directing rocket missiles at the characters on the screen.

As I turned to leave, I stopped and scanned the bulletin board by the door. There was a car for sale, an apartment for rent; someone was looking for a vegetarian housemate, someone else was selling a crib and two bicycles, someone was offering to do baby-sitting. . . . "Experienced babysitter looking for a playmate for my four-year-old son. Phone Damayanthi Fernando." My eyes stopped at the name. I read the notice again, murmuring the name beneath my breath: "Da-ma-yan-thi." I ripped off one of the phone numbers.

Half a block down the street, I found a public phone.

"Yes? Hello?" The voice was soft, with a lilting accent.

"Ms. Fernando?"

Yes, she said, she was the person who had looked after Mark, and yes, she would talk to me—but soon, please, because she was going out after lunch. I told her I'd be right over.

She was a slight young woman with dark brown skin and a thick black braid that grazed her bum. She spoke English better than I did, although she'd only been in the country for five years. "In Sri Lanka," she explained, "we learn English in school. But it is going out of fashion; nowadays all the children are being taught in Singhalese."

Damayanthi told me that she had looked after Mark five days a week for a total of three weeks, and her son was still asking why Mark never came to play anymore. "They got along so well. . . . I am trying to find another such arrangement—but most people want me to go to their house, and I don't want to do that. But why are you asking about them? Has something happened?"

As tactfully as I could, I told her why I'd come.

"No!" She clapped her hands over her mouth as if she'd been gagged. Intrigued, her child came running up and peered into her face. When he tried to pull her hands away she hauled him into her lap and held onto him tightly. Finally, when she'd recovered and had allowed her child to escape again, I started in on my list of questions.

Damayanthi said that she'd first met Sherry at the playground at Trout Lake. Their children had climbed onto the opposite ends of a teeter-totter, and Sherry had struck up a conversation with her. "She was excited," Damayanthi said. "She told me that she had just found a new job and she wanted to know if I knew anyone in the neighborhood who did baby-sitting. I do know of one person, but I said I couldn't recommend her. But our conversation got me thinking. Why shouldn't I look after Mark? We have only the one child, and he gets a little lonely—it might be good for him. I told her I would think about it and talk to my husband, and I gave her my phone number.

"When she phoned me back, I said that I'd look after Mark on a trial basis. I wanted to see how the boys would get along. At first Mark was very shy but he soon got used to us, and for the children, it worked out very well. But I was not comfortable with Sherry. In the playground she'd seemed so friendly, but now she began to treat me like an enemy. She never stopped to talk; she just wanted to get Mark and leave. I began to realize that she was probably a bit crazy."

"Was she the one who ended it?"

"Yes—and I must tell you how it happened. One day I took the boys to the same playground at Trout Lake. I was pushing my son on the swings, and Mark was a little ways away in the sand pit. I looked over and noticed a man standing near him—an older, white man. At first I didn't think anything of it—but a few minutes later I noticed that the man was still there and he was talking to Mark! Mark was alone in the sandbox, there was nobody near him—and I wondered if the man thought that Mark was in the park by himself—because, of course, I do not look like his mother.

"I called Mark to come—just to let the man know that Mark was not unsupervised. And immediately, the man went away.

"But on the way home, I stopped at the corner store to pick up a few groceries, and when I came out I saw that same man again, across the street. He was watching us. Of course this made me even more uneasy—but there was nothing I could do about it. With two small children one cannot hide, or hurry, and I didn't want to frighten them. Fortunately, once I'd turned onto my own street, I didn't see him again.

"That afternoon, when Sherry came to get Mark, I mentioned the incident. Perhaps I shouldn't have said anything—but I hadn't seen anyone else that day and it was on my mind. When I described the man Sherry became distraught; she paced back and forth, shouting at me. She told me that if I ever saw anyone near her child, I must go over to Mark immediately; I must not let anybody near him. 'But who is he?' I asked. 'It doesn't matter!' she yelled at me. 'Just do what I say!' I understood that she was upset—or I might have taken offense.

"Then the next day after supper Sherry phoned and told me that she was quitting her job and would no longer need a babysitter. Her manner was quite cold—so I didn't feel that I could ask her any questions. I was sorry for my son's sake, but I was glad that I wouldn't have to deal with her anymore. But later, thinking about it, I felt sure that her decision had something to do with that man in the playground."

I reached into my bag, pulled out the photo of Fred Dunbar and handed it to her.

Damayanthi looked at the photograph, and her forehead stitched with little V-shaped wrinkles. "This is him!" Her eyes lifted—upbraided me. "You—where did you get this? Who is he? Have the police—Is this the man who—" She broke off, looking alarmed.

"I don't know what his connection is to Sherry. I'm trying to find out."

"But why is his picture in the newspaper?"

"Because he's dead."

She shook her head, bewildered. "I don't understand."

"I don't either. Are you quite sure that this is the same guy?"

She studied Dunbar again. "Of course I never saw him up close—but it certainly looks like him. I noticed that he had a limp," she added.

"He limped?" But yes—now I remembered Dikeakos saying something about an injured knee.

"Why was he following us?" Damayanthi demanded.

"I don't know."

I told her the little I did know, and when I'd finished she asked, "Do you think I should I tell the police that I saw him?"

I agreed that she should. I wanted Dikeakos to get this corroboration of my own theory—that there was some connection between Fred Dunbar and Sherry Hovey.

Stopped at a traffic light on my way back to the office, I pulled out my notebook, flipped back a few pages. Vicky had visited Sherry at Copper's restaurant on Monday, March 5th. The next day, Tuesday, Fred Dunbar had showed up at the Trout Lake playground. Was there a connection? It occurred to me that Sherry might have moved—not to avoid Vicky, but to escape Fred Dunbar.

But Ed knew Fred Dunbar too. Had Fred Dunbar known Sherry? Somehow, Ed must be persuaded to talk.

16

I SAT AT MY DESK, looking at the telephone. Finally I picked up the receiver, dialed.

I asked Randy McConnell what it would cost me to find out if a Will Fischer was listed on any flight from Thailand to Vancouver since March 10th, which was the date he'd flown to Bangkok.

"What airline?"

"Well—start with Sky Pacific—but you'd have to search them all."

"Sorry, baby—but my connections aren't that good. I can get you Sky Pacific all right, and Northern Air, Kanata and— Hmm. Maybe Global too."

"What would that cost me?"

"Ooh. Depends what you've got to offer," he said salaciously.

"Money, Randy," I answered, icily.

"You're a hard woman," he reproved me.

"And your lines are so hackneyed, you deserve to be stuffed," I retorted. "They can prop you up alongside the mastodon."

"Four hundred," he said, and by the tone of his voice, I knew the price had just gone up.

"Don't be ridiculous."

"Take it or leave it."

"Three hundred."

"Three sixty. And that's final."

I debated. Was it worth it? If Randy found out that Vicky's husband wasn't on any of those flights, I'd be no further ahead. Will Fischer could have booked a ticket on some other airline, could have flown from Bangkok to Vancouver via Portland or Seattle, then taken a bus or rented a car. But if Randy learned that Will *was* on one of those flights, the money would have been well spent.

"O.K.," I said. "Do it."

Half an hour later, I received a call from a Mrs. Dubois, who said she was the girls' counselor at Capilano Secondary School. She'd known both Jekubik girls, Kasia as well as her younger sister, Lydia. But she'd known Lydia better. "She got herself pregnant," she commented despairingly (although, presumably, Lydia couldn't have accomplished this feat without assistance). "She was only fifteen years old. I think she gave the baby up for adoption, but she dropped out of school."

"And that was the last you heard of her?"

"I'm afraid so."

"You don't know what became of Kasia."

"I know their parents died in a car crash a couple of years later. The story was in the newspaper. But that was long after Lydia had dropped out of school and I'm sure that Kasia had moved out by then too."

This was bad news indeed. I asked for the names of friends or other people who might have kept in touch with either of the Jekubik girls. "Lydia's boyfriend's name was Mike Ferreira—I remember that much. He was the baby's father." Mrs. Dubois spelled Ferreira; I wrote it down.

After I'd finished talking to her, I reached for my telephone directory, looked up "Ferreira"—and found eleven listed under the initial M. I got through to about half of them and I found one Michael, but he'd attended high school in Moose Jaw, Saskatchewan.

After that I tried all six Jekubik's again—but this time I asked to speak to Lydia. "Who?" No Lydia.

I told Vicky she was wasting her money, I reminded myself as I locked the door to my office.

*

Opening my front door, I was greeted by the mingled smells of frying onions, ground beef, brown sugar and peanut butter. I peered into the kitchen and found Ben making spaghetti, one of his dietary staples. And on the table, beyond him, were several trays piled high with peanut butter cookies.

"Wow!" I commented, staring at all the cookies and wondering how I was going to prevent myself from eating them. My weight-control strategy is very simple—I don't bake, and I try not to buy anything with sugar in it. "No classes today?"

"Nope." He smashed another garlic, tossed it into the frying pan.

"Isn't this your last week?"

He didn't answer, aligned a big green pepper on the cutting board, sliced it in half.

"Ben—" I called, sotto-voce.

He turned his back on me, dug out the insides of the pepper and dumped them into the compost bucket. "I decided that I don't want to do it anymore."

I studied his back. "When did you make this decision?"

He returned to the chopping board, began dicing the green pepper. "Oh, I've been thinking about it for a while now."

"Are you failing?"

"No."

"Are you behind?"

"A little."

"Since when have you been cutting classes?"

He cleared his throat, started in on the second half of the pepper. "Well I—I didn't go yesterday."

"Yesterday and today."

He nodded.

"You've got two more days of classes—and then exams, right?"

He nodded again.

"Finish the term," I said, in my "and-I-mean-it" tone of voice.

"Mum—there's no—"

"Look! I've invested several hundred dollars in this whim of

156

yours, and when you've completed the term, you may reconsider. But first, you finish what you committed to do. You've got about two weeks of work left—you don't quit now."

"But I don't want to become a computer tech—"

"You don't know what you're going to do! And even if you don't get a job as a technologist, those courses may still be useful to you for something else."

"I'll pay you back," he assured me, aggrievedly.

I strode over to the stove and switched off the burner under the frying pan. "Sit down," I ordered, jerking a thumb at the kitchen table.

I'm amazed, sometimes, that this six-foot-tall man still does what I tell him to. He gave me a look—but went and sat down.

"Now," I said, more mildly, sitting opposite him, "why did you decide to move back home?"

"Well, I um. . . . " His voice creaked to a halt; he was starting to blush.

I looked out the kitchen window at my neighbor's washing line, which, as usual, was sagging under a heavy weight of laundry. I admire her pragmatism—she never takes in one load until she's got another all washed and ready to hang up.

"Tiara and I broke up," Ben blurted.

Good riddance, I thought, trying to control the expression on my face. "And she's in some of your classes, right?" Ben's skin was a painful shade of pink, he was staring fixedly at his thumbnails. "So you want to avoid seeing her." He almost met my eyes, gave an infinitesimal nod. "What does that have to do with moving back home?"

Here we got stuck again. He shifted in his seat, turned, if possible, an even deeper shade of pink.

After about a minute he said, "She's dating Aziz now."

Ouch. Why, I wondered, is life so trite—why must each generation re-enact the same old soap opera? By my age, one gets pretty sick of the plot. After a while, I said, "It was her idea to break up?"

He nodded. "We didn't last long," he commented ruefully, but couldn't quite pull it off. His mouth skewed sideways, his voice wobbled, and I felt that age-old maternal ache at finding myself, yet again, unable to protect my children from pain. "She uh—she does that," he said.

"She does what?"

"Goes from—goes from one guy to the other."

"Plays the field?" I suggested.

"So it won't last," he concluded with bitter satisfaction. "She'll dump Aziz too. But meanwhile...I don't want to be around them. Much." He puffed out his cheeks, exhaled. Obviously, this was an understatement.

I reached across the table, picked up a cookie, started eating it.

"I don't really blame Aziz," Ben said after another minute.

"Why not?" I asked, munching.

"Because if Tiara doesn't want to be with me, then.... It's her choice, right? Besides, when she goes after a guy that way, it's pretty hard to—she's hard to resist."

Ah, I thought, the old siren myth. But when young women get pregnant, people don't say, "It's not her fault—he's irresistible."

Ben added, "I think she's sort of a collector."

"A collector?"

"Yeah. She collected me because—by her standards, I'm—um—sort of poor." He glanced at me, afraid that I might take this as a criticism. "No skis," he explained, "and no car. And where she grew up everyone was white. So she thinks Aziz is exotic. It's true—" he argued, "she even told me so. She said, 'I've never slept with anyone who wasn't white.' "

I thought of all the professional female "exotics"—pictured in travel brochures, soliciting in doorways downtown—who are similarly exploited. Then I thought about Aziz, who has been Ben's friend since grade eight. He's affectionate, cheeky, and clever. If he was being used, it wouldn't take him long to figure it out.

"But Ben," I said, leaning across the table, "you have to finish the term—Tiara or no Tiara. You can ignore her existence, you can refuse to speak to either of them—but you mustn't throw away a whole term like that."

"But I can't imagine myself getting a job for some company that—"

"You didn't decide to quit until Tiara jilted you," I pointed out.

"Yes, but—"

"Did you?" I demanded.

He balked. "You're not my boss!"

"As long as you're living off my money I am!" Christ, I thought—and why do parents keep saying the same things, generation after generation, over and over again? "Besides which— I'm right! Aren't I?" I asked, lowering my voice. "You can't quit just because of Tiara and Aziz."

He said nothing. I pressed my advantage. "Now. I'll finish the spaghetti. You go rustle up your textbooks or whatever, find out what you missed, do what you have to do to catch up. Where are your books?"

He looked stubborn. "Most of them are at my place."

I got up, went into the hall, returned with my car keys, dropped them onto the table in front of him. "Go get them."

He wouldn't look at me.

"Phone first," I suggested. "Tell them to clear out so that you can come and pick up your stuff. Make them feel guilty. Or ask Luan to stuff it all in a box outside the door. Do it any way you like—but do it."

His gaze moved to the keys—but he didn't touch them.

I went over to the stove and turned on the front burner, picked up the knife, relieved my feelings by chopping the rest of the green pepper into little bits. Then I found the can opener, opened two cans of tomatoes.

About five minutes later Ben got up from the table, walked past me into the hallway. The front door closed behind him.

That evening I went out again. The sky was baby blue, the clouds pink-tinted—all they lacked were a few lambs, simpering as they bounced over them. I turned right off Main and found St. Joseph Street, drove south for several blocks peering at house

159

numbers. I finally pulled up under a tree. Fred Dunbar's house stood on the other side of the lane, about twenty yards in front of me.

I turned off the engine and sat in the car looking at the house. It was little better than a shack, with asphalt shingles and lush patches of moss on the roof. It was probably built around the turn of the century when this neighborhood was a raw clearing of stumps and slash, intersected by rutted tracks, dotted with the homesteads of those who had been lured here by the gold rush, and who stayed on to butcher the rain forest. It had a small, odd-shaped lot overgrown with weeds, a dilapidated picket fence. I wondered who had inherited it.

In Vancouver, most houses front the east-west avenues, not the cross-streets, like St. Joseph. But in older neighborhoods, like this one, occasional houses get squeezed in on the streets running north-south, their lots truncating the back yards of their neighbors. Dunbar's house was one of these, alone on its side of the block, tucked up against the alley. And there were two others across the street: one that looked like a concrete bunker, the other a white cottage, with a rose trellis arching over its front gate.

As I was studying these houses, I heard the click of a door latch and saw that the front door of the white cottage was opening. A small black terrier jumped down its front steps. "Now you wait there," a female voice commanded, her voice carrying clearly in the still evening air.

The dog stood on the front sidewalk, ears pricked, waiting, looking back at the open door. An older woman emerged and descended the front steps, carrying a leash in one hand and firmly gripping the handrail with the other. When she was safely on the sidewalk, she clipped the leash to the dog's collar and together they proceeded down the front path, under the rose trellis to the street.

She had a soft, puckered brown face, a plump, pear-shaped body. She turned south, heading away from me, and walked slowly along the sidewalk while the dog made little side trips, peeing and sniffing at trees and lamp-posts. She crossed the street and returned north, and by the time she'd come abreast of my car I was standing beside the passenger side door, waiting for her.

"Mrs. Storey?"

She glanced at me and quickly averted her eyes, as if I'd asked her for money.

"Mrs. Storey?" I stepped forward; the dog backed away from me, yapping frantically.

Her sweater was askew, misbuttoned over her flowered dress; her nyloned ankles were wrinkled and thick above her heavy, black shoes. "I read about you in the paper," I said. "This is Mr. Dunbar's dog, isn't it?"

"Rocket," she introduced me, wrapping the leash tighter around her hand. "Stop that now! Stand!" she commanded. She gave me a sidelong glance. "You knew Mr. Dunbar?"

"Not well," I answered. I crouched and snapped my fingers in an attempt to placate the dog, which was running back and forth and hurting my ears with its staccato, high-pitched barks. "Here Rocket," I coaxed.

"They said he was named after a hockey star."

Who? "Oh—the dog. Rocket Richard." I nodded, remembering that this was one of the names in Canada's pantheon of hockey players. Rocket, working himself up to a real display of ferocity, started growling. I gave up on him and stood up. "I guess he's a good watch dog," I said, trying to be gracious.

"He makes enough noise," Irma Storey agreed, jerking hard on his leash. "Quiet now—that's enough." Rocket whimpered and peered at me from between her ankles. He barked again, but less assertively.

"I was wondering if you know what's going to happen to Mr. Dunbar's house." I nodded in the direction of the over-grown lot behind her.

She turned and looked at the house, as if the sight of it might supply her with an answer. "His sister was out from Winnipeg last weekend; she said there'll be an estate sale. She looked through the place, but she didn't know what to do with all his stuff—she's only got an apartment. I don't think he had much of value anyway."

"According to the newspapers, you were the one who

found him. Is that right?"

"Yes." She gave a deep sigh.

"It must have been awful for you."

She gazed up into my face. "It was the worst experience of my life. Horrible. Absolutely horrible." She continued to stare at me with dark, shocked eyes, as if demanding reparation.

Unnerved, I looked over her head at the windows of the house.

"I couldn't even recognize him," she said.

"No?"

"He'd been beat to a pulp. All swollen up and discolored, covered with blood. And the smell—ugh!" Her eyes were still sticking to my face like cobwebs.

"Where did you find him?"

"In the kitchen—on the floor."

"The cops didn't say anything about how he'd—"

"Nothing." She was emphatic. "They keep all that to themselves, you know."

Finally her eyes released me; we watched a car pass down the street.

"Did you know Mr. Dunbar well?" I asked.

She shook her head. "By sight—nothing more."

"Did you notice if he had a limp?"

"Oh yes. He always limped. Was it the war?" she inquired solicitously.

"No, I don't think so. An injury—at work."

Her expression became confiding. "I wouldn't want his things in my house. Would you?" She watched me expectantly —apparently she really wanted to know.

"Perhaps not," I agreed.

"I suppose people will buy anything," she said resignedly, "but I can tell you his furniture is hopping with fleas. The dog certainly was. I had to take it in for one of those shots. Twenty dollars it cost me."

At this point she noticed Rocket, who was snuffling at the remains of something furry in the gutter. She tried to disengage him from it. Finally she started walking again, dragging him after her. "He's got photographs all over his walls—like

162

wallpaper," she called to me over her shoulder. "Pictures of hockey teams. Who'll buy them?" She left this question hanging, unanswered, turned and continued down the sidewalk to the end of the block.

I climbed into my car, and watched her cross the street and return through her front gate. As I drove past Dunbar's house I gave it one last, apprehensive glance. Beat to a pulp? Maybe Ed had come back for more.

But as Dikeakos had said, beating someone up is not an effective way to commit murder. From the sound of it, Dunbar's death—like Sherry's—was unpremeditated, "accidental."

But whoever killed Dunbar evinced no belated compunction; no one had picked him up afterwards and carried him off to bed.

At nine-fifty-five the next morning I was parking my car outside Copper's restaurant. As I opened the driver's side door, my eye was caught by the telephone booth, which was about two car lengths in front of me. Today the booth was uninhabited, but I stared at it with a strange, sinking sensation. I closed the car door again. I was remembering that other time, when I'd waited to use the phone, when the booth had been occupied by a heavy-set white man, who'd stood with his back to me, smoking a cigarette. He'd turned and I'd caught a glimpse of his face: a thick nose, a rectangular jaw...and he'd limped! Was my memory playing tricks on me? And now I remembered that when I'd seen Fred Dunbar in his car outside Sherry's house, I'd thought he looked familiar.

My hands were trembling, and the car shook too with the vibrations of passing trucks. A draught was leaking through the hole in the floor under my clutch pedal, making my feet cold. If I was right—and I wasn't sure that I was—then had Fred Dunbar also been trying to find Sherry? Or had he been waiting to ambush Ed?

From down the block, where the red Coast Welding sign protruded over the sidewalk, I saw the group of overalled workers approaching. I glanced at my watch—I'd timed it just right.

They were a motley group—of Asiatic, African and Indo-European descent; even from this distance I could see that Ed was among them, at least four inches taller than any of the others.

I watched the workers amble up the sidewalk and file, one by one, through the door into Copper's. Then I got out of my car. This time, I said grimly, as I mounted the curb, he won't be able to hang up.

As I entered the restaurant, I saw the workers sliding into one of the big booths, and Ed, still standing, was waiting his turn to sit down. I marched straight up to him.

"I have to talk to you. It's important."

Caught off guard, the eyes of his co-workers turning to us, curiously, he hesitated—gave in. "Order me a coffee, will you, Sadik?" he said to the older man beside him. "I'll be right back."

I led him to one of the small tables against the opposite wall; we sat down. "What?" he demanded.

I handed him Dunbar's photograph.

Ed stared at the photograph for a long time, with an expression of distaste. "Who is he?"

"That's what I'm asking you."

He sneered sarcastically. "Is he dead too?"

"You saw the article in the newspaper?"

"What article?"

"Then why do you ask if he's dead?"

"If he's dead, I must have known him—isn't that how it goes?" He let the photograph dangle between his forefinger and thumb, offering it back to me as if it were a worm.

"Come on—knock it off. This guy was sitting in a car outside your house the night before Sherry was killed."

"What—you figure *he* murdered her?"

"Who is he, Ed? What do you know about him?"

His gaze was opaque, about as communicative as a cement wall.

"You know him. I know you know him."

"Who says?" He straightened, glanced sideways to where Patty was serving his co-workers coffee.

"Because you were seen arguing with him that same Saturday night."

That got his attention. He looked distinctly ill-at-ease.

"Who is he, Ed?"

"What article? What did it say?"

When I wouldn't answer, he began to get up.

"It said he'd been murdered."

I caught the shock in his eyes; he sank back into his chair as if he'd been winded. But he recovered fast. "Good," he declared, and stood up.

"Ed—for Christ's sake!" My voice rose with exasperation. "This guy was outside your place, and he was seen hanging around Mark. I'm trying to figure out what the connection is between his death and Sherry's."

"And you think that connection is me—right?"

At the same moment we glanced around, suddenly conscious that we'd become the center of attention. Ed's co-workers were staring at us and I caught sight of Alexis, glowering at us from his stool behind the till.

I lowered my voice. "I don't *think* anything. I'm trying to find out. Would you please tell me how you know him, and what you know about him?"

"Sure." He placed both hands on the table, leaned over me and murmured venomously: "He's a bully and a racist pig. And I hope his murderer gets away with it. Now leave me fuckin' alone or I'll get Alexis to throw you out of here."

He strode back to join his co-workers.

17

I SPENT A COUPLE of hours in office that afternoon and soothed my savage feelings with paperwork. Then I made two phone calls—one to Vicky, one to Glen. Vicky said that she'd be home for the rest of the afternoon; Glen suggested that I come round to his house tomorrow evening, after he'd put Mark to bed.

I drove out to Richmond, turned left after the Market Garden Plaza, through the portico that warned me that I was entering "Greenwood Estates—a Security Patrolled Neighborhood." At Vicky's door I was greeted by a girl of about eight, who took one look at me and yelled, "Mum!" then vanished from the doorway, abandoning me on the porch. Finally Vicky appeared, toweling her wet hair as she descended the stairs.

She led me into the kitchen and turned on the coffee maker. I handed her an updated list of my activities and costs to date and while she was glancing through this document, I watched her daughters. They were crowded around the end of the kitchen table, poring over a family photograph album, discussing the snapshots. Mark was securely settled in the midst of them, sitting in the eldest girl's lap. "Look Mark—there you are!" the eldest girl said, turning the page. "I told you you were in here. See—aren't you cute?"

"It's a baby," Mark said, peering at the photograph.

"But that's you, Mark. You used to be a baby!" The two older girls smiled at each other, maternally, over the top of his head.

I wandered over and stood behind them, looked down at the photograph. A rather floppy-looking baby with profuse dark hair was propped in a high chair. As my eyes scanned the page opposite, Vicky's youngest daughter, Shannon, looked up at me shyly. "Is that your Dad?" I asked, pointing to a photograph in the middle of the next page. She glanced down at the album, nodded. Will Fischer, like his daughters, had ginger hair and eyes that crinkled when he smiled. His square, pudgy face had an engaging, puckish look; he had a highball glass in one hand, a fishing rod in the other, and was sitting in the back of a yacht getting sunburnt.

Vicky arrived at my elbow, handed me a mug of coffee and a check for the invoice I'd given her. "Let's go into the living room," she said.

She settled herself into the armchair opposite me, placed her hairbrush and coffee cup on the table beside her, and continued towel-drying her long heavy hair. After I'd answered her questions about my report, I told her Damayanthi's story. She listened carefully, and when I got to the part where Dunbar appeared beside the sandbox in the playground, she let the towel drop into her lap, and forgot about her hair. "And this is the same guy you showed me the picture of?" she asked, when I'd finished.

"Yup," I said.

"And now he's dead," she murmured. "Jesus! What's going on here?" She sounded worried, and angry.

"Just wait," I warned. "It gets worse."

Now I repeated Georgia's account of Ed's fight with Fred Dunbar. This time, as the story progressed, Vicky seemed to lose interest; she picked up the hairbrush and began pulling long clumps of hair over her eyes, working out the tangles. I wound up with a description of my latest encounter with Ed.

By the time I'd finished, Vicky was concealed behind a waterfall of clotted hair. "It seems to be getting more and more complicated," she commented, clenching her jaw and attacking a recalcitrant knot.

"But certain patterns are emerging,"

Vicky peered up from under her eyebrows, trying to get a better view of the tangle she was working on. "Like what?"

"The link between Ed and Sherry, for example. Not only did they frequent the same restaurant and live in the same house; now I've established that they had a mutual acquaintance in Fred Dunbar. And neither of them seems to have liked him very much."

"Yes. That is odd." But she was only being polite. Her eyes were screwed up; she was flaying the tangle with her hairbrush.

I watched her, unamiably. "You'll get split ends."

"My blow-dryer's on strike," she answered through gritted teeth. "And I haven't got the patience to use a comb." She finished with that clump, started on another. "Did you tell the police?" she asked, offhandedly.

"That Ed punched out Fred Dunbar a day or two before Dunbar died?"

The brush hesitated—continued with a burst of new energy.

"Wouldn't you?" I inquired.

This time the brush stopped. Then it moved to the crown of Vicky's head and swept down over her face with long, smooth strokes. The cascade of hair, which now completely concealed her face, rippled and shone, its ends lapping and curling over her shoulders and breasts.

"When I last talked to Dikeakos," I said, "he mentioned the fact that Dunbar had a black eye—an injury that had already started to heal before he died."

The brush kept sweeping—all the tangles were gone.

"Vicky," I said finally, "you were the one who got me involved in all this. Don't you think it's about time that you told me what's going on?"

"I don't know what you're talking about." Nor do I intend to find out, her tone of voice added.

I was beginning to lose my temper. "No?"

"If I knew what was going on, I wouldn't have hired you." She tossed her head, began brushing the hair on one side back, past her ear.

"But perhaps you only wanted me to find out some things, not others. Unfortunately, it's not working out that way."

"You're telling me you want to quit," she taunted, as if scoring a point. The tip of her ear was turning pink.

"No, that's not what I'm telling you. I'm saying that you're withholding information—and as a result, you're making my job harder than it has to be."

She stared at me. "You're out of your mind." She flung her hair over the other shoulder and began brushing that side. Her scalp hadn't had such a good massage in weeks.

"What's going on between you and Ed?"

"Ed?" Her eyebrows arched. "What a question," she remarked, as if scandalized. "You never did like this job—did you? You were squeamish right from the beginning." She pointed the end of the brush at me. "Go ahead then—quit. But stop making up excuses."

"That's what you want, isn't it? You want me to quit."

She narrowed her eyes. "I want you to find out who killed my sister."

"But if you don't trust me, I see no reason to trust you. And I'm warning you right now that your behavior looks goddamn suspicious. Your friend, Ed, is going to end up charged with somebody's murder if the two of you don't start talking—soon. And yes, that's a threat." I stood up.

"You're fired," she retaliated—but more in fear, I thought, than anger.

"Good." I swung my bag over my shoulder and stomped into her front hallway. "That'll make my job a lot easier."

"I said, you're fired!" she shouted after me. This time she sounded more convincing.

I had my hand on her front doorknob. "When I'm really motivated," I informed her, "I work without pay."

I slammed the door behind me.

I went straight to Vicky's bank, got there five minutes before it closed and cashed her check before she tried to put a stop on it. Then I drove to my Aikido class—which was the best possible conclusion to a day like this. I needed to clear my mind, center myself.

It was the last practice before the workshop, which was scheduled to take place the following weekend. Dean showed up—I hadn't seen him for some time—and we practiced together for a good part of the evening. In Aikido one usually works in partners, and the people one likes personally aren't necessarily the people one likes to practice with. Dean is a case in point. He's a supremacist of the worst order, a paternalistic left-wing fanatic who despises everyone who isn't a card-carrying member of the proletariat. I never talk to him if I can avoid doing so, but as long as we don't talk, we communicate beautifully, our bodies establishing a rhythm that becomes almost hypnotic. I sometimes wonder what it would be like to make love with him. Would we, if we kept our mouths shut, achieve Tantric enlightenment?

But the following morning found me dull-witted and depressed; I sat in my office and brooded, thinking about Vicky, about Damayanthi's story, about Ed's fight with Fred Dunbar. I wasn't happy about any of it and, worse still, I wasn't even getting paid to be unhappy anymore.

Finally I remembered that I'd never finished phoning all the Ferreiras in the phone book—a nice, routine, and probably irrelevant task. But routine tasks impose an order and a discipline upon the investigative process, and make disheartened detectives feel competent and professional. I pulled out my telephone directory, found the column I'd marked. The very first person I talked to told me that she had a brother named Mike Ferreira who worked on an oil rig up north. Both she and her brother had gone to Capilano Secondary, and although she was four years younger than he was, she did indeed remember a girlfriend named Lydia. "In fact, my best friend's sister was her best friend," she added helpfully.

I asked her if she knew how I could get in touch with that friend, or better yet—with that friend's sister.

She gave me her friend's name and phone number, and her friend gave me the phone number for her older sister, Nancy Mok (now Nancy Lo) who, reputedly, had once been Lydia's best friend. But Nancy Lo didn't answer her telephone.

I hung up the receiver, but just as I let go of it, the telephone rang. It was Randy McConnell, the sleazy P.I. I'd hired to track down Will Fischer. "Well, baby—you're lucky," he said, in answer to my greeting.

"Oh yeah?"

"I've got you the goods."

I picked up my pen, pulled my notebook towards me. "You found something?" I didn't believe it.

"Sure—wasn't that the idea?"

When we'd finished sparring, Randy told me that Will Fischer had flown into Vancouver on Global Airways, Flight No. 606, on the night of March 23rd, a Friday. And he'd flown back to Bangkok on Flight No. 414, two nights later—Sunday—ten hours after Sherry died.

I was stunned. "Are you sure?"

"My sources are good, lady—very good," he snarled. It appeared that I'd hurt his feelings.

"Yes, but—"

"And if you find out I'm wrong, I'll give you your money back," he added belligerently.

I said nothing more. I was remembering that I'd asked him to check all flights since March 10th, when Will Fischer had left Vancouver for Bangkok. I hadn't told Randy why, or which dates particularly interested me.

"...I found him listed with both companies—Sky Pacific and Global," Randy was saying. "And I was told he'll be coming this way again on April 9th—Sky Pacific this time—Flight No. 169." Yup, I thought, adding this number to my list of flight numbers and dates, that's what Vicky said—next Monday.

"That's amazing," I breathed. I made an effort. "Good work, Randy. I'm impressed."

"Hey—does that mean I get a tip?"

I stared at the receiver, too dazed to come up with a suitably squelching rejoinder. Without saying anything more, I hung up.

Will Fischer had been in town that same weekend! He'd been in Vancouver when Sherry moved from Glen's house; he'd been here when she moved for the second time, to East 6th; and he'd flown back into town for the weekend of her death. He'd once made advances to Sherry—had they led to something more? I remembered the photograph that I'd seen in Vicky's album: his smooth, pale body, his impish smile. Glen had said that Vicky put a stop to it. But putting a stop to a love affair is sometimes easier said than done.

This last piece of information was the final, shattering blow to my morale, so I did something very sensible: I closed up shop for the day and went to visit my favorite second-hand store. I bought myself a pair of pants, a set of screwdrivers, a beautiful moss-green spring jacket and a stainless steel pot that looked like it had never been used. Total: thirteen bucks.

But at eight-thirty that evening, I was back on the job, standing on Glen Hovey's front porch in the leaf-dappled light, and admiring his security features: the intercom above the doorbell, the peep-hole in the stained oak door, the keyless combination lock over the doorknob. It was a house that looked like it might well be worth breaking into: with wide granite steps and mullion windows, set on an angle in the center of a generous, tree-studded lot. It reeked of old-fashioned comfort (and lots of paid help), of the early years of this century when Asian immigrants could be imported by the shipload and made to work for next to nothing. Crocuses and narcissi had naturalized in the lawn around the rhododendrons, and an enormous magnolia stood on the front lawn in a pool of its own petals.

I rang the doorbell. Almost immediately, the dead bolt clicked, the door slid open—a smooth, oiled weight—and Glen stood before me, head slightly ducked—his characteristic stance.

"Come in," he said, with more warmth than I felt I deserved. Perhaps he wasn't enjoying these long solitary evenings of enforced domesticity.

Entering Glen's house was like walking into a public building. He ushered me into a lobby with an open ceiling, the most striking feature of which was a curved, sweeping staircase that led up to a banistered landing on the second floor. The major rooms of the house opened off from this central space: the living room to my right, the kitchen straight ahead under the arch of the staircase. On my left was a study, and through the uprights of the banistered landing on the second floor, I could see the doors to the bedrooms.

As Glen hung up my jacket, I walked over to the banister and patted the top of the smooth, polished end-post, my eyes following the long ascending curve of the handrail. "That must make a nice slide for Mark," I commented. "No," Glen rebuked me, "it doesn't."

He led me into the living room—which had all the appurtenances of its period: a hardwood floor, bay windows, wainscoting, and a handsome stone fireplace. The furniture, however, looked like it had been lifted—along with its accessories: drapes, carpet, cushions—from a department store showroom. The result was characterless, and relentlessly color coordinated. There were no photographs on the mantelpiece, no magazines on the coffee table, no dints in the cushions. I've been in hotel lobbies that felt a lot more homey.

Glen offered me a drink and I followed him through the dining room (where the furniture was exactly positioned, static—like a room in a museum) and into the kitchen, where he mixed two drinks. The kitchen had been renovated—modernized and streamlined—and unlike the other rooms, it felt lived-in.

"When did you buy this place?" I asked, settling myself on one of the tall stools at the counter.

"About eight years ago," he answered, uncapping a bottle of scotch. "Before I met Sherry."

That explained it. House prices had nearly quadrupled since then. Still, it must have been a hefty investment for someone on a restaurant manager's salary.

He handed me my drink, then led me back to the living room. I sat at one end of the chesterfield, he sat at the other, and I told him Damayanthi's story.

"You're saying that this is the same guy—the one you showed me the picture of?"

"That's right."

He considered, then shook his head. "This is like some— like a T.V. show or something. I can't believe that Sherry was involved in something like this."

"Something like what?"

"Well—being pursued, or whatever. I mean, what did this guy want?"

"That's what I'm trying to find out. Does the name Ed Jeffreys mean anything to you?"

"No. Who's he?"

"Just a guy I met who happens to know Fred Dunbar."

"What does he say about him?"

"Nothing to the point."

Glen looked exasperated. "But why is this guy hanging around my kid?" His legs were crossed, and his suspended foot had started to jitter.

I took a sip of my drink. "Did you ever play hockey?"

"What's that got to do with it?"

"Ever take Mark to play hockey?"

"Come on," he answered irritably. "He's too young. And he's not very coordinated, either."

"Has he ever been skating?"

"Sure. Sherry took him a couple of times." He watched me, impatiently. I took another swallow of scotch and waited while his blood pressure rose another notch. "Did you ever play hockey?" I asked him for the second time.

He exhaled, audibly—like a breaching whale. "Of course I played hockey. Doesn't every boy in this country play hockey? In fact my brother was training to go professional before he got crushed in that car. But I was never into it like he was. A bunch of guys shoving and pushing at each other to get hold of a stupid puck."

"Where did you skate?"

He hesitated. "We went to a lot of places. Back then, there was no rink anywhere near us, so we had to take the bus— played all over town. At least my brother did. And I often tagged along."

I decided to leave it at that. There was no point questioning him any further since I didn't know where Dunbar had coached twenty-five years ago, and I wasn't sure that I'd be able to find out.

I changed the topic. "Exactly when was it that Vicky caught her husband trying to make out with Sherry?"

Glen looked pained—as if I'd offended his sensibilities—although he was the one who'd told me about it. "Mark was about two years old—and it was summer, so...maybe two years ago? But it had been going on for quite a while before that."

"Are you absolutely sure that Sherry found his attentions unwelcome?"

He stilled, then raised his glass to his lips. "Why? You know different?"

"No," I said. "I'm asking, that's all."

"What does Vicky say?"

"I haven't talked to Vicky about this."

"Yeah." He wiped the back of his hand across his lips. "I guess it's kind of a touchy subject."

"*Are* you sure?" I prodded. This man was an expert at side-stepping questions.

"Well—" He prepared to be expansive, clasped his hands around his knee. "I only know what Sherry told me—and she said he gave her the creeps. But I didn't ever—" He stopped. "No, that's not true," he said, correcting himself. "I did see them together occasionally—not often—after Vicky's big show-down. And I noticed that whenever Will was around Sherry, he looked a bit hang-dog. But Sherry...." He considered. "Nah. She hated him. She was no good at hiding things—and it was written all over her. Every time Will got too close, she'd freeze."

"Even after Vicky bawled him out, Will was still trying to get too close?"

"I can't say that I ever saw him try—but I wasn't over there much. I wouldn't put it past him."

"Vicky or no Vicky?"

Glen cocked his head. "Yeah, well—he'd certainly be dis-creet about it. But Will is one of those guys who never grows up, you know? If you give him a rule, he's got to break it—

regardless of the consequences. And I bet Sherry's attitude towards him was a bit of a challenge. So he might have kept trying—Vicky or no Vicky."

"Assuming he kept trying," I said, "can you imagine him making such a nuisance of himself that Sherry would go into hiding to get away from him?"

Glen pursed his mouth as if to whistle; his eyebrows lifted. "So that's your gist," he said. "Interesting." He took a sip of his drink. "I wonder. . . . " Then he nodded. "It's possible. Because Sherry had sort of a phobia about him. Of course—" he warned me, "she had phobias about all kinds of things. But it wouldn't have taken much to make her feel desperate. She really wasn't up to dealing with that kind of situation. And she wouldn't have talked to Vicky about it."

"Why wouldn't she have talked to you?"

A troubled expression crossed his face. "I'd like to think she would." He lowered his eyelids. "But I have to admit, we weren't very close this past year or so. I was so damn busy and—and half the time, she was off her head." He glanced at me apologetically. "It was like we existed on different planets. But see—often when she did come to me with stuff, it was—it was nuts! So I'd dismiss a lot of what she said—her fears, her crazy ideas. And maybe after a while. . . . " He faltered. "Maybe she figured there was no point talking to me anymore." Now he looked upset.

I studied the painting above his mantelpiece: a pastel-colored abstract which, in my opinion, would have looked better on a bolt of material than it did on Glen's wall. After a decent interval had elapsed, I changed the subject again. "What does Will's company import?"

He considered for a moment. "The usual: knick-knacks, cheap clothing, electronic stuff from South Korea and Hong Kong. But—" His foot had started twitching again. "I'll tell you. He makes one hell of a lot of money. Which makes me wonder sometimes if all that other stuff isn't just a front."

"A front for what?"

"For whatever it is that he really imports."

Everyone in Vancouver knows what this means. Our city,

176

picturesquely situated on the eastern rim of the Pacific, is the drug capital of Canada. "But you've no proof of this."

"No. Except that he's capable of it. Morally, I mean. Plus the fact that he makes far too much money. He paid cash for that house, he owns a yacht, and he's bought real estate all over town. And he started out a poor boy. Like me," he added, giving me a look that was self-deprecating, almost flirtatious.

I had no more questions to ask. As we finished our drinks I let the conversation move on to more general topics: Glen's search for a housekeeper, Mark's night terrors and bed-wetting problems. ". . . One night I took him to the bathroom three times—and still, in the morning, the bed was wet. I'm going nuts, I really am. And every night, just when I finally get to sleep, he wakes up, crying and screaming—hysterical. I get him up, take him to the bathroom—and then he won't go to sleep again. I've tried reading to him, talking to him—and sure, after two hours, he finally can't keep himself awake anymore. But I can't go on like this."

"Does he have a night-light?"

Glen nodded. "Sherry bought that for him years ago."

"Why don't you try sleeping in his room for a while? Make up a bed on the floor or something. But you've got to give him time—lots of time. Don't pressure him."

I swallowed the last of my drink and thanked him, but when I got up to leave Glen looked surprised, as if he'd expected me to stay longer.

"But Mark is supposed to be going to kindergarten this fall," he expostulated, rising and following me to the door. He took my jacket down out of the cupboard.

"Maybe he should wait a year," I said as he helped me into it. I saw the stricken look on his face. "Each kid develops differently—but they all eventually grow up." I smiled, reassuringly, and reached for the doorknob.

He escorted me out. "Sometimes—" he began.

I'd already started down the steps, but now I turned and looked back. He stood framed in the big doorway, dwarfed by its proportions. He appeared smaller and suddenly vulnerable.

"Sometimes," he confessed, "when Mark looks up at me,

it's like I see Sherry again, staring at me out of his eyes. Like she's still alive—you know?"

I had the feeling that he'd been working up to saying this for the past half hour, and had only found the courage now that I was leaving. "How does that make you feel?"

His right hand twitched and suddenly clenched. "It scares me," he admitted. "I feel like—uh—it's like I'm being haunted, eh?" He finished in an embarrassed rush, his voice high and tense.

"If it's too much for you," I said, wondering how it was that I'd become this man's confidante, "admit it. Get help. Have you considered doing that?"

His eyes, shadowed by the porch light above him, were like empty sockets; his skin looked bleached. "Yeah. Yeah, I think about it sometimes," he answered distractedly. "But, well . . . bye." He pushed the door shut between us.

18

FRIDAY WAS AN IRRITATING and useless day. I dawdled around at home for most of the morning, but Ben was dawdling around there too (supposedly getting settled down for a good day of studying), and his dilatory tactics were so much like mine that they finally drove me out of the house. It's all your own doing, I reminded myself as I drove down to my office. You were the one who kept his room ready and waiting. If you'd moved to a smaller place, he'd have camped at his father's house instead.

Then I sat down at my desk and tried to organize my thoughts. I mapped out every possible scenario . . . who'd killed whom (and why), or hired whom to kill whom, and who'd found out about it. Vicky and Ed were lovers, Will and Sherry were lovers, Ed and Sherry were lovers . . . Glen and Vicky were lovers? By the end of this exercise, I'd reached a state of complete mental paralysis.

I opened my notebook and stared at the last entry: Flight No. 169, Sky Pacific, April 9th. Perhaps, I thought, marking it with a big asterisk, I should be at the airport to meet that plane.

Then I succumbed to a long daydream in which Vicky and I had a heart-to-heart chat. I told Vicky about her husband's secret trip home; she cried and admitted that she'd always feared that something like this was going on. "He's such a bastard," she wept, "he's been after Sherry for years." By the end of the daydream, I'd settled it all: Will and his partner were the biggest heroin importers in the Pacific Northwest; Ed and Dunbar worked for them (but hated each other), and for years Vicky had

179

suspected that something fishy was going on. When Sherry disappeared, Vicky knew that her sister must have become somehow involved, and decided to act. She'd hired me in the hope that I'd blow the whole mess to smithereens.

By that time it was mid-afternoon, and I was feeling like I'd just eaten a whole box of chocolates. Ashamed, I managed to make myself phone Sky Pacific, and found out that Flight No. 169 was due to arrive in Vancouver on Monday at noon. Then I tried phoning Nancy Lo again. This time she was home. And she made my day by telling me that as far as she knew, Glen's ex-girlfriend, Kasia Jekubik, now lived in Toronto.

"Toronto!" I protested, quelling the urge to wail.

"First she moved to Edmonton. But then she met some man there and he got a job in Toronto."

"Did she get married?"

"I think so. But I'm not sure."

Worse and worse. "And you don't know her address?"

"No—but Lydia would."

And the last Nancy had heard of Lydia, she was working in a health food store. "A friend of mine ran into her a couple of months ago. She's changed her name—she doesn't call herself Lydia anymore, and I'm trying to remember. . . . It was a weird name. You know—like Ozone or something."

"Ozone?"

"Not ozone, but something like that."

"Look—can you get me the name of the health food store?"

"Sure," she said. "I'll call you back after I've talked to my friend. And maybe she'll remember Lydia's new name too."

"That'd be very helpful," I agreed.

It was with relief that I went home, knowing that I could now forget the whole business and think about nothing but Aikido for the entire weekend.

That evening the workshop started. There was a demonstration, a few speeches and a potluck supper. The visiting senseii was a charming, rotund little man—all ease and smiles, with neat wrists and plump hands. A casual turn, a flick of the wrist, and his assailants bounced off him as if he were a human trampoline.

The next day I got a chance to assail him myself—an experience that was like trying to jump my own shadow. Afterwards he showed us the moves in slow motion, demonstrating that he wasn't doing anything we didn't know how to do ourselves, only he'd refined the techniques and gotten the timing down perfect. For the next two hours we practiced, while he walked among us, correcting and commenting. It was a wonderful class, and after lunch there was another. By the end of the day I was almost euphoric.

I got home around eight o'clock, tripped over Ben's shoes in the hallway, found a mess of unwashed dishes on the kitchen counter and a message taped to the refrigerator door: "Phone Vicky." My euphoria curdled like sour milk in a fresh cup of coffee. Vicky was finally ready for that heart-to-heart chat?

"Meg, would you come over?" she asked softly, as if not wanting to be overheard. "Ed and I would like to talk to you."

My eyebrows went up. Ed and I?

"All right," I said, and grabbed a box of crackers—supper—on my way out the door.

Vicky preceded me into her living room, where Ed was sprawled in one of her spacious armchairs, his cheek resting against his hand, his eyes staring out the big picture window, through which there was nothing to see but the muted reflection of Vicky's living room. I sat down on the couch. Vicky sat in the chair nearest him. "They've had him down at the station all afternoon," Vicky said, as if Ed were a convalescent who couldn't speak for himself.

I looked at Ed—who was ignoring us. "Maybe it's time you got some legal advice."

He shrugged.

"I know a couple of decent lawyers, one who adjusts her fees to the income of her clients."

"I don't talk. That's all. They can't do anything to you if you don't talk."

"You don't even have to let them in the door, you don't have to go down to the station with them. Make them charge you with something if they want to interrogate you."

Ed glanced at me but said nothing. I turned back to Vicky, waited, expectantly.

"Ed and I—" she began, then cleared her throat. "We've decided that it might be best to tell you a little more. It's not really relevant—in fact, it's not relevant at all—but we haven't told the police because we know that the police might not see it that way. But we want to tell you—in confidence, of course—because it does confuse things a bit and—"

"I might not see it that way either," I pointed out.

"That's what *I* said." Ed directed his comment at Vicky's drapes.

"No, I think when. . . ." Vicky looked at me, then at Ed, and didn't finish.

I sighed. "Well, go on then—spit it out."

At this Ed stirred, finally turning around to face me. "We've been sleeping together," he announced bluntly.

"Since when?" I snapped.

"Oh, a long time now."

Vicky explained: "We met at a softball game about a year ago. On second base."

I gave her a look of incredulity.

"We belong to a mixed softball league—maybe you've heard of it? There's teams all over the Lower Mainland and we play off against each other. It's just for fun. We're not real serious or competitive or anything. Anyway, Ed's team happened to be playing mine; he was second baseman and every time I went up to bat I'd make it to second and then I'd get stuck there. They had a pretty good pitcher," she acknowledged. "So by the end of the game Ed and I had sort of—um—become interested in each other."

"Then you did know Sherry," I said to Ed, annoyed.

"No, that's—" "He didn't!" They denied it in chorus.

"That's why the cops won't understand!" Vicky leaned forward. "That's what they'll think too! But it was a coincidence!"

"*What* was a coincidence?" I inquired scornfully.

"Ed never even met Sherry! Not once. He doesn't know my family. He just comes—" She broke off.

182

"I sleep here," Ed sneered. "When *he* doesn't." I assumed he meant Will.

"You were here the other afternoon."

"Yeah. Since Sherry died, I've been here a couple of times. Because of...." He shrugged; now it was his turn to leave his sentences unfinished.

"I wanted him here," Vicky said, as if I'd forbidden it. "And that's why Mark wasn't afraid of him. Remember when you asked me about that? Well, Mark and Ed were already acquainted. Ed had been over the day before, when Mark got a big splinter stuck in his knee. Mark freaked out. He wouldn't let me near it; he was convinced he was going to die. But Ed...." Vicky gazed at Ed admiringly. "He's wonderful with kids—he really is."

Ed looked uncomfortable. "I'm the oldest of six," he muttered. "I've had a lot of practice."

"He turned the whole thing into a game," Vicky explained, "a story with all these characters. There was the Big Bad Splinter, the Nosey Needle, the Trusty Tweezers—and Mark got so involved in the story that he just sat there with his mouth open and watched Ed extract that Big Bad Splinter right out of his knee. Now whenever Ed comes, Mark gets him to tell the story all over again. He's going to remember that splinter for the rest of his life."

Vicky was smiling at me, fondly, but I felt unable to reciprocate. "If Ed didn't know Sherry, how was it that Sherry ended up at Copper's restaurant?"

"See?" Ed turned to Vicky, jerking his head in my direction. "I told you she wasn't going to believe it."

But then, having proved his point, he went on to try to convince me. "I knew Vicky had a sister who was a bit nuts, eh? But I'd never met her, never seen her picture—nothing. So when Sherry showed up in Copper's restaurant, I didn't know who she was. Vicky had never been to Copper's—I'd never talked about it or anything—she didn't even know that Copper's existed! It wasn't until her sister was *dead*—" He stabbed a forefinger at me, "that Vicky and I figured out that her long lost sister had been living in my basement all along."

"Refresh my memory," I demanded acidly. "How was it that Sherry ended in that basement?"

"I told you," Ed retorted.

"But now I'm being informed that half the things you told me aren't true."

"No. Maybe Vicky lied to you, but I didn't. You asked me if I knew Sherry—not Vicky—and I didn't know Sherry. I saw her at Copper's, but I didn't know who she was. I never talked to her—nothing."

"So you're sticking to your story. Sherry overheard you talking to Ahmed about the basement suite, and she picked up the telephone number that you left on the table."

"Maybe. That's what I *think*—I don't know. I did talk to Ahmed about the suite, I did write down the telephone number, and Sherry was there at the time. That's all I can tell you."

"You knew that Sherry was missing?" I was now being more careful to conceal my skepticism.

"Sure. Because Vicky and I had talked about it. She'd told me that her sister had run off with her kid and disappeared. But I'm not looking at every new waitress in town thinking maybe that's Vicky's lost sister!"

"No, of course not," I agreed.

"And when I hear that a lady and her kid have moved into the basement, I'm not going to think: Hey—maybe it's her! It's a big city, for Chrissakes—there's single women with kids every-where!"

"I understand," I said emphatically. He was getting pretty worked up.

"We were as surprised as you are," Vicky joined in. "When I phoned Ed and told him that my sister had been killed—"

"I thought, Hey—that's weird!" Ed interrupted her. "Because there was this woman killed in the basement and I mean—how many women get murdered in one day? Then I re-membered the kid and I said to her, 'Vicky—what's your sister's kid's name?' And she says, 'Mark.' " Ed spoke Mark's name with a kind of hushed wonder, and they suddenly glanced at each other.

"But later," Vicky went on, "when we found out that

Sherry had given Ed's name to the landlady, and when the police started treating Ed like the number one suspect, that's when we realized that this was going to look bad, real bad for Ed. Because if the cops found out about us—about me and Ed—then they'd never believe that he didn't know Sherry. Not that it's something we would have wanted to talk about anyway. I mean it's. . . . "

She looked at Ed; he looked at her—again the connection between them was exposed, like a band of heat shimmering in the air. I wondered how they categorized this relationship—was it love, or just sex? "I assume that Will doesn't know about this . . . ?" I sketched the link between them with my hand.

"No. He doesn't." Vicky tightened her lips; the dimple indented her cheek.

I decided to probe a little deeper. "What's this story I hear about Sherry and Will?"

"What story?" Vicky looked irritated.

"I was told that you caught your husband making out with Sherry in the basement one night."

She began shaking her head in angry disbelief. "Hey," she said, "I catch my husband making out with other women *all* the time. It's a routine procedure. But some women are out of bounds, and my sister happened to be one of them."

"Why?"

"Why?" Vicky demanded rhetorically. "Because my husband was making Sherry upset," she spat at me. "She's had a pretty sheltered existence—and she didn't think that Will's behavior was right. *I* didn't think it was right, either. If he wants to mess around, he can do it in someone else's house and with some woman that I'll never have to meet. He's got plenty of opportunities."

"So you have a sort of . . . open marriage?"

Vicky eyed me, sourly. "I'm just a pragmatist, that's all. I know his limits, and I know mine."

I gave some thought to Will's limits. "Glen tells me that Will's company is very successful."

"Yeah." She made it sound like a challenge.

"What's the secret of his success?"

185

She hesitated—wondering what dirt I'd raked up this time. "His partner, Somchai, put up the capital to get the company started, and he's got connections all over Southeast Asia. But he didn't know the scene here, so he needed someone like Will to talk up the buyers at this end. That's what Will is good at—talking up buyers," she added, with acerbity.

"But it's all legal and above-board?"

"You mean Glen told you otherwise?"

I didn't answer.

"That bad-mouthing, stuck-up little bastard!" Bright circles of pink appeared in Vicky's cheeks. "He's an envious turd—that's what he is! He just can't stand the fact that Will makes more money than he does—and you can tell him I said so!"

I held up my hands in surrender. "I just wanted to check it out," I explained appeasingly.

I thought some more about Will, and his secret trip home from Bangkok. But I wasn't going to bring that subject up here; I was saving that discussion for Will, personally, and I didn't want him briefed in advance by Vicky, who clearly retained at least a few wifely loyalties where Will's interests were concerned.

Instead I turned to Ed. He was slouched in his chair, one of his fingers tapping rhythmically against the armrest, as if keeping time to a tune inside his head. "Now," I addressed him. "Tell me about Fred Dunbar."

"Yeah." He looked puzzled. "You said he's dead, eh? What happened to him? And what was he doing outside my house that night anyway?"

"I asked you first."

"I don't know—that's what I'm telling you! Goddammit!" he burst out, raising himself into a more upright position. "You're worse than the cops—you know that?"

"But who is he?" I insisted, with a feeling of déjà vu. "Where do you know him from?"

Ed folded his arms across his chest.

"Tell her, Ed," Vicky intervened, persuasively.

He made me wait for a while longer, then yielded ungraciously. "He's a hockey coach—or he used to be. I knew him when I was a kid. And he's a real. . . . " Ed pursed his lips, contemplating various epithets. "Asshole," he decided.

"You played hockey?"

"When I was kid I did—yeah." He paused, seemed to reflect. "Not too many black kids play hockey. Baseball, basketball . . . but you don't see them in hockey. It wasn't something I thought about much—until I met up with Dunbar."

"You said he was racist."

Ed's long legs shifted. "You might say he singled me out for special attention. Whenever I got separated from the other players, whenever I was alone for some reason, Dunbar would come past me and whisper things like, well—I remember one time he said, 'Kind of cold for you in here, isn't it? Why don't you get back to the jungle where you belong?' Stuff like that." He gave me a brief look—a look that took me back to that night on East 6th, when rectangles of light swung around the walls, moving our faces in and out of the darkness. "I'd be tying up my skates, standing in a line-up and suddenly there'd be this hiss in my ear—" he brushed at the side of his head as if swatting away a mosquito, "calling me 'nigger-ass,' 'pickaninny,' 'ape-face'. . . . " Ed projected these names at me like gobs of spit. "And every time Dunbar looked at me I could feel him thinking up more names, watching to see how I was taking it."

"How old were you?"

"About ten."

"What rink was this?"

"The Albion. It's torn down now."

"Where was it?"

"Down on Southeast Marine. They've got a hospital there now."

I searched my memory and finally remembered the hospital—which was between Cambie and Main. It wasn't close to Glen's father's house—but it was as likely a place as any for the Hovey brothers to skate. "You never told anyone that Dunbar was abusing you?"

"You gotta understand," Ed explained. "This was the ace team—we were the best in the city, and I wanted to stay on that team, Dunbar or no Dunbar. And I was the kind of kid who—I was stubborn, you know? So when Dunbar started picking on me, I tried to pretend it wasn't happening."

"How long did this go on?"

Ed flexed his fingers, like a boxer. "Months. Right up until the day I finally put a stop to it."

"How did you do that?"

He was silent for a long time, as if the events of the past were replaying in his mind; I could even hear him breathing. "It was just after a playoff game, eh? And we lost by one point. We'd been tied right up to the end of the last period, but then, when there was only one minute left to play, the puck was passed to me—and I blew it. For a split second I got distracted—the puck bounced off my skate and a guy from the other team came up on my left, intercepted it and took it back down the ice. So when we came off the ice I was feeling pretty sick—not talking, not looking at anyone. And right away Dunbar sneaks up beside me and he says—" He broke off and looked at Vicky, who was hunched in her armchair, gazing at him with visible distress. "Well, I don't need to repeat it. But he'd pushed me too far. Right there in front of everybody I clobbered him across the head with my stick."

For at least half a minute, no one spoke. The low bushes outside the picture window scratched against the glass, and someone—a child who was supposed to be asleep?—flushed a toilet upstairs. "I guess that put an end to your hockey career," I concluded.

"Yep." Ed flattened his lips and fluted air through them, like a trumpet player. "But it also put an end to Dunbar as a coach. Because when they hauled me into the office and told me they were considering laying charges in Family Court or whatever, I finally went home and told my mother the whole story."

Ed gave an embarrassed grin, lowered his eyes and, noticing a piece of tape stuck to his pant leg, reached down and peeled it off. "You'd have to meet my mother to really appreciate what that meant," he said, sitting up again. "When my mother gets her back up, she's a terror. She sailed into that ice rink and threatened them with the Charter of Rights, the Race Relations Board and God knows what-all. They didn't know what had hit them—and they had to bring in some bigwig from the Parks Board to deal with her. But she didn't get it all her way. The hockey club people felt that they had to suspend me from the team because so many of the other kids had seen what had happened. In the end they made a bargain with my mother—I was thrown off the team, and Mr. Dunbar was relieved of his coaching duties. Which I think—I don't know—but I think that was a big deal for him. Coaching was his life."

Away in the distance I heard a siren heading south down Highway 99, and as we paused to listen to it I found myself staring at Ed's feet, which were encased in a pair of large, grubby running shoes. I asked, "Did you ever hear of the Hovey brothers when you were playing hockey at the Albion?"

"Hovey? Is that Sherry's husband?" Ed glanced at Vicky.

"Yeah," I said. "Or his older brother, Brad. I understand Brad was a hotshot player and was training to go professional. Maybe you heard of them."

He shook his head. "Before my time, I guess." He looked down at his hands and started rolling the piece of tape into a tiny wad with his fingertips.

"Which brings us," I proposed, "to the next part of the story."

Ed's forehead crinkled. "I don't follow you."

I obliged with a summary. "On the Saturday night before Sherry died, I saw Fred Dunbar sitting in a parked car outside your house. About an hour and a half later, one of your neighbors saw him pursuing you down the block, yelling at you. When he persisted, you punched him and kicked him in the stomach."

I heard Vicky's breath hiss—as if in protest—although I'd told her this story before. But maybe she was listening more closely this time.

"Yeah, well—" Ed stretched and wriggled his neck, as if his shirt collar were too tight. "That wasn't the first time I saw him, you know."

189

"So I gathered," I said.

"No. I mean, he'd been following me around. I saw him in Copper's a couple of weeks before that."

"You did?"

"Yeah. I was on my afternoon break, sitting in a booth with my buddies and suddenly I look over and see this old guy staring at me. I didn't recognize him at first, but it was obvious that he'd already figured out who I was. He was looking at me exactly the way he used to look at me when I was a kid."

"When was this?" I was watching him intently.

Ed shrugged. "Like I say—"

"Before or after Sherry had quit working at Copper's?"

Ed sighed. "As I told you, I never paid too much attention to Sherry. I don't remember exactly when she quit. But I'd guess that this was after."

"After." I did some calculating. "Do you remember the day I was there? It was a Tuesday, five days before Sherry died."

Ed frowned at me.

"It was lunchtime. I was standing at the till talking to Alexis when you guys came up to pay for your lunch."

Ed looked enlightened. "So that's where I'd seen you before."

"Was that the same day you saw Dunbar?"

"No. It was before that."

Then Dunbar was there twice, I thought. Ed saw him in the restaurant and some time later, I saw Dunbar in the phone booth outside. I turned to Vicky. "And you went to Copper's about a week before I did, to get Sherry's address from Alexis."

"But I wouldn't have recognized Fred Dunbar," Vicky said.

"You would have recognized Ed."

"Yes, but I never ran into him at Copper's."

This is farcical, I thought. We seem to have been running around at cross-purposes, narrowly missing each other. I addressed Ed again. "When you saw Dunbar at Copper's, what did you do?"

"Nothing. I ignored him."

"He didn't say anything to you?"

"With all my buddies around me? Hell, no. And I certainly

wasn't anxious to renew our acquaintance. He waited until later when he could get me alone."

Or he may not have been waiting for you at all, I thought. He may have been looking for Sherry and in the course of that search, he kept bumping into you. "Tell me what happened when he saw you outside your place on Saturday night."

"It was pretty much the way you said. I came home that evening—that was the night I saw you again, right? Coming down the steps?" I nodded. "I ate supper, had a bath, then I was going out to a party. And as I was walking down the sidewalk to my car, I heard someone calling, 'Hey you—nigger!' When I didn't answer to that, the guy remembers my name. 'Jeffreys,' he says. So I take a good look at him, eh? And there's old Fred Dunbar again, for the second time. I tell him to get lost—or words to that effect—but Dunbar keeps following me down the street, threatening me, saying he'll get me in the end—real Ku Klux Klan stuff. And he was going on about some woman, telling me to keep my hands off her if I knew what was good for me—"

"What woman?" I demanded.

"I don't know. I had no idea what he was talking about."

"Did he mention a name?"

"He called her Mrs. Something-or-other, but I didn't catch the name. And whatever it was, it meant nothing to me."

"Mrs. Hovey," I said.

"Hovey? Vicky's sister, you mean?" He looked dubious. "But I never heard that name until after she was killed. Besides, why would he think I knew Sherry Hovey?"

You tell me, I thought. But more diplomatically I answered: "For the same reason everybody else does. Because you lived in the same house and spent time in the same restaurant."

There was a silence. I was wondering if Fred Dunbar, knowing that there was some connection between Ed and Sherry, had found out that Sherry was living on East 6th by following Ed. "Finish your story," I said. "Dunbar was pursuing you down the sidewalk, going on about some woman—and then what?"

"Then when I got to my car, he grabbed me."

191

"He grabbed your jacket," I corrected him.

Ed's anger was instant. "That's called assault, lady! And I don't have to put up with it!" But like a wave, the rage rolled over him and was gone; he lowered his gaze to his knuckles, as if ruminating on their part in this story. He turned his hands over, examined his palms. "You're not going to believe this," he added, making it sound as if he didn't care whether I did or not, "but I think of myself as a pretty peaceable kind of guy."

His eyes lifted—and bumped into mine just as I was concluding that, given the right provocation, he was certainly capable of murder. "You punched him," I said. "Exactly what was the damage?"

"I knocked the wind out of him—maybe gave him a black eye. A bruise or two when he fell. He wasn't dead."

"Not yet."

I was treated to another display of outrage. "Look, lady!" He used that word, "lady," primarily, as an insult. "He walked away. I gave him a black eye—that was it!"

"Calm down," I said irritably. "You saw him walk away?"

"As good as. I circled the block and by the time I came around again he was trying to sit up. So I didn't bother calling in an ambulance crew to scrape him off the sidewalk." His eyes returned to the wad of tape in his fingers; then, as if taking aim at a dart board, he flicked the piece of tape into the solid glass ashtray that was on the coffee table in front of him.

"Have the police found out about your encounter with Dunbar on Saturday night?"

Ed let his head rest back against the cushion; his eyelids flickered as if he were falling asleep.

"I think you should tell them. Soon. Before somebody else does."

"Who's going to squeal?" he inquired laconically.

"Well—I found out about it. And at nine o'clock in the evening on a residential street . . . I bet you had plenty of witnesses."

"Then how come they haven't said anything yet? It's been two weeks."

"I'm just warning you—it'll go badly for you if the cops find out."

"Then don't you tell them," Ed whispered, enunciating each word and pursing his lips as if offering me a kiss.

I went over his story with him a couple more times, but he had nothing to add. When I got up to leave, Vicky trailed after me onto the porch. "Meg," she remonstrated, touching my sleeve as if to prevent my departure, "if we were lying to you— if we were guilty, I mean, or had anything to do with this..." Her tone was apologetic. "Why would I have hired you?"

I considered various answers to this. "As a bluff?"

"Is that what you think? That this is all some elaborate coverup? That Ed and I killed my sister?"

I gazed steadily into her eyes. "I try to keep an open mind. Good night," I added, and headed down her steps.

"Meg?" she called. As I stopped and looked back, I was reminded of the last time I'd seen Glen. It was a different porch this time, a different character standing under the light. "Will you work for me again?"

I turned and stared away down the empty, flood-lit street; the smell of fresh-cut grass wafted up from the lawn. "No," I answered.

19

THE NEXT MORNING I was stiff. I didn't wake up until nearly nine, and by that point I was too late to catch the meditation session at the Aikido workshop. I longed for a hot shower, but didn't have time to wait around for Ben to get out of the bathtub. I hurried off to the community center, anxious to get there in time for the first class.

The class loosened me up a bit. After it was over I went down to the cafeteria and bought myself a salad and a bottle of juice, then took my lunch outside and found a grassy nook in the sunshine where I could be by myself. But as soon as I was alone, the previous evening's scene in Vicky's living room began replaying in my mind; I reviewed everything that had been said, analyzed each gesture, each glance that had passed between them. Then I reconsidered all the scenes that had preceded last night's denouement to see if I could find the tell-tale places where the pattern didn't match up, where the rents in the truth had been patched over with lies.

Unrefreshed, unenlightened, I returned inside for the afternoon session, but I was too preoccupied and worn out to concentrate. I left the class early, went downstairs to the whirlpool and lay back against the jets. The thunder of churning water filled my ears and emptied my brain; I let my feet rise to the surface and floated around like a dead fish.

Then I started home. I turned left out of the community center parking lot, tried to take a shortcut through an unfamiliar subdivision and ended up in a maze of circular, winding streets, intended to confound anyone attempting to cut through the neighborhood to some destination on the other side. Finally, when I'd escaped and had recovered my sense of direction, I found myself on an east-west street lined with prim, stucco bungalows—a street which looked familiar. Then I saw the house with the privet hedge. Remembering that I'd left a piece of unfinished business there, I pulled up and parked.

"I figured you'd be back," Glen's father said with satisfaction, peering at me through the mesh of the screen door. He ushered me in, and as I followed him into his living room I felt like Little Red Riding Hood going to visit the wolf. "I notice the police haven't done much," he commented, easing himself down into the armchair behind the footstool. Again, I sat on the couch in front of the window.

"Oh they're probably busy behind the scenes. They don't communicate with me, though."

"No." He looked as if he understood full well why not.

"I wanted to talk to you a bit more about the Sunday morning that Sherry died."

He lifted one shoulder to ease a cramp in his side, then settled again. "I went over all that with the police. More than once."

"Yes, but I'd like to hear it firsthand. Can you go over it again with me? I know it was a while ago now."

"I remember it perfectly well," he snapped, as if I'd implied that he was going senile. "I've had to repeat it so often that I've got it memorized by now."

So, I thought, the cops don't like Glen's alibi any more than I do. "But I don't want you to just repeat what you said to the cops. I want you to recreate that morning for me—to remember the ways in which it differed from other mornings. Starting right from the beginning." I paused—but he continued to scowl at me. "Do you remember what time you got up?"

"The usual time."

For a moment I thought that this was all the answer I was going to get.

"Seven," he finally added. "I'm an early riser—always have been."

"Even on Sundays?"

"What's Sunday to me?" he asked peevishly. "Every day's like any other when you reach my age."

"You got up at seven," I prompted, pampering him.

"Had my bath. Then I changed the clock." He tilted his head in the direction of the old-fashioned clock that sat on the mantelpiece. "It's a finicky thing—I don't let anyone else touch it."

"You have to wind it, do you?" I wondered what there was to change.

"No, no. The time, girl! Yes of course I had to wind it—but I do that every Sunday. But that day I had to change the time as well."

"Oh, right!" Daylight Savings Time—I'd forgotten.

"Damn fool nonsense it is too. Why don't we just leave the time the way it is? Last year in Newfoundland they made them jump two hours ahead. Created havoc—they hated it! But these bureaucrats—"

"You changed the time on the clock," I interrupted him quickly, heading off the harangue, "to what? Forwards or backwards?"

"An hour forward in the spring," he rebuked me, like a school teacher testing knowledge I was supposed to have memorized.

"So instead of being seven thirty, it became eight thirty."

"That's right."

"And then what did you do?"

"Took my walk."

"Your walk?" I thought Glen had said he couldn't go out.

"Just up and down the sidewalk out front. Got to keep the joints oiled, you know. And I can still get around. It's just the back steps give me trouble. They're too steep."

"And after your walk?"

"I made breakfast."

"What did you eat?"

He looked at me as if I'd asked how often he changed his underwear.

"I want the details," I reminded him, "the things that made that Sunday morning different from any other."

"There was the clock," he pointed out.

"Yes, I'm glad you remembered that."

He was silent for a moment, his yellowish eyes reflecting the light from the window behind me. "Well, I put the porridge on—and then I made the coffee."

"How long does that take?"

"Oh—I perk it, you see. And I like it strong. So—fifteen minutes, thereabouts."

"By that time, Glen had arrived?"

"No, he didn't show up until later, when I was eating my breakfast."

"But I thought—" I stopped. I reached for my bag, dug into it and found my notebook, began flipping through the pages.

He continued: "When the coffee was done, I sat down at the kitchen table, drank my first cup and read the newspaper. I always do that."

I finally found the page I was looking for. I scanned my notes and there it was: Dikeakos had told me that, according to Glen's father, Glen had arrived at his father's house at eight-forty a.m. Yet the old man had just told me that after setting the living room clock at eight-thirty, he'd gone for a walk, cooked his porridge, made coffee, read the newspaper...and Glen hadn't arrived yet.

"...By the time I'd finished my first cup of coffee the porridge was cooked. So I poured myself a second cup and ate my breakfast." He added, offhand: "I do the same thing every morning, you know, so I'm not likely to forget."

"When Glen arrived, you were sitting in the kitchen?"

"That's right. He came in at eight-forty." He lowered his chin, secure in the knowledge that he was verifying the facts he'd already given to the police. " 'What gets you up so bright and early this morning?' I said. Usually he doesn't show up until after I've had my breakfast."

I got up from the couch. I walked through his living room and into the kitchen.

"Where are you going?" he objected, swiveling his head and trying to see me over his shoulder.

It was a small, old-fashioned kitchen with a tiled countertop and floor. There was a short, rounded fridge and just room beside it for the little arborite-topped table pushed up against the wall. At this table was one metal-framed chair, facing the fridge. I glanced around and finally located the clock, high on the wall above the kitchen sink, easily visible to anyone sitting at the table. I stared at its homely numbered face and felt a sudden, strange calm—like the slow-motion silence in which one perceives an imminent head-on collision.

I walked back into the living room, where the old man awaited me, fidgeting with curiosity, but unwilling to make the effort to get up and find out what I was up to.

I stood in front of him. "Who changed the time on the kitchen clock?"

His eyebrows met, disapprovingly.

"You changed the time on the living room clock, but when Glen came in, you were sitting in the kitchen, right? Do you wear a watch?"

His right hand covered his left; his fingers massaged the bare skin under the cuff of his sleeve.

"How do you know that Glen arrived at eight-forty?"

"I looked at the clock." His face gave a convulsive twitch.

"The clock in the kitchen, over the sink."

"That's right."

"And when did you change the time on that clock?"

He was silent.

"How did you get up there to change it? You must have stood on a chair or something."

"I can't climb on chairs," he sputtered furiously. "I have trouble enough with the steps!"

I walked back to the couch and sat down again. "When Glen arrived, you were sitting in the kitchen eating breakfast, and you looked at the kitchen clock, which said eight-forty."

He opened his mouth—abruptly shut it again.

"But when you changed the time on the living room clock,

you set it at eight-thirty. After that you went for walk, cooked the porridge, made coffee, read the newspaper. . . . "

He was shaking his head vigorously, like a dog coming out of the water.

"In other words, nobody had changed the time on the kitchen clock. So when did it get changed?"

He waved me away, crossly. "How do I know?"

"It says the right time now."

"Of course it does!" he snapped. "Glen probably changed it that same morning, after he did the dishes."

"When Glen walked in and you looked at the kitchen clock, you didn't notice that you'd forgotten to change it, you didn't remember that it was an hour behind?"

He wouldn't answer.

"In other words," I said quietly, "Glen arrived here at *nine-forty*—new time."

"And eight-forty—old time," Mr. Hovey proclaimed, as if vindicated. But his knotted hands were pulling and clutching at each other.

"When Glen arrived you commented that he was early and—what did he say?"

"I don't recall," he answered, haughtily.

"He walked into the kitchen, you looked at the kitchen clock and you said, 'What gets you up—"

"No." He couldn't pass up the opportunity to correct me. "I was in the kitchen, and I heard the front door open. I knew who it was, of course—who else would it be? I looked up at the kitchen clock and I said, 'What gets you up so early this morning?' I heard him walking through the living room and he said—" He hesitated, frowning. "Something about having a lot to do today and—yes, that's what it was. He said he had a busy day ahead of him and couldn't stay long." He stopped twisting his hands and folded them complacently over his small, rounded paunch.

"Then he came into the kitchen?"

"That's it."

"Did he look at the kitchen clock?"

He frowned. "Not that I remember."

Does he understand, I wondered, the significance of these details? Does he realize that he's just destroyed his son's alibi? At eight-thirty, Daylight Savings Time, Corinne and her kids had picked up Mark from Sherry's place; by eleven a.m. at the latest, Sherry was dead. Glen got up at seven-thirty, arrived at his father's house at nine-forty. That gave him plenty of time to make a detour to Sherry's house. I tried to remember what Glen had told me about that morning, his exact words. Something about not noticing the time, but that his Dad, who was a clock-watcher, had told the police that he'd arrived at his father's house at eight-forty. But if Glen had changed the time on the kitchen clock himself, he must have realized that his father, confused by the time change, had made a mistake.

"When you talked to the police—did they ask you whether you'd changed your clocks?"

"Yes indeed. And I told them." He nodded towards the clock on the mantelpiece.

"But you didn't tell them about the kitchen clock. You didn't mention that you were sitting in the kitchen, not the living room, when Glen arrived."

"They never asked," he protested. "I never thought of it."

Pretty sloppy work, Dikeakos, I thought. "What happened next—after Glen arrived?"

"I finished my breakfast, then came in here."

"What was Glen doing?"

"He did the dishes, took out the garbage. Or maybe that was the day he forgot the garbage—I can't remember!" He was suddenly angry that I should expect him to.

"And what were you doing?"

"Sitting. Here. I brought the paper in with me," he added loftily, gazing out the window.

"In other words, Glen was only here for fifty minutes."

His face started twitching again, his hands plucked at each other. Now what's bothering him, I wondered, and pressed the point home. "You told the police that Glen left here at ten-thirty."

Turtle-like, his head seemed to be shrinking into his

shoulders. "Woke me up when he slammed the door!" he blurted, indignantly.

Ah. I sat back and breathed a long sigh. So you fell asleep, you old bastard, I addressed him silently. You've no idea how long Glen was here.

"He always slams it," he appealed to me plaintively. "There's absolutely no need for it. I've told him time and again."

Presumably his confusion about the time was genuine—because if it wasn't, why admit to it now? If he'd lied once to protect his son, why not lie again?

I decided that he deserved a reprieve and offered to make him some tea or coffee. As if I'd lost status by the offer (or to make up for the humiliations inflicted upon him), he began ordering me around. "Make me tea," he demanded, like a tyrannical three-year-old. "And be sure you heat the pot. There's a tea egg in the drawer—I don't hold with bags. . . . " Finally, having successfully carried out his instructions, I returned to the living room with a tea tray: the pot, cups, milk and sugar. He sent me back into the kitchen for the proper sugar spoon and a package of biscuits. "O.K?" I asked caustically, preparing to sit down again. But no, we had to have plates for our biscuits.

After he'd been fortified with tea and I'd let him rave for a while about the stupidities of the new tax system, I guided the conversation back to his son. "I understand that both your boys played hockey. Glen told me that Brad was training to go professional."

He ruminated, chewing his biscuit. "It's a stupid game, if you ask me. Now soccer—" He lifted a reproving forefinger. "There's a sport. Takes skill, that does. But this hockey stuff is for louts." He said the word "louts" with damning contempt, and a distinct British accent.

"You didn't approve of them playing hockey."

"No." He clamped his mouth, decidedly.

"Where did they play, do you remember?"

"No." For some reason this subject had reduced him to monosyllables. Finally he added: "The wife drove them—I wouldn't. And then when they were old enough, they took the bus. Paid for it out of their own allowance too. That damped their enthusiasm a bit—with Glen, at least."

"But where's the nearest rink? Where did they go to skate?"

He stared out the window, masticating his biscuit.

"Did they go to the Albion," I suggested, "on Southeast Marine?"

He ignored me.

Why wouldn't he answer? After destroying his son's alibi, why would he balk at the name of a skating rink? "Have you ever heard of the Albion?"

His gaze turned upon me, like the cold glare of an eagle. "Of course I've heard of it. They tore it down years ago. But don't ask me if my boys ever skated there because I made it my business not to know where they went. If they wanted to play hockey, they did it on their own time, with their own money, and I didn't want to hear about it. That was the rule in our house—I would hear no talk of hockey."

And the rule still applied—he refused to discuss the matter further.

People are weird, I thought grumpily, as I climbed back into my car. I'm no hockey fan myself—but when Ben, at the age of eight, begged and pleaded to be allowed to play hockey, I got up at six in the morning to drive him to his practices. Fortunately, in Ben's case, the enthusiasm didn't last.

As I drove home I noticed I was feeling apprehensive, jumpy—and glancing at the speedometer I saw that I'd better slow down. I kept thinking of Glen, standing in his father's kitchen, looking up at the clock. He'd been on his way to the restaurant that morning so he must have had some awareness of time. . . . Perhaps he'd changed the time on the kitchen clock, intending to tell his father that he'd done so, but when he went into the living room he found his father asleep. Later that evening, when questioned by the police about his movements, he'd fudged the times and claimed he didn't remember . . . in the hope that his father would mistakenly provide him with an alibi?

Proof? No, not proof. When faced with a dead wife and two police interrogators, most suspects—even if innocent—would be tempted to take advantage of exonerating circumstances. But

202

I'd established one thing—that if Glen had arrived at his father's house at nine-forty, he'd had time to kill his wife.

Assuming, of course, that he knew where to find her.

As soon as I got home, I noticed that Ben had finally got around to washing the dishes. That was a relief—I don't take kindly to being turned into a nag. He was now sitting in the kitchen, slurping leftover spaghetti, a textbook propped on the table in front of him. As I sat down beside him, I accidentally kicked his foot and I wondered why he seemed to take up so much more space than he used to. Hadn't he stopped growing yet?

"Is that the tomato sauce you made last week?" I asked him. "Isn't it getting kind of old?"

"I froze it," Ben said, twirling more noodles around his fork.

I gave a small sigh—of weariness, satisfaction. Sometimes I can't figure out how I ended up with such competent children.

"Katie phoned," he said.

"Yeah?"

"She's coming over."

"Tonight?"

"To see me," he explained.

"Oh." I was surprised. I know that my children do talk to each other sometimes, but Katie still thinks of Ben as being light years younger than she is—an immature adolescent whose experiences can be automatically discounted.

"She talked to Tiara," Ben commented, still ostensibly reading his textbook.

"*Katie* talked to Tiara?" I was appalled. "About you?"

"They ran into each other at a party." His eyes moved up to the next page.

"Oh." Phew. For a moment I'd thought that Katie had sought out Tiara in order to remonstrate with her, an act that would have been, in my opinion, disastrously officious.

But I wouldn't have put it past Katie, who had been going through a particularly didactic phase of late. She's not happy, I thought. She hasn't been happy ever since she broke up with

203

that cyclist—whatever his name was. When Katie can't solve her own problems, she tries to run everyone else's life. Should I intercept her at the door and tell her to leave Ben alone?

I looked at Ben, who was inhaling noodles, his irises flickering back and forth across the text. He seemed to be doing pretty well, considering. He was moping, of course, and he wasn't talking much—but at least he was functioning. And if anyone was immune to Katie's didacticism, it was Ben, who'd been a captive audience to her lectures ever since he was a baby, when he lay helpless in his cot, kicking his heels at the ceiling.

So when Katie arrived, I left Ben to deal with her, and they disappeared into his room. About an hour later, Katie emerged and found me at the kitchen table, surrounded by a year's worth of receipts.

"Taxes?" she inquired.

I grunted.

She took the lid off the teapot and peered into it to see if there was any tea left. There wasn't.

"Make more," I suggested.

She put on the kettle. "How long are you going to let him stay here?"

I felt a twinge of guilt, as if I'd been accused of favoring one child over the other, although I don't think that Katie meant it that way. "I don't know. I haven't thought about it."

"I wouldn't let him hang about here too long. After all, he's a big boy now. And if he didn't have a mother—"

"He *does* have a mother," I said defensively.

"Yeah, but you don't want to baby him. He's been living in a bit of a dream world, I think. A little reality would be good for him, help him see things in perspective."

I was not impressed by this sudden altruistic interest in Ben. "I thought we mothers of today were being exhorted to raise a softer, more sensitive breed of men. A little less of this grin and bear it stuff."

"Well, I've got no patience with him," Katie said candidly. "I mean, why shouldn't Tiara sleep with whomever she likes?"

"Of course she can. It just happens that Ben's feelings got hurt in the process."

"Yes, but that's because his expectations were totally un-realistic. That's what I was telling him. What made him think she was only going to sleep with him? I mean—how possessive can you get?"

"In my experience," I said dryly, "most people are posses-sive."

"Especially men," Katie amended resentfully. She threw an-other tea bag into the pot, poured water over it, sat down across from me. "I've been reading this book—it's really good, Mum, you should read it. It's written by this woman—she's a sociol-ogy professor somewhere—and she says that women, if they want to make it in the business world or have careers or whatever, have got to stop squandering all their energy on men. She cites all these statistics and it's true—time after time, two people get married, and it's the woman's career that suffers, she's the one that makes the sacrifices, that raises the family, makes the lunches, stays home when the kid is sick, whatever. It's so unfair!"

I wondered what, if anything, this had to do with Ben. "The problem is," I suggested, "that many women do want to have children."

"Nonsense!" Katie snapped, and I was taken aback by her vehemence. "They *both* want to have children, but the man as-sumes that looking after them is his wife's problem. And nine times out of ten, she lets him get away with it."

"Yes, I suppose that's true." I was remembering that only three years ago I'd feared that this daughter of mine was going to marry at the age of nineteen, have three kids and move to sub-urbia.

"The woman drops her career, stays home and raises the kids for ten years, then her husband divorces her, the children grow up and there she is—left with nothing!"

She's talking about me! I thought, and was momentarily up-set. "And what does this book propose that women should do about it?"

"Forget children. And men."

I picked up the teapot and poured out some tea—but it was still too weak. I put the pot down again.

"If you want sex, she says, do like men do—look for short-term relationships, no strings attached. Or be a lesbian," Katie added. "Lesbians are much more successful in their careers than heterosexual women."

"Is that what you came to tell Ben? That this is the new face of womanhood and he'd better adjust to it?"

"Not exactly. But Tiara and I both agreed that it can be a big mistake to get tied down to one man. She's quite ambitious, you know. It was interesting, talking to her."

I reached for the teapot again but Katie, intercepting me, poured out a cup of tea for both of us. I submitted to being served, my hands in my lap. "Sometimes people fall in love?" I suggested. "Women and men, I mean."

Katie rolled her eyes and put down the teapot.

"That doesn't happen anymore?" I asked, exasperated.

"You're talking about lust, infatuation, hormones—"

"No, I'm not. I mean love!"

"But love doesn't last. Everyone knows that."

"Oh." I picked up my cup, and gave her a long, rebellious look over its rim. So much for my illusions. "You've finally converted to feminism?"

"No," Katie retorted.

We'd had this argument before. Katie seemed to think that the young women of her generation were going to achieve all the powers and privileges that men have, without upsetting the status quo or acquiring any labels in the process. And dreading the day when I'd get to say I told you so, I often attempted to alleviate her naivete.

"But the book you're recommending to me presents a feminist analysis. Feminists have been saying these things for years."

"It's statistics, Mum; she's just presenting the facts."

"Yes," I said gently, "but facts are not necessarily self-evident. Your grandmothers and their grandmothers struggled long and hard so that statistics like these could get published and read by young women like you. Even if you don't want to call yourself a feminist, remember that you're learning something from women who do."

Katie eyed me in silence—she preferred giving lectures to receiving them.

I changed the topic and asked her how her job search was going. But as Katie chattered on about her various options, I watched her, wistfully, thinking that the development of a human being is a truly extraordinary process, and that no experience of my life had been more interesting than motherhood. But I suppose Katie would tell me that a profession would have provided me with more long-term rewards.

Later that evening, I went over to Tom's place. We drank hot almond milk laced with brandy, went to bed, made love. But afterwards I couldn't sleep. Although my limbs felt like they were buried under sand, my muscles wouldn't relax, and the mood that had come upon me when talking to Katie returned. I remembered what a sweet two-year-old she'd been, dimpled and demure (although autocratic, even then), given to bestowing upon me sudden and passionate hugs. Now she was taking Business Management courses and had decided to become a cutthroat career woman. But shouldn't I be grateful that (unlike Vicky Fischer) she wasn't likely to marry a lecherous alcoholic? "Touch wood," I murmured, reaching for the headboard of the bed.

But I want her to be happy, I protested silently. Who says she isn't going to be happy? Without love? Without, I reproved myself, romance. She wasn't talking about love at all—she was talking about romance. And she's quite right, romance has probably done more damage to North American women than girdles and high heels combined.

Finally I wrapped myself around Tom's warm back, matched the rhythm of my breathing to his, and managed to get myself to sleep.

20

ON MONDAY MORNING, there was a message on my machine telling me to phone Nancy Lo at work.

"Lydia's new name is Aural."

"Oral?"

"As in aura." She spelled it. "And she works at the Whole Foods Store on West Broadway."

I phoned the Whole Foods Store, but Aural wasn't there. The man I talked to wouldn't give me her home phone number, but said that Aural would be in at ten-thirty—twenty minutes from now. I left my mail, unopened, on my desk, and returned to my car.

My entrance was heralded by a shimmering of chimes. The store smelled of sandalwood, and the few customers inside spoke in hushed voices, as if they were in church. The woman at the cash register had a sallow complexion and very long brown hair, which was tied in a loose knot halfway down her back. Her face seemed slightly askew (the right side didn't quite match the left), and she had big, shining brown eyes.

"Are you Aural?" I asked.

She nodded, gazing at me in anticipatory pleasure.

I introduced myself and, while I explained that I was trying to get in touch with her sister, she studied my card with an air of distress.

"Meg is short for Margaret?" she asked when I'd finished.

"Uh-huh."

"Did you choose that name?"

"No," I said warily. "My parents did."

"That's what I thought. It isn't you. It's not right at all."

"Perhaps not," I said, "but I'm getting good use out of it."

"But names are so important; they're like mantras. Your name is the symbol of who you are—isn't it?"

Fortunately, before I could answer, she was diverted by a customer who wanted to purchase some herbal skin conditioner and a bottle of kelp pills. Aural tried to talk her into buying dried seaweed instead of the pills because, as she explained, there was less processing involved and it would bring the woman closer to the real nutritive source. But the customer said that seaweed made her gag and finally Aural allowed her to pay for her purchases. When the customer had gone, I asked, "Do you know where Kasia is?"

"Oh sure," she said. "She was living in Toronto, but last year she moved back to the coast. She got a job in Squamish."

Squamish—yeah! A mere thirty miles up the coast. "Do you have her address?"

"I think so. I know I have her phone number. And she works for the Department of Fisheries, so you can always call her at work. She was so glad to get that job. It's secure, you know? And that's what she really needs right now." She nodded at me, as if I'd know how Kasia felt. "Here—I'll look it up."

She pulled a woven bag out from the under the counter, dug into it and found an address book, began thumbing through the pages. "You know, if you ever do start to feel that your name isn't quite right—isn't comfortable, you know? Oh, here it is." She put down the book, rooted through her bag again and pulled out a packet of business cards, selected one and wrote on the back of it. "Kasia . . . Farris." She printed her sister's name in big childish letters. "That's her married name. I've told her that it's not working for her. The wrong name can actually be a handicap—did you realize? I mean, think about those kids who get teased in school because of their name. Anyway. . . ." She added two phone numbers. "This bottom one is her work phone number." She handed me the card. I took it, turned it over. In lilac script, it read: "Aural Mist—Name Diviner." Then underneath, in pink quotation marks: "The right name can change your life."

"That's me," Aural explained, unnecessarily. "I also do numerology and birth charts. You'll find that my rates are quite reasonable. . . . " She gazed at me, blinking.

"Right," I said. "And thanks for the help."

"Oh, anytime," she assured me. "And I hope you and Kasia really connect—you know?"

"I hope so too," I said, enduring another sprinkle of chimes as I headed out the door.

But when I connected (technically speaking) with Kasia Farris on the telephone, she gave me the third degree. I called her at work, which might have been a mistake, because it took me a long time to persuade her to see me. She wanted a detailed explanation—who I was, who was employing me, who I was investigating, and why.

"His wife was murdered?"

"She wasn't living with him at the time; she'd left him about two months previously."

"Well, well," Kasia murmured. "And he's a suspect?"

I hesitated. "One of several."

She wanted to know how I'd got hold of her name. When I said that Glen had given it to me, there was an ominous silence.

"He told you to look for me?"

"In the course of a conversation with him, I asked him if he'd ever been involved in any other serious relationships, and he mentioned you. However, he didn't know where you were, and he didn't think I'd be able to find you."

Another silence, during which I could feel her debating. She knows something, I thought, but she doesn't want to talk to me. Finally she said: "Listen. I'll see you on one condition—that you never, ever let him know that you found me. Got that?"

I got it.

But she didn't want me to drive out to Squamish, and suggested that we meet that evening in a restaurant halfway, about ten miles past Horseshoe Bay.

"You go in first," she said, "and see if you can get us one of the tables in the back. Leave your name with the hostess and I'll join you in a few minutes. What kind of car do you drive?"

"A Datsun," I said. "Green, with rust spots and a dented front fender. But look—I'm in the business. I'll make sure I'm not followed if that's what you're worried about."

"You do that," she ordered. "Because if I find out that you're not alone, I'll turn right around and drive back home again."

After that I went over to Julio's and bought myself a cafe latte and a cinnamon bun, took them back to my office. I'd just finished the bun, and was licking the brown sugar off my fingertips, when there was a knock at my door.

"Come in," I called, crumpling up the wrapper and pitching it into the wastepaper basket. The door opened, and before I could renege on that invitation, Detective Dikeakos came striding into my office.

21

I STOOD UP. "Wait a—"

"We need to talk," he interrupted me.

"You mean you need to talk."

"You'll talk too if you know what's good for you."

"Threats, Detective Dikeakos?"

This gave him pause. We eyed each other, like boxers circling a ring.

Dikeakos seemed to have aged ten years in the last two weeks. The bruises under his eyes had spread, like ink blots, halfway down his cheeks; the skin around his jaw seemed to have loosened from the bone. "I'll charge you if I have to," he informed me, testily, "but I'm hoping that won't be necessary."

"With what?" I sneered.

"Interference?" Taking his time, he looked me over as if I were on an auction block. "We should be able to make that stick," he decided, when he'd finished his inspection. He appropriated the chair beside him. "Whose side are you on, anyway? Vicky Fischer's?"

"No." I sank back down behind my desk, my mind scrabbling, calculating probabilities. . . . Obviously they'd got hold of something. But what? "I don't work for her anymore."

He didn't believe me. "Then perhaps you'll tell me what you were doing at her house last Saturday night? Just a social evening, was it? You and . . . "

Ed! I thought. For God's sake—of course! They've had a tail on Ed! Why didn't I think of that?

". . . You fell out, perhaps? We noticed you left early. But Ed Jeffreys seems to—"

"Have you arrested him yet?" I interrupted sarcastically. "You finally got tired of chauffeuring him back and forth and decided to charge him with loitering or something?"

His bloodshot eyes drove like nails into my face. "He's under twenty-four hour arrest."

"He's what!" I'd been joking—but Dikeakos wasn't.

"Of course we've charged him!" Dikeakos exploded. "And you know why as well as I do! I understand that you've been sitting on this story for weeks!"

"You exaggerate," I informed him.

"He's saying that you've got a witness to that fight on Saturday night—"

"Oh." The fight. No wonder they'd arrested him. "Is that what you're talking about?"

"I'm talking about Dunbar's black eye—yes. You remember I've asked you about that before? And I'm talking about a man who claims he doesn't know the woman who got murdered in his basement, even though he's been sleeping with her sister for months! None of which, I understand, is news to you."

"But one hears so many things. . . . " I trailed off and looked at the jade tree that sits under my window, accumulating dust. "About so many people," I finished. "And *my* promotion doesn't depend on making arrests. This case isn't closed, Dikeakos—not by a long shot. You've focused all your attention on Ed Jeffreys just because he happens to be more conspicuous than some of the others."

"I knew we'd get to that," Dikeakos assured me acidly. "With your kind of people, we always do. So enlighten me, Ms. Bleeding Heart—who have we been neglecting?"

I hesitated for a moment, but I wanted to get back at him too much to be discreet. "All right." I sat back. "For example. It so happens that I went to see Mr. Hovey Senior yesterday afternoon and we figured out, between us, that when Glen showed up on the Sunday morning of his wife's death, Mr. Hovey was sitting at his kitchen table, and looking—not at his heirloom

213

living room clock, but at his *kitchen* clock. And guess what, Detective Dikeakos?"

He didn't want to guess.

"No one had changed the time on that clock. Daylight Savings—remember? Well, it happens that his kitchen clock hangs above the sink and old Mr. Hovey can't get up that high. So when Glen arrived Sunday morning, it wasn't eight-forty at all. It was—" I paused, triumphantly.

"Nine-forty." Dikeakos' face was dead pan.

"Good for you. And now I'll leave it up to you to find out who changed the time on that clock, and when. And why Glen decided not to say anything about it? Mm? A little project for you?"

Dikeakos' expression hadn't changed, but his fingertips were fluttering against his leg like the wings of a moth trapped inside a jar. "Give me another example."

"Sorry," I said—and I was. I shouldn't have told him that much. "But my generosity has its limits."

Dikeakos pushed back his chair and stood up.

I got up also, moved to the door and stood with my back to it. "Did Damayanthi Fernando come to see you?"

He stopped two feet away from me. "Yes."

"Sounds like Fred Dunbar knew Sherry, right?"

"Maybe. And Ed Jeffreys knew both of them."

"That's a crime?"

"We just want to talk to him," he explained soothingly (as if being interrogated under duress was like taking a spoonful of cough syrup).

He took a step towards me, expecting me to move out of his way. But I wasn't ready to let him leave.

"Those two murders are connected," I stated. "Even you must see that now. Dunbar knew something about Sherry's death, knew who killed her, probably. And he died the same way she did."

"Did he?" Dikeakos moved his face even closer to mine, so close that I could see the webbed capillaries in his eyes. "Dunbar was beat up, sure. But after he'd been . . . incapacitated, shall we say?—his murderer, kindly putting him out of his misery—"

Curving his nicotine-stained fingertips like talons, Dikeakos moved his hand menacingly up and under my chin, as if to encircle my neck. "Gave his trachea a good squeeze—" He suddenly snapped his fist shut and brought it to within half an inch of my nose so that I went cross-eyed looking at it. "And crushed his windpipe."

I swallowed, with difficulty, the saliva struggling to work its way down past every tracheal bump.

"Throttled," Dikeakos concluded, with satisfaction. *And—*" He removed his fist, smiled at me like an alligator. "His murderer wore gloves."

We stared into each other's eyes, as if we were connected by elastic bands stretched to the breaking point.

"Deliberate," he whispered. "Premeditated. Not like Sherry's murder at all. You see?"

I saw. He reached behind me for the doorknob; I stepped aside and let him out.

When he was gone, I stood there, staring into space, Irma Storey's voice coiling like smoke through my brain: ". . . beat to a pulp . . . discolored, covered with blood. . . . " Then I glanced at my watch. I grabbed my notebook, stuffed it into my bag, charged for the door—stopped—went back to the window and peered out between the slats of the venetian blind. The unmarked cop car was still in Julio's loading zone, its engine idling. As I watched, the driver finished speaking into his mike and Dikeakos lit a cigarette. The car slid away like a shark into the traffic.

Ten seconds later I was unlocking my car door. Fifteen seconds after that I was on my way to the airport.

Driving west along King Edward Avenue, I noticed I was feeling upset. What's bothering you? I asked myself as I joined a line-up of cars in the left-hand turn lane. Ed's arrest? A gap was coming up in the approaching traffic; the cars in front of me turned left. It just doesn't feel right, I answered, inching forward over the white line. The traffic light turned yellow. "Call it feminine intuition," I grumbled, hitting the gas pedal just as some punk in a TransAm accelerated through the intersection, leaning on his horn. He missed my right front fender by inches, and I

215

braked so fast that I almost gave myself whiplash. He waved as he went by. "Jerk!" I screamed after him and hastily completed my turn under the eye of the red light.

Flight Number 169 was late. I stood in front of the big green-tinted windows and stared out across the runways, watched the jets lumbering in and out of the sky like modern-day pterodactyls, the ground crews swarming around their wheels, ministering to their needs. Why, I wondered, did I tell Dikeakos about Glen's alibi rather than about Will Fischer's secret trip home? But if I'd told Dikeakos about Will, I realized, there'd be a posse of police detectives here at the airport to meet him and I'd never get a chance to talk to him myself. Of course Vicky might show up . . . I glanced around, uneasily. Had the cops told her that they'd arrested Ed?

Finally a massive Sky Pacific jet touched down, burning rubber on the runway, and I went back to the waiting area outside Customs. After an extended wait, the first passengers began appearing through the doors, greeting their friends and relatives. I hope he looks like he did in the photograph, I thought, my eyes leaping from one briefcase to the next and inspecting the faces to which they were attached. He did.

He had a breezy, disheveled style, pouches under his eyes and thinning ginger hair. He looked like the kind of guy who has lived hard and now, pushing forty, is beginning to pay the price. He was carrying a large suitcase, a shoulder bag and an attaché case.

I intercepted him. "Mr. Fischer?"

I introduced myself and suggested that he might be aware that I'd been working for his wife. "I'd like to ask you a few questions," I said. "It won't take more than fifteen minutes."

"Right now?" he objected. "Couldn't it wait a day? I'm dead tired and I'd like to get home to see my family."

"Hello, Will," Vicky said quietly, materializing beside us. She gave him a restrained hug, a kiss on the cheek. "Hello, Meg," she added. Her tone was cool but polite. Then she looked over her shoulder at Mark, who was standing about ten feet away from us, not wanting to be introduced.

"Here's your uncle Will," Vicky said to him. "You haven't seen him for a while, have you?"

"Hi there, Mark!" Will saluted him, and Mark took a step backwards.

Vicky turned to me again. "I'm sure you have nothing to say to Will that couldn't be said to both of us?"

I didn't share this assumption—but could tell that I wasn't being given a choice. "I guess not."

"Good," Vicky said.

"But don't blame me if you don't like what you hear," I warned.

Vicky turned back to me with an expression of forced amiability. "Then perhaps we should adjourn to the house. The kids will be home soon, and somehow I don't think this is quite the place. . . . " She glanced around at the rows of molded plastic seats, then smiled up at Will. "Tired?" He grimaced, but looked gallant, and handed her his shoulder bag.

"We'll meet you there," Vicky said, hefting the bag over her shoulder. Together they turned away.

Again, the scene was Vicky's living room. Will was sitting in the chair that Ed had occupied—drinking scotch on the rocks. Vicky was in the armchair nearest him, pouring me a cup of tea; Mark had been parked upstairs in front of the VCR. The other children were still at school.

I got down to business. "I'd like you to give me a description of your activities on the weekend of March 24th," I said to Will.

He glanced at Vicky as if asking her if she really wanted him to go through with this. Vicky, ignoring him, spooned sugar into her teacup.

Will took a sip of scotch, then sat back and smacked his lips. "Jeez—but it's good to be home, eh?" He looked around the room as if in search of an audience—but I was the only one attending. "The 24th, eh? That would be about two weeks ago? When I'm going back and forth like this I lose track of time.

Let's see." He put on his thinking face. When this failed to produce results, he reached into a pocket of his suit jacket and pulled out a daybook. He flipped back through the pages, stopped.

He couldn't act worth beans. He shut the book immediately, like a child who's just encountered a dirty picture in his textbook. "Yes, well. . . . " He cleared his throat.

Vicky was holding out her hand. "Give me that," she commanded, in tones of resignation.

"Honey, I. . . . " But he could think of no reason not to give it to her, and handed it over.

Vicky, her face impassive, flipped through the pages, found the relevant dates. "Apparently my husband was out of order that weekend," she commented, and chucked the book across the coffee table at me. It hit the armrest of the couch and I caught it on the rebound; together they waited while I, in turn, searched for the weekend of March 24th.

Will was a busy man. Almost every date in the month of March was annotated with names, times, and phone numbers. But March 24th and 25th were stroked out with a single line, as if they'd been eliminated from his life.

"So what does it mean?" Vicky addressed this question to the ornate light fixture in the center of the ceiling.

I closed the daybook, put it on the coffee table in front of me. "It means," I said, "that on the weekend of March 24th, Will made a trip to Vancouver, a trip that he didn't want anyone else to know about."

"What!" Vicky went white.

Will, who'd been inspecting the contents of his glass, looked up sharply. Vicky's fingers were clenched into the upholstery of her chair. "No!" she breathed. "No!" She started to get up, stopped—stared at her husband in horror. "You didn't!" she begged him. "No, you couldn't—"

Will was gaping at her. "What the hell?" He turned to me defiantly. "So? So yeah! I made a trip home." He appealed to Vicky. "I know I should have told you, honey, but I wasn't going to have time for visiting or anything; it was just one meeting after another, sign a few papers and get the hell out again. So I thought, why even tell them I'm here? They'll only get—"

Vicky made it onto her feet. "Where the hell did you *sleep!*" she screamed at him.

"I—I—"

I saw, in her hand, the solid glass ashtray that had been sitting on the coffee table and as her hand went back, I leapt up and grabbed her wrist. The ashtray flew sideways and plummeted to the carpet with an ominous thud. "Sit down!" I pushed her back into her armchair. Vicky collapsed, and huddled into the cushions.

"Mr. Fischer," I said, returning to the couch, "I'm still waiting for you to give me a description of your movements on the weekend of March 24th."

"I—" He was gazing, with what seemed to be genuine concern, at Vicky, who'd started trembling convulsively. "Like I say, I had these meetings. . . . "

I picked up my notebook and pen. "I want exact times, and I want the names and phone numbers of the people you were with."

"I can't give you that." He seemed dazed, but spoke with conviction. "Some of these meetings were absolutely confidential."

"Take your pick, Mr. Fischer. You either tell me, or the police."

"The police?" Then, finally, he figured it out. "You mean that's the—You think that I—Hey, Vicky." He leaned towards her beseechingly. "Come on, honey! You know I didn't have anything to do with that! Is that what you thought? Oh my God. . . . " He gazed at her mottled, frozen face, and I saw tears in his eyes. "Jesus, Vicky!" One of his ginger-haired hands reached across the living room in a gesture of entreaty—but Vicky made no reciprocal response. She continued to stare, as if she were seeing straight through him, into some hellhole beyond.

He turned to me again, noticed the pen and notebook. "But I can't—"

"This is a murder case, Mr. Fischer, and I need a verifiable alibi."

He stared at me for several seconds longer—then lowered

his head and accepted defeat. "I spent the weekend with a woman named Monica Sotheran," he admitted dully. "She's one of our sales reps." He glanced at his watch. "If you want to talk to her, she's probably at the office right now."

"The whole weekend?"

He nodded, glanced at Vicky. "There was a bit of a mix-up; she called me in Bangkok. . . . " Vicky's gaze was expressionless, implacable. "It was sort of an emergency," he mumbled, looking down at his shoes again.

"Phone her," I said.

"Now?"

"You have an extension phone, don't you?"

"Yes."

"I'll take the phone out there in the hall, you find another; phone this woman, tell her who I am and tell her that you want her to answer my questions truthfully. Then get off the phone, and I'll do the rest."

Again he looked at Vicky, as if still hoping, somehow, that she was going to get him out of it. When this appeal failed, he got up and disappeared into the kitchen. I took my notebook into the hall. I sat down at the desk in the little telephone alcove under the staircase.

He phoned. He spent a moment making obligatory small talk with the receptionist, then asked to speak to Monica. "Hi, Will," Monica answered, with obvious pleasure. "How are you?"

He told her he was fine—tired, of course—and then asked her, with what seemed rather pointed concern, how she was feeling. "Better," she answered. "Much better. This morning I almost managed to eat my breakfast. So?" She paused. "When am I going to see you?"

He sidestepped that one, explained that he was in a bit of fix and needed her assistance. He described the circumstances of his sister-in-law's death, and asked her if she'd please talk to the detective who was on the line and—

"She's listening—right now?" Monica was affronted.

"Yes, so if you'd. . . . Just tell her whatever it is she wants to know," he finished, in a rush. "Please. I'm sorry to drag you

220

into this, but. . . . I'll be in the office tomorrow—we can talk more then. O.K?" He hung up quickly before she had time to say no.

"Ms. Sotheran?" I began. And the rest was straightforward. After a minute of conversation, Monica Sotheran informed me, stiffly, that Will Fischer had spent the morning of Sunday, March 25th, beside her in bed; they got up around ten-thirty, then went out to the Bayshore for brunch.

As I hung up the phone I heard Vicky saying: "What do you mean—a mix-up? What kind of mix-up?"

I stopped in the living room doorway. Vicky appeared to have recovered from her shock, and was gearing up for a good, old-fashioned marital showdown.

". . . When Shannon was in the hospital for a week, you didn't think it necessary to come home. When my own sister got murdered, you suggested I go stay with your mother, for Chrissakes! Some comfort she'd be! But when dear little Monica gets upset about something, you'll fly all the way across the Pacific to comfort her? Isn't true love something?" Vicky finished, with grand sarcasm.

"It—it wasn't. . . . She was very upset and she was—uh—threatening me so I thought that I'd better—um—come back and d-deal with it."

"Threatening you with *what*?"

In spite of myself, I smiled. It's hard not to like a woman who shows spunk.

"Monica—um—she found out she was pregnant."

"She *what*?" Vicky's voice dropped to a reverberant stage whisper.

"And she—ah—" Will, like a little boy, was twisting his hands between his knees. "She doesn't believe in abortion, you see."

Vicky's face lifted; her mouth formed a perfect "Oh."

The front door opened behind me. "Daddy?" Vicky's second daughter, Tanya, was standing in the doorway. When she saw me, she frowned—I wasn't what she'd expected—but then she saw her father's suitcases parked in the hall. She looked back over her shoulder. "He's here!" she shrieked. There was a sud-

221

den commotion on the porch and then all three of their daughters burst in at once. Discarding a trail of lunch boxes, jackets and exercise books, they ran to where their father was sitting in the armchair. One climbed on the armrest, another into his lap, the third latched onto him from behind and hung around his neck. Laughing, he lavished hugs and kisses on them all, calling them his little princesses, trying to extricate himself from Tanya's stranglehold while Shannon jumped on his feet.

I looked at Vicky, and found her watching me. Without either of us saying anything, a communication passed between us—sympathy for the many victims of a marriage like this one.

"I'm going," I said to her.

She nodded.

Again I remembered Ed, and wondered if she knew about his arrest, but this was no time to bring it up. As I turned to leave, I noticed Mark. He was sitting halfway up the staircase that led to the second floor, his elbows on his knees, his chin in his hands. He looked like he'd been there for hours.

I hesitated, not sure whether to acknowledge someone who was so obviously excluding himself. "Good-bye, Mark."

"Bye," he answered indifferently.

In the living room the noisy reunion went on: one of his cousins squealed, another clamored for presents. "Presents?" Will expostulated, in what was obviously the ritual denial that led up to them.

Mark's eyes flickered sideways. I left him sitting there, listening intently.

22

WHEN I GOT BACK to my office, I found my mail, still un-opened, littered across my desk. I sat down, intending to deal with it, but ended up idly shuffling the envelopes through my fingers, thinking about the collective failures of monogamy, marriage and the nuclear family. I was remembering my own children, and the traumas they'd suffered when my husband and I divorced. It's ridiculous, I thought, to make the emotional and physical security of our children dependent upon the success of one sexual relationship. When that relationship fails, the children's support structure goes with it, and, like little spiders clinging to the strands of a broken web, they dangle in the breeze. What is it about this society that it can keep twenty-four-week-old fetuses alive, can transplant organs from one infant to another, but can't guarantee that its children will grow up in a secure environment, with adults capable of taking good care of them?

The telephone rang. It was Vicky. She'd finally heard about Ed's arrest; he'd called about five minutes after I'd left. She was understandably upset—but I'd had my fill of Vicky's problems that day, and wasn't feeling very understanding.

"You knew!" she upbraided me.

"I wanted to tell you," I defended myself, "but there was so much else happening. . . . "

There was a knock at my door. I covered the mouthpiece with my hand. "Hello?" I called. The door opened. Glen's head poked through the gap.

I stared at him—taken aback—and wondered if he'd somehow found out that I'd tattled on him to the police.

"May I come in?" he inquired archly.

I nodded and glanced at my watch. I needed to leave soon to meet Kasia Farris.

Vicky, unaware that I'd been interrupted, went on: ". . . I'm trying to bail him out but they haven't even set bail. And they're holding him without charging him—how can they do that?"

"They can only hold him for twenty-four hours," I said. "They're trying to get him to talk. They don't have enough evidence to charge him with anything, but they hope that by the end of the twenty-four hours, he'll have confessed to something."

She asked me for the names of some criminal lawyers, and while I read these out to her I watched Glen, who was sitting on my sofa, leafing through the newspaper that he'd found on the cushion beside him.

"Meg," Vicky asked when I'd finished, "haven't they got anything on anybody else?"

"Well—" I hardly wanted to go into it with Glen in the room. He was now deep in the business section and looked like he intended to be there for some time.

"I know you're not working for me anymore, but—do you think. . . . Are *you* getting anywhere?"

Was I? "Maybe," I said. "But I can't talk about it right now because I've got an appointment to meet someone. . . . " Again I looked at my watch. "But I'll keep you posted," I added, with finality, and hung up.

"Vicky?" Glen inquired, without taking his eyes off the newspaper. He turned the page.

"How did you guess?"

He lifted his eyes from the print. "I phoned her before I left work. She's looking for lawyers, right? Who is this guy anyway? What have they charged him with?"

I explained briefly that Ed was Sherry's upstairs neighbor and that the cops were holding him for questioning.

"Maybe they're finally getting somewhere. Why's Vicky so worked up about it?"

I didn't answer. He read the expression on my face. "Well, I didn't come to interrogate you. You've got your job, I've got mine." He closed the newspaper and threw it back down on the cushion beside him. "But how about putting our businesses on hold and going out for some supper? You doing anything tonight?"

"I—ah. . . . " I had absolutely no desire to eat supper with Glen Hovey, and thought the feeling should be mutual. Then I remembered our last talk, and his attempts to confide in me.

"You ever tried that Italian restaurant two blocks down from here? I've heard it's pretty good."

"I—um—No, I haven't." I finally recovered my powers of speech. "But unfortunately, I've already arranged to meet some-one tonight. Soon, in fact."

He shook his head, regretfully. "I knew you were a busy woman, but I thought you might take time out for supper."

"Yeah, well." I was putting on my jacket. "I don't keep what you'd call regular hours. I only eat when I run out of other things to do." Hearing myself, I squirmed—it was the sort of pretentious comment that one of Glen's friends might make. I turned off my desk lamp, he got up from the sofa. We started towards the door.

"Now that's a mistake," he admonished me. "People like you could put me out of business." He reached the door before me, closed his hand around the doorknob. "How about tomorrow then? Instead."

He continued to smile—but his arm blocked my exit. If I'd possessed hackles, he would have seen them, rising.

"Tomorrow? Sure. That'd be fun." Like hell it would, I thought.

He opened the door, allowed me to precede him through it. "Six?" he said.

"Sounds good." We exchanged insincere smiles. He sketched a wave, then set off down the sidewalk.

What brought you out of the woodwork? I wondered, watching his tailored shoulders as he strode away through the other pedestrians. The news about Ed? Or had his father briefed him about my visit yesterday afternoon?

I climbed into my car, pulled out into the traffic. I checked my rear-view mirror, drove clockwise around one block, counter-clockwise around another, checked the mirror again. Why, I asked myself, did you agree to have dinner with him? Out of guilt? Pity? A lone cyclist was coming up the side street behind me. The cyclist passed; I adjusted the mirror and encountered my reflection. (The lines etch deeper, the wrinkles accumulate, but that same old self stares out through my eyes, like a prisoner denied parole.) "You're not going out for dinner with Glen," I warned my reflection, "so you'd better come up with a good excuse—fast." Having delivered this ultimatum, I finally set off towards the Second Narrows Bridge.

I'd caught the tail end of rush hour and over the bridge, the cars were bumper to bumper. But once I'd passed the intersections into North Vancouver, the traffic cleared and I hit fifty miles an hour. I opened my window, drank in the smells of fir, broom and sun-baked granite. Toy freighters dotted the outer harbor below me (full of idle sailors who'd been waiting weeks for a berth); the city spread to the south like a vast cancerous growth, devouring the rich farmlands of the Fraser Delta beyond it, where the river branched like the veins in a big maple leaf. A jet plane floated down over the Pacific, a giant container ship was sliding up the Strait. Far away in the distance I could see the encircling rings of mountains and islands, like paper cutouts in a pop-up picture book.

When I was a child this highway didn't exist and the communities up Howe Sound could only be reached by boat. In the fifties they blasted the first section of the road out of the mountainside, and got as far as the ferry terminal at Horseshoe Bay. Now the Squamish Highway continues up the Sound, twisting and turning above the deep green inlet, affording spectacular views of the mountains which pile, island upon island, inlet after inlet, into the glaciered plateaus of the interior.

Too soon I reached the turnoff. As I pulled into the exit lane and circled under the causeway, I glanced once more into my rear-view mirror, but no one followed me down the hill. When I reached the water, I turned right and saw the restaurant.

There weren't many cars in the small parking lot beside it.

As I walked from my car to the restaurant entrance, I glanced around and pretended not to notice the Honda parked out on the street under a giant cedar tree, and the solitary figure sitting behind the wheel. I pulled open the restaurant door and went inside.

The decor was trite—old-fashioned nautical, bedecked with anchors and tillers, dimly lit by fake hurricane lamps. The hostess was a seventies-style champagne blonde, whose eyelashes were as improbable as the monster starfish glued to the hollow beam above my head. When I pointed out the table in the back corner beside the window, she gave me a big wink and said, "We reserve that one for adulterers." She led me to it.

I was still perusing the menu when I saw Kasia come in. In style, she was very different from her sister. Her short wavy hair was swept back off her ears; she wore a pale blue pantsuit with padded shoulders, and dress shoes with pointed toes. She had a brittle look, an aggressive thrust to her chin. She said something to the hostess, then walked directly across the restaurant towards me.

"I guess you're Meg Lacey." She sat down in the chair across from me.

Close up I could see the resemblance to her sister. But in Kasia's face, the features were more symmetrical and seemed to fit together better. "Thank you for coming all this way to see me."

She pulled out a package of cigarettes. "I got the impression it was important. Mind if I smoke?"

I did—but shook my head.

While she lit her cigarette I returned to my study of the menu, and decided upon the scallops and a salad. "Don't order the crab," Kasia said. "The fishermen around here sell them—but they won't eat them."

"How about the scallops?"

"They're probably just as bad."

A waitress appeared, and Kasia ordered a Caesar. "Aren't you going to eat something?" I asked. "This is on me."

"Thanks, but I'm not hungry. And I can't stay long. My kid's at a friend's house, but it's a school night so I don't want to get back too late."

"Share some nachos with me," I suggested.

"Well, maybe a couple."

Deciding not to risk the seafood, I ordered a beer, a plate of nachos and a salad.

"How old is your kid?" I asked, when the waitress had gone. Kasia took a long drag on her cigarette, looked out across the restaurant. "Seven." She blew smoke in the direction of the bar. "I'm a single parent. We left his Dad back in Toronto."

She was sitting sideways in her chair, minimizing our contact, and her manner was brusque, offhand. She was having trouble looking at me.

Finally she turned, made herself meet my eyes. "So you want to know what I know about Glen Hovey, right?" She took another drag on her cigarette. "See this?" She presented me with a view of her profile, patted the end of her straight, short nose. "This was his parting gift—the only one I kept. Not bad, eh? They could have just reset it, but Glen decided that I deserved the best that plastic surgery could produce. It's a lot straighter than the original."

I felt myself go still. There's knowing and there's knowing, and despite my premonitions, this blunt confirmation buried into my stomach like a meteor hitting Earth. Kasia went on. Like Coleridge's Ancient Mariner, she kept this story under pressure, bottled inside herself—and it spurted out of its own accord as soon as she took the cap off.

"And while I was lying in the hospital with my face plastered in bandages, Glen sat right by my bedside holding my hand, telling me how sorry he was, how beautiful I'd be, and how he'd make it up to me. He loved doing that," she added, acrimoniously. "In fact I finally realized that that was the whole point. Afterwards, he was so nice to me that I almost felt like it was worth it. He'd buy me flowers, earrings . . . he'd blow his entire paycheck. Every time I left, he'd come crawling, crying. Shit! I never knew a man could cry like that." Her mouth gave an ugly twist; she placed both elbows on the table and cupped her hands around her face, like visors. "First it was just a bruise or two, a black eye, a broken rib, then we got to a little internal hemorrhaging. . . . I tried to get away from him, but he'd comb the city to find me, he'd phone up all my friends. But that last time, when I was lying in the hospital bed with the taste of blood in my throat, looking at the plans for my pretty new nose, I couldn't feel anything anymore. He'd lost his hold on me. I'd finally realized that I was going to have to leave town, leave everyone I knew, my family, friends, job—everything. Because if I didn't, he'd kill me."

Our drinks arrived. Kasia sat back and stirred her Caesar, took a sip. She pulled out a second cigarette, lit it from the butt of the first. "I got to know the signs," she continued, stubbing the butt in the ashtray. "First he'd get grumpy—he wouldn't talk or if he did talk, he criticized me. Then he'd start working himself up. He'd get mad at me for anything, for having friends, for forgetting to buy the milk—it didn't matter what it was. I could see it coming—like a thunderstorm—and I'd try to get out of the apartment before it hit. But he was jealous. He never wanted me to go anywhere without him. Then, if I did get out, I had to make sure he couldn't find me. If I had enough money, I'd go to a motel. But usually I slept under a bush in a park."

The waitress set down a plate of nachos on the table in front of me; I rearranged the glasses and cutlery, moved the plate into the middle of the table. "Help yourself," I said. By now I didn't want them either, but knowing that I'd better put something in my stomach to counteract the beer, I selected a chip from the edge of the pile.

Kasia ignored the offer, and took another gulp of her drink. "I was living a double life. I went to work, Glen and I planned vacations, we had people over to dinner . . . and meanwhile, I kept an old sleeping bag and an overnight case hidden in an abandoned garage down the alley. I lived like that for nearly two years—until I finally understood that it was getting worse, not better. That he kept going one step further than the last time. As if he were daring himself."

"You never told anyone?"

She shook her head. "Now I would. But I was only nineteen, and back then I didn't know anything about this kind of stuff. I thought this was a unique situation and it never even oc-

229

curred to me that—well, that it was crime! When you're in a situation like that, it seems so personal. Like when he was mad at me, he'd list all my faults—and they *were* my faults, I knew it. So I'd start thinking, well, he's right. I *should* stop pigging out on potato chips before bedtime and I shouldn't leave my clothes all over the floor. I thought that if I stopped doing the things he didn't like, he'd stop hitting me. When you're in that situation, that's how you think. You've become part of it. You feel like you're responsible, you should be able to make it stop. It never occurred to me—ever—that I could go to the police."

"Or to a women's shelter."

She shook her head. "It's stupid, I know, but I didn't think of myself that way. If I even knew about women's shelters back then I would have thought: Oh yeah, those are for poor immigrant woman whose husbands get drunk and beat them up. I would never have thought of going there myself."

My salad was now in front of me. I stared down at the brown-edged curls of iceberg lettuce, the unripe tomato wedges, the orange salad dressing pooling onto the plate. I looked at Kasia again, and noticed that the light brown freckles that sprinkled her cheeks didn't span the bridge of her nose.

"One day," Kasia said, "instead of going to work, I went down to the bus depot and got on a bus to Edmonton. I had a business card from a lady I'd met once, a consultant who'd visited us at work—and she put me up for a week. I found a job, and ended up with a new boyfriend, who couldn't hit a badminton bird, let alone me. Turned out he couldn't support himself either. That's Jason's Dad. Anyway, we moved to Toronto and about eight years later, I bumped into one of my old friends in a movie line-up, and she told me that Glen was married. I'd been homesick ever since the day I left Vancouver, and I started thinking that now that Glen had a new punching bag, it might be safe to come home. A couple of years after that, when it became obvious that I was going to have to choose between feeding two mouths and feeding three, I finally found the courage to come back to the Coast."

Her eyes came to rest on the plate of nachos in the middle of the table; she seemed to see it for the first time.

"Have some," I said to her. "I can't eat them all."

She picked a chip from the top of the pile, nibbled it without enthusiasm.

I stabbed a tomato with my fork. "Would you be willing to tell this story to the police?"

Her gaze dropped to the tourist map that was reproduced on the plastic placemat in front of her. "I was wondering if you'd ask me that." With a forefinger she began tracing the lines on the map; she followed the dotted ferry route to Langdale, circled the Sechelt Peninsula, stopped at the fisherman who was trolling past Gibson's with a salmon twice the size of his boat dragging on his line. "You think I should, huh?"

I didn't answer. I was pretty sure that she could figure it out for herself.

"You think he killed her?" she asked, as if the subject were only of academic interest.

"You do."

She didn't deny it. Her finger moved down the inlet to Port Melon, returned up the other side to Gambier Island. "What was her name?"

"Sherry. They have a little boy. Fortunately, he was at a neighbor's house when she was killed."

The finger started stubbing out the ferries around Horseshoe Bay.

"He's four years old. He's living with Glen now."

"How did Glen—like how did she . . . ?" Kasia couldn't finish.

"He punched her until she fell over; she hit the back of her head on the kitchen counter as she went down." Kasia's eyes slowly lifted, as if pulled towards mine by magnetic force. "She died of a brain hemorrhage."

With a jerk her hand moved and covered the package of cigarettes beside her, as if to protect it.

"After he killed her," I said, "he carried her to bed, closed her eyes and tucked her under the blankets."

Kasia gripped the cigarette package; her facial muscles sagged. Abruptly she snatched up her napkin and covered her mouth as if she were going to be sick. "I'm sorry," she

231

whispered. She stuffed the cigarette package into her purse, got up and hurried away, walking heavily, on her heels, through the tables to the washroom.

I wondered whether I should follow her—but was sure she'd rather be alone. I picked at the plate of chips, pulling off the cheesiest bits, and poked at my salad. I stared out at the shoals of islands, at the mountains silhouetted against the darkening green sky. I felt curiously stranded. Nobody knows where I am, I thought. Then I realized that, by nobody, I meant Glen.

Now I felt nauseous too—as if a colony of tent caterpillars had taken up residence in my intestines. You see? I pointed out. A perfectly typical, textbook case. That's why, when you heard that Ed was arrested, you knew something was wrong. Not because you're blessed with intuitive powers, but because you've read the statistics. And that's why you decided to tell Dikeakos about Glen. Because Dikeakos knows those statistics just as well as you do.

Finally, after ten minutes had passed, I got up and followed Kasia to the washroom.

She wasn't touching up her makeup in front of the mirror, and both toilet cubicles were empty. I went back out into the hallway and saw that it led to a door labeled "Staff Only" with an Exit sign above it. I opened this door and found myself in a short corridor with more doors to the left and right, and some cement steps beyond them descending to an outside exit.

I went down the steps and pushed out the door. I was standing at the side of the restaurant, facing the street. I could smell seaweed and an unpleasant punky odor—the contribution from the pulp mill at the head of the inlet. Somewhere, frogs were chirruping and I could hear a stream, swollen with runoff, pummeling down a cliff face into the sea. A single streetlight highlighted the entrance to the parking lot; the triangular bulk of the cedar tree rose right in front of me, blending into the blackness of the mountainside behind it.

The Honda that had been parked underneath the tree was gone.

23

I WAS IN SIGHT of Vancouver again, its grid of streetlights below me, the red beacons of the airport twinkling on the horizon. Ahead, the Lion's Gate Bridge described a glittering parabola over the narrows, its farthest end quenched in the dark hump of Stanley Park.

I drove over the bridge and was funneled into the causeway that cuts through the park. Daffodils, bleached of color by the streetlights and buffeted relentlessly by the gusts of passing traffic, bloomed along the banks on either side of the road. After the roar of the causeway, downtown seemed strangely quiet, cars idling meditatively at the intersections, traffic lights blinking, people strolling along the sidewalks. I left downtown by way of the Cambie Street Bridge, then headed southeast into the untidy neighborhoods of Mount Pleasant. I drove slowly up St. Joseph Street and parked under the tree where I'd parked before, alongside a gutter choked with dirty white petals.

I turned off the engine and sat in the darkness looking at Fred Dunbar's house. I wasn't sure what I expected to accomplish by being here—except that this house knew things that I needed to know, and I was hoping to discover its secrets by some kind of proximate osmosis. I was in search of an essential link, and I had a piece that I knew must fit in somewhere, a homeless clue called Fred Dunbar, who floated around the fringes of this case, like a piece from some other jigsaw that had gotten into the wrong box by accident.

A dark brown youth, his black hair slicked into elaborate waves, slammed out the door of the concrete bunker-style home across the street. He climbed into one of the vehicles parked in the driveway, slammed the car door too (slamming doors was clearly an integral feature of his style), backed out onto St. Joseph and accelerated south towards 25th Avenue. An elderly Chinese couple shuffled past me on the sidewalk, the husband about three yards ahead of his wife, who carried two fat shopping bags which alternately dipped and grazed the sidewalk as she rocked from one foot to the other. A step-van rumbled past, a cat scampered under a hedge. The street was empty again, blue-tinted under the streetlights.

"...She said there'll be an estate sale...photographs all over his walls...who'll buy them?" Again, Irma Storey's words were drifting through my mind. But there was still no For Sale sign attached to the picket fence. Dunbar had probably died intestate, and the government would take its time settling his affairs. Photographs all over his walls.... Was it worth taking a look?

I drove around the corner and parked again, about two-thirds of the way down the block. I got out of the car and unlocked the trunk, dug into my tool chest and pulled out a screwdriver, a prybar, my Swiss army knife and a flashlight. I checked the batteries—which were still good—but found a package of new ones as well. I rummaged through the junk on my back seat until I found my navy blue track pants, my old black jacket with the big pockets, and dark grey rubber gloves. I deposited these articles on the front seat with the tools, glanced at my watch. It was still a bit early. I turned on the radio. I listened to the news, the sports, the marine weather forecast. Then I got a fifteen minute excerpt from some award-winning Canadian novel, and a concerto by Dvořák. At eleven, I managed an awkward change of clothes, pocketed the rubber gloves along with the tools, and went for a walk around the block.

When I turned the corner onto St. Joseph, I saw that the bunker-style house across the street was now in darkness, but in the living room of Irma Storey's cottage next door someone was still up, watching television. I strolled slowly past Dunbar's

234

house, noting its structural features and surmising the layout within, then turned into the lane.

Fortunately, there were few windows—none on the south side and only one upstairs—and all of them were curtained. Even so, I wouldn't be able to turn on any interior lights. Everyone in the neighborhood must know that a man had been murdered in this house, and glowing curtains would certainly attract notice.

I followed the path to the back door. This side of the house was in deep shadow; I almost tripped over something—it looked like an old car battery—that lay buried in the weeds. Dunbar's back yard consisted of a strip of wasteland about twenty feet wide in which he'd stored various pieces of junk: a rusted push mower, a pile of tires, a tattered goalie net, a heap of broken boards. His back neighbors had protected themselves from this sight by building a tall wooden fence between their lot and his, thus affording me good cover.

Obviously security was not Dunbar's number one priority. Around the side of the house I found a small frosted window and giving it an experimental prod, I discovered that the inside latch had snapped off. Standing on a tire, aided and abetted by my prybar, I jimmied the window open and squeezed through it into the house.

I landed in a bathtub, one of the old-fashioned kind with a curled rim and clawed feet. As I closed the window behind me, I was assailed by a smell: mildew, dog, drains—death? Whatever it was, I didn't like it. I turned on my flashlight, surveyed the peeling, murk-green walls, the round wash basin, the stained toilet bowl. Dunbar's electric razor was on the shelf beside his cup, his beard hairs were in the sink, his gnawed yellowed toothbrush dangled from its metal holder.

Overcoming an intense desire to leave, immediately, I climbed out of the bathtub and moved through the doorway into the blackness of the hall. Straight ahead was the living room, the front door was to my right, a narrow wooden staircase rose above me to my left. And grinning down at me from the walls were rows and rows of tiny faces, thousands of boys, stacked in neat formations on bleachers, bedecked in their team sweatshirts, barricaded behind their criss-crossed hockey sticks. As Irma Storey had said, the walls were literally papered with team photographs—from the waist-high wainscotting to the ceiling, around the hallway and up the stairs.

I stood there for some time, my flashlight picking out one photograph after another. I felt like I was standing in front of a memorial, paying tribute to generations of boys who had been gobbled up into adulthood. Finally, I crossed the hall and entered the living room.

It was a shabby, nondescript room containing a few well-worn pieces of furniture, a bouquet of team pennants wilting above the mantelpiece, a large television screen in the corner. Against the north wall of the room stood an old glass-fronted case, with framed photographs formally arrayed around it. In these photographs boys and men stood on podiums, on stages and under banners; they cut ribbons, accepted diplomas, exchanged handshakes and trophies. In the display case I found the trophies themselves: gold-plated cups, skates, hockey sticks, figurines frozen in mid-flight and mounted above engraved plaques: "Fred Dunbar, Coach of the Year," "The Tigers—Bantam All-Stars," "Consolation Playoffs—1957."

I returned to the hallway and as hundreds of little eyes followed my progress from the bleachers, I proceeded towards the kitchen at the back of the house. Here, instead of teams or trophies, the walls were decorated with action shots: bodies sprawled on the ice and driven against the boards, saves, shoots, scrimmages; blurred arms, legs and sticks. Apart from this documentation of drama and violence, Fred's kitchen was unrelievedly squalid. The tattered linoleum on the floor was smeared and encrusted with years of filth and what might well have been bloodstains; cobwebs draped from the ceiling, the stove was caked with grease. A bowl of water, littered with dust and dead insects, had been left out for the dog.

I retraced my steps and glanced into the closet (where Dunbar's coats and jackets still hung, smelling of Camel cigarettes), then followed the team photographs up the stairs.

There was only one room on the second floor, an attic bedroom with sloping ceilings. Being less suited, perhaps, to

Dunbar's style of wallpaper, these had been left bare. But on the vertical end wall above the head of the bed, Fred paid homage to the stars. He'd slept under a constellation of glossy, autographed faces: "To Fred, Best Wishes from Gordie Howe," "Regards from Bobby Hull," "All the Best, from Rocket Richard, Guy LaFleur, Gump Worsley, Jacques Plant, Frank Mahovlich. . . . "

As I returned down the stairs I decided to concentrate on the team photographs, in the hope that they would provide me with a complete visual record of all the boys that Dunbar had coached. I stood in the hallway and tried to figure out how they had been organized—by year, team, rink? But I could discover no logic of time or place in their arrangement. Black and white photographs were intermixed with color, hairstyles and fashions were jumbled. I figured there must be over a thousand photographs, and armed with a single flashlight (and two extra D-cell batteries), I'd come to study them all.

I worked methodically, stubbornly, one area at a time, left to right, top to bottom, one face after another, then on to the next photograph. From time to time, when I found a boy with a narrow face and dark hair who might have been Glen— maybe—I pulled out my knife and pried the thumbtacks out of the wall. On the backs of the photographs I sometimes found a list of names or a date, by means of which I managed to eliminate some of my suspects.

But it was a hopeless task. Although I'd commandeered a chair from the kitchen, within fifteen minutes I had a crick in my neck and my eyes ached from straining to decipher the minuscule features captured in my spotlight. By the end of the first half hour, the flashlight was noticeably dimmer. At twelve-fifteen I replaced the batteries. Half an hour later, I found Ed.

But finding Ed was easy—and did not reassure me. One black face among all those white ones, one bony-looking boy with prominent cheekbones. Nevertheless, I took the photograph off the wall, and glanced at the back of it. "The Albion Astronauts 1975," someone had penciled.

This is futile, I thought. My new batteries were fading fast; I was tired, I had a headache. Think again, Meg, I said to myself, as I carried the chair into the kitchen.

Then, as I was about to climb back into the bathtub, something occurred to me. I returned to the living room, stood in front of the trophy case and surveyed the framed photographs that were mounted on the wall around it. After inspecting them all, I selected a photograph of a tall, brown-haired boy with a lopsided grin. He was standing on a podium with two other men (one of them Dunbar), clutching a gold cup to his chest. I know that grin, I said to myself, and opened my knife.

My hands were sticky; I felt jittery, overcharged, like an engine going too fast in first gear. I cut off the back paper and lo and behold, someone had made my job easy. "Brad Hovey," they'd printed, "Best Player—1961." Carefully, I separated the photograph from the matte-board and replaced the empty frame on the wall.

So far, so good. With renewed hope I returned to the hall, identified the row where I'd left off, and continued my search. About ten minutes later I spotted Brad Hovey again—in a photograph that was high above my head, under the sloping ceiling where the stairs turned the corner. He was a little younger this time, beaming at the camera and looking more than ever like his nephew, who'd inherited his crooked smile.

I went back to the kitchen and retrieved my chair, carried it up the stairs—but then couldn't figure out how to balance it on the narrow staircase. Finally, by shoving the chair into the corner and getting three of its legs onto one step, I managed to climb up onto the chair seat and reach the photograph. But as I was prizing up the last thumbtack, it popped out of the wall; my weight lurched—and the chair fell out from under me. Fortunately I managed to land approximately upright. I banged my elbow, bruised my hip, staggered and clutched the banisters. The photograph came drifting down after me, grazing my neck like an affectionate autumn leaf. The chair clattered down the uncarpeted staircase, hit the wall at the bottom, and a dog started to bark.

The dog wasn't far away. In fact, within seconds, the high-pitched yapping was right outside the front door, and I could hear toenails scrabbling on the porch. I switched off my flashlight. Hide? Or attempt to escape from the house? But if the dog heard me climbing through the bathroom window, it would surely run around the side and catch me coming out. I finally headed upstairs—away from the noise. I crouched under the front window in Fred Dunbar's bedroom.

"Yap-yap. Yap-yap-yap-yap-yap. . . ." From somewhere down the street another, larger dog took up the alarm and then a man yelled, "Shad-dup!" and the distant dog was silenced. But the frantic yapping coming from the porch right below me sounded louder than ever.

A door latch clicked across the street. "Rocket?" The voice was querulous, inquiring. "Rocket—what are you up to?" I closed my eyes and crossed my fingers—and indeed, Rocket stopped barking for all of three seconds, gave an expressive whimper, then started up again with renewed vehemence, barking without surcease, and seemingly without breath.

How long can it keep it up? I wondered in despair. I felt like such a fool, as if I'd been caught doing something embarrassing and childish—like snitching a lick of icing from the edge of someone else's piece of birthday cake. Finally, when nothing seemed to happen for a very long time—nothing, that is, except for Rocket's incessant barking—I moved to the window, shifted the curtain fractionally aside and peered out. Irma Storey was descending her front steps with her coat pulled over her dressing gown and a leash in her hand. Hastily, I dropped the curtain and sank back onto my haunches.

"Rocket!" Irma demanded, when she reached her front gate. "You get back here this minute!" Again Rocket paused, and I could imagine him, intrepid and feisty little investigator that he was, making the headlines in tomorrow's newspaper. "Dog Apprehends Intruder," with a picture of Rocket, his beady eyes gleaming, his tongue hanging out. Now he began barking more furiously than ever, running back and forth across the porch (to judge by the sounds of his toenails), getting increasingly excited as his mistress approached.

"What on earth has gotten into you?" Irma Storey wondered aloud, as she started up Dunbar's front sidewalk. "I shan't let you out alone again if you can't behave yourself. Stop that now!" she commanded, as Rocket retorted with more frenzied whines and a new bout of yapping. "Did you hear something—is that it?" There was a silence, during which I could imagine her, standing on the sidewalk and surveying the front of the house, inspecting each window in turn. She's a courageous old woman, I remembered grudgingly. Next she'll decide to have a look round the back just to make sure, and she'll find the tire outside the bathroom window. Then Rocket renewed his barking, and was echoed, once again, by the larger dog down the street.

"That's quite enough! You'll have the whole neighborhood awake!" And to my immeasurable relief I heard hard-heeled thumps on the porch, the click of the leash as it was attached to Rocket's collar. Footsteps and clicking toenails descended the steps and receded along Dunbar's sidewalk. After a short wait I heard Irma's gate squeak and then the solid, secure sound of a front door being locked.

Silence. It was as palpable, as delicious as a mouthful of icy water. I continued squatting under the window, inhaling great gulps of it, and feeling it pass through my system like Valium. Finally, remembering the photograph that had caused all this commotion, I switched on my flashlight and directed the beam down at it. Brad Hovey stared up at me from the middle of the back row, looking like he figured he was somebody important.

Turning the photograph over, I discovered that it had been autographed by the team members themselves. Some names were written, others printed, they sloped uphill, and down. My eyes scanned those that were easiest to read and they fell upon a row of small, printed capitals: "Glen Hovey."

My heart hit the ceiling. But that's Brad, I protested—not Glen! I turned the picture over again and stared in confusion at the brown-haired boy in the back row, who stood as Glen would never have stood: chin tucked, chest stuck out, as if waiting for someone to pin a medal upon it. I continued reading the list of names. In the middle of the second column, in an almost illegible scrawl, I found the name I'd expected to find: "Brad Hovey."

There! I was right. But my eyes returned to that line of carefully printed capitals. . . . I glanced at photograph again, scanned the rows—bright faces scoured pink by the cold air of the ice rink. I tried to envisage those faces as they might look now, thinned down or jowled, transformed by wrinkles and beards. Could Glen have been absent on the day they took the photo? I counted the players, then the names on the back. I was short of names, not players. I had only sixteen boys to choose from, but it took me at least five minutes to find him.

It was the eyes that finally gave him away. At the right end of the bottom row was a pudgy boy who had splotchy cheeks, over-large hands splayed on his kneepads, and sunken, haunted eyes—the kind of eyes you see looking up at you from the trenches of World War I. But without that neatly printed name on the back, I would never have recognized him.

I parked in front of my house, ran up the steps. Although it was two in the morning, the living room lights were on and the front door was unlocked. I bolted it behind me. "Ben?" I called tentatively. He answered from the kitchen, "Yeah?"

He was not alone. Ben and Aziz were seated on either side of the kitchen table, a chess board between them, various white and black players distributed over its surface.

"Hi," I said.

Ben grunted, not taking his eyes off the board; Aziz gave me a smile. There were empty glasses on the table, dirty plates in the kitchen sink. A loaf of bread was sitting out on the breadboard, unwrapped, beside an open jar of peanut butter and a crumpled potato chip bag. "Who's winning?" I asked.

"I am." Aziz looked up at me again; it was Ben's turn to play. "But he won the last game."

Ben's lips were pursed, his hand hovered over a white knight. And where is Tiara? I wanted to ask. Was this how they were working it out—by competing at chess?

Ben finally moved his knight, shifted position, stretched.

"How are your exams going?" I asked him.

"Pretty good. I had two today, and the next one's not till Friday."

I went to the counter, wrapped up the loaf of bread and

threw out the empty bag of potato chips. "Leave it, Mum—I'll do it," Ben called over to me, irritated.

The lid of the peanut butter jar was in my hand—I placed it back on the counter where I'd found it. "Well," I yawned, "I'm off to bed."

"You won't get out of it that way," Ben threatened. I glanced at him and saw that he was addressing Aziz, whose eyes were on his bishop.

"Just looking," Aziz informed him. Their eyes met.

I left them to it.

But as I drifted at the edge of sleep I found myself driving the Squamish Highway again, as if the curves of the road had become etched into the underside of my eyelids. And at every corner I encountered formations of boys ranked up the mountainsides, smiling, smiling... determinedly denying Dunbar's vituperative whispers and the belt that hung behind the kitchen door at home, ready to weal their bottoms if they shamed their fathers and missed the puck. "Hey, Meg," I muttered, adjusting my pillow and rolling over, "it's just a game—remember?" Sure, I remembered. When I used to go to those practices with Ben, there was one father in particular who hung over the boards yelling, "Smash the buggers! Give it to him!" and who cuffed his kid's ear every time the boy came stumbling off the ice.

At six I was awake again, my headache grating against my skull, my curtains luminous with sunshine. I buried my head under the blankets. But now, instead of the highway, I saw Glen hunched at the end of the front row beside his teammates, gazing up at me with hollowed eyes. And I remembered him saying: "...it's like I see Sherry again, staring at me...it's like I'm being haunted, eh?"

My eyelids opened. I too had been visited by Sherry's troubled spirit, and I knew I wouldn't sleep again until I'd avenged her.

24

To my surprise Ben was up before me, sitting at the kitchen table and contemplating the chess board. His hair was tousled, a glass of milk was on the table beside him.

"You're still playing?" I greeted him. "Didn't you go to bed?"

"I woke up." He stared at the chess pieces, gnawing at the edge of his thumbnail. Feeling my gaze, he glanced up. "See— this is how it was." He gestured at the chess board. "And I thought I had him. I should have had him." He frowned. "But then he did this—" He put his hand on a black bishop, slid it diagonally across the board, "and I did this. . . ." He started to move a white castle, stopped. "That's it! God damn! What a stupid—" He broke off, scratched his head, took a large swallow of milk. "See, I should have come round him with this pawn— here—and then moved the castle here, and then I'd. . . . No, that doesn't work. But if I'd—"

"Ben," I said gently.

"Huh?" He looked up, perfunctorily.

"What happened about Tiara?"

"Oh," he said. He had his finger on a black pawn. "She went to the Caribbean. Her Mum took her off on one of those love boat cruises." He lifted the black pawn, jumped a white knight and removed it from the board. "In fact, I meant to tell you. I'm going to move back into the apartment today."

"Oh good," I said—then realized that I'd been tactless. Ben didn't seem to notice. "What happens when Tiara comes back?"

"Well." He shrugged. "Like Aziz says, 'We've been done.' "

"Done?"

"Yeah. She's a tourist—you know? And we've been done."

"She's finished with Aziz, as well?"

Ben looked uncomfortable. "He says it's mutual."

I studied him in silence. "So now you and Aziz are being friends again?"

Another shrug. "Sort of. Yeah. I guess."

I guess. Relationships, I thought, grow old just like bodies do, acquiring scars and tumors (that may or may not prove malignant), and old wounds that throb when certain memories are touched upon.

I went back to my bedroom and got dressed, downed a few painkillers for my headache. I put my purloined hockey photographs into an envelope and packed up my bathing suit, towel and shampoo. Since it was still too early to go to work, I planned to catch the Early Bird Swim at Britannia Pool.

I returned to the kitchen where Ben was now eating a bowl of cereal, and reading the newspaper comics. As I reached over the counter to dig some quarters out of my change jar, the corner of my jacket grazed a smear of peanut butter that was on the edge of the bread board. I gazed at it for a moment, then picked up the dishcloth and removed the offending smear.

"Ben," I said, rinsing out the dishcloth, "I've been thinking that I should move." I hung up the dishcloth, then turned around and faced him.

"Mm?" He wasn't paying attention.

"Now that I don't need three bedrooms anymore."

He continued reading.

"Ben?"

"Good idea," he agreed, with his mouth full of cornflakes.

"So I want you and Katie to start going through all your stuff—because I won't have the space to store it anymore."

"It's mostly junk," he said. "Just throw it out."

"No. You throw it out."

"O.K.," he said good-naturedly, and finally looked up. "When?"

244

"I don't know. I'll have to find somewhere to move to first. That might take a while."

"Why don't you get one of those condominiums with a swimming pool and a rec center and all that stuff? That'd be neat."

"I think that's out of my price range."

"Yeah. Probably." His eyes returned to the comics.

Now what brought that on? I wondered as I walked out to my car. What happened to your attachment to history? Or were you just testing out the idea, hoping Ben would protest? But in my mind I was picturing a gracious, airy apartment—something close to my office—or near Tom's place? I considered. It would be kind of nice to be able to just walk back and forth. I'd hold a big yard sale and get rid of everything I didn't like; I'd start with bare empty rooms and furnish them very gradually, refusing to acquire anything that wasn't aesthetic as well as functional. It would be a home all my own—it would inaugurate a new era of my life.

The city streets were hazing over with green. The early morning sun sloped over the silhouette of the North Shore mountains, the downtown office towers steamed in the mist that had crept off the sea in the night. In the park beside the pool, the tennis players were thwacking their balls across the nets, and a cluster of elderly women were practicing Tai Chi under the basketball hoop.

I left my envelope in the safe-keeping of the cashier and stashed my clothes into a locker in the dressing room. I ducked in and out of the shower, walked out onto the pool deck and dove into the long, empty blue swimming lane.

I don't think I've ever enjoyed a swim more. Theoretically, I go swimming two times a week; in practice, I'm lucky if I get to the pool at all. I've noticed that the less I exercise, the more I appreciate it when I do. The water bubbled over my limbs, massaged my eyelids and scalp, succored and supported me. I swam thirty lengths, then drowsed on my back. I climbed out, had a sauna, showered, washed my hair, put on clean clothes. Then I retrieved my envelope and strode back out into the morning.

By now the co-op bakery on Venables was open so I

detoured in that direction, bought myself a cup of politically correct coffee and a scone which beat anything my mother used to bake—hot out of the oven and oozing with blueberries. But as I drove up to my office exhaustion reclaimed me; my eyes, irritated by the chlorine, felt scratched and swollen. I went into my office, where the red light on my answering machine was glowing, insistently. But I phoned Dikeakos first.

He wasn't at the station. The receptionist told me that she expected him in any time now, and I asked her to tell him to call me, stressing that it was urgent.

The first message on my machine was from Vicky. "They've let him go. They didn't charge him with anything. Call me as soon as you get in."

Not enough evidence, I thought. I wondered whether my tip about Glen's alibi had helped secure Ed's release.

Glen's voice came next—too close for comfort. "Sorry, Meg, but I have to cancel the dinner date. Childcare problems. Call me at work."

Thank God, I thought. I couldn't have made it through another meal with Glen. I would have spent it evading his gaze, mesmerized by the sight of his long square-tipped fingers toying with the silverware.

Tom's voice succeeded his—such a safe, familiar sound. He'd been invited to stay at a friend's cabin on Hornby Island this weekend and wanted to know if I'd like to come along. I did a swift calculation; it was only Tuesday—for sure I'd have this case wrapped up by the end of the week.

I phoned him first. It sounded just the ticket. A waterfront cabin on a bay full of oysters, a spit of white sand, grassy walks along the ocean bluffs. "Rain or shine," I implored. "Let's go. I'll even cook."

"*I'm* cooking," Tom objected. "I've got the menus all planned."

Oh. "Then I guess I'll wash the dishes," I offered, less enthusiastically. Once upon a time I'd done all the cooking, and Tom had washed the dishes. But nowadays it was always the other way round. The time had come to renegotiate.

246

After that I phoned Vicky. First we discussed Ed, who, Vicky said, was "right on the edge. I'm afraid he's going to do something desperate, quit his job—maybe go into hiding or something. I'm going over to see him this evening." There was a pause, and then, answering my unspoken question, she added: "I've told Will. I mean, if I have to hear all about Monica's anemia and digestive disorders, he can hear about Ed's problems too. Why let him go on thinking he's the only one with a sex life?"

Another pause. When I failed to come up with a response, she went on: "I've decided that if Monica wants him, she can have him—as long as I get a good chunk of child support and enough money to live on for the rest of my life. He can afford it. I know exactly what he's worth; he's been sheltering his assets under my name for years."

I finally summoned up enough energy to change the topic. "How's Mark doing? Glen mentioned something about child-care problems?"

"Well. He's surviving, I guess. He's not here today. Glen says he's got some kind of flu or something so he kept him home. Which is probably just as well. Mark is going through a difficult stage right now and I'm not sure how to deal with it. Yesterday about an hour after you left, he stole a knife out of the kitchen drawer, went into Shannon's room and stabbed her favorite doll full of holes. We were all so shocked—I've never known him to do anything like that before. But maybe this is a normal reaction, I don't know. I'd like to get him checked out by child psychiatrist, but I don't think Glen would like the idea. What do you think?"

I thought too many things—and didn't answer the question. "Glen is at home with him?"

"Yeah. Apparently he's got a fever and Glen was worried it was something infectious. I said, 'My kids are at school, and I'm sure he's no more infectious than half their classmates.' But Mark wants to stay in his own room, his own bed—and if that's what he wants, that's probably what he needs."

But Glen told me to call him at work, I thought. Had he

finally found a housekeeper? Then I remembered that this was Tuesday—the day Teresa Minero came to clean his house. Would he have asked her to look after Mark?

After I'd finished talking to Vicky, I debated for a minute or two, then, stoically ignoring the fermenting feeling in my stomach, I called Glen at work. Sure enough, he was there. "How's it going?" he greeted me.

"Well enough," I said.

"Have they charged that guy yet?"

I hesitated. "I haven't heard. Vicky tells me that you've got a sick kid on your hands."

"Yeah. Poor little guy. That's why I canceled—sorry about that."

"Who's looking after him? Have you found a housekeeper yet?"

"No—but there's a teenager down the street. She's taken care of him a couple of times. She's great. Plays games with him, reads to him; she's a real gem."

"Well, I hope he gets better soon."

"It's just a bug. He'll probably be over it by tomorrow. Maybe later this week, we'll make up that dinner date."

"Maybe," I said.

I put down the receiver and then sat there, looking at it. I knew exactly what was bothering me. I looked down at my notebook, where Glen's home phone number was written right under the number for his restaurant. I lifted a finger, dialed again.

I got an answering machine. "This is Glen Hovey speaking. I'm not available to take your call right now but if you...." I hung up.

So? He'd told the babysitter not to answer the phone. His answering machine could take messages as well as she could.

Again I tried Dikeakos. This time the receptionist told me that he was out on a case, but that she'd make sure he got my message just as soon as he called in. "What about Detective Baker?" I asked. But Detective Baker was away at a conference.

The painkillers were wearing off; my stomach bubbled and

seethed like a bread dough sponge. Lack of sleep. Anxiety. What was I going to do—sit around waiting for Dikeakos to call? If he was out on a case, he might not be back for hours.

I left the office, went next door and bought a cheese sandwich from Julio. Then I drove up to the credit union on the corner and locked the envelope containing the Hovey brothers' hockey photographs into my safety deposit box. There. That felt better.

As I continued across town I ate my cheese sandwich, which helped settle my stomach. I stopped in at a toy store on Broadway, bought a sticker book that contained all sorts of bright-colored stickers: furry insects, glittering rainbows, flowers, boats. (If Mark didn't want it, I'd give it to my niece, who would.) I drove south and turned onto the quiet, winding street where Glen lived.

The driveway beside his house was empty, the garage door was closed, the venetian blinds in the front windows were shaded. I pulled up at the curb in front of the house.

Armed with my sticker book, I walked up the front sidewalk. I mounted the stone steps, stared at the push-button combination lock above the doorknob. Hm. I rang the doorbell.

Nothing happened. I rang it again—held the button; I could hear the buzzer droning away inside the house. But no one came. Was this the latest security strategy for babysitters? I leaned over the porch railing and inspected the shaded windows. Each window was secured with an inside lock, each pane of glass was marked with a neat foil strip. I listened for a long time. No voices, no footsteps, no clatter of dishes from the kitchen.

I glanced up and down the street. The neighborhood seemed deserted. The men were out making money; maybe the women were out making money too—either that, or they were in the malls, supervising its expenditure. A gardener's truck was parked in front of a house half a block down, and I could hear the high-pitched whine of a weed-eater coming from that direction.

I walked around the house to the back where two old apple trees were just coming into blossom and white sprays of spiraea arched over the path that led to the porch. I mounted the steps and knocked on the back door, where another panel of numbers was mounted above the doorknob. No answer.

Again the windows were locked and protected with strips of foil; the French doors that led out onto the patio were similarly secured. The basement windows were barred, the basement door was bolted from the inside. Glen, unlike Dunbar, protected his possessions; keyless combination locks are pick-proof—they pose a challenge to any pro. And when it comes to B & E jobs, I'm a rank amateur.

But we amateurs have other resources—like cunning and charm. I went back to my car and drove around until I found a pay phone. First I dialed Dikeakos (who was still out on his case), then rooted through my notebook until I found Teresa Minero's phone number. She was home.

I explained that I was a friend of Glen Hovey's, and that he'd recommended her to me. I said I was looking for someone to come in and do the heavy cleaning in my house on a regular basis.

"Moment, please," she said.

"Hello?" This was a different voice—one I'd heard before in my attempts to talk to Teresa. "I'm sorry. Teresa cannot speak English very well and she has difficulty on the telephone. She asks me to translate for her. Can I help you?"

Again I explained, and waited while my explanation was repeated to Teresa in Spanish.

"She asks how much work you have. She is pretty busy right now."

I said one day a week would be ideal—though I'd settle for less. Preferably Tuesdays. Again, I waited.

"No, sorry, Tuesday is not possible. Teresa already works on Tuesdays."

"But she's not working today," I pointed out, feeling like the kind of pushy employer Teresa would do well to avoid.

"No, because this morning the employer calls to say don't come today. But Tuesday is his regular day. Teresa says maybe Saturday is possible."

I explained that Saturday was not good for me. I said I'd think about it some more and call her back.

After I'd hung up, I continued to stand in the phone booth, staring at the well-dressed shoppers who passed by on the sidewalk. This was Kerrisdale, a neighborhood of established money, British bakeries and fashion stores for genteel ladies.

Where was Mark? If he was sick, the babysitter wouldn't have taken him out of the house. After a few more minutes of contemplation, I turned back to the telephone and dialed Vicky's number.

She too was home. "Are you alone?" I asked her.

"Yes. Why?"

"Because I don't want anyone to know about this phone call. As soon as it's over, you must forget that it happened. O.K?"

"But—"

"O.K?"

"All right," she grumbled.

"Now listen. Glen told you he was staying home with Mark today, right?"

"Yes."

"But he's not at home. He's at work. And he tells me he's hired a teenager from down the street to look after Mark. Have you ever heard him mention this teenage babysitter before?"

"No." She sounded puzzled.

"Can you think of anyone else who might be looking after Mark today? How about your mother?"

"Mum works today."

"Who else?"

"But—but why wouldn't he ask me? I don't get it! Isn't Mark at home?"

"I don't think so."

"Then where is he?"

"That's what I'm trying to find out."

"Well why don't you just ask—"

"No," I said, sharply. "Absolutely not. And you won't either—understand?"

251

"But this is—"

"Vicky," I interrupted her. "You wanted to know if I was getting anywhere—remember? The answer is yes. But I can't tell you what's going on because the information I have is dangerous to the person who has it. Now please—can you think of anyone else who might be looking after Mark?"

There was a pause. "Well, there's that real estate lady," Vicky began doubtfully. "Although she works. And I don't think Mark has seen her for months. But she did look after him once or twice before."

Right. I'd met her. She was the one who thought Mark would grow up twisted because he still wet his bed. Her number should be in my notebook somewhere. I started flipping back through the pages. "O.K.," I said. I'd found her name and number. "Anyone else?"

"Let me think." She thought. "Doesn't he have that cleaning lady?"

"I've already talked to her. No dice."

She had no other suggestions to offer. I reminded her again that this phone call had not taken place. She said she understood. I sure hoped so.

The real estate agent was not in her office; however she had been in all morning and was expected back shortly. Would I like to leave a message? I said not.

I went back to my car. By now it was early afternoon and the streets were heating up; high clouds were seeping over the mountains from the north, and the air was muggy. I felt muggy myself, and my headache was getting steadily worse. What do I do now? I asked myself, swallowing more painkillers.

He'd told Teresa not to come. Why? Because Teresa's presence in the house might make Mark and his babysitter uncomfortable? But Mark and his babysitter didn't seem to be there. Perhaps Glen had taken Mark to the babysitter's house, but in that case, why cancel Teresa? And why use a teenager rather than Vicky? "What I need," I said to myself, "is to get into that house."

I remembered, then, that the last time I'd tried to talk to

Teresa Minero, Sherry was still alive. Now that she was dead. . . . That might make a difference? I decided that it was worth a try, certainly better than sitting around waiting for Dikeakos, nursing a stomach that was quaking like quicksand.

I drove back across town. The address was in my notebook, but I didn't need to look it up. I remembered the street, and the house—though neither was memorable. I got out of the car, walked up to the front door.

The woman who answered the door was the one who'd talked to me on the phone. She left the chain latched, watched me through the six-inch gap. "Yes?"

"I've come to you for help," I confessed. "I want to talk to Teresa Minero, and I know that I'll probably need you to translate for me. I tried to talk to her before, but she didn't want to talk to me. But since the last time I came, the situation has changed. I was looking for Sherry Hovey, who had disappeared. Now Sherry Hovey is dead, and I'm afraid that her little boy might be in trouble. I'm trying to find out who killed Sherry Hovey, and how. And I think Teresa can help me."

"You called on the telephone," she said suspiciously.

"Yes, I did. I was trying to find out if Teresa was working in Glen Hovey's house today. I was tricking you then—but I am not tricking you now. I am a private investigator. I think the last time I came, Teresa did not want to talk to me because she suspected that Sherry was in danger and she was trying to protect her. Now that Sherry is dead, perhaps Teresa will agree to talk to me."

She stood silent, watching me. "Wait," she said. She closed the door and disappeared.

She was gone a long time. While I waited for her to come back, I stared at the squat, stucco houses, at the spindly trees planted down either side of the street. But this neighborhood—unlike Glen's—was a place where people did things. The man next door was shoveling manure into his vegetable beds; in the driveway beyond him two youths were disassembling the engine of a car; and a woman across the street was running a day care center out of her home. About eight small children were playing on her lawn, charging up and down the sidewalk on tricycles, while she and a friend sat on the porch steps, knitting and chatting.

Teresa's housemate came back, and Teresa was with her. "You come before," Teresa said to me, her eyes examining me through the gap.

"Yes, I did. At that time I was trying to find Sherry Hovey. She had disappeared."

Teresa said something to the other woman in Spanish. She stepped aside, out of sight, and the other woman took Teresa's place in the doorway. "She asks, did you find her?"

"Yes."

I heard Teresa ask another brief question; her housemate met my eyes. "You said she was killed?"

"Yes," I said.

"Murdered?"

"Yes."

Teresa started talking. I couldn't see her, but I watched the face of her housemate as she listened and made comments. Teresa went on for some time; she sounded angry. When she paused for a moment, her companion turned to me and explained, politely, "Teresa didn't know that Mrs. Hovey is dead."

"I understand," I said, and waited while the two women discussed the situation, wishing—oh how I wished—that I could understand what they were saying. Finally the woman in the doorway turned to me again. "Teresa is a refugee," she said, "and she waits for her hearing. She comes from El Salvador. Her father was imprisoned and tortured by the soldiers because he would not tell them how Teresa got out of the country. She cannot do anything that will make trouble for her at the hearing. If she does not get refugee status she will be sent back home and killed. Do you understand?"

"Yes," I said. "I am not working for any government department—nor with the police. What Teresa says to me is in confidence; I will not repeat it to anyone else."

This was translated; there was a moment of silence. Suddenly Teresa appeared, replacing her friend in the gap. She just stood there, staring at me. She was about five feet tall, in her mid-thirties; a stocky woman with grim lines around her mouth and a severe expression in her dark brown eyes.

She didn't say anything. She just watched me steadily, and I stared back, knowing full well that this woman was trying to read my soul.

"O.K.," she said abruptly—but there was no welcome in her face. She unlatched the chain and opened the door.

"Thank you," I said, and entered their house.

25

THEY LED ME into their small living room, which doubled as a bedroom. There was a single bed (neatly covered with a shiny gold bedspread) and a chest of drawers on one side of the room, a couch and side table on the other. Although it was the middle of the day, the curtains were drawn and the room was lit by a single overhead lightbulb, covered with a pink glass shade. The floor was uncarpeted linoleum and very clean; what furniture they possessed looked new, but cheap. The only personal touches were two brightly embroidered cushions on the couch, an arrangement of silk flowers on the side table, and a photograph on the mantelpiece in which three children, arms around each other, laughed up into the camera. They were obviously siblings—with thin faces, big grins and diamond-shaped eyes.

When I paused before this photograph, Teresa's housemate said, "They are my children."

I turned to her. "Where are they?"

"In El Salvador. I send them money; I am trying to get them out. Their father has been killed, so my mother is looking after them." Then she introduced herself. "My name is Natalia."

"My name is Meg." We smiled at each other.

Teresa was already sitting on the bed, facing the couch—as if she were in a witness box, waiting to give evidence. I sat down on the couch; Natalia sat down beside Teresa on the bed. When we were seated Teresa's eyes fixed on my face, and she began talking in Spanish, pausing at regular intervals so that Natalia could translate.

"It was me who told Mrs. Hovey that she must leave her husband. I will tell you how it happened. From the beginning I knew there was trouble in the house of the Hoveys. Sometimes Mr. Hovey said to me when he left for work, 'Don't disturb Mrs. Hovey; she is still in bed, she is not feeling good.' At first I thought that she was sick—but later I realized that the sickness was in her mind. I would hear her talking to herself from behind the bedroom door, and when she came out, she sometimes behaved very strangely. I felt sorry for the family, especially for the little boy."

Natalia's translation was hesitant, but Teresa showed no impatience; she sat erect, both feet on the floor, hands clasped in her lap. Her eyes never left my face. When Natalia finished, she went on:

"One day, Mr. Hovey took the little boy with him when he left for work. He told me his wife was asleep; I must be careful not to disturb her. I was cleaning the downstairs bathroom and I ran out of cleaning powder—I knew there was more in the bathroom upstairs. The upstairs bathroom is beside Mr. and Mrs. Hovey's bedroom and it has two doors—one into the bedroom, the other onto the landing. I entered it from the landing—the door was not locked. But Mrs. Hovey was in there; she was naked, sitting on the toilet. Of course I was embarrassed—I apologized and turned to go. But then I saw that her breasts and stomach and thighs and here—" Natalia stopped, glanced at Teresa. "What do you call this?" Natalia asked me. She raised her shoulders, patted the sides of her rib cage with both hands. "They were purple and red—swollen with many, many bruises. I forgot to leave; I stood there, staring at her; I could feel my face getting hot." Teresa's fingers lifted to her cheek, remembering. "Of course, I have seen such things before, but not here—not in Canada. I said, 'Who did this? Your husband?'

"Mrs. Hovey said nothing. She stared up at me and in her eyes I saw she was afraid. I said to her, 'This is no good. You must leave him. One day he will kill you.'

"Mrs. Hovey said to me, 'If I leave him, he will kill me. He has told me so many times.'

257

"'Then you must hide,' I said to her. 'You must ask your friends to help you.' I tried to say these things. You know that I do not speak very good English, and it is easier for me to understand than to speak. I told her to come to my house until she found somewhere to go.

"'But he will find me,' she said. 'He will look there.'

"I didn't know what else to say, or how to say it. I just kept telling her, 'Come with me. You must come.' But she kept shaking her head and I could see that I was making her upset. So finally I took the cleaning powder and left her alone.

"Maybe about ten days later the police came to our house and asked me where Mrs. Hovey is. I said I knew nothing. The next Tuesday when I went to the house, nobody was home. But I saw that only a few of her clothes were in the laundry baskets—and there were no clothes for the little boy. I saw that many things were missing from her room. I thought that she had run away and I was glad. Later you came and I didn't talk to you because I didn't want anybody to find Mrs. Hovey. Then, two weeks ago, I noticed that some of the little boy's clothes were back; I saw that he was living there again. But his mother's things did not come back. Now you tell me that she is dead."

Teresa stopped as abruptly as she'd begun; her eyes were angry—as if she blamed me for the way this story had ended. Yet if she'd told me all this the last time I came. . . . Would it have made any difference? I would have stopped looking for Sherry immediately—but it was Dunbar who'd followed her home from Copper's, Fred Dunbar who'd told Ed to keep his hands off Mrs. Hovey if he knew what was good for him. Perhaps, having no children of his own, Fred Dunbar had taken an avuncular interest in Glen, had kept up the acquaintance and looked for ways to make himself useful to him. When Sherry disappeared, Fred Dunbar must have taken it upon himself to find her. I now believed that it was Dunbar who'd betrayed Sherry, who'd told Glen where she was.

"I have a problem," I said to Teresa, "and I think you may be able to help me. As you saw, the little boy, Mark, is living again with his father. But I'm worried about him. Something is

258

wrong—his father is telling lies about where he is and who is looking after him. I want to know why Mr. Hovey didn't want you to go to his house today. I want to get into his house to see if Mark is there, to see if I can figure out what is going on, and why Mr. Hovey is lying."

Teresa digested this for a moment, her face uncommunicative. I asked, "Were you given an access number to the lock on their door?"

Teresa listened as Natalia translated this—but she didn't answer. Instead she asked a question, her head turning towards Natalia, her eyes remaining on my face.

"Do you think that it was her husband who killed her?" Natalia asked me.

"Yes," I said.

Natalia looked at Teresa, who asked another question. "Will you tell the police?" Natalia asked.

"I have been trying to get in touch with the detective all morning. I believe that I now have enough evidence to convince him to make an arrest."

Then the three of us sat in silence, watching each other. Or rather, Teresa and I watched each other while Natalia waited, her eyes going back and forth between us. A car went by, its radio blaring, a child begin to wail in the yard across the street. Teresa's face was set; it gave no clue to what she was thinking.

"El numero es," she said, and the hairs prickled along my arms, "quatro, zero, siete, nueve."

Natalia translated, and I closed my eyes, repeated it several times: four zero seven nine, four zero seven nine . . .

"Thank you." I got up. "Thank you very much." Teresa replied with a grave nod. I wanted to say more—to thank her for trusting me, to wish her success at her hearing. But her face seemed to forbid this and in the end I said nothing, turned to Natalia. "Thank you for your help."

"You have a dangerous job," Natalia commented, getting up.

Although Natalia and I were standing, Teresa remained on the bed, her eyes still focused upon the cushion where I'd been sitting. "Good-bye," I said to her. She glanced up with a slight frown, as if irritated by these courtesies, then bowed her head again. "Good-bye," she said.

Natalia accompanied me to the door. "Be careful," she warned me as she unhooked the chain.

"I will," I said, and she locked the door behind me.

Back to the other side of town. (Quatro zero siete nueve . . .) The impossible had been achieved—there was only one thing that could go wrong. If, after Glen had phoned Teresa, he was really feeling paranoid, he might have deleted her access code from the lock—just to make sure she couldn't get in. I didn't see why he would go to such lengths—but he might have.

When I got to 41st Avenue, I pulled up beside a telephone booth and tried Dikeakos again. He still wasn't there. "Can't you page him?" I begged the receptionist.

"Is it an emergency?" she asked cagily.

"If I say yes, will you page him?"

"If it's an emergency," she said, "I'll put you through to emergency."

"Then it's not an emergency," I snapped. "But it's important, and it's urgent."

"He'll get the message," she assured me huffily.

Then I phoned The Blue Heron and asked to speak to Glen Hovey.

"He's on the other line," said Kaye. "Would you like to hold—or can he call you back?"

"I'll try him again later," I said.

Good. The coast was clear. It was two-fifteen; he'd probably be there for a few more hours yet. I climbed back into my car and continued west on 41st, turned left on Arbutus, right on 49th, left on Holly. "Four zero seven nine . . . " I chanted softly, as my junky little Datsun sped through the tunnels of budding elm trees.

This time I left my car about three blocks from Glen's house. My disguise was simple. I stuffed my hair under a cap, stuck a handkerchief and my rubber gloves in my pockets, donned a pair of large, mirrored sunglasses. Then I locked the car and walked the rest of the way to Glen's house.

The house looked just as I'd left it. The gardening truck was gone; the only person in sight was a very old woman, bent almost double with osteoporosis, who was inching along the sidewalk with a cane in either hand, the soles of her shoes scraping over the cement. I walked up the path to Glen's front door, put on my rubber gloves, rang the doorbell. No one came. I wiped the doorbell and the doorknob with my handkerchief, trying to remember what I'd touched the last time I was here. I glanced up and down the street; the old woman had her back to me and was now past the house. I walked around to the back door.

First I knocked. Loudly. Then, when nothing happened, I did a little more cleaning up, wiped the doorknob, the jamb. Then, with a rubber-gloved fingertip I pressed the buttons, one at a time: four, zero, seven, nine. The dead bolt clicked, I turned the doorknob. Home free.

I stepped into the utility room, pulling the door closed behind me. As it shut, the dead bolt relocked automatically. I took off my sunglasses and slipped them into my jacket pocket.

In front of me was a laundry tub, beside it a washing machine, a dryer, a freezer; to my right was a row of boots. Three plastic laundry baskets, stuffed full of clothes, were stacked on the floor in front of the washing machine—waiting for Teresa? Who'd been told not to come.

I moved cautiously through the kitchen. The refrigerator hummed, and somewhere outside a truck was backing up: "beep, beep, beep. . . . " I peered into the dining room. All was quiet and tidy, the chairs pushed in around the table. As I walked through the room I passed an antique chiffonier and I stopped and looked at the framed photograph mounted above it. I didn't remember it being there before. It was a wedding portrait of Glen and Sherry, Glen standing slightly behind Sherry, his hands placed possessively over her lace-covered shoulders. Sherry looked as brides are supposed to look—radiant and beautiful—but Glen's expression was preoccupied, as if he were troubled by thoughts that were at odds with the moment. I re-

261

membered him saying, "I know we both believed that our marriage would be different."

Below the photograph stood a graceful, translucent vase containing a bouquet of flowers: baby's breath, white irises, and something tall and deep blue—delphiniums? On either side of the bouquet were two long purple candles set in ornate silver candlesticks. Taken together—the photograph above, the bouquet and candles underneath—it looked suspiciously like a shrine. "You never got a chance to make it up to her. Did you?" I murmured, meeting the eyes of the man in the photograph.

There was a small noise above my head—a muffled bump—as if something had been dropped onto a carpet upstairs. I stared at the ceiling, then I strode swiftly through the living room and into the hall. I stood at the bottom of the stairs, gazing up the wide, curving staircase to the banistered landing. All the doors that opened off the landing were shut; everything was silent.

Quietly I mounted the stairs and stopped outside the first door to my right. I noticed a small sliding bolt, like the kind used on bathroom doors, mounted on the door about five feet up. The bolt was locked, and looked new; the paint around the screws was scratched. Cautiously, I put my ear to the door.

About half a minute later there was another slight sound—like someone bumping against the wall. I lifted my head, glanced around. I conducted a swift survey of all the other upstairs rooms, opening and closing each door in turn: guest bedroom, sewing room, master bedroom, bathroom. Then I returned to the door that was locked.

I slid back the bolt, opened the door. The room was in semidarkness, a Venetian blind shaded the window. The air in the room was warm, humid; there was a strong smell of urine and something else—apple juice? It took me several seconds to find the small figure sitting on the far corner of the bed. "Mark?" I whispered. "Is that you?" I stepped inside, closed the door behind me, took off my rubber gloves and flipped the light switch on the wall.

He was almost unrecognizable. Both eyes were a dark, shiny purple, the right one swollen shut. The flesh of one ear was puffed up and inflamed—the color of a mottled plum. His left cheek was several shades of blue; his bottom lip was distended and starting to scab.

He didn't react to my presence; I doubted whether he could either see or speak. He continued to sit in the corner of his bed, his head tilted, expectantly. He was wearing pajama bottoms without a top; there was a tiny pickup truck in his lap, a toy bull dozer halfway up the mound of his pillow. As I approached he lifted his chin, trying to see me through the one partially closed eyelid, and I noticed other bruises all over his body, fat thumbprints on his upper arms, red abrasions on his chest, a long welt across his stomach. I walked around to the head of the bed, inspected the clusters of oval bruises on the backs of his shoulders and on the sides of his ribs where his father had gripped him with both hands. Just above his left kidney there was bruise as big as a football—or to be more precise, the size of a man's foot. I exhaled through my teeth, and realized that I'd been holding my breath.

On the night table beside his bed there was a bent straw, a carton of apple juice, a spoon beside an unopened container of raspberry yoghurt, and what looked like a bowl of congealed instant oatmeal. Glen, with characteristic thoughtfulness, had provided Mark with food that he wouldn't have to chew. A yellow bucket stood in the corner by the cupboard, but Mark hadn't used it. He was sitting in a dark, circular stain of pee.

"Mark," I said, trying to keep my voice steady, "I think you'd better come with me. I'll take you to a doctor and then to your aunt Vicky's house. Let's find you a shirt and some pants to put on."

I looked around the room but couldn't see any clothes. I opened the cupboard and was suddenly hit, broadside, by a wave of nausea and despair, a feeling that I'd been confronted by a job that was more than I could cope with. I blundered towards the window and opened the slats of the Venetian blind, found myself staring into the branches of an apple tree, its greenish-white blossoms droning with bees. Why did life go on like this? People torturing each other, children dying of starvation....

263

Sickened by the fug of urine and apple juice, I reached under the blind, unlocked the window and pushed it open. I inhaled, gratefully, sucking in currents of cool, scented air.

I faced back into the room, focused on a chest of drawers. I made myself walk over to it. I pulled opened the top drawer, found a pair of underpants, some socks; tried the next drawer down, picked out a T-shirt, a sweatshirt; the bottom drawer—pants. Shoes? I looked around the room, under the dresser, under the bed. . . . Oh God—no shoes. They must be downstairs. "Just put on the sweatshirt for now," I said. "And these pants. We'll take the rest of the clothes with us; you can finish getting dressed later."

I managed to get Mark's wet pajama bottoms off, discovered more bruises on his bottom and thighs—and wriggled him into a pair of elasticized track suit pants. Carefully, gingerly, I tried to ease the neck of the sweatshirt over his head—but when it compressed his swollen ear, he gave an abrupt, piercing scream. "O.K.—ssh!" I hushed him, pulling it off again. I went back to the chest of drawers, found a button-up sweater instead. With this we did better, although he whimpered when I tried to get his arms into the armholes and my fingers fumbled with the small, slippery buttons. I pulled the pillowcase off the pillow, stuck the rest of his clothes inside it, then noticed his toy puppy tucked under the bedclothes, only its head sticking out. I stuffed it in as well.

It was hard to figure out how to pick him up, where to hold him without hurting him. I tried—and he began to cry; he was as flaccid as a corpse and making no effort to help me. "Can you walk?" I asked him. I tried to see into his eyes—then remembering that I'd left my car three blocks away, I finally understood that what was needed was an ambulance. "Wait. I'll be right back," I said, giving him a light touch on the shoulder.

As I crossed the room, the downstairs door slammed. I stopped—petrified; someone was bounding up the stairs, taking them two at a time. I turned off the light switch, opened the bedroom door and stepped out onto the landing just as Glen's head appeared over the top stair.

26

"You!" Glen came to an abrupt halt. "How the hell did—"

He broke off and I watched the blood draining from his face; he was realizing, I think, that I'd seen Mark, that now I knew.

"It's over," I said quietly, closing the bedroom door behind me. "I know that you found Sherry, and I know how you found her. The police know it too. I'm going to phone an ambulance."

His Adam's apple bobbed. "Get away from that door."

He was out breath—he'd been running. His eyes flickered over me. Slowly he climbed the last few stairs until he stood on the landing. I moved away from Mark's door, taking a few steps sideways along the wall.

"You lied about knowing Dunbar," I said, "because he was the one who told you where Sherry was." My voice was shaking, but I tried to sound calm and matter-of-fact. I wanted to convince him that he might as well give up.

Glen took a step towards me. His big hands were hanging loose and slightly out from his sides, ready and trembling. "It was an accident," he pleaded. "She fell backwards—she hit her head."

He was telling me the truth—his version of it. He hadn't meant to kill Sherry, anymore than he'd meant to hurt Mark. His fists were like vicious, undisciplined dogs that escaped his control. "But first you hit her," I reminded him. "And you did mean to kill Fred Dunbar."

"Oh for Christ's sake!" He was disgusted. "So I did the world a service. That bastard was trying to blackmail me."

265

"Was he? And he used to be your hockey coach, right?"

"He was *Brad's* hockey coach," Glen corrected me, sneering.

"And yours," I said.

"Oh, I didn't count—the only reason he hung around me was so he could talk about my big brother. 'Brad would have done this, if only Brad had lived to see this, you should have seen the day that Brad did such-and-such. . . . ' When I worked at the Shamrock, Dunbar used to come in and sit at the counter, trying to get free refills, repeating all his old stories. Brad was his hero," Glen finished with contempt.

At least I'd got him talking. But I was finding it extraordinarily difficult to keep up my end of the conversation—because it distracted me as much as it did him. He took another step towards me; I edged further along the wall. I had to keep out of the range of those hands. He came closer; I moved again.

"But after Sherry disappeared. . . . Why was Dunbar looking for her? Or did he just run into her by accident?"

"Because I hired him," Glen said, obviously surprised that he should have to tell me this.

"You hired Dunbar?"

"About two weeks after Sherry disappeared, I bumped into him on the street. And he started whining about his knee and how he'd had to quit work and I thought: Hey, he's an ex-security guard—why not put him to good use? Because I knew Vicky was lying—Sherry never went anywhere without Vicky knowing about it. So I hired Dunbar to tail her."

"To tail Vicky? But Vicky didn't know where Sherry was."

"Sure she did. She went to that two-bit restaurant and had coffee with her."

"And Fred Dunbar followed Sherry home from Copper's restaurant."

Glen's answer was a supercilious smile.

His arm shot out like a jack-in-the-box and I twisted, leapt aside, and backed up fast, hard into a small table. It fell over and the telephone that was on it clattered to the floor. I grabbed the table and held it by its top so that its legs were aimed at Glen, then I backed up some more, disentangling myself from the tele-

266

phone wire and keeping the top table leg pointed at his face.

"This'll do you no good, Glen." But even to my own ears I didn't sound convinced. "The police know. I've already told them." (If only.)

"I just need a little time," he said quietly, as if working it out.

He kept shifting from side to side on the balls of his feet, so that it was difficult for me to keep the table leg aimed at him. He was herding me to the right, past the closed doorways and along the wall. Pretty soon I'd reach the other end of the landing.

"Time for what?" I taunted. "You're planning to hop a plane to South America? Go ahead—do it. I'll stay here with Mark until you're out of the country."

"Mark comes with me," he protested, shocked that I should suggest he would leave his son behind. He took his eyes off the table leg just long enough to give me a reproachful glance. "I need him. We need each other."

Right, I thought. And everybody thought that it was Sherry who was crazy. "You think you'll get out of the country with a kid who looks like that?"

Then I lunged—pushing the top table leg straight into his face. But he sidestepped just in time, grabbed two of the legs and twisted them, almost wrenching the table out of my grasp. Again I charged, forcing him to retreat to avoid the other two legs, one of which gouged him in the stomach. But still he had hold of the top leg and catching another, he rammed the table back into me, slamming my head against the wall and pinning me there, the table top squeezing my chest. He pushed—I pushed—but he was stronger than I was and abruptly he stopped pushing. He yanked the table away from me and flung it across the landing.

Now we were both breathing hard, staring into each other's eyes. He'd worked me all the way along the landing and I was at the end wall, the long banister to my right, the bathroom door directly behind me. If I ducked into the bathroom, how long would the lock hold? Long enough for me to get out of the window? And what would I do from there? Fly?

Talk, Meg! Make him talk. Cunning and charm—

remember? "But then Dunbar lost her again," I said breath-lessly. "Sherry moved, and after she'd moved, even Vicky didn't know where she was."

He was still driving me to the right; now my back was to the railing. Not good.

"How did he find her the second time?"

Glen stopped dancing. He looked at me, curiously. "Don't you know?"

As soon as he said this, I did know. And with that realiza-tion, I disintegrated, my legs dissolving like wet toilet paper.

Seeing the expression on my face—Glen sprang. Warm, damp hands encircled my neck, thumbs dug into my windpipe. "He followed *you*," he proclaimed vindictively, gritting his teeth and giving my head an extra hard shake for emphasis. I gagged, tried to get my chin down. Already black and red spots were exploding before my eyes and in my mind I was seeing Dunbar in the phone booth, Dunbar behind the driver's wheel, and I was thinking, Then it's my fault. I was the one who led Glen to Sherry. I was about to die as Fred Dunbar had died and I had no one but myself to blame for it.

But it was as if some other part of me stepped in and took over. As the world turned black, as a thick rock of pain severed my head from my shoulders, I took my weight off my feet, and Glen staggered. In one swinging movement I brought both el-bows to my chest, stamped on his arch and rammed my fists straight up into his chin. His head snapped back, his fingers loosened, and thrusting my forearms up and out past his face, I broke his hold around my neck. I ran. But he came after me. He seized me by the arm and again, acting without planning or thought, I stepped in towards him, turned and, using the force of his momentum, flipped him over my shoulder. He landed on his back. He hit the banister and with a slow-motion, sickening slither, his arms and legs flailing, he went over it.

I was doubled over with pain, coughing, gagging, hawking—breathing? I couldn't tell. Something large and jag-ged, like the spiny burr of a chestnut, was lodged halfway down my throat; my diaphragm had cramped, my lungs were going to implode. There was a horrible retching wheeze in my ears—I couldn't figure out where it was coming from. Finally I realized that it was me, breathing, trying to get air through my windpipe.

I became aware of a sound—a high, insistent beeping. I looked around and saw the telephone. It was lying on the floor a few feet away from me, the receiver still attached by its wire to the base, emitting peeps of protest. It worked! I threw myself after it as if it were being swept away from me in a current, righted the base, tried to remember what to dial. Emergency—yes. This time it was an emergency. I took time out to inhale, then tried to aim a shaking forefinger at the numbered buttons. On the second attempt, I got through.

"Fire, police, or ambulance?" a nasal voice inquired. "What is your emergency?"

"Police," I tried to say—but all that came out was a croak. "Cops—get the cops." I sounded awful—like someone in the terminal stages of emphysema. "Ambulance," I added as an afterthought, but the line had already clicked.

A different voice—male. "You have the police. What is your problem?"

Oh please, I begged silently, sucking more air past that godawful boulder in my throat. "Murder," I rasped. That should make them sit up.

"Give me your name and address please. Your name, and address."

"Meg Lacey," I whispered. It hurt like hell to talk. The address? "Holly Street," I said, which was as much as I knew. And then I saw it—the address, neatly printed in Glen's writing on a small label that had been stuck to the base of the phone. "6790 Holly."

"6790 Holly Street—in Vancouver?"

"Yes."

"Someone is on the way," said the voice. "Just stay where you are. Don't go anywhere, don't do anything."

I won't, my lips mouthed. The line went dead.

I sat with my back to the wall, hauling air into my lungs and clutching the telephone receiver as if it were a crucifix. I couldn't pull my eyes from the top of the stairs where I kept expecting

Glen to reappear, battered and bloodied, but back for more. Again the receiver began to beep, and I let it drop into its cradle. In. Out. In. Out. Every breath brought new pain, was like a wave dragging gravel back and forth along the raw innards of my throat. If he'd crushed my windpipe, would they be able to fix it?

Finally I remembered Mark. What must he be thinking, cowering in his room? I managed to get onto my feet, balanced precariously, then walked over to the top of the stairs and looked down.

Glen, eyes wide open and staring, was lying like a broken marionette in the middle of the hall floor. He was half on his stomach, half on his side, one leg and arm pinioned beneath him, his chin jammed into his collar bone. From this perspective he looked two-dimensional, as if he'd been hit with a flyswatter and flattened against the floorboards.

My legs shook violently. I felt myself swaying towards him like a tree beginning to topple. . . . I dropped to my knees, back to the safety of the floorboards. I huddled there, eyes closed, breathing, breathing.

I crawled to Mark's bedroom door. I knocked, reached up to turn the doorknob, entered.

"Mark?" I croaked.

I pushed the door shut behind me. Still on my hands and knees, I peered around the room like an inquisitive dog. Everything was as I'd left it—dim, quiet; the shades of the blind shifted and clicked in the draft from the open window. The pillowcase stuffed with clothes was in the middle of the bed. But I couldn't see Mark.

"Mark?"

No sound, no answer.

He wasn't in the closet, nor under the chest of drawers, nor buried under the snarl of blankets on the bed. Had he slipped out, somehow, while his father and I were trying to kill each other?

Finally, putting my ear to floor, I looked under the bed and found him huddled into the farthest corner right up against the wall. "There you are!" I rasped, and lowered my voice to a whisper, which didn't hurt so much. "It's O.K. now. Everything's going to be. . . . "

Fine? I asked myself. Was that what I was going to say? There he is, so bruised he can hardly move, his mother murdered, his father. . . . "The police will come," I whispered. "Someone will take us to the hospital. Then you can go to Vicky's house."

He made no response at all, but I knew he was watching me because I could see the slit of one eye glinting in the dim light. "You can come out now if you want to. Your Daddy's. . . . " I couldn't finish.

But he didn't want to. I lay on the floor and concentrated, again, on the task of obtaining air. But after a few minutes I couldn't bear seeing him so far out of reach and I squeezed myself under the bed, getting as close to him as I could. Now we were almost touching—holed up like two wounded animals hiding from predators. "We're safe," I said, and attempted a smile. But I felt tears threatening at the sight of his smashed, discolored face.

Safe, I thought bitterly. Safe from what?

A bird, close outside the open window, gave a long, liquid warble, and the voices of children wafted up—children released from school into the warm spring afternoon. Mark's slitted eye closed. He was falling asleep? Thus do babies survive earthquakes, hibernating under the rubble, curled like fetuses in the air pockets. But I was less adaptable, and was going to asphyxiate. I managed to get my arm under my head. . . . There, that relieved my neck a bit, though my top shoulder was now wedged against the bottom boards of the bed. I let my eyelids close, tried not to resist the inexorable inhalations, which burned down my throat like gusts of fire. The bird outside the window let forth another liquid warble, and another, and as I began to slip into a thickening swirl of unconsciousness I heard sirens, wailing in the distance.

271

About the Author

Elisabeth Bowers was born and raised in the city of Vancouver and now lives with her family on the Gulf Islands off the West Coast of British Columbia. She has made a living as a bakery worker, reporter, tree-planter, teacher, library technician, postal worker and writer. Her first mystery novel featuring private investigator Meg Lacey, entitled *Ladies' Night,* was published in the United States, Canada, England and Germany and is currently being made into a film.

Selected Titles from Seal Press

LADIES' NIGHT by Elisabeth Bowers. $8.95, 0-931188-65-2
Meg Lacey, divorced mother and savvy private eye, tackles a
child-pornography ring in Vancouver, B.C. First in the series.

GAUDI AFTERNOON by Barbara Wilson. $8.95, 0-931188-89-X
This high-spirited comic thriller introduces Cassandra Reilly as
she chases people of all genders and motives through the streets
of Barcelona.

VITAL LIES by Ellen Hart. $9.95, 1-878067-02-8 Jane Lawless
and her unpredictable sidekick, Cordelia Thorn, unravel a
gripping story of buried memories from the past that wreak
havoc on the present.

GLORY DAYS by Rosie Scott, $8.95, 1-878067-72-5 Glory
Day, streetwise artist, nightclub singer and uncommon heroine,
makes her debut in this dazzling thriller from New Zealand.

ANTIPODES by Maria Antònia Oliver, $8.95, 0-931188-82-2
Lònia Guiu, the hardboiled Catalan private eye of *Study in Lilac,*
returns in this intriguing mystery set in Australia.

The Pam Nilsen Series
Three riveting mysteries featuring feminist sleuth Pam Nilsen,
by Barbara Wilson:
MURDER IN THE COLLECTIVE, 0-931188-23-7, $8.95
SISTERS OF THE ROAD, 0-931188-45-8, $8.95
THE DOG COLLAR MURDERS, 0-931188-69-5, $8.95

DISAPPEARING MOON CAFE by SKY Lee, $18.95 1-878067-11-7
A spellbinding first novel that portrays four generations of the
Wong family in Vancouver's Chinatown, by one of Canada's
brightest new literary talents.

SEAL PRESS, founded in 1976 to provide a forum for women
writers and feminist issues, has many other titles in stock:
fiction, self-help books, anthologies and international literature.
Any of the books above may be ordered from us at 3131
Western Ave., Suite 410, Seattle, WA 98121. Please include 15%
of total book order for shipping and handling. Write to us for a
free catalog or if you would like to be on our mailing list.